UNDE [barcode]

t i

T0166754

a novel

One source of destruction, in my own opinion, is the ignorance in ten fingers. Even harmless ignorance can bring destruction. A simple ignorance, like failing to recognise a guava sitting in the palm of the hand, can destroy all the things you love, or failing to see a favour sitting in the hand, or a friend, a rupee, a memory.

Khalid is an ambitious young cook who invents a miraculous tandoor; his transport, he fervently hopes, from the world of cooks and bearers to the non-stop rich man's wedding of the sahibs' world. When his design is stolen and copied by an English sahib's factory, his grief is so great he is blind to the deepening love of Zeythi, the beautiful new aya. Not without ambitions of her own, Zeythi has meanwhile been spending secret erotic afternoons with the young grandson of the household, intent on confirming rumours that the love-making of the sahib-types is different. Around them other lives play out their passions, petty and huge, as all of Chittagong swelters under the impending Monsoon.

With Rushdie-like sweep and power, combining absorbing sensual narrative with wonderfully realised characters and moments, *Under A Tin-Grey Sari* is a seductive tour de force of storytelling, marking the arrival of a major new literary talent.

Book club notes available from www.fremantlepress.com.au

Wayne Ashton is a writer and painter. *Under a Tin-Grey Sari*, his first novel, was published by Fremantle Press in 2002. His second novel, *Equator*, was published by Fremantle Press in 2010. His radio dramas *The Aunt, The Tasman Angel from Hell*, and *The Oils and Mirrors of Dorothy Hoffkoff* were produced and broadcast by ABC Radio National. He has exhibited in twelve solo shows, including the group shows *Australians in New York* at Gelabert Galleries Broadway (1994), and *Australians in London* at Mall Galleries Trafalgar Square (1995). His paintings are in private collections in Australia, New Zealand, Britain, India and Canada. He is director of The Chilli Rooms Sydney, a space for international and national guest speakers in residence. Wayne Ashton has British and Pakistani family origins.

www.wayneashton.com

UNDER a tin-grey SARI

a novel

First published 2002 by
FREMANTLE PRESS
25 Quarry Street, Fremantle
(PO Box 158, North Fremantle 6159)
Western Australia.
www.fremantlepress.com.au

2nd edition first published 2010

Consultant Editor Ray Coffey
Original cover design Marion Duke
Cover design Ally Crimp
Cover photograph Steve McCurry
Author portrait Christian Mushenko

Printed by Everbest Printing Company, China
Typeset in Palatino (TT) Regular 10.5/13.3 pt and
printed on 67 gsm Alternative Book

National Library of Australia
Cataloguing-in-publication data
Ashton, Wayne, 1959– .
Under a tin-grey sari / Wayne Ashton
2nd ed.
ISBN 9781921696138 (pbk)
ISBN 9781921696329 (ebook)
I. Title.
A823.4

Department of
**Culture and
the Arts**

Publication of this title was assisted by the Commonwealth Government
through the Australia Council, its arts funding and advisory body.

for my grandparents
Marjorie and Cassim Auzam
and my mother
Saleema

UNDER *a*
tin-grey SARI

a novel

WAYNE ASHTON

FREMANTLE
fine independent publishing PRESS

A Collaboration

The ayah came up to check the rumour that sahib types grunted less hard. With her nose under the window ledge she watched the glistening backside hump away between the memsahib's expert thighs. Noise was starting but the ayah was forced into the darkness by headlights.

In those days the rumour was fresh, it had a strong hold on the ayah. She would do plenty more checking in dim bungalow windows for polite grunting.

Back in that time of hot nights I lived at the bungalow, but these days you'll find me past Zakir Hussein Road, in a cooler place, down a slope of guava trees and headstones. A moss has blotted out the name on a headstone near the stream, my name.

The ayah, now a young woman, might visit my headstone to sit on the cool grass in the shade of the guavas, maybe stuck silently in remembering, for she will burst into laughter, and just as quickly might weep. She might place to the rock a kiss. Then I also weep, holding onto a sorrow. In some lore this is sad, but it is a sorrow to cherish, for it comforts with warped memory. Besides, a bargain is a bargain, and I possess the other facts: I have in my heart's cheery pocket secrets to which only the brave, the happy, the sorry and the foolish might choose to bring the quieter attention.

I sometimes long for a stroller brave or happy—or sorry or foolish—to pass by and take to the headstone with a brush and bucket against that obstinate moss. But I should be grateful, only the name is blocked out. The rest is there for all to see:

A wise friend educated in the simple
and the difficult things in life
1950–1967

In those days I was plenty less than wise. A dunderhead, I admit. Nowadays I sprout a bit of wise stuff. It passes the time and amuses the mynah birds.

One source of destruction, in my own opinion, is the ignorance in ten fingers. Even harmless ignorance can bring destruction. A simple ignorance, like failing to recognise a guava sitting in the palm of the hand, can destroy all the things you love, or failing to see a favour sitting in the hand, or a friend, a rupee, a memory. As for the simple things in life: my reverence of the simple things was too fast—it was one of the culprits behind my downfall. But these days I have plenty to say about the simple things because I can see everything from a different angle. I can see the flesh of the schemes sahibs carry in their important heads.

Not every memory is etched in stone. Take Iqbal. He works as a letterwriter. If not for his unusual ear, his third ear, it would be difficult to record this tattered collection of rumours and secrets. He has a fine place at a junction by the harbour, sits on a cushion at his roadside desk and is protected from the sun by an old Thames black brolly. He utters very little. His age, though the arrow chin has grown into the knee by saying hello and farewell to uncountable monsoons, is any sabjantawallah's guess. His eyes are the deepest pools of wonder I've ever encountered. A strangely neutral wonder, though you would assume his is the heart stung with the aching cries and shitty declarations of countless others, that's what you would reasonably think. I could not look into Iqbal's eyes without knowing he was full with the rumours of a bustling town under the flaking delta.

So, yesterday I asked how many other 'jobs' he had performed over the years. How many love letters had he taken down? And how many desperate cries for help? How many decomposing secrets had finally rested by his hand? Iqbal's are not the fingers of ignorance. From his hand the rumours are able to flow like a monsoon drain. I am able to remember what I remember, but Iqbal can complete the picture by using other memories too.

So Iqbal looked up from the page into a distance beyond the busy road. A smile came to his coarse lips, and his finger released the pencil.

He said, 'I have not been asked about other letters for a long time. Usually a customer can forget I do other jobs. Are you sitting next to me?'

'I am,' I said.

Iqbal leaned out from his Thames brolly and whispered, 'Hundreds, my friend!'

'And still you like the work?'

'Oh yes,' he whispered, 'very much. Thousands of strange jottings, and it becomes more strange, not less. Some even you—in your present state of wisdom—might not believe to be so.'

'What about this job for me?' I asked.

'Yes, yours is peculiar too. I remember those days. Do

you want to tell your name?'

'No.'

'Not at all?' Iqbal asked abruptly. He was disappointed.

'Maybe later,' I said to reassure him.

'Okay. Shall we continue?'

'Yes,' I said. 'Let's dig into these rumours.'

The Hotel of Moans in the Night

When the ayah arrived nobody took any notice. The diamond stillness stole any interest in matters outside your own hand. The wail from town, tireless in its resolve to raise the earth, carried on the ancient air, and she rode into the fumes of Chittagong on the long notes, easily smoothing out the voice like a worn carpet at a landing. Her eyes were outlined in lovely black. The silver ring at the nostril glinted and lay on her skin as if it too had been born when she was born.

The boy placed her into the scheme with no more effort than a lazy stare. He then returned to the front garden of grass, shrubs and flowers to resume watching the household try to breathe. On the porch three sahibs simply gazed downwards at the grass, but they were puzzling a pathway to themselves. The boy did not ask them who she was; he knew who she was. And there was no hello. Unseen arrivals brush forgotten departures. Low clouds kiss roads coming to 'Ten-ten Zakir Hussein, next to the Sleeping Camel Hills please'. And a moment in the kitchen on a markless day brushes destiny: that too is as it should be.

Brooms, toilets and groans on the hot darkness; these became the routine. The household thought of her as shy.

They thought of her as sweet and honest. But the cook knew sahibs could be idiots. He had a different idea. At every opportunity he grabbed a long look. Watching when she was not looking he saw tension, but this he didn't mind putting down to homesickness. He saw cleverness, maybe cunning. But this he didn't mind too because you have to get by. He could not shake the feeling that she was somehow a troubled child.

It was a big household: The Grand Old Man, a West Pakistani; The Grand Old Woman, English, very long ago from Leicester; and the seven adult children, mixtures who were given various labels—Anglo-Pakistani if you felt like keeping a straight face, Anglo-Banglo if you didn't, or Paklish as Khalid the cook preferred. Then there was the boy, the eight-year-old grandson, who lingered when he discovered anything of interest. Then the tumbling stream of friends and visitors.

One visitor came with the start of a play he had written to show the Old Man for advice. He was the engineer from a factory in the industrial estate. Writing plays was his hobby. When he first came out from Bristol he was inspired, he said, by the huge amount of raw material Chittagong offered. The Old Man took the first act and promised to read it. He read the first few pages but found it no good.

'His Bengali characters talk as if they are stupid,' he said. 'Listen to this. A Bengali guy at a factory asks, "What is the putting of respect into friends meaning?"'

'Wow,' the Grand Old Woman chuckled. 'All the characters talk like that?'

'Yes.'

'Oh well, seems to be about important feelings,' she said, 'but I do wonder why these writers make their

Bengalis talk in broken English.'

'It is a stupid device used by stupid people for stupid effects to amuse other stupid people.'

'That's a bit harsh,' she smiled. 'Don't go telling Brian to his face.'

'Here, do you want to read it?'

'No. I can wait until his production at the club.'

Often many visitors arrived at once and a small party sprung up. Khalid would make pakoras, samosas, maybe a feast. He called it the Paklish hotel. The ayah called it the hotel of moans. The cook liked her for the remark.

'Yes,' Khalid said as he turned off the flame under the giant pot he boiled for drinking water, 'The Hotel of Grunting.'

'No,' the ayah said. '*Moans.*'

'Okay,' Khalid said and smiled.

The ayah's own household, which she had left behind in the hills, ached with sex when it felt the urge, and no doors of fancy stopping jute would keep the entertainment from her eye. She often moved into position to see what she could see. It all became a bore, and she got on with life in the small village, welcoming the urges as a normal part of things and with the simple knowledge that one day they might involve her.

Late at night she crept up to a window to watch a sahib and memsahib making love. To confirm the rumour that these sahib types moaned differently. A candle burned a flickering circle on the far wall. The weak light fell across the naked limbs of one of the adult children and his wife. The wife had him in the hand, stroking him, and after she kissed his belly there was pulling and sudden sucking. The sucking became slow. Outside the window Zeythi caressed her thigh. The couple began to make love. A car arrived into the driveway, and the ayah stepped behind the hibiscus. She moved down the laneway to her quarters. But it was how Zeythi became tangled in her own wishes in the last days of the dry season. It was how she would come to fall in love. That's what it really was. Sleep arrived, and her spirit curled into it with a deep sense of it belonging especially to her.

The morning was market day, club day, petrol day, and, by nine-thirty, the house was mostly empty. With a cake of yellow tar soap, she went to work outside at the cement tubs in the compound. The heat and the stillness baked the dusty compound. It was a rectangle of pale dirt, hard as a road. Tall trees of mango, mangosteen and almond gave it good shade in the corners, and behind the crumbling back fence rose a wall of thick jungle.

The boy stood solitary out on the paleness of the smooth dirt, lingering. He leaned on his bamboo stick, and he watched.

The scrubbing's making her bums bounce, he thought. When he'd had enough he called out that he was off to the pond. Nobody took any notice, but he liked announcing the bicycle journey to the pond.

But then Khalid came out the kitchen with a bag of garbage. The boy tossed away the bamboo and walked after the cook.

'When are you going to make the flying fox?'

'Tomorrow,' Khalid replied without stopping.

'You said last week.'

'Tomorrow, I'll get the rope from the bazaar.'

Satisfied, the boy rode his bicycle through a gate in the back fence and down a narrow path in the jungle. Riding down the shaded pathway to the pond, the boy considers what he's seen since yesterday, and he concludes with satisfaction: She's a lot older than I am, but that doesn't matter a bit. She's good compared to the stinking boring grown-ups around here ... all they do is nothing and more nothing.

It's Nothing, Nothing

Khalid stood at the top step. Today he became, he felt with a sense of new manliness, seventeen. He noticed the stillness in the compound seemed strange, something more than simple heat. A touch slid over the shoulders, unlike a thought, more like what they call a premonition. The new day was as hot as standing next to the tandoor but he shivered. Drops of water from the clump of wet cloth in his hand darkened the cement. He took the loongie to the clothes line. As he crossed the compound dark spots appeared on the dry dirt like a trail of small footprints, maybe an invisible thing, just a *thing*, following him into the quiet morning. The days of stillness would soon end, replaced by a violence that came to remake the delta into another bold and sparkling image of itself. The arrival and departure of the season that had no use for the passport would destroy rambling bungalows and lovers holding hands.

Khalid shook off the eerie feelings and returned to his new day. He felt full of what he thought of as 'sahib stuff'. A polish shined in his eyes. Carefree pleasure lifted his hands to the clothes line and the cool water brushed the sparse hair on his forearms. He sensed in himself a refinement, or maybe today at the wild teahouse he could call himself a man. As he pinched the loongie with clips he whistled his favourite radio song into the curious quiet, and his head responded by bouncing to the tune. As he hung it, the loongie dangled and bounced too.

The boy would ride back around lunchtime with a bag of clay shovelled from the shores of the dark green pond. Khalid decided he would have to ask for a supply. Khalid needed clay. For clay he had the type of grand plans sahibs had for jute.

Spooky feelings returned. The cat, a wild creature with big fighting paws, was nowhere in sight. Every morning he would emerge from the vines to sit on the wall. Then he would cross the compound on slow, relaxed legs. Khalid would put out a plate of leftover meat. The cat would clean the plate with his sandy tongue, and then bathe in the invisible sun before disappearing into the jungle. Maybe Khalid had nothing to worry about. He switched on the radio hanging from the beam. Not much happened in '67, especially just before the monsoon. The Fall of Dacca was four years off. In '71 came Mujibur Rahman's declaration of independence on the twenty-sixth of March; Ziaur Rahman's competing declaration came two days later on the twenty-eighth when he made a speech from the Chittagong radio station. But for now the radio simply played another hip-shunting love song.

The ayah had settled beneath the skin of the bungalow, under a protective layer. Over the delta the bitterness of hunger did nothing to make girls outside the bungalow want to smile. Zeythi had heard of bungalows like this since she was very small, and she had dared to hide away from hunger. She turned off the tap and used her arm to sweep the foam over the side. She stopped to watch it slide down the outer wall of the stone tub, and she felt a small lightness.

She called out to Khalid, 'Have you seen the Minisahib?'

The Minisahib, Khalid thought. Yah, funny, I will say nothing. Let this clever new idiot carry on with it. She is very strange, this girl. Tonight I will ask that smelly sabjantawallah Khan to check her out.

'Yah, funny,' Khalid called back. 'Let him catch you calling him the Minisahib.'

'Don't worry, he will not find out,' Zeythi said.

She learned quickly from the memsahibs certain ways of saying things. But Minisahib she made up herself.

'Do you know where he is?'

'The pond,' Khalid said.

Zeythi carried on with her work, but she had caught the cook's blank expression.

'You look worried, what is it?'

'Everything is fine.'

'Truly?'

'Yah.'

Khalid frisked his forearm of the icy chill of the premonition and he walked back inside to the kitchen.

The Scent of a Small Wisdom

And the moan of a Minisahib? Is this also different? Finding out had to be under cover of the gully of banana leaves. You can fly off a broken trunk into the green light and flap your wild arms before falling to the grass. You roll down the slope until your neck is twisted like jute on the bridge past the teahouse.

They spoke in whispers.

'It's your turn,' Zeythi said gaining her breath.

'No, I've had enough,' the Minisahib said.

'Why?'

'I'm tired. And all this grass on me, it's too itchy.'

She ignored him. When she reached the ledge she removed her shirt and flung it away into the gully. She jumped down to the slope after it. He followed into the green air, landing on the soft grasses and then rolling down the slope.

They fell to their backs on the grass. He rolled over and he watched her chest swell. Catching his eye, she looked down to see grass sticking to her chest.

She said, 'Wipe them off …'

'They're all over you.'

'Wipe them off …'

He began at her breast. One of the greatest sources of

destruction, I believe, is the ignorance in ten fingers. But here was not the hand of ignorance. Neither was his the hand of innocence. He picked at the grass on his fingers to toss them over his head one by one, and he brought his fingers down to his nose. He smelled a hint of coconut oil. And he could smell a strong sweat, but he was trying to bring back what he hoped would be the smell of her breast. He gave the fingers a powerful sniff.

'Quiet!' She sat suddenly upright.

'What is it?'

'Listen!'

The voices near the compound grew more distinct. She held his head.

'Lick them off,' she said.

A tongue too can store a world of ignorance. She drew him to her chest, and his head was the right height. He could see nothing of the exciting world but her chest. And he could now breathe the scent. He ran his tongue up a small rise. She drew a breath, and they continued.

They went on enjoying the sensation. They were falling into a still rhythm of embrace. Well, from its tenderness their hands gained the scent of a small wisdom. Bigger wisdoms would come to them later—as the big shifting of sky drew itself nearer to remake the delta.

The Featherduster

Outside the secret dark shade, in the glare and heat of the compound, a visitor arrived. Mohendra the chickenwallah was a bony twenty-year-old forever in shirts that had been ironed to a shine. He had long been one to rub his hands together when alone, rubbing them good to generate the respectability for which he grit his teeth. But you could not call these the hands of ignorance, for his chicken stall at the bazaar did good trade in the boom, and he was a bastard inventor of smart plans to keep customers coming back. He devised a plan for giving away a featherduster, made from the fated birds, to every customer who took more than three chickens a week. He displayed the dusters on the overhead rung at the counter. The colours made an eye-catching sight, gaining the interest of passers-by. The many reds and blacks and browns and yellows, he thought with satisfaction, make the stall come to life.

To expose himself further, he stood for a position in the bazaar's meeting of bosses. They did nothing of use to the stallkeepers, but he liked the important boom-talk that buzzed. After the meetings, when he found time to relax and boast, he would visit his friend Khalid the cook. Mohendra was a bit prosperous and very thrifty. He was also sneaky.

Mohendra walked down the side of the house. A featherduster was hooked into his belt. He strolled across the compound.

'What is that?' Khalid said.

'This is your prize!' Mohendra called out.

'But what is it?'

'A duster!' he barked.

'A duster for the house dusting?'

'Yah!' he said loudly as he came up to the chopping block and stood next to Khalid.

'Quite nice, but it is useless to me.' Khalid returned to slicing onions.

'Then give it to Zeythi!' Mohendra called out.

'Why are you shouting?'

'Today I have inside me *energy*!'

Khalid continued working.

Mohendra was here to make a sly advance on Zeythi. He had already visited once before when he saw the ayah. He had approached her but she vanished into the house.

'Where is she?' Mohendra asked quietly.

Khalid ceased his work to look into the chickenwallah's eyes. The merchant's shirt fluttered as he moved a foot. The purple nylon carried the glaze of heavy-hitting ironing.

Mohendra said, 'I am only asking where she is.'

'I do not know where she is,' Khalid said.

'Will she be working in the inside laundry?'

'Maybe.'

'Maybe I'll check it out?'

'You know how to find it.'

Khalid returned to his work. He sliced with a nimble movement, and the feeble breeze had just the gusto to brush away the sting before it pierced his eyes. At one point the fumes did catch his eyes. He lifted his head and blinked to flush, and he saw a dark figure at the fence. The figure stood very still. He was deeply under the shade. Khalid called out, but the figure fell into the shade and disappeared.

Mohendra returned.

'I cannot find her,' he said flatly.

'Oh well,' Khalid said to make noise, but he cared about nothing now.

'How are you today?' Mohendra asked.

'Why are you talking so much?'

'What else is there to do?'

'You can close your mouth and just think,' Khalid said as he peeled an onion.

'Thinking is a boring activity.'

'Then try to think before you talk.'

'I can talk without thinking.'

They were silent for some moments while Khalid sliced the onions.

'I have twenty sweet ducks,' Mohendra said. 'Shall I keep some? You can make fantastic tandoori duck.'

'Sweet you say? You mean tender?'

'Yah, terribly tender.'

'Terribly miserable probably.'

'What is the matter with you today?' Mohendra said with sharp displeasure.

'Okay, I'll try two, but it will be too soon for my new tandoor.'

Mohendra rebounded into feeling fine.

'They are getting a new tandoor? What happened to the tandoor in the kitchen?'

'Not just some bastard new tandoor—*my* new tandoor,

a new design, I've done drawings. I'll show you. I have a feeling it will make the meat better. Lock the life inside it.'

'How will you make it?'

'I have to get clay.'

The chickenwallah knew he had completed the duck pitch so he fell quiet and gazed at the clouds. A moment later he wanted to talk.

'How come so many onions?'

'Big dinner tonight, guests from Karachi and London,' Khalid muttered.

'Always with you there is a bastard pack from London. Why don't you take a break?'

'No, I'll finish these and then we'll have some chai.'

'Good idea. You have any beer?'

'No.'

'I have some.'

'Where is it?'

'On my bicycle.'

'What is it doing on your bike?'

'Okay. Hold on, I'll fetch it.'

Mohendra walked off. Then he called back, 'Why not put on your transistor? … Hoi … Khalid!'

'What?'

'Switch on your radio!'

Khalid fetched the radio and hung it by the strap on a big rusty nail. It flung a trail of bouncing music into the hot air.

Mohendra returned, took up the opener and used it against the bottle top. A sharp hiss, but the bottle top remained fast. The bottle emptied out in a continuous spray before he could remove the top entirely and, after waiting for the bottle to settle down, he poured from the remains a small tumbler each. Mohendra threw back his head with a genuine laughter. He then held out his tumbler.

'Cheers,' he said. He liked the saying of cheers. Copying the sahibs was something everyone did in one way or another. Not copying, but using bits and pieces to feel bigger and better. To enjoy the boom.

'Yah,' Khalid said instead of cheers. Khalid had other ways of copying the sahibs.

'Lovely beer,' Mohendra murmured.

'You got it from Farooq's?'

'Not a chance. I got it cheaper at the club.'

'I heard they clamped down like stink at the club.'

'There's a new guy, just started, Swimmingpool-bearer.'

'He'll get caught just like the others. Who's been snooping on all these stupid bearers lately?' Khalid stole a glance into the chickenwallah's eyes. 'I heard,' he continued, 'it is the Chief Bearer-bastard.'

'Him? I think not,' Mohendra shook his head.

'Why not? He is your cousin, you should know.'

'Akram is the Chief Bearer, he is too important to worry about what fool takes home English beer. As if he would go telling me.'

'He is a bigmouth, he would relish digging. Anyway, he definitely steals the beer himself.'

'He has no need, his wages are very high.'

'I heard they are shit.'

'His wages are big. Plus the amount of bucksheesh he gets from the club President-sahib makes me want to be sick fifty times.'

They continued enjoying the slackness of the day, sipping at their good fortune—good lives—and feeling lucky to be part of so exciting a town as Chittagong.

Mohendra boasted of plans to open a fish shop in Dacca because of the boom, but Khalid had never been to the big city. Flies settled on a gleam of fat and blood from slicing the meat. Khalid flicked his hand at them. They settled back down to the block. He went on gazing silently at the flies.

'What is the matter?' Mohendra asked. He waited.

'Nothing. Yah, nothing.'

The chickenwallah sighed, 'It's a fine day, don't you think so? And sometimes a dazzling life.' He took up the duster and flicked at the flies.

'Oh yes,' said the cook, 'this monsoon will dazzle everybody.'

'I have been thinking,' Mohendra said seriously, 'about buying a new bicycle.'

'Buy mine.'

'Yours is a shitheap. Truly you have no beer?'

'No beer.'

'What about inside?'

'There is plenty in the house.'

Mohendra got up to see if he could find a hawker who would ride to the club and bring back two bottles.

It was the boom that made you wish to be enterprising. A boom to a servant working in Chittagong was a fantastic time.

He did not walk two steps when he turned back. Could be, he proposed enthusiastically, he'd find a hawker to bring the beer in return for the duster. He picked it up, held it at arm's length to admire it and then shook it at the flies before walking off.

'Yah, I'll find someone who wants to have a featherduster. Save cost.'

'You'll never catch a fool as big as that,' Khalid said.

Mohendra stopped.

'You,' he retorted, 'presume I am just a chickenbutcher. You should stop thinking that what people do is their heart's happiness. I am more than just that. I am a man who has a great understanding of human dunderheads. Very successful as well. Why? Because I make people happy by giving them what they want. If you want to copy my success, you should stop thinking people are feeling okay, and start thinking people are unhappy. Last week I met a woman who is unhappy. All her friends are unhappy. I offered her the work of plucking the feathers, and her friend the work of making the dusters. Now they are happy. I will find this unhappy hawker dingling into town, you will see.'

Khalid returned to the onions. 'May luck come falling down to infest it.'

'You want the beer?'

'Yah.'

'Then show your senior friends proper respect.'

Mohendra decided to pursue his proposition, but he turned to see Zeythi and the Minisahib stroll from under the giant frangipani behind the laundry hut. His enterprising vigour took a back seat for a sly advance.

He emitted a greeting from big teeth: 'Aaahh ... look, Miss, what I have for you. Come over here, come, come.'

'What is it?' Zeythi called.

'A present.'

Khalid said, 'It is a testicle-tickling contraption.'

'What is it with you today? From jealous you go to stinginess and at the end you come to sickening crudeness ... you have a mouth like a septic tank.'

'What does she want with a testicle-tickling contraption?'

'Do not listen to him, today he has been slingshotted from his senses.'

She came up and stood. It was a blank look, and she intended to keep moving to the house to work.

He held the featherduster out proudly.

'It is a duster,' Zeythi said without interest. 'I already have one.'

'Take two,' the chickenwallah said. 'Take two of things every time. Emergency type of thinking.'

'No thank you.'

'You look nice today. What have you done to your hair? It is blown out like a film star.'

'I fell down.'

'Looks nice.'

'It is none of your business.'

'I'm just saying it looks nice.'

The Minisahib said, 'She knows it looks nice, you don't have to tell her.'

'There is grass on your clothing, let me show you what my featherduster can do.'

'I do not want to see what your featherduster can do.'

Mohendra was not perturbed.

The figure in the shade appeared. Only Khalid faced him. The posture was a defiant one, the head thrown back, feet set proudly and the hands resting insolent. He remained deep in the shade, and he was further hidden by the sight line with the tree trunk.

Mohendra's new proposition unfolded in a mess of tugging and pushing. He implored Zeythi to be still, and Zeythi was fighting off chicken feathers, and then gripping them to rip them from the stick. The Minisahib seemed to be kicking at Mohendra's pants leg, but Khalid could not tell what, really, was going on, for he kept his attention on the figure. But the figure turned away and again moved into the gloom under the big trees. Became a shadow.

Mohendra reversed his efforts. He gave a final mighty wrench. The featherduster came free, and he resumed his enterprising search. His boom-look. Put the eye right upon bottle-top opportunity. What stink.

'Off he goes,' Khalid said. 'Strange fellow. He's holding his purple future, every hour he's holding onto his future.'

'That boy is horrible,' Zeythi said.

'He is not a boy, he is a man,' Khalid said. 'Anyway, he's all right.'

'How come he came around?' the Minisahib asked.

'I don't know. Where have you two been?'

'We went to the Smiths' house,' the Minisahib lied.

'Them? What for?'

'New kite.'

'You flew it?'

'I didn't. Zeythi did. She ran up the field with it. Like a real expert she was ...'

'Okay, yah yah okay,' Khalid said abruptly.

When the cook began to work, Zeythi went inside and returned with two knives. They stood at the big block, slicing and talking. Here, the Minisahib's small hands were perhaps a little ignorant. Maybe lazy. But he pressed on because it was the teamwork.

Then the Minisahib stopped. He said to Khalid, 'I have a secret to tell you.'

'You are always telling me a damn secret: who is this one about?'

'Him.'

'Mohendra?'

'I saw him with that liar bearer-bastard at the club.'

'Say bastard again,' Khalid rolled his head, 'and I will kick you.'

'I saw him with that liar guy you know at the club.'

'The club has many liars. Which one?'

'The Chief Bearer.'

'Yah? So?'

'They were talking about money.'

'Yah, payment for chickens.'

'You said bucksheesh,' the Minisahib insisted.

'From the Chief Bearer to Mohendra? What for?'

'Do you like them?'

'Yah, they are fine manly bastards like me,' the cook smiled, 'not small-boy smells like you.'

'They're smells like you!' the Minisahib spat with disgust.

They continued unlocking the onion fumes into the growing heat of the afternoon. A breeze came up, and a few moments later dropped away. With three working the wooden block, the onion became the enemy. The Minisahib and Zeythi gave up. Khalid offered his thanks. He sat to rest a moment, and to watch them walk. A kite, he thought. He let go a wide smile.

In the silence he recalled the figure. He wiped his forehead and looked up to the roofline. There was no wind. Then he glanced at the shade under the mangosteen. He turned to search the perimeter of the compound, the scruffy edges, crumbling walls, old fences. He removed his shirt, took up an onion and continued working.

After a long while Mohendra returned. On the surface there is nothing to complain about. Nothing lacking. Cold beer. Sweet ducks and chickens. Plenty of dahl and rice. A coastal plain of fruit and vegetables. Fish for the tandoor jump from the sea. Goats for the pot clutter and fall from the hills. The government is building a new ring road. The year is 1967, and the whole country is experiencing good growth. A 'boom' some say. And the stall ticks along like a Hong Kong watch. Yes, nothing to growl at.

'Did you get the beer?'

'It is coming.'

'From the club?'

'From the club.'

'Where is the featherduster?'

'Don't mention it.'

'Some twit is doing it for the duster?' Khalid said. The memsahib often said 'twit'.

'Don't mention it I said.'

Khalid continued working. He finished it off by the time the hawker arrived.

The hawker walked in. He brought the two bottles of beer up and placed them on the block. Khalid thanked him, and Mohendra did not. Khalid then realised that neither man acknowledged the other. Mohendra only gazed at the sky. And the hawker began to leave.

But, without warning, the hawker exploded into laughter. He then walked off, across the compound, laughing more clearly as he grew more distant. When he finally disappeared round the house, his laughter receded in the hot dusty air.

'He did not want your featherduster I suppose,' Khalid smiled.

Khalid said nothing more. He took up a bottle and, with a clean lift of the opener, removed the cap. He poured out the drinks. The beer was warm so Khalid took the second bottle inside to the icebox. He walked back outside, bounding off the steps, and they sat together enjoying the drinks.

A shrill and long laughter came in from a distance. In the emptiness of heat and dust it seemed to come from all directions and have abundant song.

'Yah,' Mohendra said, 'very nice—now the bastard sounds like a girl.'

'No,' Khalid said, 'it *is* Zeythi.'

'It is the hawker.'

'No, it is from the back of the fence. Listen.'

'It is on the road at the front,' Mohendra insisted.

'You have a strong mind,' Khalid said to piss in his pocket.

'That's right.'

They drank the beer. The onions were done. Now the garlic, the ginger, the fresh chillies. Things were well in order.

Mohendra reminded Khalid about the evening.

'Don't forget the teahouse tonight.'

'Yah. I'll see you there after this big dinner,' Khalid said. He looked forward to the new maturity he would take to the teahouse.

'Will you bring Zeythi?'

Khalid looked up. He stared into Mohendra's eyes.

'I am only asking if you will bring her,' Mohendra said with some anger. He shook his head in disgust and walked off.

The Teahouse

He was done. Dinner turned his kitchen upside down, ten times the mess of a normal household meal, and he knew it would, so he had cleverly worked the cooking, the serving and the cleaning as three jobs running together. The bungalow hummed with glad noise. Seventeen sahib and memsahib mouths in the dining room. Two from London, one from a place he heard they called Hay-Stings. What a name, he thought. Onion, he reasoned as he worked, stings, but hay? Sahibs, he thought ruefully as he shook his head, how they can be so stupid and still be sahibs is too kooky.

Another sahib at the table was from Karachi. One even from Dacca. Dacca had a powerful hold on the cook's ambitions. He had never been north to the glittering city, but he had plans now that he was a man. Also present was Abdul the history teacher, who at these dinners did his best to sit beside Fatimah Westcott. But Khalid noted that his favourite memsahib was missing. Where is Fatimah Westcott the Arab? 'Never mind,' he said aloud to himself as he worked. The real memsahib entered the kitchen to thank him.

'You can go now,' she said with a smile, and she slipped him a note. His eye caught the number, and he thought with excitement: What a generous one she is, this memsahib. He was done good.

In the laundry he jumped under the tap and soaped off the day's work. He dried off and slipped into his shalwar kameez. The shalwar kameez was torn at the armpit, and the collar was rubbed out by the love of it. He was excited but his legs and arms ached.

Now Khalid was hurrying, and his shirt stuck up his neck.

Zeythi was perched on the wall. A small figure against the night.

'You want to come?' he asked.

'No.'

'Why not?'

'I'm too tired.'

'You should come. Everyone will be there. Iqbal the letterwriter will be there.'

'So?'

'You told me you like him,' Khalid said.

'I never told you such a thing.'

'Not like that.'

'He is okay, but he is a strange man.'

'One day this, one day that. You are not happy?'

'I am happy, yah. But he …'

Khalid waited patiently.

'He talks to the dead,' Zeythi said quietly.

In the dimly lit shadows under the porch light, Khalid smiled. He looked down at the small forehead.

'He makes letters,' Khalid said. 'You must stop all this worry. Come to the teahouse.'

'They won't let me in.'

'Rubbish. With me, they will let you in. Where's the Minisahib?'

'He went to sleep long ago.'

Khalid leaned forward and gave her shoulder a squeeze. 'You are sad. Soon I will take you to Iqbal so that you can send your thoughts to your mother and father. Maybe that will help. Chittagong is not so bad, you'll see.'

She said nothing.

'Okay?'

'Yes,' she said.

He swung his leg over the bicycle and took off. Pedalling up the side of the bungalow, merry noises floated from the windows and followed him to the front gate.

Zeythi sat in the dark. She felt an unpleasant loneliness, and she went to her quarters. She lay on the bed. She thought of home, and of her father and mother. During the next few weeks she would 'write' and send many letters. Khalid would talk to Iqbal to see if he wouldn't mind doing them cheap, and Iqbal would happily roll his head.

Zeythi would walk from Iqbal's corner to the post office and then make her way back to the bungalow. It became as regular as once a week. She did not tell anyone that her mother and father had passed away before she left the hills, she just kept sending the letters.

The teahouse was a short ride, and Khalid might have walked but he wanted to feel the night air on his chin. It was good to ride up to the place on your bike. Swing it in, climb off, park, walk up, say hi, all in one smooth swish. He took a neat pleasure in the arrival. One way or another most of them made an arrival. It was their place where they could argue about rumours in free Bengali, high or low, and it enjoyed a small notoriety.

It was a crumbling bungalow, built in the forties by a Greek trader. He had used the ground floor for his office and the top for living quarters. He became, down the decades, known by the 'expatriates' as the Pirate, until his health sent him home one last time. On the final approach Khalid could see the place glowing in the night, and it seemed to fling a tint into the cloud. The balcony was loaded heavily with the jolly and full types.

These days, many years after independence, I see full and jolly types on wide balconies all over Chittagong. It is the thin balconies that are stuffed with the unhappy and the empty.

Downstairs you could buy a sweet tea, or a cold beer—which nobody talked about. You could talk about the boom but you did not talk about the beer. Khalid decided to start with a beer. The costly English type, he thought.

As the warm night air flew past his chin he concentrated a moment on Zeythi. Rambling thoughts: Where did she get this idea about Iqbal? Damn spooky girl. Must remember to ask that stinking sabjantawallah to poke his nose into it. Sometimes in her room the low whining sound. Oh well.

He patted his pocket to feel the money. Look at this. Damn good woman. Thank you, memsahib. Thank you thank you.

Making his entrance, Khalid pulled up with a bounce to the balustrade and slipped off the bicycle. The place was busy. Bearers from the club, a gang of rickshaw drivers, a gardener, many other cooks, ayahs, a sabjan-tawallah. And Iqbal not writing letters.

Here, at the decaying teahouse, they sang and fought

in Bengali, Urdu, a bit of Hindi. No proper stuff like at work. No pretending to be a good boy. Khalid went inside. He looked about and reckoned on at least forty bastards tonight. Good, he thought. He felt mature. There was no more doubt in him about it, he was now a man.

He shouted out to the canteen for a beer, 'English lager!' They were his last English words for the night.

At the table a young guy was telling a story from his day at work as a bearer. He was pushed around by the President of the foreigners' club, and his tale was a quick one of revenge. The President, an Englishman, had ordered a beer with his lunch in the lounge, and the bearer spat in the glass before taking it to the 'President-bastard'. The bearer described it as a 'big, mixed-up, ugly spit.'

Khalid called out: 'You are a filthy pig.'

'Khalid!' the Spitting-bearer smiled widely. 'How are you?'

'I am fine,' Khalid said dismissively. He continued walking.

'Watch out, cook, I can eat fire!' the Spitting-bearer called. Lately he had begun to allow the fine hairs on his lip to grow long, and he thought of the material as a moustache.

'People say I look like a baby catfish, but I do not care,' he would boast, 'I can eat a burning tree!'

Other tables were in full swing, and the night grew larger. Everyone knew what everyone else knew—the country was running through a boom. They liked saying the word, but the merchants used it over and over. Stallkeepers from the bazaar, hawkers, taxi drivers: 'Boom times, my friend!'

'Boom?' a man in the corner said. 'A boom? What does it mean to us? It means nothing to us.'

To Khalid it was a heady time, but he felt it in a slightly different way. There is cheer, work, plenty, praise, a spark in the ayah's eye when she's not tired, a place to stay, a 'fantastic' memsahib, and, such as it is for a cook in whites in Chittagong 1967, there is *position*. Things are fast and glorious, and everyone knows the thing to do is keep a beady eye out for opportunity.

'Think quick like a catfish!' Mahfouz the Spitting-bearer said loudly.

Khalid swung back to the table. 'I don't care, you are still a filthy pig! Give his glass to me, I'll spit in it!'

Mahfouz took up his glass. 'Get lost! What are you talking about?'

'Give his glass here!' Khalid barked.

'I warn you, cook, I can eat stones!'

From the staircase Mohendra the chickenwallah appeared. He was Wandering. Out in the night of great things, the chickenwallah's habit: to Wander. Mohendra made Wandering into a special activity not to be interrupted. Seeing Khalid, he came to the table and then called out to the canteen, 'Two English lagers!'

Odd. Mohendra's custom was never to blow money off into space.

Another tale was rolling, but the Spitting-bearer interrupted, 'Khalid! We heard the news!'

'What news?'

'Beautiful new girl at your place. Did you bring her?'

'No, she's too tired.'

'Too tired? What have you been doing to her?'

'You should learn manners, drainhead. Come to the house tomorrow, I'll show you how to eat fire and stones.'

'Yah, like bulldust. I will eat the fire from your kitchen and make you useless!'

The young men at the Spitting-bearer's table laughed loudly.

Mohendra the chickenwallah then spoke with Khalid for a moment. To hide a sly question, he first asked unimportant nonsense. How was the big international dinner? Khalid mumbled a few unimportant words. Then Mohendra got to Zeythi. Was she on her way up? Khalid shook his head.

'Really? She is not coming?'

'By now she is fast asleep.'

'What a pity.'

'Come,' Khalid said, 'let's go upstairs. Anybody up there?'

'Yah.'

'Who?'

'Iqbal is there. Ajit Mookerjee. Leila also.'

'Leila Ghosh?'

'Yah.'

'She is back from Dacca?'

'Yah.'

'Then? Let's go up!'

Leila Ghosh worked for the Jordanian Egyptian, Fatimah Westcott-memsahib, though only on a month-by-month basis. So Leila had taken the bus with her uncle to Dacca to try her luck. Fatimah Westcott, who was retained by a trading firm, liked Leila and so offered to keep things open if the girl returned. No, she would not, Leila had said, 'Dacca is for me, but thank you.' Fatimah Westcott knew the trading houses of ugly Dacca, and she smiled and said all right. She would let

Leila go the magic circle.

Why Fatimah Westcott called it the magic circle I did not know back then. She was what they call a little jumping eyebrow. Funny but a bit suspicious.

Standing with friends and a costly beer at the balcony wall was a big pleasure: the jungle on the hillside glowed, and the open expanse of the balcony created a sahib sense. You also had the view back inside to the talking types bullshitting on about basically nothing.

Khalid was excited. The city he had not seen for himself, he had seen in his daydreams. Daydreams are worse than dreams, but the cook needed to find out this petty sting for himself.

'Hi Leila,' the cook said.

'Hi Khalid.'

'Back so soon?'

'Dacca is rubbish, don't listen to what everyone says.'

'But it is a city, no?'

City. Sometimes you catch someone saying something you want her to say. It has the sound of a bell all going utterly fanatic. Stinking with opportunity. Everyone's pockets in Dacca jingled like a hundred bells. Work, a man or woman could pick and choose. Crossing this *city* choosing a job would take days it was that big, that bright, that festooned with floating paisas and rupees.

Leila and Khalid stood at the balcony wall, and the night was warm. Two small groups on the other side of the balcony talked and laughed. It was less boisterous upstairs.

'They tell me,' Leila said, 'there is a new girl at your place.'

'Yah.'

'Is she nice?'

'She is okay.'

Khalid turned to the gardener. Ajit Mookerjee had recently landed a new job at the Bengali mayor's bungalow. His expertise with hibiscus, roses and orchids was legend, and most expected him to start up his own small farm at the foot of the hills behind Chittagong.

'New job okay, Ajit?' Khalid asked.

'Very good.'

'What is the latest news on this place?'

'The sahibs couldn't care less about it. What about you? How is the new girl?'

Khalid turned to Mohendra, 'Anybody left to tell?'

They all laughed and Leila smiled a short smile.

Then Khalid asked Mohendra if his pottery friend from the bazaar was here tonight.

'Aranthi? You never showed any interest before. Why are you asking about her?'

'Because,' Leila said, 'he is just asking only.'

'Because,' Khalid replied with firmness, 'I want to ask her about making a tandoor, but a new type.'

'Oh, this thing you were telling me about today.'

'Yah.'

The sabjantawallah shuffled past, and he squeaked in his small voice, 'Because he wants to finish it before the rain!'

Every village has a sabjantawallah, its Mister Know-It-All, but in the town of Chittagong we had about twenty-seven sabjantawallahs, give or take. Our sabjantawallah, Khan as he was simply known, was a long-standing friend of Iqbal's. He was more than the town's Mister Know-It-All. Khan could also divine what you were not saying. That is, he could hear what you were thinking. Never did I believe this myself, fully. But he used to shrug his bony shoulder and mutter, 'What do I care what you do not believe?'

'You should take more notice,' Iqbal used to advise me on the side. 'It is quite a nifty talent. Shitty—but nifty.'

When the sahibs went away on a holiday, Khan could tell me what they did and said.

Even though Khan did not disguise the fact that back then he thought I was a stupid fool this never stopped him from showing off. He passed onto me plenty of filthy stuff. He liked it, the telling, very much. His mouth would water. But these days I have more than just Khan's lowdown knowledge. From my headstone I can also touch the living shoulder of the club President-sahib to eavesdrop on his memories.

Khan shuffled past, wailing lightly, 'The rain is coming! The borders of the living and the dead will disappear!'

Inside the building, hopes were being brewed in the excitement of the boom. Another crack near the door was ignored. Like any teahouse, the seers and the blind were thrown together and the place between was the luxurious balcony. The balcony from where you might crash into the river of life or crumble into the sky of life or career into the heart of life. The balcony was already fishing for a soul or two.

'Let me tell you a story,' Khalid said to the sabjan-tawallah, 'about a bad feeling I had yesterday.'

'Story,' Leila said. 'What high-and-mighty ideas you have inside your head.'

'Are you listening to him?' Mohendra asked and leaned in to Leila.

'Yah,' she said without removing her gaze from the cook.

'Don't. He's a sagawallah.'

Leila stood comfortably. She folded her Dacca arms. All fine and smooth Mohendra decided these were.

'Why are you with your long face?' Mohendra asked her. 'Let me entertain you.'

Iqbal said, tapping his foot, 'I think the floor is making me slip. Is it making you slip?'

'Me?' Khalid said. 'No, I am standing on cement,' he said confidently.

They continued enjoying the night until late. Khalid felt good taking beer. The thrill of reaching beyond the rules made him say bold things. He was starting to know what it must be like to be one of the men around town. He started saying 'How are you?' to people here and there on the balcony and also inside. He started telling stories. Talking about his new tandoor.

They did not ever say it, but they patted the balcony like they embraced a friend. It was easy for sahibs or foreigners to say, with some pity but without feeling, that these folk of the teahouse had nowhere to go. Let them have the teahouse. No hope, they'd say, really, if you look at it square-on, if you think about it unsentimentally. Well this was of course from the outside. There was plenty of hope, especially back in those days. And the boom was coming into full flower. Along with the monsoon.

What did we care about these sahibs? About dam builders, lawyers, World Health people? The English, Dutch, Australians, Irish, Greeks, Japanese? Before Khalid was born the Japanese bombed Chittagong. Now they were Chittagong's friend and they built the Kaptai dam. One hundred thousand Chakma people in the hills had to move, but the sahibs were happy because electricity was needed for the coast to become modern. Yah, the sahibs had grand plans for the place. But in the teahouse nobody wanted to know about such useless bulldust.

Then there was the other sahib. The Bengali upright who wanted to see the place leap ahead. Abdul the history teacher always liked to tell his 'European friends' that 'Ptolemy called Chittagong the finest of the Eastern ports.' It was true, now that I can say it these days, Chittagong the ancient port traded with everybody. Why suddenly change a good thing?

No, in '67 they encouraged a great tide of all that old stuff. There was nothing wrong in that. And in the teahouse, Mohendra and his friends believed in the boom; mostly didn't mind the men and women they worked for. That is not strictly true. It is better put like this: they knew how to keep a good eye on the opportunity.

Besides, Khan the sabjantawallah knew what the sahibs were thinking. So the teahouse people knew every stinking thing. If the club President sat alone in the library, pondering his future in East Pakistan, a bearer somewhere who was throwing back a sweet tea with Khan could tell you what the Englishman was hoping Chittagong's fertile future would bring. And this place, Chittagong, was not like the catastrophic boils of Calcutta or Dacca. Abdul the history teacher insisted it was beautiful: ancient and lovely.

Mahfouz the Spitting-bearer emerged from the staircase to see what was going on upstairs.

Khalid leaned over to Mohendra, 'Somebody should give that kid an idea on how to get ahead.'

'Mahfouz? Don't be a dunderhead. Mahfouz is

doomed,' Mohendra said dismissively.

The sabjantawallah squeaked as he shuffled away, 'Doomed!'

Two Forecasters Sitting
in the Shade

The next day Khalid and Mohendra the chickenwallah paid for the long night at the teahouse with painful heads and deep thirst. Khalid sipped at a glass that glinted red when he lifted it. This was a new potion he made to cure the exploding head and quench the unending thirst. Mohendra did not like the look or the smell of the potion, so he sipped plain lychee juice instead. They had been sipping for a while, wasting no effort on talking.

'Is yours working?' Khalid said lazily.

'No,' Mohendra said. He emptied his lychee to the dust. 'Give me some of yours.'

Khalid poured the mixture of tomato juice, chilli and lime into Mohendra's glass.

'My head is damn bad,' Mohendra said.

'It will be soon okay. Drink.'

'It looks horrible.'

'Drink. What goodness can it do waiting in your shaking hand?'

'You say the sahib does this?'

'Yah. It is a bloody mary,' Khalid said and they fell silent. Khalid had left out the hard stuff. He knew if the sahib caught him putting in the hard stuff he would be sacked.

Zeythi strode from the house to hang clothing. She kept to herself. She flung the basket to the dirt.

'Where have you been?' Khalid called out.

'To the club,' she grumbled.

'It has made you angry?'

'No, your stupid friend Mahfouz has made me angry.'

Mahfouz the Spitting-bearer was not one to sit back. Yes, he maybe had a word with Zeythi as he worked the tables at the swimming pool. Or grabbed his groin with both hands as he stood in front of her and shovelled the hot air with his bony hips. Big nasty smile full of charm. Mouth full of boasts.

Zeythi hung the washing in silence.

'Yah,' Mohendra said quietly to Khalid, 'that Mahfouz, eating fire, he has no idea.'

But that, according to the sabjantawallah, is not what Mohendra was thinking. According to Khan, Mohendra was thinking, Wow, that girl, maybe one day soon she will see my business and then she will want to let me have her. Look at her damn legs. Look at her damn arse. Look at her damn fine temper—look at everything. Argh, bastard, I am getting near to getting hard. Better take this horrible drink and cool off …

'Yah, that guy, eating fire,' said Mohendra quietly, 'he has no idea.'

'He acts like a bigshot,' Khalid agreed. 'Iqbal told me he thinks he is Khudiram Bose.'

'Mahfouz? What a joke. The stupid idiot does nothing every day except pull a stunt.'

'Pulling a stunt is okay,' Khalid said, 'My sahib says in these boom times every bastard is pulling a stunt.'

'I cannot pull a stunt.'

'I am pulling one,' Khalid said with a smile.

'Yah? This new tandoor you talk about?'

'Yah.'

They sipped the sour drink in silence. Khalid patted water to the back of his neck.

In a lull waiting for a monsoon, it is impossible to foresee things. Khalid could not know that the future world into which the fifteen-year-old Mahfouz would throw his heart was to be torn by the chilling cries of insurrection and the abrupt noises of executions. The Spitting-bearer would one day arise, join the liberators, the Mukti Bahini, to chase unwanted sahibs from the coast. But then, Mahfouz himself did not yet know.

When I look back on Mahfouz, I think that he might have carried on ejecting until there was nobody left to eject. But I am wrong, because in time to come he would be taken along to my headstone. And he would sit in the cool shade of the guava trees, staring. Eyes of exhaustion. By then he would be a grown Bengali man, and his time with the revolution would be over. He would no longer be eating fire. I suppose it was the cool silence he liked. He sat on the grass by the headstone for long stretches, sometimes very long. He was twenty-three and strong when he fought in the Insurrection in '75. He fought the West Pakistani army, and some men convinced him he also fought Bengalis. He had felt the execution of Abu Taher in the gallows of Dacca Central Gaol, and the death of Mujibur Rahman, Rahman's sister, the children.

Then one day, as if by complete surprise, when Ajit Mookerjee the gardener took him along to the guava grove, he sat by the headstone for over two hours. He was not eating fire, but sipping from a glass of cool water.

If Mahfouz once believed he was the great freedom fighter Khudiram Bose, he did not seem to think so after the years of destruction had fallen silent.

It never occurred to the thirsty forecasters that Mahfouz the Spitting-bearer was tumbling into the explosions of independence.

'Tell him to go to school with you,' Mohendra said to Khalid as he lifted his glass.

'Why?'

'He can learn manners, like you said last night.'

'He has no interest in manners. Is the drink working?'

'Yah, I think so. Cheers.'

Clean!

Dry afternoons in the compound offered nothing to do so the place was left idle. To finish work Zeythi decided to clean the outside toilet.

The Minisahib squatted, and then he pushed, and he was empty. He reached out for the roll of paper, but Zeythi interrupted and held his wrist.

He was startled. How did *she* suddenly get in?

She hissed at him: 'Dirty!' She produced a tin pail. 'Water!' she said. 'Wash!' she ordered. Then in a calm voice, 'Wash … like this.'

He pulled away his hand. He slapped the air against the possibility of touching his shit with his fingers. Between his whispered shouts she impressed on him the cleanliness of washing himself, and he kept fighting off her many hands, fending, squatting, not considering any 'filthy thing' of washing.

It was their first disagreement.

But she let him have the paper. He ran it wildly from the wall, bunched it up as he had been taught. Again a fresh wad, and again a hasty scudding.

He stood to reach for the flush handle. He pulled it down. He waited for her to step aside.

The moments floated in the pungent air. But she stood.

'Get out!' the Minisahib whispered.

But she began to lift her small loongie with one hand, and she held his shirt collar with the other, stronger, working hand. Her belly appeared. She brought their bodies about, positioning herself over the hole, feet set on the cement footpads.

'Iqbal?'

'Yes?'

'Are you taking this down?'

'Can you not see the writing?'

'No, I cannot, I've decided to lie back for a minute.'

'Tired today?'

'No. You are not altering any of this?'

'Alter it? Why should I change it?'

'I don't know, maybe you think it's not fit to put in.'

'It is none of my business,' Iqbal said quietly. 'Shall we continue?'

'Yes, let's continue.'

The Minisahib wanted to bolt outside, but she held him hard. She squatted and let loose a healthy spray. She fixed her eyes on his. And then she pushed. With this she felt she could release his collar. She was right. All he did was stand there against the cool cement wall.

She lifted the pail up behind herself with one hand. With the other hand she reached under the thigh and washed. Again she tilted the pail, and again she rinsed herself. A third pour for luck, and she stood to pull down the flush handle. Her loongie slid to the ankles.

She took him by the hand outside. He walked behind, limbs loose, until they reached the laundry tub. There, under the afternoon sun, which was invisible, she worked

53

her hands in running water with a cake of yellow soap.

'Clean,' she said with a pleasant smile.

She lifted the Minisahib's hands to the tap and worked them with the soap, loosely rubbing to the rhythm of her humming.

'Also clean,' she said.

Then, slowly, so that the Minisahib could not mistake the approach, she brought her hands up to his cheekbones. She held his head, smiled into his eyes and placed a kiss to his nose.

'Iqbal?'

'Yes?'

'Good thing to teach the Minisahib?'

Normally Iqbal will say nothing. But here, the unusual. Iqbal offered an opinion.

'Yes,' he said. 'It is a good thing to teach people proper cleanliness.'

Deep into the Night

Khalid lay awake with his hands open. The type of ignorance in his palm was one he wished to fling away forever. He would wish it more or less every night. Shuffle up, into a sitting position. A near-monsoonal moon would peek into the dark room, a diluted light that settled across the knee. The jungle over the back wall would call out with a ticking sound. Over the other wall, at the side of the compound, the Sleeping Camels would rise against the dim light. The entire compound, his room included, had been cooled by the night. Things were settled. Without noise. Then he would imagine the big city. How unlike this calm. Bold maybe, never asleep, cars always, and hot with excitement maybe. Dacca. So damn bold, Khalid would think, that it was maybe the one place that could stick its nose up at the monsoon. He would light a cigarette and think of the way that Leila said it was a dump. She had said it with a throwaway certainty.

Then he would make the wish. He would give himself thoughts of Leila. In the stillness of the deep night. Lovely Leila. And he would let himself fully start to think. By the time he had finished thinking of Leila, poor Leila wasn't even Leila any more but just a jumble of things he'd always wanted to do with a kind of Leila. There were Leilas all over the place for a young cook like Khalid. Chittagong was a misery for him like that. Leila-land. Someday I will marry, he decided, that's for me. He would be rid of that snorting ignorance in the palm of his hand.

He then lit a cigarette and looked out at the dim sky. It brought happiness to the plate of his face. Blank, but happy. If the cat glimpsed his head, the cat would get a bad shock, because the calm, dreaming, happy head in the window would appear to be some kind of new beast the rat-catching animal had not yet known. But the night felt good. The ticking quiet felt like a gift. And he appreciated the wetness on the sill of the open window. He ran a sticky finger along it.

Then a proper thought would overcome his empty smile. He'd wonder, How can I have a night with the real Leila? Are such things possible? But again the night would catch him, draw his attention to new pleasures. They were lighted nights, airy and cool, bigger than the jam-packed days full of the grabbing eagerness of the boom.

A Tuft of Caution

The next day Leila called in. Pleasure walked down the side of the bungalow into the compound, and Khalid lingered on her appearance. He thought pleasure looked very modern in her new Dacca outfit. She strolled across the dust on long brown legs—which showed through the thin skirt, which he liked suddenly a lot, and he invited her to sit at the table under the shade and have a pot of tea. Stupid, he then thought, dunderhead; the table has blocked the modern Dacca legs.

'I cannot give you a strong drink, I have plenty more work to do,' he said.

'It's okay,' Leila said gladly. 'I took enough at the teahouse. If my father knows, he will beat me with my broom.'

They sat and talked. Khalid wanted to ask about the big city of his dreams. Instead, Leila talked about Zeythi. When she had met Zeythi a few days ago, she came to the secret conclusion that Khalid ought to exercise care and caution. Now Leila said it openly.

'What are you carrying on about?' Khalid said. 'She's a know-nothing child from the hills.'

'She is not a child,' Leila said. 'More than that—I'm

telling you—she is too strange.'

'Like fun she is strange. What you are seeing is the sorrow of homesickness. Today I will take her to Iqbal, and she can send a letter off to Mummy and Daddy.'

But Leila's cloudy suspicion was almost right. Zeythi did possess strange gifts, certain abnormal powers. These were not fully developed as she was still only young, but they amounted to Zeythi possessing a *knowing*.

Zeythi came down the steps carrying a basket. She hung bed sheets on the clothes line, joining the corners, and when she made a complete wall, she went back inside.

'Homesickness my foot,' Leila said. 'She has a shifty look in the eye. Plenty just like her in Dacca.'

'Yah rubbish. Slap from the village bang into town—what kind of "look" do you expect? When you know her, you will like her.'

'You like her, that I know,' Leila said.

But that, according to the sabjantawallah, is not what Leila was thinking. Khan says she was thinking: You damn well want to fool around with her, and she's very beautiful, you filthy guy. You stinking pig.

'You like her, that I know at least,' Leila said.

'Yah, she's nice. How come you're not working today?'

'I'm going to the bazaar. Want to come along?'

'No,' Khalid stated, but suddenly he realised he had said no. He stumbled along, 'I only need ducks, nothing else for now, and the ducks Featherduster is delivering tomorrow.'

'Featherduster?'

'Mohendra.'

'Why do you call him Featherduster all of a sudden?'

'Check him out when you go into town, you'll see.'

When Leila left, Zeythi came outside and sat with Khalid.

Khalid suggested he take Zeythi to Iqbal the letterwriter.

She remained silent.

'You don't want to?'

'I do.'

'Then what is the matter?'

'It will be no good to say things to a stranger.'

'Iqbal? No no, Iqbal is a very good man. He never tells anybody else about anybody else's business.'

'But my umma told me to take it carefully with these letterwriters.'

'Your umma is right. The other fellow, and that other one far up near the bazaar, they are shitheads who don't give a damn and they flap their smelly mouths whenever they can.'

'Does he really talk to those on the other side?'

Khalid smiled. 'No,' he said.

He went inside to work his way through the evening meal. He thought for a long time about Dacca and he decided to ask Leila for tips about the place. Zeythi completed the bedrooms and they rode off on his bicycle. Khalid dropped her off at Iqbal's roadside table under the brolly, and then rode away to find a rickshaw to follow him to the club. He was to collect the Minisahib from the pool because the Old Man would be staying late for snooker.

Khalid returned with a rickshaw. They pulled up alongside the big drain. The rickshaw carried the Minisahib and two French girls who were staying at the Smiths' bungalow.

'Everything okay?' Khalid asked the letterwriter across the giant drain.

Iqbal rolled his head and smiled back.

The traffic flowed past.

The Spitting-bearer rode up. He smiled at Zeythi and pulled up.

'I am Mahfouz, remember?' he said with charm.

Zeythi made a half-hearted smile.

Khalid ignored the Spitting-bearer and asked Zeythi, 'You want to go in the rickshaw? Or with me?'

'Rickshaw?' the Spitting-bearer said and looked over his shoulder. 'Hey …! Two English … hi darlings!' he called out sarcastically.

'They are not English,' Khalid said flatly.

'Then?'

'French.'

'Who are French?'

Khalid ignored the question.

Zeythi decided on the small platform on the back of the cook's bike, and they pulled away. Iqbal waved goodbye and smiled.

Riding along, Zeythi considered the short note she had made, and she decided that it was all right but not enough. She decided that she would 'write' another in a few days' time.

The Spitting-bearer followed alongside, smiling, weaving skilfully in the heavy traffic, and Khalid warned him off. The bearer swung away easily and disappeared.

Outside town the rickshaw set down the French girls

at the driveway of the Smiths' bungalow. The driver was on his way again, following the cook's bicycle to the house. Zeythi had taken a seat in the rickshaw beside the Minisahib.

'Did you do the letter?' the Minisahib asked.

But Zeythi changed the subject: 'Who is Leila?'

'She's from the Arab woman's house.'

Again she altered the subject: 'So did you swim in the big thing?'

'Yes. Today it was crowded like the blazes,' he said excitedly.

He whispered, 'Tomorrow I'm going again, but I'll stay a bit later, swim in the dark. Do you want to come?'

She forgot about the letter she had posted. But next week she would again remember to send another.

The Minisahib followed Khalid into the kitchen. Khalid walked briskly so the Minisahib was trotting in order to keep up. He was firing questions again. First he asked why the generator at the club was not working. Khalid replied by asking how the hell he should know and he didn't care. Then the Minisahib asked why everyone did such a filthy thing like using paper to wipe their arses. Khalid did not answer and continued to the kitchen to prepare dinner. At the kitchen door he stopped. He turned to the Minisahib.

'From where do you get these endless questions?'

'I'm only asking one question,' the Minisahib said.

'You ask a thousand questions a day, what is wrong with you?'

'Why do they use paper?'

Khalid stared at the Minisahib. 'You know what you are?' Khalid said. 'You are a question generator. Now leave me alone, I have work to do.'

The Minisahib wandered outside to sit high in the money plant to watch the evening turn to night. He didn't mind. He'd wait until dinner was over to sit with Khalid and ask again.

Somebody Vacuumed the World

Outside had been hot and the Minisahib could feel the sun burning his nose, but he finally decided what to do. He went inside and made his way quietly to a broom cupboard. In the corridor his footstep squeaked. He drew aside the door to the shelves, exposing bland darkness. His hand went for the jar, but he had to pat about. When he held up the jar to the light of the corridor the clear water sparkled. Khalid had bought it for him. He simply went out one day and returned with the household goods, from which he took the small jar.

'These,' the cook said, 'give the fish these worms. The fish will sing for you like film stars.'

Outside, he twisted off the lid. He teased a pinch from the ball of hair-thin worms and lowered the morsel into the guppies. A big guppy shot into position, holding off to tighten up and vibrate before jabbing at the worms.

Khalid was forever showing him into the world of curious things. He was the Minisahib's friend and guide. And here, between the laundry and the crumbling back fence on a forgotten patch of dirt, under the shade, no grass, the world was as big as it was anywhere, maybe bigger. The tank, the size of two boxes side by side, looked fine today, the Minisahib decided. The guppies were in a frenzy of feeding. Right again, he thought, they're singing like the dancers on the radio.

But that was done. It didn't take long. Now there was nothing to do. Big world all right.

He walked along the crumbling wall. He kicked a tin. It rolled into the air. He picked up a pail and strolled to the good wall at the side. He laid the pail upside down and placed a broken brick on it. He stood looking at it and wondered what he could place on the brick. He looked about the compound as if this would make a flagpole appear, or a statue of a giant catfish. He placed the jar of worms on it. Then to make it look like a machine he ran a length of electric cable from the brick to the pail handle. Then he put two used batteries at the ends of the brick.

Satisfied, he stepped up to the vine at the wall. The vine rose on solid loops that he climbed easily. The grown-ups were forever saying that he looked like a monkey, but they were ignorant. It was as simple as climbing steps the branches were so curled and thick. On top of the wall he sat in the money plant for the comfort of the matting of leaves.

When is Khalid going to make the flying fox? he wondered.

In the leaves he found a bottle of guava juice. It would be stale and sour but he lifted it to his mouth. He spat it out to the field. Flecks of cattle grazed in the stillness. Beyond the cattle, the hills shouldered up under a shawl of dust.

Mohendra the chickenwallah walked down the side of the house. When he was in the compound he stood for a moment. He called out for Khalid. Then he called out for Zeythi. No reply.

'Boo!'

Mohendra's head jerked. He looked up and he thought, Little Paklish bastard.

He then asked politely, 'Have you seen Zeythi?'

'No.'

'Khalid?'

'No.'

'What are you doing up there?'

'Nothing.'

'What is this?' he muttered, pointing to the pail. He thought it would be best to be nice to the Minisahib since being nice could help when it came to getting messages to Zeythi. Mohendra thought like that, always a step in front, always with reasons.

'What do you think it is?' the Minisahib asked.

'How should I know? What is it?'

'It's a generator.'

'Why is it not making noise?'

'Because it does not generate electricity.'

'Then what does it generate?'

'It's a question generator.'

Mohendra decided he would play along. Good sense.

'How much do you want for it?'

'Ten rupees.'

'Ten rupees! What use have I for a question generator that is so costly?'

'Why do you want to fuck Zeythi?' the Minisahib asked dismissively.

'You are saying "fuck"? You filthy little bastard. Anyway, who told you that?'

'See what I mean, it works very well—ten rupees is cheap.'

'Tell Zeythi I called in, okay?'

He walked up the side of the house and rode away on his bicycle.

The Minisahib heard the kitchen door tap shut. Zeythi had come outside. She began to load runner carpets on the clothes line. Tonight, the Minisahib thought with satisfaction, wait until they close the pool, then we swim, she and me alone.

How Much for the Emerald?

An emerald glow danced on the water. It reflected a bat falling into flight from a mango tree. The pump had been switched off. They stood at the far end, a taller figure and a small figure on bony legs, watching the slow bounce. She took her foot to it, and the Minisahib watched the breaking away of the reflections.

It was late, it was an opportunity; when would this come again, this moment alone, unattended, the Old Man too busy in the snooker room?

She looked over the surface, a long sweep, and no smile came to her mouth; it was too actual for a smile. And the uneven silk, the beautiful, bouncing smoothness; enter a dream of the deepest pleasure. Even the big river pools, the forgotten curves by the banks under a warm moon, did not look like this.

How, she thought, would this strange water feel?

But she sensed the answer. With her customary knowing, she already had an answer.

She lifted the loongie and swung her ankle into it. She looked about once more. It seemed secure. The Minisahib sat down at the edge, and he watched as she removed her clothing. She placed the folded bundle on a nearby table. She lowered herself into the emerald-coloured shallows, and a breath left her mouth. With a small push she glided away under the surface, concentrating as she went, on the light dancing above her eyes.

Far away, so that the night expanded into the whole enclosure, she stood up. Her hair fell against her back in a shining sheet, but she replaced it to a shoulder. She looked at what she had come from; the huge trees glistening in the darkness, the cement water tank, the Minisahib dangling his legs over the edge, the slope rising up to the well-lit club building and a low cover of cloud. It was so. This was like bathing at a palace. Not a palace of silk where forbidden things are too numerous; more like a palace of some small, modest self, where to glide aimlessly is to discover a flesh-felt paradise.

These were the moments of thinness and transparency. The moments in which she was to recognise the true payment for leaving her home to come to Chittagong. She pushed off the floor of the pool to go further, and she turned chest up, watching the light, which now came slicing into the deep. Halfway into the far deep she came up. She floated on her back and closed her eyes.

But her knowing had failed her. She had not realised that this small moment was the murmur of a new and sparkling experience, one that brings a shimmer to these sheltered trees, so that things are forever changed, are never the same.

And, from a less intimate viewpoint, it was also a moment when a girl holds another scent of growing into the larger world; of, maybe, a kind of womanhood approaching quicker at this moment than at other moments. Another of the thousands of hesitations had vanished into the clouds.

Even her mother's reigning guidance over the years

('We mustn't be too proud and take things for granted') now paled against the lush harmonies which she experienced as she floated over the deep. She now most definitely wanted to take this for granted.

Patience, forbearance, a rich love of life; destiny can encourage these qualities in ways both dreamed and undreamed, but none seem as right and true as a presence, as floating right there.

The Minisahib had never seen her in the pool. To him it looked good: all empty, calm, her naked legs afloat on the glowing expanse. It looks very good, he thought, I wonder if she likes it.

Her skin and the water's skin, she felt no difference existed to tell them apart—but this was not so. What she maybe felt was the completeness that appears the one time only. Her idle daydreams never foresaw the moment with such clarity. They were not able to foretell the existence inside of untouched pleasures that can make all things suddenly hum with inviting glows. It had always been easy to like the Minisahib—and to warm to that idiot Khalid—and to like the family, for under the house forever ran a hidden stream, flowing with kindnesses. And it had been fascinating to watch, with disbelief, the spectacle of the club. To see the comings and goings at the house. To watch as strange women walked into the door from their strange lands, to witness their odd habits, and to hear with surprise their voices of untrembling and unconcerned bigness. It had also been a shock to see the ocean, the wall of foam crashing to the sand. All these things, and many more, were very easy to like, and had been a big thrill. But after tonight, Chittagong will transform into a town of beauty that will lay across her heart in a pose of welcome against the spite of the Bay of Bengal.

'I'm here at last,' she whispered. 'I have arrived.' And she lay on the undulating emerald water, looking up the rising trees, a smile on her face.

The Minisahib set his curling toes to the water, whispering to himself. 'It looks like she's being hugged by the sky. Is she smiling? She's not smiling. She never smiles.'

Later she dressed and they stepped together up the hill to meet the Old Man. When he came out, they drove home marvelling at the low sky. It collected an orange glow.

'Raining suddenly?' the Old Man asked.

'A bearer came out with a hose,' the Minisahib said.

'What! Which one?'

'We couldn't see who it was—he jumped out behind her.'

'You didn't get just a glimpse?'

'No,' the Minisahib said.

'Well that's it, we'll never catch him the bastard toolbrain.'

The Old Man steered hard. He took control of the car as it joined the main road.

'Never mind, little one. You can have a shower, when we arrive home you can have a warm shower,' the Old Man said as he weaved into the night.

He took hold of the steering wheel and almost hit the trunk of an almond tree, and then loosened his grip to veer towards the road. They went home almost hitting pedestrians; they almost hit a goat, they almost hit the tin end of a hut, they almost hit a rickshaw at the rear wheelguard, and they took a chip from the cement gatepost when they did arrive home.

The next afternoon the club President called an emergency meeting. To the bearers the Englishman was simply 'President-bastard'.

He was another nameless sahib. He had come to Chittagong long ago, and he was shocked to find all kinds of stuff he liked. He wrote to his wife: 'a beehive of international activity, friendly locals, abundant opportunity and a flash clubhouse stained by the weather.' His wife arrived and they made a fine home of the town. He opened a small factory that made road signs and a line of domestic goods. He hoped the venture would secure reasonable riches while at the same time flick a personal switch to a personal engine that might address the country's call for help and development. He called it a 'symbiotic relationship'.

Iqbal and I have asked everyone if they know what this means, but nobody can say. To me it sounds like a disease. He loved his life in Chittagong. Doubtful he would ever return to England.

At the emergency meeting Abdul the club secretary made a quick announcement. He was a Bengali who taught at the polytechnic. He was forever dreaming about Fatimah Westcott.

Abdul-sahib and President-bastard met when the President first came to Chittagong. They became friends in a week, and the friendship deepened the more Abdul discovered how well the President felt about Chittagong 'and its people'.

In the meeting Abdul quickly got to the point to state the quarterly earnings from the bar, which was the biggest source of the club's income. A murmur rose around the room. Abdul banged his pipe on the edge of a snooker table, and the green-brown room fell silent.

'The cost,' Abdul concluded, 'exceeded the damn earnings.'

The committee broke into a long period of scattered talk. The President remained quiet. He allowed the rambling chatter to exhaust itself. No solution would emerge, that he knew. They would babble on about increasing the fees on this and that. He waited with a casual patience. He leaned into the chair, and he raised a finger to the Chief Bearer, who went away and returned with a gin and tonic on a tray. The Chief Bearer stood by.

Akram the Chief Bearer was in reality the President's personal assistant, and took extra secret pay each month, a glad bucksheesh regular as clockwork, he could bank on it.

Then the President stood. He said, 'We shall close the pool.'

A long confusion followed where the bearers became very busy.

The Old Man approached the President. He didn't feel too good from the previous night.

'Why shut down the pool?' he croaked.

'The pool is our biggest cost. You're not having a drink?'

'No thank you. What do you expect the children to do?'

'Children are expert at inventing activity.'

The President stood up and called for order. He arranged an informal vote, which was taken and then counted. It came out half and half, and the President, who had not bothered to vote, seemed to hold the balance.

By dinnertime Khalid gave the Minisahib the news. He waited until he cleaned the kitchen, when he could concentrate on telling the boy a plan. They sat next to the laundry, under the twisting vines.

The Minisahib was confused. No pool? It was difficult to see.

Zeythi came out and sat beside Khalid. She sat beside the cook to keep things with the Minisahib out of sight.

She listened without expression. She understood the news not as 'no pool' but as a sensation. The sensation of things being taken away. It was a feeling she had grown to know as hollowness.

The Minisahib was attempting to see what it would look like. He tried to see no more shark hunting, no canoeing up the Karniphuli, no diving on shipwrecks. And no swimming carnival. Pictures sprang into his mind, and he let his thoughts flow. No more glimpses of naked girls in the showers, or swimming behind, under their legs, with the mask. No secret swims at night. No pushing the Swedish bastard into the deep end: Somehow I'll have to bring him to the pond, push him in at the pond, up at the boulder, yeah.

Khalid's Price for the Pool

Khalid was ready for the plan. He knew the simple fact that these two liked the pool, but he was not aware of the sultry new boldness it had heated up for them. Besides, he was not thinking only of Zeythi and the Minisahib. He had ideas for himself. He could see how the plan was about to bring him a fat amount of boomtime bucksheesh. Money he would put to use to making dozens of his new tandoors. Thanks to the tandoors, and with his new sense of manliness, he was beginning to see himself as some kind of specialised tandoorwallah. When the afternoon heat had loosened his mind, his eye snapped for one second into a far future: when plenty of his new tandoors were bought by every bastard up and down the coast, he could see himself also as some kind of actual ... Yah, he thought, say it: Some kind of actual *sahib*. This was a quick moment, but he did see it. He fell back to the plan with a thump. The plan is damn good, he thought. It was a smart plan, he decided. Like a sharp new shalwar kameez from Dacca. *Yah*.

Khalid then unfolded the plan. It did not take long to show them the steps, and he went through it again, moment by moment. When he concluded the instructions, they looked at the cook with dumb, open eyes.

'And remember,' he said to Zeythi, 'when you go for his pants, I will be this side with the camera. Got it?'

'Yes,' she said quietly.

To Zeythi and the Minisahib it seemed fine. After all, Khalid was older and wiser.

But it was full of springy optimism. Full of stuff that comes bouncing out of the head of an excited young man who wanted to copy the sahibs in every way except weak, polite grunting. Maybe excited young guys in Dacca didn't have the same feverish stuff pouring from their heads like excited young guys in Chittagong.

Khalid shuddered.

'What is wrong?' Zeythi asked.

'Excitement. Yah, *excitement*!'

But it was the premonition again. Khalid ignored it.

The next afternoon the Minisahib and Zeythi rode to the club with the Old Man. The drive was dusty and the traffic moved slowly. The dry plain carried the sour smell of sludge from the monsoon drains. The Old Man took the wheel and pushed hard at gaps in the traffic. He also used the horn a lot. At the turn-off to the club he pulled over and bought a hand of bananas from a hawker.

The Old Man drove up the laneway at a good speed, weaving around great potholes.

'Like to have a banana, you two?'

'Yes please,' the Minisahib said.

'No thank you, sahib,' Zeythi murmured.

He snapped a banana from the ridge and then held the bunch over his shoulder. The Minisahib took it gratefully and snapped one away.

At the club the car looped bouncing into a bumpy spot

under a great almond tree. The asphalt cracked where the thick roots burst into the air, and he eased the wheels over the mountainous breaks for the cool shade. The car came to a stop at a massive tilt. The bananas lay on the seat and lifted slowly and then tumbled to the floor.

The Old Man took big strides up the steps onto the verandah. Halfway up he stopped.

'Well? Are you coming in?'

'We'll just wait here—her sandal has broken, but she's fixing it.'

The verandah was busy with afternoon tea. The Old Man went on inside, saying hello here and there as he walked.

When he disappeared into the entrance, they scuttled along the tree line to proceed quietly up the side of the club as Khalid had instructed. They were to find a minor rear entrance at the top of a flight of stairs. This was not the service entrance for the kitchen; search for the small orange door.

They walked steeply downhill until they emerged near the kitchen entrance. Two bearers were smoking and drinking tea. They waited for the men to go inside, but another came out. He cleared his throat, spat into the grass and then lit a cigarette.

They waited in the bamboo tunnel. The small orange door, located two storeys up on the far side, looked a long way off. The Minisahib took up his banana. He held the woody tip and began to bring it to one side to snap it.

'What are you doing?' Zeythi whispered.

'I'm eating it.'

'Put it away!'

'I'm hungry.'

'You can eat it later.'

The bearers started to move. One cleared his throat into the grass at his feet. He walked up the steps, his whites blaring off the red brickwork. A second white uniform burned against the red wall. His foot, too, fell heavily. When the third bearer had returned to work, there was no reason to wait and they moved under the windows along the back of the building. He held the banana, as he had no pockets. The hand sweated.

Khalid had insisted on staying clear of the bearers.

'If a bearer sees you, then do not go up the staircase. And no giggling. Definitely no stupidity—this is a proper plan, and it will work if you follow the instructions properly. Behave yourselves, do as I say, and all will be well. Okay?'

They had nodded.

'Better still … promise it.'

They had promised.

They climbed the stairs, and the iron spiral gonged lightly under their feet. The Minisahib pushed first. He thought about the option of going second so that he could watch her bums, but he wanted to hurry. He realised this was the proper start. Not the lead-in, this was the true start of the plan. As they stepped upwards through the iron he felt a surge of excitement. He quickened his pace, and the gonging became louder. Zeythi reached high above her head and caught his pants. His free hand pulled hard on the rusted bannister, but she held him down.

'Let go!'

'Be quiet!'

'We must move like the blazes—Khalid is waiting!'

'We must move quietly!' she hissed.

'I hate you! Let go!'

Zeythi smiled, 'Like fun you hate me.'

She poked her fingers up his pants leg, tickling him. 'You like me, you like me,' she sang quietly.

'Wasting time!' he groaned through his teeth.

He tried everything. He pushed and kicked and nothing worked: she held him with a strong arm. The staircase gonged loudly as they wrestled, but he could not break the hold she had on the pants.

'Let me,' she whispered. 'Khalid said I should go first …'

'No!'

'You can watch my backside.'

'I don't want to see your backside … Let me go!'

But she quickly slipped under his arm, stepping ahead of his hold on the iron.

'I'll slap your arse!' he barked.

'Then do it quietly,' she whispered as she looked up. The orange door was still a long way off, three spirals maybe four.

'I'll poke this banana in it!'

'Then do it *quietly*!'

He gritted his teeth, and, as he watched with bared eyes, he squeezed the banana until it crushed in his hand.

He flung the banana away and watched with satisfaction as the two main pieces crashed into the mangosteen tree. He wiped his hand back and forth on his shirt and then followed her up the stairs. Bits were stuck between his fingers so he ran his hand along the iron bannister.

At the landing she stopped to search over the treetop for Khalid, and she could see in the distance, behind the big water tank, his hand wave a flutter of encouragement. It was an excited hand and it was happy and it was a hand belonging to all good fools. She responded by raising fingers into the air thinly. Her heart began to race.

They entered the crisp air of the building. She had not been into this part of the club. She felt a dampening cool sensation. The chill came from the silent, windowless walls, and from terrifying heads that were looking down—the Queen, Ayub Khan, Jinnah, former club presidents. And it was all wood. The corridor, the parquetry, the wall panels, two credenzas and the endless shelving of trophies, shields, bats, wickets, caps and a brass plaque displaying a quote.

They walked slowly up the corridor. Her chest began to pound.

As he followed along the shelving, the Minisahib peered into the oddments until he stopped at the plaque.

It read, 'None Of Us Knows Anything'.

He ran up the corridor and stood by her side in mock obedience. She pretended to be satisfied, but with no warning she brought a slap to the back of his head.

It stung.

Ringing in the Minisahib's head, on and on.

At the entrance to the library she posted him on watch as planned. With a hand on each of his shoulders, she held him against the doorway. The corridor was cool and quiet.

'Will you be okay?'

'Yes,' he said, 'I'm all right.'

'You think I am nice, that's what you think,' she said softly.

'Yes,' he said, looking down at the cool carpet.

'Because I agree to the plan,' she said.

'No!' he hissed out.

'It is the plan.'

'It is not the plan,' he insisted.

According to the sabjantawallah, the Minisahib was thinking other things. According to Khan, the Minisahib was thinking that she was nice because she was kind and wise and funny and full of dirty fun, and because at the pool in the night she shined like the moon and was happy.

She placed him on watch next to the door. He began his tiny but important part of the plan. The corridor travelled to the front of the building, disappearing sharply to the left and taking with it Baluchi carpets. She drew a deep breath to try to settle her racing chest, and then she gently opened the door, slipped inside, and closed it behind her.

The Minisahib stood in the corridor. He was alone. Zeythi was gone, proper.

She had arrived into the deepest vault of the club, a never-seen mysterious place, further in than the snooker room. Her skin instantly lost its heat. She folded her arms over a pounding heart and stood very still, but could hear nothing, only a faint strumming, which she supposed was the air-conditioner.

Her heart beat loudly in her eardrums. The fear made things start to become strange. In a room you never encounter you see only contortions. She took a slender step backwards into a shelf of books.

Where is he? she thought. Maybe Khalid is wrong, all these 'contacts' he boasts about, all with these bearers—and how would they know anything? Maybe the English sahib is not here.

She felt as if she moved upon sponge, or upon the Minisahib's knobbly mattress, but not upon the hard sheen of parquetry. And she floated into disturbing, silent distortions, forces that were present but not visible.

She waited and held onto an upright in the shelving. She breathed slowly and closed her eyes for a time. Briefly, she saw herself in the warm embrace of the pool. It returned glowing and real.

She proceeded down the aisle with a soft footstep, passing the tall rows left and right. Then came a sound of cracking. She slowed her footstep, but continued towards the window. Three small tables with chairs were settled in the afternoon light, an open bay, but still nobody.

When she cleared the final shelf a figure seated on the far left was brought into view, but hidden by the upheld newspaper. At his side, shining in bursts of unpolished silver on the sill of the window, sat a tray of samosas and a bottle of golden whisky beside a glass bowl of ice.

She took a long, slow breath and then walked into the open.

Bringing down the *Guardian*, the President-sahib looked up.

She was looking right back at him, from underneath her brow.

A hint of pride, the President thought lazily. The Bengali woman, a striking sight; a rare and strange one … a distinctive physical beauty … drawn from some superior mixture of invisible forces …

His half thoughts fell away.

For years the mixture had mystified him. One day, after two decades working and enjoying the sprawling paradise of East Pakistan, one fine and sunny morning, taking dark coffee and a generous strip of papaya, he decided it was no longer something which troubled him. Pride, he decided it was, mingling with a profound melancholy.

He gazed on the image of the girl.

She stood.

It amazed him that his own kind reviled Bengali women as 'ugly', or what is it the Australian Consul often said? 'Festering'—like a moveable jungle floor. Festering eyes, that was it. He sighed a sigh at the idiocy ... The extravagant idiocy. The same idiocy, he thought slowly, that was responsible for diminishing and degrading a whole vast world of rich and endless superabundance. Too bloody extravagant, and he shook his head twice. He returned his mind to the Cuban Crisis.

'Sahib.'

His head stayed in the newspaper, pasted to Castro conducting the two chief powers.

'Sahib.'

He looked up. 'What is it?' he asked with a gentle patience.

'Chief Bearer.'

'What about him?'

'Chief Bearer sends a message.'

Castro evaporated, beard, hat, strategy. The President put aside the paper.

'He wishes to meet you.'

'Then where is he?'

'He wishes to meet you behind the water tank at the swimming pool.'

'And who are you?'

Khalid had instructed her.

'I am his friend. He has a special woman waiting.'

The President began to fold up the newspaper.

'Just a minute then,' he said, 'I shall have to break camp.'

Zeythi quickly retreated up the aisle. She opened the door fast and very quietly.

'Go! *Now*!'

The Minisahib ran down the corridor and out to the landing. He waved at Khalid who waited behind the swimming pool, and then he checked for any bearers down the far end of the building. He signalled Zeythi, and then fell expertly down the iron stairs in leaps of twos. He ran across the plain of brushes and long grasses, then under the canopy of almond and mango trees. Inside three breathless chants of 'Here Comes the Old Bastard' he was concealed in the shade with Khalid.

'They're coming!' The Minisahib was jumping up and down on the spot.

Khalid calmed him, and they waited. An explosion of thunder shook the sky behind the tall trees. It started as a low rumbling and grew until it made a crack and growled away into the yellow air. Khalid looked up at the cloud. This, he thought, is going to be a big monsoon, everyone'll lose houses and sisters and brothers and mothers and fathers all over again, but this one looks like it might be the worst. Yah, damn, he thought. Cholera, typhoid, floating goats blown out like balloons, dogs and kids … after this plan is done, I'll make my new tandoor and sell hundreds and then go with my chin up and get a place on a hill like a *sahib*.

He gazed at the cloud reach and roll, not ending anywhere.

A shiver travelled up his spine. The premonition again.

'What are you looking at?' the Minisahib whispered. 'What?'

'Are you okay?'

'No problem, no problem.'

'They're almost here!' the Minisahib whispered fiercely.

Khalid could see Zeythi leading through the undergrowth. He quickly swung the Minisahib and himself into position behind the dense grasses. The thought of his new tandoor made him very serious.

Zeythi walked fast over the leafy floor and came to rest at the two-storey water tank. On the other side of the tank the pump house hummed and the low wall held a gate to the poolside.

She waited for the President-sahib to catch up. She cast her eyes around the gloom for Khalid and the Minisahib.

The President arrived, and he stood comfortably at the base of the tank. He looked about for the Chief Bearer.

'Well? Give the wanker an inch, he takes a bloody mile. He's a greedy fellow. Cunning, but his arrogance lately ... staggers and boggles. And so where is this "special woman"?'

Zeythi made no answer.

Then the President called abruptly, 'Bearer ...!'

Zeythi stood on one foot then the other, shifting her weight imperceptibly, swaying under the looming grey curve of the tank.

'Well, young lady?'

Zeythi swayed silently. It appeared she stood still, but she swayed. Khalid could only see that she stood perfectly still.

Then, without warning, she fell at the President, a swift grab, yanking at the trousers where she knew the zipper to be, and her force along with the surprise pushed him against the cement.

She had a grip on the belt, by both hands.

The President's head rolled back and forth a little as she shook him from the belly.

But that had not been the plan's intention. The intention had been to hold onto his pants, turn the head while the photograph was taken.

She continued holding the buckle. Then she turned her head.

Khalid breathed a sigh of relief and finally took the photograph, and he then jumped into the open.

The President stumbled backwards.

The Minisahib followed behind Khalid.

Khalid called out with glee, 'See here? Camera! You give me one thousand rupees.'

Khalid could now see his tandoor.

Zeythi hit the cook's shoulder. 'No money!'

Khalid took no notice of Zeythi. He said nothing. He knew the boomtime bucksheesh would be in his hand the next day.

The Minisahib said, 'Can I have some then?'

Finally, Zeythi said perfectly, 'Sahib, if the swimming pool is closed, these photos will be delivered to your memsahib.'

That was all that had to be stated. Khalid knew it. It was that simple. He looked into the President's eyes, and said to him, 'Every good plan is a simple plan, sahib?'

A curious thing though. In the moments which followed, Zeythi thought not of herself. She thought of others. What would others do to save their paradises? Perhaps it is a shield to consider others. In a moment like that, maybe it is a protection.

Khalid, the Minisahib and Zeythi were running off, over the sparsely littered floor, dried leaves bouncing up, Zeythi and the Minisahib exchanging quick, nasty names.

'What are you two squabbling about?' Khalid called out as he bounded for the bamboo tunnel.

They ceased the names and concentrated on running up the slope behind the cook.

Population Density Zero

When they arrived at the bungalow Zeythi slowly closed her door. It did not have a proper lock, but she joined a hook and loop she had made herself. A grey light fell across her hand. She heard a tapping. Then silence.

The room was still and soundless. Sweat slipped from her forehead. She let it go without wiping at it. There was always wiping. Brass, glass, wood, floor.

The knocking returned, this time far off. She heard a calling-out. It was the Minisahib.

She collected a slab of soap, and then walked with the Minisahib to the edge of the compound. She ran the tap into the stone bath.

Khalid was now sitting on the steps. He was daydreaming, filled with the spectacle of his tandoor in every bazaar up and down the coast.

'What stink,' he murmured.

Zeythi brought her attention to the bath, swirling the clear water. The Minisahib got in. He sat against the stone. She sponged the soap, scrubbing and rinsing. Cleaning the small washboard of the Minisahib's back. Empty hands. Hands that made the plan succeed.

Interrogating a Lighted Darkness

Mahfouz the Spitting-bearer cleared the last table by the pool. He stood with a spoon dangling from his hand. Then he raised the spoon and hit the table. He spat into the pool and walked up the hillside to the brightly lit club.

The Minisahib and Zeythi had been hiding behind the orchids. They slid into the water at the shallow end. She brought the tip of her finger to the floor of the pool. Then she moved away. She scraped again, bringing her finger round into a full circle.

'And this one?' she said, bursting from the surface.

'It's big,' the Minisahib said, bursting up along with her.

'And that one?'

'It's bigger!'

They swam half the night and made more circles through the thin layer of slime and settled dirt.

Later the Minisahib hurried up the stairs. He returned with two drinks and a plate of roast chicken on rice. They shared the chicken with all hands, and drank the iced lychee juice separately.

When they arrived back at the bungalow Zeythi took off alone to the President-sahib's house nearby where Khalid had told her she could do more checking on the rumour about these sahib types. She found nothing and came back complaining to Khalid. He said she made a mistake. She had gone too late and on the wrong day.

'Tuesday,' he smiled, 'every Tuesday—and go at six o'clock not ten. You will see I am right.'

The following morning Mahfouz came to set up the bar and the tables. He found the pool keeper relaxing in a chair. The pool keeper had gone in to cool off, and he was seated under the sign of the regulations. The pool was used as a toilet, and smaller children could often be seen floating wide-eyed and still before paddling off to another location, so the regulations were placed prominently.

BATHERS:
SPITTING NOT PERMITTED
URINATING NOT PERMITTED
SHOWER PRIOR TO ENTERING POOL
ONLY BATHING COSTUMES ALLOWED—NO
UNDERPANTS OR PANTIES
DO NOT THROW FOREIGN OBJECTS INTO THE POOL
By Order the Committee.

The pool keeper chewed paan and gazed absently into the water. He had one eye that shot off to Burma. With his straight eye he gazed absently for a long, comfortable time. The pool floor was alive with circles. Small circles and big ones overlapping, and, under the bouncing surface, dancing in the light of the new day.

The Spitting-bearer said sleepily, 'Hoi! Drainbreath! Did you do that?'

The pool keeper from behind paan-red teeth rolled his

head: 'Me? I tell you, I wish I did that.'

'Well? Are you going to sit there like a sahib-pig, or clean it up?'

'No, I'm going to carefully scrape the green fungus for your breakfast.'

Mahfouz forced a great spit into the shallow end. 'That is nothing,' he growled, 'I can eat the whole damn pool!'

'How come,' the pool keeper asked, 'you are not working up there in the club?'

'What business is it of yours?'

'I'll tell you why.'

'Yah, tell me.'

'Because you are no good. Soon you won't even be working down here.'

Mahfouz cursed the pool keeper and continued setting up the bar.

'Iqbal?'

'Yes?'

'What is the matter?'

'A small thing, not important. Zeythi and the Minisahib went back to the pool to celebrate the victory.'

'That is what I said, is it not?'

'Perhaps, but they also played first in the change rooms. To celebrate.'

'Played? What kind of play?'

'Small things.'

'Like what they did in the banana trees behind the compound?'

'It was to celebrate I suppose.'

'Okay, and is that all?'

'Yes.'

'Thank you Iqbal.'

The President Changes His Mind

After leaving the polytechnic Abdul drove through the heat to the President-sahib's factory. In the cool office the sweating teacher fell comfortably into a sofa. He looked forward to moving onto the club.

'Is it too early?' Abdul asked as he lit his pipe.

'Not at all,' the President said cheerfully. 'In a minute Brian brings in a file and then I'm finished.'

'Good day's work?'

'Yes indeed.'

'Shall I show you how to play snooker?' Abdul said.

The President smiled. 'You may try.'

'What about the vote on the pool? Do you think we should get it out of the way tonight?'

'No,' the President said, 'I've postponed it.'

'Okay then,' Abdul said, 'let's go.'

There was a knock on the door. Brian the engineer from Bristol walked in. Under his arm he carried a report on a new lathe. He placed it on the President's desk.

'Thanks Brian,' the President said.

'Hi Brainy Bristol,' Abdul said. 'Like to join us at the club?'

'Hello Abdul. Thanks, but it's home for me tonight.'

'Utter rubbish. What can a single fellow do at home

after work on a Tuesday night?'

'A bit of writing on the play.'

'Oh yes, this play. How is it coming along?'

'Fine thanks.'

'Do you still wish to put it on at the club?' Abdul asked. As club secretary he was keen to encourage activity.

'Yeah,' he said with a note of thanks. The engineer was new in town and he was never heard to say very much. He seemed to keep mostly to himself. He rented a very small bungalow and had bought a second-hand jeep.

The men strolled together from the building and drove away separately. Abdul followed the President to the club. He looked forward to a game of snooker, and he hoped to see Fatimah Westcott.

Leila told us, so we all knew, that Fatimah grunted with someone else. Not the French husband in Delhi, but someone else. But this Abdul did not know. As he drove through town Fatimah floated before his eyes. She lifted her skirt to reveal for him her thighs. Abdul's thoughts also created her naked belly. She exposed herself by pulling her underwear sideways.

The Theatre-sahib drove home to his small bungalow. After a shower he continued to the President's bungalow. He knocked on the door and the President's wife appeared. She said nothing and turned to walk into the house. He followed her across the lounge into a corridor. At the end of the corridor she stopped at a door. Without turning she stood silently up against the dark wood for a few moments. She opened the door and went inside. He followed. They began to undress. He noticed a movement at the window. He walked over and drew the curtains closed. Outside in the gathering darkness Zeythi sat under the window.

The Theatre-sahib and the President's wife began to make low, muffled noises but nothing of any real note that Zeythi could say confirmed the rumour about these sahib types grunting less hard. After a while she heard the memsahib moaning deeply but that soon died away. Zeythi crept away into the darkness and strolled down the road.

Rungamati Alone

The Theatre-sahib left Chittagong for the weekend. He drove an hour from the coast into the hills to the village of Rungamati. He turned into a winding road that left the village and came to a deserted cove on the lake.

The shack was perched on a bluff of red earth and boulders. It belonged to the trading firm where Fatimah Westcott worked and she had offered it to him for two days.

He sat on the verandah to take in the expanse of the lake. The small islands that comprised Rungamati were once hilltops. After a while, when the silence had seeped into his bones, he sensed the dark water giving off what he could think of only as a distinct mystery. He thought of the dark, chilled waters of the Severn at home in Bristol; he reasoned that although it was a river, under a grey day its waters would also give off mystery. But he felt there was a deeper silence about this lake. Maybe villages, he thought, drowned by the building of the Kaptai dam, maybe only drowned memories, give off this deeper silence that seems unsilent. He began to think of the notion of voices without sound. He decided to somehow bring the paradox of silent voices into his play.

He went inside and worked on the play until dusk. He came outside and he drank a glass of wine while he watched the night descend on the lake.

The Flying Fox

The difficult part was getting the rope. It had to be good rope, woven tight so it was as hard as wood to hit. Where would Khalid obtain such rope? He had seen a clump at the polytechnic. Stained by oil, it lay forgotten behind the mechanics building.

'Nobody will notice,' Khalid said to the guard.

'Like fun,' the guard said.

'It is shitty old stuff.'

'You can take it if you give me ten rupees.'

'I don't have ten rupees.'

'Then eight.'

'I have two.'

'Okay five.'

Khalid handed over the money. He wanted to spend it at the teahouse, but he also knew as well as anyone that in the boom dumping five rupees now might bring twenty later.

'Help me to put it on the bike.'

'No, you do it, I am going away,' the guard said without care. He concentrated on folding the note over and over into a small tight square.

'Just put your hands on the other side,' Khalid said.

'I am going,' the guard said as he wedged the square

into his belt, before strolling away.

Khalid thought it might be helpful that the rope lay in a coil. He looked around for a lever. He found an iron pipe. He brought his bike up to the coil and kicked the stand down. He skewered the pipe under the rope on one side, and over it on the other. Lifting it, he jammed the end of the pipe into the hard dirt. Using a swift burst he lifted the pipe, and the coil lumped onto the raft at the back of the bicycle and tipped the bicycle over.

'Damn.'

He let the pipe go and the coil slumped back down. He moved the bike over to an engine block. This, he reasoned, would hold the bike. He dragged the coil across and repeated the lift. The coil slumped onto the bike's raft. The front wheel sliced into the air. He jumped away as the bike came crashing down. He was sweating heavily. The rope had scored his whites with grease and rust. He looked around to see if the guard had returned.

Gutless bastard, he thought.

He made one more attempt but the bike sliced into the air. Khalid stumbled and fell across a patch of grease.

Gutless idiot. The fucking gutless idiot.

He got on the bicycle and rode out of the polytechnic. On the main road, he signalled a rickshaw.

Together they lifted the coil into the rickshaw. Khalid rode past the mechanics building. The rickshaw followed.

A guard came forward.

'What are you two doing?'

'We are carting rope for the teacher,' Khalid said.

'And you?'

'What does it look like? I am a rickshaw-wallah.'

'Don't try to be big around here.'

'We are taking it to Building Number Four,' Khalid said.

'Who is the teacher?'

'The history teacher. Abdul-sahib.'

'Okay. But next time ask the driver of the polytechnic van. Not the son of an ugly pig off the roadside.'

At the house Khalid tied the rope high on the almond tree. The other end he tied to the base of the mangosteen. The Minisahib and Zeythi wound it under a large nail Khalid had driven into the trunk. They wound it many times and then Khalid fastened it with loops and two large knots. Then came the hub of an old scooter and bicycle handlebars. Zeythi went inside for a jug of lychee juice. The Minisahib climbed the wall to the perch in the almond tree, and Khalid sat on the steps to rest.

Leila Ghosh walked into the compound and came to sit by Khalid.

'What is this thing?' she asked with interest.

According to Khan the sabjantawallah, Leila actually said, 'What bulldust are you up to now with this pesky scum from the hills?'

'What is this thing?'

'It is a flying mongoose.'

'What a clever man you are,' Leila said.

According to Khan, she said, 'What a pathetic show-off you are.'

Khalid kept an eye on her bare shoulder to keep it in mind for later that night. All she had bare was a shoulder. But that's all he needed. Chittagong was a misery for him like that.

The Minisahib took hold of the handlebars. He stepped from the wall and flew like a monkey across the compound down to the hard dirt. He landed badly and scraped his knee, which turned bloody, but he wiped it down and climbed the wall again. He flew all the afternoon.

Zeythi came outside with the jug and poured a glass for Khalid and then continued on to the wall.

She was very good at flying, smooth, and her landing was graceful. She was able to skip away from the handlebars. The Minisahib and Zeythi laughed a lot.

Khalid was about to ask about the beautiful city of his dreams. But Leila talked about Zeythi.

'She is being very nice to you,' Leila said.

'She is a nice girl.'

'Is she nicer to you than me?'

'Yah? How to measure that?'

'Measure by just saying.'

'She's nice in other things.'

'Which?'

'She helps around the place, also in the kitchen.'

'Does she wash your loongies?'

'No, I wash my stuff.'

'I have seen her washing your loongies.'

'Yah?'

'She dances with you sometimes.'

'Do you want some lychee?'

'No. Are you going to the teahouse tomorrow?'

'Why tomorrow?'

'Because I am going.'

'I cannot,' Khalid stated with a sudden regret.

'Why?'

'I am going to my classes.'

'You are still doing these classes?'

'Yah.'

'Why?'

'Because I want to use my brain.'

Khalid had lied. It was true that he liked the classes, but it was also true that the Old Man had made an agreement. 'Take the classes,' the Old Man had suggested, 'and I'll give you bigger wages.'

Leila didn't flinch. 'I know schooling is important.'

But if you believe the sabjantawallah, 'Give your flying mongoose to the sickly Chakma bitch.'

'Yah,' Khalid said, 'schooling is good.'

Mohendra the chickenwallah came into the compound and sat with Khalid and Leila. He watched as Zeythi flew from tree to dust.

'She is strong,' Mohendra said, and he smiled. According to Khan he wanted to say something else.

'You also?' Leila said to Mohendra.

'Me? What?'

'Never mind.'

From Slave to Sovereign

The teacher started with a bang of excitement. This was a bit pathetic with a class of three. Also, who wanted history? Your pockets would never sag with history. Students were chasing a diploma for bastard wages as mechanics. Even less wanted in lower East Pakistan was *Indian* history. Indian history might have been a stout engine in the mind of the teacher—a subject long before partition, and well beyond the days of plump lazy rajahs, but it was not a popular subject for the moment. Not so soon after a war. Fine, Ayub and Shastri signed the peace treaty in Tashkent as long ago as the year before, but that's no reason to suddenly bounce off into the peculiar life of one of the early kings of Delhi. But the teacher had a funny reason. Abdul-sahib often did have funny reasons for peculiar things. He fell into a stirring account of the first slave to rule the desert.

Khalid made curving doodles of the two-hump hills. For these doodles, and for clay, he had big plans. A couple of years before, the sahib had fixed things to get Khalid a place in secondary school. The cook did not want school. He wanted work, wanted to be 'a man'. The sahib said the wages would lift. A few classes to secure a place in the polytechnic. The sahib made it a project, and would not let it go away into dreams of manhood until he was satisfied that 'This unusually smart bugger is given the right opportunity.' So here Khalid was, in a bright room of new cement. At the polytechnic no less. Two punkahs moving the air in each room. Blueish-white lights. Feeling damn big. Making lines with a pencil that would become big plans for the tandoor. No polytechnic had history classes, but Abdul persuaded his good friend the principal to give it a try for a while and so the principal gave him one of the empty rooms to use.

The second student, a paanwallah's son from Cox's Bazaar, who possessed a quiet intellect, rested his chin on the backs of his hands.

The third student was a visiting English girl. Her father promised to buy a radio set to take back to boarding school in Yorkshire as long as she took the class while she was on summer holidays in Chittagong. She sat quietly and stole glances at the boy from Cox's Bazaar with the say-nothing intellect.

Abdul-sahib continued with hot excitement: '… and so Razia Iltutmish became the first slave to rule Northern India! In fact, the early Muslim dynasties held northern India for how long?'

The teacher gleefully cocked his eyebrow.

'… for two hundred years! Long time, no?'

He continued: 'It is not known if Razia Iltutmish was a sorcerer, but we know she was a spellbinding personality of immense beauty. One of her servants, the Abyssinian Master of the Horse, fell hopelessly under her spell. And the young queen fell under the spell of the Abyssinian. A slave-queen and a dirty soldier? In love? You think I am inventing this?'

The paanwallah's son thought so. A slave does not

become a queen. A slave does not even become a bearer.

But the teacher slapped the story along.

'Together they dragged a scandal into the palace halls; they turned many other commanders into spies with fistfuls of jealousy who lurked at bedroom doorways, and they coloured for eternity the mist of India's history with the shine of a slave girl's passion for her military commander!'

Khalid continued to make important pencil marks that had nothing to do with spies and slaves.

'… brushing a big chunk of India from the high rocks west of Karachi to this glum fertility of Chittagong, her father Shamsudin cleverly kept his empire of the subcontinent warmed like a saddle. He had many important charters. His highest charter after he was purchased by the rulers of Delhi, when he fled Persia, was vital business with his daughter. Crucial, a big occasion …

'… and what do you think the charter was? What is this thing that he gave Razia?

'… the father gave her schooling.'

The teacher broke off. He walked up the length of the blackboard.

'Yes,' the teacher repeated slowly, 'a big round education.'

The paanwallah's son raised his hand. Khalid and the girl turned to him.

'Yes?' the teacher called.

'Was Razia's father a slave?'

'Yes, he was.'

'How did he become the king?'

Good question, thought Khalid, damn good question, and he brought his attention up. The doodles could wait.

'Shamsudin became the king by using his mind. First, he had to flee the horrible Mongols. They were putting stink into Persia, his homeland. One of the golden rules of life lived by stupid people is this: next door is always uninhabited. You see that? Completely vacant? Shamsudin was not one of life's stupid ones—he knew India was next door, and so he took off into the deserts of Shiraz, Baluchistan and the Thar until he arrived in Delhi. In Delhi he was purchased by the ruling clan. In those days it was customary to train a prize slave. Slaves became very trustworthy figures and they rose up the ladder of fortune. You see that? Trustworthy? Shamsudin clawed his way from poverty and slavery to such a height that he very soon put his personal stamp on Delhi by founding his own ruling clan. Ultimate success from beginnings as a total nobody!'

The paanwallah's son came round a bit. He thought, Fine, seems simple enough.

Khalid twitched with interest.

But the teacher had lied. What he had failed to tell the class was that Shamsudin, in Persia, before the brutal Mongol destruction had fallen to the streets, had been from a wealthy, ruling family of highly learned people: all the waves of Persian immigrants were of ruling families. With the means of long-distance escape at their disposal, it is they who fell into the safety of Delhi. Shamsudin migrated from great wealth into slavery, then back into position as ruler. But the teacher did not mind his lie one dot. He had a point to make. And, truthfully, in the larger scheme, he harboured a determination to make his ignored history class as useful a tool as a spanner.

He was fond of the ruse. Nothing confidential about it outside the class either. He enjoyed feeling the good that it might accomplish. He had once bubbled it out to a colleague during lunch conversation in the staff canteen. Stupid spot for it.

'Vandalising history,' the colleague had reacted flatly. 'Plundering the stuff for your own fake view.'

The teacher then told his colleague that he believed the colleague's intelligence to be a blunt one. Filled with headfuls of generalisations about teaching history, and 'damp with spectacular pretensions about history itself.'

Abdul continued to omit the fact that Shamsudin had arrived from a ruling clan. His class remained, he proudly believed, the one place that students like the paanwallah's son and the Zakir Hussein Road cook might touch the true potential lurking inside their Brylcreemed heads.

The teacher continued.

'So you see how success belongs to the spirit who breeds the desire for it, and ... do not forget this ... the spirit with the education to run after it. One day you will become a trainee mechanic, then a mechanic, okay. But what will stop you from becoming the assistant manager of the operation? What will block you from advancing to manager?'

The teacher paused.

'And what about it—the managing director! The sahib! Fistfuls of happiness!'

Khalid shifted in his chair.

The teacher drew a large number on the blackboard. 'Shamsudin,' he said, 'attended classes just the same as you lot. Here, at five, Shamsudin arose from slumber. After his prayers, he started work around the house—quiet work that could be done peacefully without waking the sahibs. He swept the floors and dreamed of his future.'

The teacher continued to draw large numbers. 'At six,

he took morning chai. At seven, he assisted with preparations in the kitchen. Nine o'clock, after washing and cleaning the kitchen, morning study would take place. With the sahib's scientist he would read, listen and ask questions. At noon, he took a lunch of fruit and biryani rice. Then he went into the grounds for a walk along the shores of the lake. Nature refreshed his soul; waterfowl, deer, monkeys.

'Two o'clock, the sahib's historian. Yes, history, my dear girls and boys.

'Three o'clock, and the Master of the Horse, soon to be his daughter's boyfriend, gave him expert training for two hours. Evening meal, seven o'clock. At night he would complete the exercises set that morning by the scientist. Around midnight he would turn in.'

Khalid thought, Big deal, I do just as much. Same as me, what stink.

The girl from Yorkshire said, 'It seems like a complicated day. Did he do these activities every day?'

'Oh yes. But complicated? Not so. The reverse, in fact. To live in this way brought to him a tremendous simplicity. Which in turn prepared him for the rigours of gigantic success.'

Gigantic success. The words floated around Khalid's ears with a hiss. He looked down at the curves of his new tandoor. He would give them a try to be definite. After class, he thought, fly to the house, find the Minisahib, tell him to dig the clay from his famous pond.

'Next week, girls and boys, we will meet another guy who reached the top, fellow by the name of Oliver Cromwell. Heard of him?'

'I have,' said the girl.

'Is he Indian this time, or Pakistani this time?' Khalid

asked.

'He is neither, he is an Englishman. Class dismissed. Except Khalid.' The teacher called him forward.

'Have you been reading?'

'Yes, sahib.'

'You are lying.'

'No, sahib.'

'If you do not read, your teeth will drop from your mouth like ripe figs and your ears will clog up like a drain. Your eyes will see nothing but the kind hand of your sahib and your head will be as empty as a gunnysack and full of just as many holes.'

'Yes, sahib.'

'Now go!'

On his bicycle Khalid flew through town with his transistor radio slung from his neck. It flung out a tune, tabla at full ecstacy, and the voice of his favourite singer lamented the man she had lost to angry storms.

At the junction he caught Ajit Mookerjee the gardener riding in the other direction. Khalid sang out and they stopped for a quick paan, and then Khalid was on his way to the bazaar. On the corner he said hello to Lall Thankee the goatmeatwallah, and next door stood the chickenwallah's stall festooned with the colourful feather-dusters.

Mohendra the chickenwallah took Khalid down the hill to the potter's stall and introduced Khalid to Aranthi the new potterywallah. Aranthi and Khalid discussed the sketches over a cup of chai, and it was decided that she would produce the first oven. The concave and convex sketch which Khalid handed over was, he thought, the best of the lot. Damn, he thought.

She offered to sell him a bag of good clay, but he rolled

his head and said he already had a source.

'Okay,' she said. And she smiled. It was a plain, good-natured smile of great brightness, and Khalid immediately changed his mind.

'Okay,' Khalid rolled his head, 'use your clay.'

Khalid enjoyed meeting Aranthi and he rode off into the gathering night with an image of her beautiful face afloat in his mind. He looked forward to later that night. To doing things with a kind of Aranthi. She did not have a bare shoulder, or anything bare, but Khalid decided he could invent her being all bare.

'Yah,' he said aloud as the bike flew down the hill, 'it will be good.'

Razia ... Oh Ra-zi-a-a ...!

When he swung the bike down the driveway a flock of sparrows burst from the money plant. Khalid loved his bike. He always flung it about. His transistor radio was slung from his neck and the hard swerve sent it flying out. The blazing tune, and his replacing of the song's central name with 'Razia' gave his arrival a bluster everyone in the house enjoyed. A young sahib resented it, but his excuse was that he worked at the office all day and then studied his correspondence course from the Manchester School of Economics. Khalid's racket he did not need, and he shouted out the window where the bicycle fled by, 'Shut off that damn radio!'

Khalid did not care. He was too happy thinking of the fantastic new tandoor. In the kitchen Khalid inspected the pots on the stove. Each sat quietly, resting: beef, and rice, and on the bench, a smaller pot of dahl and one of vegetables. He patted the old tandoor.

'Soon you will no longer be needed, old friend—sorry to say, but you will be proud of me, wait and see.' He smiled at his morning's efficiency and danced back outside to locate Zeythi.

He couldn't find her. The compound was already becoming dark. She emerged from a gap in the wall, which was the long-neglected gate. Her small figure looked like a jungle creature creeping into the promising light of a feast. Khalid called out the name of the empress.

'Ra-zia!'

She lumbered through the broken gap of bricks and stones, dragging long stretches of cut bamboo into the compound.

'Razia!' he called again from the top step.

Zeythi thought that the dim light on the roof made him look like a bearer from the club. She muttered to herself, 'Making people do this and that, come over here and get over there, faster faster. Who is Razia? Yah, maybe some fancy new sahib-girl from the class. Razia, Leila, who next? I used to like this twit.'

'Who is Razia?' she called out irritably.

'You!'

'I am Zeythi. Come and help me with these sticks.'

Zeythi's irritation was understandable. She had her own thoughts and ideas. Here was Khalid off to his classes at the big college, and there was she lugging bamboo she'd cut, and also finishing off a long day's work.

Khalid's springy optimism was understandable too. Zeythi did not know Khalid would be taking delivery of his new tandoor in a very short time. Aranthi the potterywallah had promised it. Such a big bark over a little clay tandoor? Well, to him, it contained a sparkling new life. His head was awash with the shimmer of silver and his ears with the ruffle of rupees. He bounded off the steps and took hold of a portion of the bamboo to drag across the compound floor.

'No, you are Razia Iltutmish.'

'And who is she?'

'She was the ayah, just like you, who became the memsahib.'

'Very funny.'

He leaned forward to whisper from his grin, 'She took someone from the house … into her bed!'

Zeythi felt a sudden wave of heat rise to her cheeks.

'Want to have a cool drink?' he asked.

She nodded, and it was a series of crooked half nods.

When Khalid brought out two glasses of lychee juice, she had recovered.

'She was very beautiful,' Khalid grinned, 'and she came from faraway hills which were full of treasures and lakes and jungle.'

'Sounds like bulldust,' Zeythi said.

'No,' Khalid grinned, 'it is true.'

'I don't believe it. It does not sound like life.'

Life? Khalid suddenly thought. For what is this girl talking about life?

It struck him as odd, and it changed his perky mood.

'It is only a story,' he said, 'it is not life.'

'Khan says life is very simple,' she said.

'I cannot say anything about it. Only a show-off sabjan-tawallah talks about it.'

They sat in silence, and Khalid wondered about Zeythi. Strange bugger, he thought over and over.

The Pond

The Minisahib lay on a warm rock face. The invisible sun was hot but the boulder was the thing that warmed the back. He sat up. His hair stuck out like a chicken's hood. He gazed out at the pond. Water, he thought, green, or brown, like it gets at the beach at Cox's Bazaar?

'Bugger it,' he said aloud, 'I can't tell what stuffing colour it is today.'

'And what?' Zeythi demanded.

'I only said "stuffing".'

'I don't care. Stuffing is not good for a small boy.'

'I am not a *small boy*,' he blurted, attaching a tone of vile sickness to the words.

'You are a small boy.'

He swore. Then he fell back into thinking about the water.

Was it black? Purple? He decided very privately that in the middle it looked deep and dangerous. I'm never going in the middle, he thought.

But Zeythi had floated over the small expanse, and he was impressed by the calm she had.

'Did you see anything out there, in the middle?'

'Like what?'

'Giant catfish? With the electric-shock moustache?'

'No,' she said with her eyes shut. She enjoyed the heat against her back.

He kept his eye out on the centre. The plop of a bubble disturbed the surface. Ripples flattened out and the pond returned to a smooth glaze. He couldn't make out if her eyes were shut. He roamed his own eyes over her chest, up her neck and into the shining black hair. There was always oil and it made the hair shine in so many colours he could catch. It was only after long staring, though, he knew, oh yes, that the colours would begin. But he couldn't tell if her eyes were her hearts.

'What have you told Khalid?' she said lazily, eyes closed.

'Khalid?'

'What have you been telling him?'

The Minisahib looked off at the air, its infinite dust.

'Nothing,' he said.

Zeythi knew it was true. She knew Khalid was guessing. Her floating mind relaxed as she soaked up the warmth of the boulder. When she had dried off after the swim, they walked back along the path.

Things Can Change

I remember the morning he decided on kisses. Khalid would kiss the new tandoor, his fresh version of the ancient oven, a thousand times.

'Good luck kisses!' he called out.

He would place his head inside the oven, planting kisses to the inside wall. He would also kiss the lip and the cute feet which he had designed into it as no-reason good looks. He would also cover the thing with the kisses of the Minisahib and Zeythi. Three thousand kisses, three thousand sales. Exact arithmetic. The sums of a happy cook.

He was excited, and he had big plans. From the bazaar he believed he would sell to the town proper. Then to Dacca, to Calcutta across the sea, invisible places to Khalid, magic big cities, then in excitement he grabbed at another big name, Delhi, and then his head ran out of big magic places so he shouted, 'And the whole world!'

The radio twanged, and Khalid shook his hips about. He reached for Zeythi's hand and they danced together around the oven, bare feet sending up dust from the bald patches of the compound. The Minisahib joined in. His shaking and shunting was awkward and stiff, and Zeythi laughed.

And it was another fact. Khalid had invented a new tandoor. It was a small example, no taller than a bedside table, but it was not a decoy. It was poised to become the tandoor of the future. He made possible the impossible: extra succulence and an extra outer crispness to the baked thigh.

Freak accident? Right time, right place, right cook? Perhaps it was plain destiny. Whatever it was, Khalid had tripped on it. He stumbled into the world of the new tandoor to say with his copper-stained teeth a big hello.

The Old Man came out to inspect it behind the kitchen.

'Uncanny,' he murmured twice as he strolled around the oven.

So what was the simple modification? How did a cook's instinct find it? Put clearly, he had made a giant hourglass. Inverted the normal tandoor. Simple enough. But a small difference from the hourglass was that the concave at the middle was only a slight curve. A gentle equatorial gully. This gully pushed the heat of the inner wall immediately to the surface of the chicken, at the final run, by simply lifting the skewer to where the chicken would take a crisping. By contrast, when baking chicken in a normal tandoor you can achieve a heat which is even, but which does not successfully obtain a brisk crispness without risking a leather-boot meat ruefully separated from its natural juices. Khalid's tandoor was no such destroyer. His inwardly curved oven was a creator. Khalid felt so powerful a charge of 'Shamsudin Success' that he believed the forces of quality and sensation would send the olden tandoor into the graveyard of the useless. Factories would produce his new tandoor at a sahib rate, and he would name it the Khalid Tandoor.

But first the kisses.

'A thousand kisses is a lot,' Zeythi protested. 'If I kiss it ten times a day, I'll be kissing the thing for many days.'

'Then kiss it a hundred times a day and it will be done in a few days—what a lazy beggar she is,' Khalid said to the Minisahib. 'No faith,' he spat. 'Think of the future!' he insisted.

Many Chittagong foreheads of ambition do that on a perpetual basis. Plenty of stuff is stuck by our lips to the future. So he decided to request her kisses again tomorrow. But now Khalid was thinking quickly, he was thinking feast!

'A big bastard feast for the household, yah! And we'll see if Featherduster has those damn juicy ducks!'

'I'm only teasing,' said Zeythi. She came forward, brushing pieces of grass from her shoulder, and she kissed the tandoor all over. Khalid leapt around the wooden block like a monkey.

A simple kiss. I now see how it changes things.

The News Spreads

'Inside out,' said Ajit Mookerjee the gardener. 'Very clever. You picked up this idea at your classes?'

'Rubbish! My classes are dusty old stories. Nothing to do with this.'

'I like it,' said Iqbal. 'So tell me. What must I do with the chicken?'

'You put it in like usual, and when it is almost ready, you bring it up to the neck for a blasting.'

'I think it is very beautiful,' Leila said. 'It shows a balance and it has a friendly feeling.'

They stood in a circle around the chopping block. Khalid had put it on the block so that it would look important. They were sipping sweet chai, casting rubbed-out shadows under the invisible sun.

'Yah,' Khalid said, 'Aranthi did a good job.'

'What are these?' Iqbal asked quietly, stooping for a close inspection.

'They are the toes.'

'Why does it need toes?'

'It keeps the thing off the floor.'

'Oh. Good idea.'

'They look like the feet of a baby elephant,' Leila said.

'Camel's feet,' Khalid said.

'Why camels?' Ajit Mookerjee asked.

'Because that is how Razia Iltutmish travelled across the desert a long time ago.'

'Who is she?'

There was a pause. Zeythi, who sat on the laundry wall nearby, began to feel a heat rise up her neck.

But Khalid replied sensibly. 'She was a slave who became the ruler of India.'

'India?' Ajit Mookerjee asked, a bit surprised. 'Why India? This is Pakistan.'

'Before,' Khalid said. 'Before, when it was one place.'

'It was never one place only,' Iqbal offered with a patient smile.

'It is the Queen's camel,' Leila said. 'I like that.'

'This is a small type, but later I'll make normal size types.'

'Will Aranthi make them for you?'

'No.'

'Then who?'

'A factory.'

Ajit Mookerjee smiled. 'Thinking big and bold!'

'My memsahib,' Leila said helpfully, 'knows many factories in Dacca.'

Dacca. Khalid's mind floated away.

'Have you tried it out?' asked Iqbal.

'It works. Damn well. Last night I made for them duck. When you bite, it bursts with the juice and flavour. Tomorrow night they are having a big bastard party, so I want to try it out for bigger numbers and see if it is good for restaurants.'

Khalid looked over Leila's shoulder and smiled at Zeythi. She returned a small smile and went inside to continue working.

The Tandoori Feast and the Shameful Ticking Off

It was in a mood of happiness that he prepared the giant feast. He was given the weight of it all, which he liked. New tall feelings. Plenty of stuff to do—but Khalid did not know he would later snarl, 'Kissed by the luck of the filthy camel driver.'

They dubbed it the monsoon feast. It seemed nothing was available under the sagging sky, so the Old Man pondered on it on the front porch. What celebration to bestow upon this 'monsoon dinner'? And there it was.

'Simple and direct,' he said pleasantly to his wife.

'You mean bland,' she said.

'Are you joking?'

'Even something a bit more pointed like the "Zakir Hussein Road feast" would be better,' she said as she smiled and took his hand.

Forty tables were delivered for the front garden. These were dressed with candles and bowls of floating frangipani and sliced lemons. The house looked like a decorated restaurant. Coloured lights crept over the rooftop into the cloud.

Before visitors beat the house and garden, Khalid

watched as the sahib and the memsahib stood on the verandah.

The Old Man and the Old Lady. Oh yah, Khalid thought, I know all about the talk around town—the Karachi man and the English woman. But look now. Let the town take a sniff at this little minute. They're even holding hands, the two old lugs. Shabash.

Khalid grinned, and carried on working his new tandoor into the night.

Cars arrived from everywhere. They parked on the field between the house and the hills. Children ran over the field. They tossed cakes of dried dung and fought with sticks. Balloons drifted up the entire body of the feast like bubbles in a fizzy drink. Some children fiddled with balloons for the whole night. Repetition, the big success behind nature—like the monsoon. But the children grew tired. In the small hours a lone pop.

Khalid and his tandoor were installed under the mangosteen tree. The cook worked seriously to conceal his eagerness and he had never felt so fine and tight with all the good and grand dreams. He could have burst into song. But the music they were playing, as usual, was English music. How they could stomach it he did not know, but tonight what did he care?

The guests came drifting past as he worked.

'Look at it! It curves inwardly!'

'Yah, a bit stupid.'

Khalid took no notice. He worked very seriously and he was too happy to care about ignorance.

'Exactly, too rickety, only a dumbo could do that.'

'How can you make chicken in a tunnel type of contraption?'

'Yah, and it's just a travesty of tradition.'

'The heat will make the middle too weak. It will break like a stick.'

'It looks ugly, that's all.'

'I agree, it just looks repulsive.'

'Yes, me too, utterly hideous.'

'Totally misbegotten, that's right.'

The opinions were enjoyed over drinks and discussed at length. But the cook and the tandoor under lights, outside in the warm noise of the cool night; I can confirm it was a sight. Khalid in pristine whites. Taking no notice of prejudiced babble. Now there's a sight I will never forget. What a sly thing it is this moment of beauty.

Then a sudden shadow fell on the feast. At the forward corner, against the gatepost, stood a strange figure, and Khalid recognised him as the figure from the other afternoon. He stood quietly, uninvited, on the edge of the evening. Khalid stopped, but the figure turned slowly and fell away into the night.

Then a good friend of the memsahib's walked up with great confidence. She chatted with the cook about the invention and she heaped the praise upon him. She had such confidence that compliments sprang off her shoulder like buttons.

She was Fatimah Westcott. Of all the nameless memsahibs only she insisted on Khalid using her name. He took a while to use it, but she persisted with firmness until one day it tumbled out naturally. It didn't feel the same as saying Leila or Iqbal, but it didn't feel too bad. From the Dutch to the Japanese back to the English, she was the only one. She was an Egyptian Jordanian. A solid frame, lofty as a Bedouin. Her success with clients had resulted in a third extension of her contract. 'She's here for good,' said some. And it was true. Fatimah Westcott did like the life in Chittagong, though she would not declare it.

Her husband, a Frenchman who lived in Delhi, came to inspect the tandoor. He was impressed, and said so directly. He took a serving of duck.

'Strange-looking contraption,' he remarked pleasantly and with approval.

'Yes,' Fatimah Westcott said, and added with a trader's gusto, 'but consider—what better to catch the eye in a shop, eh Khalid?'

This was something Khalid had not considered.

'True, Fatimah memsahib, true!'

Abdul the history teacher came up. He was small and round with a tiny head—a papaya, say, but he had the brain of ten sahibs.

'Hello Abdul,' Fatimah said with gusto.

'Fatimah. How are you tonight?'

But Khan the sabjantawallah says Abdul was actually thinking, Fatimah Fatimah Fatimah. Look at your radiance, the appealing velvet of your eyes, the elegance of your dark mouth, the glow of your breasts, your elegant hands. Jam your beautiful hand into my pants and bring out my slung pung-goo. Jam my hard pung-goo into your fattened bosom valley, just jam my pung-goo everywhere, all over that unbelievable fattened body, run it up those thighs of plenty, jam it in your smelling fragrant bulbous vagina, how can we stop this? No chance. Jam away Fatimah, push. Yah, push!

'Fatimah. How are you tonight?'

'Very well. Have you met my husband? Guillaume this is Abdul Rahim.'

'A pleasure to meet with you,' Abdul said. 'Are you visiting us for long?'

'I must return to Delhi on Friday.'

'Pity. Chittagong is great if you give it time.'

Abdul stood a while and chatted with the cook. They talked warmly about Shamsudin the slave-king. Khalid gave the teacher a plate of tandoori duck. Abdul thanked him and walked away into the night.

Zeythi and the Minisahib had been watching the festival from the far corner of the verandah. Then, called inside, Zeythi vanished.

The Minisahib sat on the railing corner to give himself comfort. For a little fellow he was very mature—he was always looking around for comfort. If nearby lurked a boulder or a branch he would seek it out and take it and only then continue with whatever was going on. The view was good, he decided. The arriving guests, the fools with the balloons, Khalid, the lights, all spread around just right.

Suddenly at the front gate stood the club President. The Minisahib sprung up and twisted through the brightly coloured night into the house to find Zeythi. She was in the kitchen with the others, and they were busy draining yoghurt from the chicken ready for another batch for the tandoor, so he sailed out the back door and up the side to the verandah. The President and his wife were being seen to by the Old Man. They were given drinks by a bearer hired from the club. Khalid had nothing to do with the decision, but Mahfouz the Spitting-bearer had somehow managed to step in, probably by sharing the pay.

'What are you doing here?' Khalid asked Mahfouz.

'Don't you worry, cook, I am strong, I can eat stones!' he grinned, and he walked off.

The President made his way into the gala occasion. He

enjoyed accepting greetings and compliments. He had the talent for stand-away friendship.

The Minisahib took a frosty glass of beer to Khalid.

'Squirtypants is here!'

Khalid put away the drink nicely, and felt the cold bitterness drift across his gut. Then he looked about the garden for the President. He spotted the tall figure standing with the Old Man on the far side. They were talking closely; rather, the Old Man was listening attentively. The President was leaning right on the Old Man's ear. Old Man nodding.

Khalid remembered the photographs, and then he remembered money—the President-sahib's money. Tandoor-bucksheesh-hillside, it was all too beautiful.

He worked the next batch of thighs. He raised the skewers to place the chicken and duck at the narrow section, when two men appeared. The Old Man and his guest.

Khalid welcomed each in turn, and then made a fresh serving consisting of a leg and thigh which were basted to a copper finish, a crescent of cucumber, tomato and lime, and a patch of fresh coriander. The President gladly received his plate. Khalid started to make a second serving, but the Old Man declined.

Peculiar. First, the sahib had not yet eaten. Second, tandoori chicken he never refused. And third, he had spent the week raving about the new design to nameless sahibs all over town.

The Old Man asked Khalid if he knew what business the President-sahib conducted.

'I do not know, sorry,' Khalid smiled.

'You do not know that the President-sahib is the owner of a big factory?'

'No, sahib.'

'You do not know that the factory makes new things, such as engineering modifications to common household goods? That the President-sahib has only just this month started making a new tandoor …?'

But Khalid did not hear the sahib's voice any longer. His attention was diverted to visions of how the hell the President-bastard got hold of his tandoor. He could only see those snobbish bearers, the slick liars and pretenders who worked a lot in the snooker room. It had to be one of those scum. Or maybe it was that opportunity-hunting Chief Bearer, Akram.

But the President smiled and complimented the cook on the duck. He said never to mind. Not to worry, he said.

The Old Man finished off by declaring, 'I am disappointed in you, Khalid … and it is only for the compassion of the sahib—luckily for you he is my good friend—that you are not sacked.

'You are a good cook,' the Old Man continued, 'but you are a jungly boy. How many times have I told you cheating is weak?'

The President-sahib entered the ticking-off and cooled his friend with easy-to-say bulldust, and one very fake compliment. Then the two men walked into the gala night of saris, balloons and lights.

Khalid stood still for a long, long while.

At the makeshift drinks bar, the President repeated the fake compliment to his host. At the tandoor, he had said, 'You're the rare individual who celebrates life rather than mourns its passage.' But away from Khalid, as they received a gin and tonic from the Spitting-bearer, he added, 'Dear man, the cost of this fundamental optimism is a weak eye in identifying thieves.' The President raised his glass to his host, and the Old Man muttered a bad-hearted toast before draining half his glass.

Khalid thrust a fresh skewer into the coals. He looked up. The scene was a fluid blur. He hissed to himself in Bengali, 'Kissed by the luck of a filthy fucking camel driver!' He pushed a second skewer into the glowing tandoor and tears fell with it. In his tough Bengali fists rose the tight pain of rage. 'I'll get the photos and see what's what!' he hissed.

From the colour-ridden distance the Minisahib noted Khalid working faster. Jumping about, jabbing at this and that in his expert way, filled by the three thousand kisses they gave it. Next to the Minisahib's head a balloon was burst. He decided to give chase into the field where he hoped he could push the little guest into a new dung that would be soggy.

The President came back to the oven.

'Let me tell you, lad, what I want. I want the photographs, and I want the film.'

Khalid put aside the skewer.

'In return I'll see the sahib doesn't sack you. There's no need to be frightened of me. Go bring what I ask for. When you return, place them inside the napkin with my chicken.'

Khalid picked up the skewer.

He called the Spitting-bearer. He told him to hold the chicken in the oven.

'What is wrong?'

'Just hold the thing!'

'Is it the President-sahib? You want me to spit in his glass?'

Khalid walked up the side of the bungalow where he

disappeared into a tunnel of bamboo to his quarters.

He reached for a wooden box under the jute-slung bed frame. The lock braces had been torn from the wood. Flicking the lid he saw sunglasses, tobacco, sketches for the oven. No photographs, no negatives. He searched the sparseness of his room, but he knew that if they were not in his box then they were not in his possession.

That night it flashed about that the cook copied the oven from Roger Reid's factory. The next day it entered the paper as a small item with a lean towards the notion of a sweet local eagerness to utilise, to celebrate, British ingenuity as and when it was given, 'even before it is placed on offer in the marketplace'. The last paragraph looped high into the air by exalting the development and the progress 'of the nation' by the sudden mention of railways, roads, bridges and schools. Somehow they were able to mention America, but who knows what stupidity can be found in the paper.

Late in the night Zeythi located Khalid. He lay on the roof of his quarters. She climbed the ladder, avoiding a step that dangled unrepaired. She brought up a plate of chicken with trimmings, and a cold drink from the memsahib.

Khalid lay back with his hands behind his head, staring at the blackness. Zeythi sat next to his shoulder. She eased a hand out from under his head and she held it. They said nothing.

After some time spent gazing, Zeythi said, 'I will take care of it for you.'

She climbed down and went to her quarters to sleep. Before she could settle, the Minisahib had crept inside. Khalid was his friend, the cook had showed him how to build things like the bamboo raft at the pond, the carrier platform on the back of his small bicycle, the tadpole net from discarded stockings. He had shown him the bazaar and the club bearer population—who was rotten, who was okay—at the pool and at the clubhouse. He even took him into the teahouse, he had shown him right through the town; he was his friend and his guide. And now, after the most severe darkness he had seen in the house since Christmas, he feared the cook would go the way of so many cooks you hear about.

'What's the matter, can't sleep?' Zeythi whispered.

'How is Khalid?'

'He is okay.'

'Will they sack him?'

'*You* are asking *me*?'

The Minisahib lay beside her in the thin jute bed. When she thought he was falling asleep, she woke him gently and sent him off. He wandered sleepily into the bungalow, found his bed and slept soundly.

'Iqbal?'

'Yes?'

'Do you remember that?'

'Oh yes. Everybody heard about it, paper or no paper. Feel like telling who you are?'

'No, not yet.'

A Quiet Moment

'The newspaper, sahib.'

The President opened it to the article. The air in the library was cool, and the hum of the club was securely locked out.

'Your friend is a fine cook,' the President said, returning the paper to the coffee table. He placed his elbow on the wide armrest.

Akram the Chief Bearer thought quickly. He decided to put a lid on things. 'Yes sahib, his cooking is okay, but it would be better if he did not steal my design for the tandoor. He is not from Chittagong, he is from a distant place in the jungle, so that is the reason for his bad behaviour.'

'You seem quite fair about the problem.'

Akram shifted his foot for a good-natured smile. 'Yes, sahib,' he said in a downcast humble way, but then added a sly gloat, 'I am a fair man.'

The President was not satisfied. He knew it was likely that the tandoor belonged to Khalid.

Akram had no idea of the incident at the water tank. And the President was not about to mention it. The photographs and the roll of film would soon be handed over, he thought, and he would burn them straightaway.

The President handed Akram a folded cluster of rupees. They were crisp and their colour was stunning for a moment, new colour.

Akram stepped forward, took the wad and turned to walk out.

The President turned to the big, low window. The view today was wide. He gazed at the unending cloud. I damn well wish, he thought, it would go right on ahead and burst.

'*Burst!*'

'Sahib?'

'Forget about it.'

Akram walked out.

'Is that all you want to say?' Iqbal asked me quietly.

'Yes,' I replied, 'because that was the extent of what was said.'

'Not really,' Iqbal countered amicably. 'Actually, a bit more. I know, because Akram at that time was sending letters to the woman in Calcutta who he was chasing. Every time he took one kind of bucksheesh or another from the President-sahib, he would shoot off a letter of encouragement saying how much he got, and how he got hold of it. He was describing a new shirt, silver pen, new bicycle, every fancy thing he could think of to lure her to Chittagong.'

'Really?'

'Yah.'

'Then what else?'

'Well, Akram did not leave the room straightaway. He counted the money. He stood casually next to the sahib, and he slowly shifted the notes from one hand to the other. He told the President-sahib more was needed.'

'And did the sahib give him more?'

'Oh yes. Had the sahib eating from his hand—at least that is the idea he wanted to give to his future wife in Calcutta. So the President-sahib gave him another five hundred rupees for the tandoor. Akram took pleasure in reporting this to his sweetheart across the sea. He took a lot of pleasure in telling how he could push the sahib around. One time he told her he gave the sahib a bit of a slap on the mouth, but that I think was just fibbing only.'

'Then he left the room?'

'Yah, then he thanked the sahib, and he left the room in a cheerful way.'

Quick Action, Lasting Result

At the club Mahfouz the Spitting-bearer lurked around the corner and then reached out for the younger bearer's collar.

'Take my shift, I am finished!' he said through his teeth.

'I don't want your shift, I am going home.'

'Take it!' Mahfouz said as he pushed the younger bearer into the recess.

'Okay-okay! Okay.'

The younger bearer returned to work, back through the busy kitchen, cursing under his breath.

Mahfouz changed from his whites, wrapped two bottles of beer in a soiled cloth, and sailed out of the club and into town where he stopped to pick up two paans before weaving down the red road of big almond trees. Mahfouz in a flow could not be stopped. Once in a while the Chief Bearer tried to stop him, but he would just push Akram out of the way and growl, 'I will eat this damn club!'

Reaching Zakir Hussein Road did not take him long. As he approached the bungalow he stood up on the pedals and swung his rusting bone-breaker down into the driveway.

'Khalid!'

The cook jumped. The oil he was decanting on the wooden block spilled between his toes and down into the joins of his sandal.

'Look what has happened!' Khalid barked.

'What is it?' Mahfouz called as he clattered over the compound standing on a pedal. He came to a stop beside the wooden stump.

'Ghee, you idiot!'

'Then how come it is not burning you?'

'It's cooling off ... that's how come!'

'Ah, sorry. Listen, I have an idea.'

He rested the bicycle against the wooden stump. He wiped his neck and forehead and then reached into a pocket.

'Here, take,.' Mahfouz smiled, holding out his hand.

'What is it?'

'What does it look like? It is a damn paan.'

'No, I won't have one. How come you're not at work?'

'They let me off early for once. Here, take one.'

'No thanks.'

'Then here, take a beer.'

'Where did you get beer?'

'From Farooq's.'

'Farooq's?'

The bearer looked at him squarely. 'That's right,' he said.

'Okay, give me one.'

The bearer opened each bottle against the edge of the stump. He passed one to Khalid and then lifted his own into the air.

Khalid reluctantly held up his bottle. The Spitting-bearer had never come to the house before. He had got himself in as the extra bearer for the feast. And now here, Khalid thought, a second time. Acting as if he's been a hundred times.

Mahfouz took a mouthful. 'Well? You want to go get him?'

'Get who?'

The bearer took another mouthful. He stood quietly. He looked about the compound. He lingered on Zeythi's quarters, then Khalid's quarters. He remained silent.

Then he grumbled, 'You think living like this will help anyone?'

'Living like what?'

'Like a jungly fool tacked onto the backside of this English house.'

'The sahib is a Pakistani.'

'Yah, and even he calls you now a "jungly boy". Who only knows what the memsahib calls you behind your back, hah, jungly boy?'

Khalid said nothing. He felt a kind of twisted pity for the bearer. He knew the guy was at least two years his junior and that he was known to have a fire inside him.

'She calls me Khalid,' Khalid said flatly.

'You are living in some other place; this is Pakistan. All these foreigners are the same, just like the President-bastard.'

Khalid sipped from his bottle and said nothing.

'Come on, Khalid. You and me. We can go to that bastard's factory tonight, and we can mess it up. At night time I am very good, I can eat the head of a cobra, crush it with my teeth like a nut!'

'I do not think it was the President-sahib. I think it was someone else.'

'We both saw his face! Boasting eyes, big mouth like a

lorry horn "BEARER … GO GET ME ANOTHER", and cheeks all pink like a monkey's backside.'

'Yah, but someone told him. One of the guys.'

'One of the bearers?'

'Yah.'

'Khalid, you have gone soft in the head. One of the guys? Take your tandoor?'

'Maybe, yes.'

'You better keep that shitty thinking to yourself.'

Khalid sat on the wooden block and looked blankly at the Spitting-bearer. The cook knew Akram the Chief Bearer was involved in the theft. The problem was he did not know who had been wrapped up with the Chief Bearer.

'So,' Khalid said, 'Akram let you go early.'

'Yah.'

'How come?'

'Don't start trying to be sneaky; I am not one of his lackeys.'

Khalid knew the young guy had strong views, causes. The biggest Khalid heard about was a scheme to eject all the foreigners and West Pakistanis. Here in Chittagong, from the teahouse where he and others held their secret meetings, the cause was no sponge wiping down windowpanes. It was a big stick ablaze and poised to strike against the dusty windows. Khalid heard rumours that the group talked about a war going on behind the hills, in a place called Sigh Gone. He had actually heard Mahfouz use the word 'war' once or twice. Yes, Khalid thought, it was unlikely Mahfouz was Akram's lackey. Someone else had done the theft with Akram, someone else.

Mahfouz sat down a moment. He finished his beer by

exalting a mysterious thing dissolved in the contents of the bottle as he held it up, tossing it back into his hard chin before he headed for the teahouse.

'See you some other time,' Mahfouz said.

'Maybe,' Khalid replied.

Mahfouz turned to leave, but he stopped.

'You know,' he said darkly, 'you must learn to pick up opportunity.'

'Don't you worry,' Khalid said, 'you will see what *opportunity* truly means. One day, when you are looking around like a dog for a bone, you will see what I mean by opportunity. Your problem is that you cannot see a rupee if it is sitting in your damn hand.'

The bearer turned and walked. The bicycle clattered.

That poor guy knows nothing, Khalid thought. Ignorant fool. Mohendra is right, the guy is doomed.

Zeythi came outside. She carried a green cloth. She sat on the steps and moved the cloth from one hand to the other.

She said warmly, 'Do not worry, I will fix it.'

Khalid stood looking blankly at her. What could she do, he thought, about someone like the President-bastard? She will learn the ways of Chittagong.

'What can you do?' he said flatly.

'I will fix it,' she said firmly. She lifted the cloth and tied its length around her forehead.

It took Khalid by surprise. 'What's that?' he said.

'I will fix it.'

Khalid took the jar of ghee inside. In the kitchen he worked, but it was automatic work while he wondered about the green cloth Zeythi tied to her head. He then continued to explore who might be mixed up with Akram at the club.

Drizzle on the Balcony

It was a hot evening. Everyone sat around like dogs. Nobody asked about the coming rain, but rain occupied every mind everywhere. Only the sahibs openly talked about it. It was always only the sahibs. It was a constant wonder to Khalid that sahibs could be so stupid.

Time for the teahouse. The place of not a single sahib. Khalid thought it would be a good idea to ask a few questions about the Chief Bearer.

Khalid arrived while it was bouncing in full swing, and the balcony was crowded. It was the kind of time when you chant in your mind *Will the rain please come will the rain hurry please*. It was an odd thing to wish, this wanting the disaster to hurry, but that's what you did when you knew full well what the rain was all about. *Get it over with* was what the chanting really meant.

Downstairs, the Spitting-bearer's table of hunched shoulders and burning eyes hissed at him as he walked past. One called out a shrill cry of abuse that involved three generations. Khalid said nothing and he walked to the stairs. On the balcony Ajit Mookerjee stood at a far corner over the stream. Iqbal was there too. Khalid lifted his hand, waved and turned to go downstairs. He paid for three drinks and took them back up.

They didn't mention the newspaper until Khalid did, and then they said nothing much of it except that there must be some dirty business going round and that it was the worst of bad luck. Khalid nodded, said little, kept his eye roaming the small crowd across the balcony. He saw Aranthi the potterywallah walk outside. A friend followed, and they searched about for a clear table. He kept his eye on Aranthi for a long time as she moved, causing Ajit Mookerjee to issue a quiet warning.

'Khalid. She is Mustapha's daughter.'

'Who is Mustapha?'

'My sahib's clerk at the council. He is not a funny man.'

'I'll be back in a minute.'

As Khalid walked across the cement he sweated like a cold bottle. He hadn't bothered to clean himself up after the night's work at the house, but he didn't care. He'd wash tomorrow. The sweat darkened his light shirt and made his temples shine. He stood off for a moment. Aranthi seemed to him so impressive and so lighted. Long hair, greasy and lovely and shining, a big set of lit eyes and a smooth smile which appeared to be full of bright things to say, and she was laughing a little with her friend, a laugh sprinkled with the light of the balcony's two big outside bulbs. Khalid took the last three steps. For a moment he stood in what he thought of as her personal light.

The friend saw the cook first, and she tugged at Aranthi's sleeve.

The potterywallah's smile grew larger and it lit the corner. Khalid thought it lit the whole balcony. In fact, he thought it lit the hillside. Someone with a bit of experience, like maybe Ajit Mookerjee, should have told

Khalid back in those days the facts about a beautiful smile. After you are kissed by the luck of the filthy camel driver, almost any smile is very, very beautiful.

'Have you heard?' Khalid asked.

'Yes I have,' the potterywallah said without overdone pity. Khalid liked that moment.

'Do you know how this happened?'

'Me? Do I know? What are you asking me?'

'Did someone, say maybe Featherduster come to you to copy the sketches?'

'Who is Featherduster?'

'Mohendra the chickenwallah.'

'Oh. I don't think so, no.'

'A bearer from the English club?'

'No.'

'The Chief Bearer from the English club?'

'No, nobody.'

A mist fell past the big bulb. People moved inside. Aranthi and her friend skipped inside, and Khalid went to the other wall to resume his drinking. The balcony was deserted, and only Ajit Mookerjee and Iqbal stood against the wall.

'I should have brought my brolly,' Iqbal said.

'Two minutes and this is gone,' the gardener said. 'It is the usual false beginning.'

'Please do not let it come,' said the letterwriter. 'Please.'

That was the other chant. Please *do not* let it come. Just as odd, because even though it was a wish, it was a resigned one. You chanted it, but not for one second did you believe it.

Khalid took a chair and sat under the overhang. He said nothing and looked away into the drizzle and the hillside. He threw an empty glass over the balcony.

'What is the matter?' the gardener asked and sat at the table.

'Nothing.'

'I told you—she is the clerk's daughter.'

'It is not her.'

'Then?'

'I am angry, yah, but it is a good cause.'

'What is this good cause?'

'The thieves are Mohendra-bastard and Akram-bastard. I know it, I feel it in my hands, but it is like they are invisible.'

'Well, they are being very careful.'

'Mohendra is a sneak,' Khalid said.

'True,' the gardener said with a shrug.

'He is just a low-down rat, but he wants everyone to believe he is a refined man.'

'He is a truth-mangler; anyone who tries as hard as Mohendra to be respected, is a truth-mangler. Even chickens he cannot cut properly—he just mangles them.'

'He has broken my hopes for the tandoor.'

They fell silent. The drizzle came down heavier, as though saying please had worked.

'Unhappiness,' the gardener said, 'yah, it is a bad thing. I have a remedy for unhappiness.'

Khalid looked sideways at the gardener. Then he glanced up at Iqbal.

'What are you looking at me for?' the letterwriter asked quietly.

Khalid turned to Mookerjee. 'Remedy,' he said to the gardener flatly.

Mookerjee rolled his head. 'Yah.'

'Don't be funny.'

'I am not being funny.'

'There is no such thing as a damn "remedy". Like what? Medicine?'

'There is, definitely.'

'Now you are a sabjantawallah all of a sudden?'

'No, but I can tell you a remedy.'

'Okay, tell me,' Khalid said without interest, and he looked at the hillside.

'The ayah.'

'What about her?'

'She likes you.'

'So?'

'Very much. I have eyes. Better still, I have a nose. I know a little about these things.'

Khalid glanced up at Iqbal.

'What are you looking at me for?' The letterwriter asked.

Khalid thought for a moment about Zeythi. 'I will fix it,' she had said over and over.

They sat out the evening on the balcony and watched the possible rising of the monsoon, and they talked about nothing. Normal teahouse nothing. The kind of empty warmth that is full of fun if you do it among those who know what it is you do. And in a peculiar way, the gardener understood what the cook did and the letterwriter understood what the gardener did and the cook understood too. The drizzle stopped, and the gardener's words had been right—it rose false. And saying please did not seem to help.

Fiddling with Dreams
of Innocence

Zeythi came silently to the wall. The night guard twitched, narrowed his eyes, but decided it was nothing: maybe a snake after the warm breath of a rat. The darkness was full of blank shapes and holes of eternity.

She climbed softly to the ledge of a window. The timber was wet and gave way to the hand's pressure. She flowed downwards to a Baluchi carpet. The double-storey house of the President-sahib lay asleep.

She tied a green band to her forehead.

Strange smells filled the air. Maybe perfumes or soaps. A swirl designed to hold off the country in which you were located. Smells into which the President's wife could fall as she surrendered to sleep and into jars of memories.

So, to interfere with the wife's dreams.

If the wife was now drifting through a place of early comfort, of her own special fantasies from the land where all things are known and nothing is strange, a disruption might mean a terrifying thing.

An approach of footfalls, and Zeythi remained under the window. Outside, the guard yawned.

She floated to the next room. A big table rimmed by chairs occupied the stale centre like a general in state. Now it became comfortable to move about. The eye was dart-good. At this depth of the house were no windows risking the night guard. The spaciousness felt fine. And the clocks kept a normal sound riding on the abnormal air. Each room had a clock and each clock spoke with a click of the tongue. She decided that it would be an uncomplicated return journey following the clocks.

At the stairway she struck a problem. Too many steps. Wood out in the weather gives way, but in here it will resist. She directed her weight to all fours, crawled up like a spider, reaching the limbs out to the ends of each step.

Getting inside and upstairs had been simple. She was calm and did not hurry. The President-sahib lay in a position on his back, knees rising over a cotton bolster. Beside him the wife curled away into a pale shrimp. Then Zeythi caught an infant smell. It gave her cause to hurry. The wife favoured a powder used on her as a child. During the day she wore a perfume, but at night, in the bedship, she secretly wore the talc.

The President's wife lying curled on the bedship puffed and sucked in surprise, and she ceased a light snore.

Slowly Zeythi moved off the stern of the bedship and floated along its side, gagged by the fragrance.

The wife's mouth started to twitch. The eyes bounced. Zeythi came up close to the wife's face. They now could touch the tips of snouts. Instead, lips moved with no sound, feeding the life of the other set of lips without touching. When the wife exhaled, the message was halted. As the wife breathed in, Zeythi's message was resumed.

Under this tidal night air, the message won much ground, tunnelling into courseways, fiddling, as it burrowed this dreaming body, with memories of innocence. Fiddling and fixing.

From Gloom to Ghee and Cheer

The President's wife always looked forward to the end of the evening when 'bath' would dissolve the French perfume of a fine-boned woman touching fifty, so that she could replace it with the talcum scent of a daughter-blob touching six. In the intervening decades the world had ruptured. Between waddling along the rosebed in Devon and worrying inside a house in Bengal came the slippage downwards of all that she was born into. To her mind, it amounted to disrespect. There had been disrespect, and the wars. Disrespect, and independence. But she grieved most the slippage of poetry, the slashing of her lyric lovers. Prepare for sleep with the talc of deep childhood breathing through the forests of pillow. But make no mention of it. At bridge they will call it a stain, a desperate unwillingness to bound healthy and wealthy into maturity.

The sahib who worked at her husband's factory and who wrote plays had begun to visit her regularly, offering a private, probing curiosity; and she welcomed this journeyer to her past-in-the-present. Not one friend in Chittagong other than this Theatre-sahib had the gloom that was vital to ask of her herself. Her friends snorted out the questions like demands. But not him. He brought along a resistance to damage, a companionship that united their useless flairs for singsong. Behind cover of the everyday 'bullshit and nonsense', his words, which were cobbled together with a kind of love, came flowing out in a crooked netting of adoration. And there was nothing dubious about them, for he did not care at first what she thought of herself, only what he felt in his own flogged heart for her. It was a torn netting that flowed out, scrappy, for some it might have needed mending, but it caught her attention, and it also caught every last one of those lost victims of her century of disrespect. He liked the way her lip hung rudely open as if she was about to fill the air with big news, and he let the messy netting tell her that too. It was only much later, after she had returned from a holiday in London, that he would be alive to the shades of its intimate possibility. For now, in the hidden moments behind the 'daily bullshit', he loved the way her lip just hung there in readiness for a declaration.

'Talcum powder?' he had laughed. 'So what! Take a running guess as to what service I put my Brylcreem.'

'You do that with your hair cream?'

'Yes, well, not always. Sometimes I use ghee.'

'That's not very nice,' she had said with sudden interest.

'Oh but it is. Would you like me to show you one day soon?'

'Yes please.'

He added tears to the dismantling of all that she was born to in summer-soft Devon in 1920. If she moodily breathed utterances admonishing the 'fall and fall of empire', he would stride into her melancholy with any kind of torn nonsense which came to mind, feed the willingness for rhyme and play. 'Just as necessity is the mother of all invention, so obesity is the mother of all convention—and a big fat bird will fall from the sky from sheer tipsy condescension.'

They would laugh a little at having been tossed to love inside the decades of irrevocable slippage.

The minor position at her husband's factory did not bother him. On a bleak day in Bristol he held his face to the icy wind coming off the black Severn. He thought well on the content of a newspaper advertisement that caught his eye over lunch, and within hasty weeks he was overseeing a small engineering shop by the Bay of Bengal. Not bad at all, he decided on arrival at the Chittagong airport.

When he was not rousing interest in his production of the play at the club hall, he was playing snooker as part of the negotiations for a contract for road signs.

These were 'small costs to shell out for a sweet and gloomy lover what smells like a baby.'

The President's wife did need to tell someone of her lover, and as the monsoon drew near she slipped into friendship with Fatimah Westcott. Neither had shyness in talking about their fucking. They had open cheer and table-thumping glee. Both had a bit of boredom from the endless days of stillness and the same dull stuff at the club, but this was a tedium that excited the glee in exchanging stories of the stolen hours. The President's wife had never spoken openly before. If she spoke of sex it had always been blandly. To hide it. Or beautifully. To give it due credit. But with Fatimah she slapped every messy detail into the air. Fatimah Westcott did not fit into Chittagong's manners. She made up her own manners. They became good friends.

At the Boss's Request

A dinner was arranged at the club, but the Theatre-sahib was dusty from the day's work and could not go directly from the factory like the President had done, so he drove the jeep home to get cleaned up. For a moment, he could see a piece of the moon. On the way back to town he picked up the President's wife.

The President's wife didn't look right. Her plain, clear beauty filled the big room, he thought, but a shadow ran round the smile. She was dressed without show, and he admired the comfortable sleekness. She poured out two Pimms. They sat on the couch holding their glasses.

'You look as if you haven't done a thing all day,' she said.

He thought carefully. Not the normal sadness, this; it's a sharper sadness.

He smiled. 'I've come to collect you,' he said.

'Yes, he telephoned from the club. So who're the dinner guests?'

'He didn't say?'

'No.'

'People from the ministry, they're down from Dacca overnight. And the Westcotts. Fatimah and the French husband—he's in from Delhi for a few days.'

She took to her glass, and the Theatre-sahib openly watched her drink, in perfect quiet. The house was well lit and thrown ajar, front door, concertina door, the porch, the windows that ran round the living room, and no sound fell indoors from the evening.

She put aside the glass for a moment.

She said, 'You look as new as a fresh towel.'

'I feel exhausted.'

She blurted out a puff, a kind of laughter.

The night guard appeared into the pool of light at the double doors to indicate his arrival, and she nodded and said hello across the large living area. He tilted his head and walked on to the darkness.

They sat in quiet again. The Theatre-sahib savoured the silent moments, and he wanted to use them to embrace but then didn't mind not embracing because it was so fine to simply look.

'Well,' she said finally, 'I am feeling quite aloof tonight so I think we shall have a good time at this dinner whether it is with the people from the ministry or with the King and the Queen of Siam … very perky indeed.'

'You slept well,' he suggested. Like a baby, he thought.

'Matter of fact I was accosted by vivid dreams.'

'Terrible?'

'No. They've left me traces, even now, of a pending festival in which I shall unleash things, setting something free. I can't remember anything much, though that's the impression I get. Perhaps I'm making it up.'

They drove to the club where the dinner was successful and the evening progressed in the lounge and the bar. Fatimah Westcott's husband took a hold of the after-dinner drinks by having a private word with Akram the Chief Bearer. The club was busy, happy, and Chittagong glittered.

They did, once, stand alone on the verandah together. Breathing the stillness, the possible, and looking out through the giant almond trees.

A Fight over the Pictures

Invisibly the rain hung in the cream air. The money plant flung itself wilfully from the wall. The money plant is cunning as a snake. It feeds from the laundry run-off. The heart-shaped leaf gives me notions, but not of money. Not to worry, like many other things on the Chittagong flats, the label is pasted a bit crookedly. The vine jumped from the crumbling wall regardless and festooned into the air better than anything else around it.

A dense patch gripped the cement, and the Minisahib used it as a cushion. He was so well immersed into the plant that it looked as if his head was a stumpy fruit bursting from the main trunk. This was comfort. Very mature little kid. Taking reward after a big day's work. He had filled the tray with new guppies from the pond. It was a hot morning's running about, but he got it done good and well. He took a large mouthful of lemonade.

'Where is Zeythi this morning?' he said to nobody. 'And Khalid, where's Khalid? I bet they've gone to the bazaar. Filthy bastards. Why couldn't they wait? They're always going without me lately. I bet they're falling in love. Old people. I hate old people. Fall in love—that's all they do, run away and fall in love. Never mind. I don't mind. Khalid's okay, he would let me play with her still.

151

What's that over there? Is it the Swedish idiot? Hope so. Is it? Push the bastard in the pond. Right in the middle of it with the demons and the electric catfish.'

He took a swig of the drink and he settled in to watch cattle graze the far side. He heard shrieking in the distance. It was the voice of Zeythi. She was chasing after Khalid. She shouted out and hurled a rock after him. Khalid laughed.

She called out: 'Son of a pig!'

She caught his head with a stone. Then she let out a string of curses, and at his head it rained stones. A second stone made contact, and he lost his footing. He came up running for the wall. Zeythi was directly behind Khalid now. She was rasping curse for curse. When he died, he would die like a rotted dog. Then he was a pig, all the types of pigs—filthy; stinking; ugly. Then he was a goat, all types. Then he was just a plain bastard.

They fell to a stop. Both were standing right underneath the Minisahib. The Minisahib hunched his shoulders into the heart-leaves, and he remained still.

Khalid turned slowly about. His chest heaved, clawing at air. Zeythi immediately raised a stone. Her teeth were bared. Her breathing sounded like the low snarl of the dog with rabies last Christmas. The rock in her hand was held far back, poised behind the head from where she could hit him suddenly right upon the bridge of his shining dark nose. Khalid knew it, and he held a defensive palm straight out. Their thin cottons were stuck to muscle.

Khalid shifted a foot forward. Zeythi responded by remaining in position.

He knew he would be forced to circle. Utter a word, a single word …

He shifted his foot sideways, then the other foot followed, and he commenced moving round her shoulder. Glided around, and she could do nothing but follow the new movement.

He simply had to wait until she dropped her eyes. Sweat fell, silent moments, and Khalid's fast arm shot out.

Zeythi finished up on the ground and under his thighs, and Khalid prised the rock from the strong, furious hand. Khalid tightened his grip on the little wrists. He began to growl his own curses and pleasures.

The Minisahib was shaking. With a sudden burst he left the money plant and landed on the hard dirt.

The Minisahib immediately stood as high as he could imagine. His throat felt insecure, voice not available. He tried to order the cook off Zeythi. He tried to copy the way they seem to make the cook pour or dish up. Khalid's eyes darkened. Again the Minisahib tried to order the cook off the ayah but again he found that no sound emerged from his dry mouth.

Khalid released a deep chuckle at the Minisahib, and he proceeded to return to Zeythi to right the curses.

But the Minisahib said, plainly, 'Get off her.'

He cocked his head a little to say it, and he said it in a feelingless way. His legs trembled. He felt a big sweat pour from his head. And the smell of cowshit everywhere.

But he very simply said, 'Get off her, right now' in a blank, sensible voice.

Khalid lifted his eyes way back to inspect the Minisahib. From far up the ridge of his nose, he contemplated his chances. He raised the idea that he might have lost the Minisahib. Also that maybe these days the boy has too much credibility. The cook calculated his chances as bad. He returned his attention to Zeythi, and removed himself piece by piece so that she could not fire a fist at his head or a foot between his legs.

Khalid stood aside, smeared with mud from the stream. He still breathed like a wild goat. He flung away the stone. It fell among the cattle, and a big white cow lifted her head. She kept her head high, and then went back to feeding on the burnt grass.

Zeythi got up. She saw that Khalid's head was cut, and it bled down to his white shirt.

'I am finished,' he spat. 'I am sacked!'

He stood, breathing less heavily. He looked at her with vacant eyes. His hands hung from the ends of the wet whites. He waited a long time.

Then he said calmly, 'You have fucked my life up.'

Zeythi didn't respond. She sat up, but she was tightly coiled.

Khalid looked off into the distance and said, 'You have fucked up my fucking life.'

Zeythi spat on the grass at his feet.

There was another long silence.

Zeythi spoke first: 'You said the pool plan would be a secret!'

'Yes,' Khalid said flatly. 'It is a big secret. Now that you have burned the photos, nobody will ever know anything. He will close the pool. I will lose my job here. I will lose my tandoor. You, he will make you also lose your work. Very clever, very smart girl, oh yes. A clever girl from the *hills*!'

'You told that filthy hawker!'

'What did he tell the hawker?' the Minisahib asked.

'What do you think?' Zeythi said angrily.

'Well,' Khalid said finally, 'nothing matters. The storm is here. The monsoon has not yet started, and the fucking storm has arrived. Very, very good. Are you happy now?'

'I have fixed it,' said Zeythi.

'Oh. You have fixed things. Bless her little heart. She has fixed it all up.'

'Yes. I went to the President-sahib's house.'

'You talked to the President-sahib?'

'No.'

'Then?'

'I'll show you. Take us to the club tomorrow afternoon.'

Khalid let his hands hang, and he looked off into the distance again. What use going to the club? he thought. What use staying around here? I might as well talk to the sahib tonight, get my quitting pay and go. At last, I'll go. Dacca. Like Leila.

'Take us to the club.'

Khalid turned and walked away.

'Take us to the club!'

A Second Warning

Khalid sat squarely at the table and smoked. The teahouse was uncrowded. He didn't bother taking the steps to the balcony, and he reasoned gruffly that it looked like rain, right this afternoon. Then he heard a call.

'Hi Khalid ...' Leila had come in.

'Want me to sit with you? Damn, what has happened to your head?'

'I fell over. Sit down if you like.'

He thought he'd wiped it clean, and he thought changing his whites had been enough.

'That looks very bad.'

'It is nothing, I fell off the bike.'

'Like a drink? Lychee?'

'Yah, good.'

Leila went to get the drinks. Khalid wiped at his head with his sleeve. When she returned Khalid wanted to talk about Dacca. Leila did not want to talk about it, but she told him where to find a junction of many eating houses where he could get work, past the slums behind the Nawab's Palace. She said Dacca was an endless place, huge. Like one hundred Chittagongs. Chittagong, she concluded, is a much better place. This made no sense to

Khalid. Leila insisted she was happy to be back and pleased to be given her work with Fatimah Westcott. Leila then changed the subject.

'I have something important you should know about.'

'I do not want to hear any more about the newspaper.'

'It is about the ayah. My aunty saw her wandering through the back village, in the middle of the night. What is a girl doing out there, among those filthy scum, so late at night? I'm telling you, watch out. I can feel something in my bones and it is not the rain, it is something bad with Zeythi. What is a Chakma girl doing down here? You cannot trust them, they tell lies and they want want want.'

'She is a tough thing. She is tough.'

'Well don't say I didn't say, that's all. You want something for that cut?'

'Yah, get me English lager.'

'I cannot get it.'

Khalid didn't mind. All he could think of was the bliss and beauty of Zeythi.

'I cannot get it,' Leila insisted.

'Yah.'

Secretions under the Bangers and Mash

The big almond trees gave the club verandah deep shade. Gusts from under the decking pushed a cool breeze up to your ankle. The President's wife sat heavily. She had been swimming in disrespect and poetry jumbled together. But she was pleased that the drink was strong and cold.

'What is it, Catherine?' the President asked.

'A little tired, not to worry.'

'Perhaps you'd like to sit inside?'

'One of these would be a nice pick-me-up.'

'Another?'

'Yes.'

'Please,' said the other man, 'allow me.'

The other man signed the chit. Akram the Chief Bearer strolled off.

'Well,' the other man began, 'I am most impressed by the ovens. Stunning operation you have, very impressive. What I find most impressive is the idea that my people could manufacture them back home under licence.'

'Yes,' said the President.

'One of my blokes deals with the restaurants. He's an effective sort, good results. He'd be damn impressed.'

The Theatre-sahib let the two men talk. He knew the meeting would conclude with success. He could drive back to the office, complete the day's work, then return to the club to spend the evening in the hall rehearsing his play.

Akram brought out the menu. He replaced the ashtrays and went directly back inside.

'What do you recommend?' asked the visitor.

'The goat curry,' the President began, 'is the very best, and I've tried goat in Butterworth, Malacca and Singapore.'

'Fine then. What will you be having?' he asked the President's wife.

'The bangers and mash.'

'What a good idea. Been out three weeks and all I've taken is curry. Karachi, Delhi, Bombay—and curry all the way.'

'They're very nice bangers and mash too. The real thing.'

'Yes, I think I'll have the bangers and mash instead. Come with peas?'

'Comes with peas,' she nodded.

Akram returned, and they ordered lunch. The visitor ordered a bottle of red wine and a bottle of white wine.

The President's wife then took a vague interest in the pleasant smiles on the verandah. A young girl caught her attention. She was the student from Yorkshire. She walked directly past the table. Her arms and shoulders glowed with a new brownness. She was followed by the student from Cox's Bazaar. When they sat at a table she was openly relaxed, and the paanwallah's son was on the edge of his chair. She had her hair tied back, and she smiled at the boy. Akram walked up the length of the verandah. He stopped at their table. The boy got up and walked off the verandah. The girl followed after him.

A light breeze came up, which surprised the President, and a cool rush emerged from slits in the floor. When the wine was brought to the table the visitor proposed a toast to the contract.

The floor of the verandah made a striped ceiling, high up, sounding-off with footsteps. Khalid was becoming noisy, and he got up to go. Zeythi convinced him to wait longer. She produced the green headband from inside her shirt and tied it round her head. Khalid pulled out a cigarette, and he leaned against a wooden pole.

'What are you doing?'

'I want to smoke.'

'Don't.'

'It can help them celebrate their little fucking agreement.'

'They will smell it!'

'What am I doing here?' he hissed.

It was too loud. They fell silent.

Zeythi said quietly, 'You will see.'

He slid his back down the pole until he rested on his thighs. He tossed the unlit cigarette away into the gloom.

Zeythi came forward and stroked his arm. She then kissed him on the cut on his forehead. She walked over the rubble until she was under the President's wife.

'You will see,' she whispered.

The Minisahib then said, 'Yeah, behave yourself.'

'You! I'll throw you off the hills into the cowshit! You shut up!'

When the lunch was brought to the table, an omen must

have come with it. The President's wife announced she was feeling 'a giddiness'.

'Perhaps you might like to go inside, Catherine?'

'Must be the Pimms. Very strong today.'

The moment passed, and the other man talked to the Theatre-sahib.

'So where are you from?'

'Bristol.'

'Oh very nice.'

'Yes, Filton.'

'Filton a nice place?'

'It's not as congested.'

'So what is it like working here, for this rather impressive fellow?'

'Yeah, very good.'

The omen must have been right there in the steam curling off the gravy, because the President's wife spoke next.

She began vacantly, 'I'll tell you what it's like, it is uncomfortable.'

The visitor said, 'A formidable taskmaster!'

But the President's wife continued, 'He steals things. His mother informed me that as a child he was quite the astonishing little thief—cunning. As for me, I can confirm things have not altered all that much. Scale perhaps, complexity yes.'

The President said nothing. He thought, let the creamy old sack go at it—it'll all fade into the next Pimms.

'Last month he stole my Keats. Why, I do not know, and shan't ask.'

The Theatre-sahib's feet shuffled, and then shifted.

The President's wife continued. It was a carefree monotone. 'Last year he stole a road signs contract from his friend the Anglo-Belgian in Dacca. What's his name ... sorry, can't remember the man's name. We haven't seen him for some time.

'And he constantly pinches my talcum powder.

'He will nick a cigar off you at any time, if you let him.

'And recently, well, he stole that oven from a wretched local who invented the thing all by himself, the clever fellow. It is uncomfortable to work for him I should think. In balance—all said and done—it would be rather uncomfortable.'

The wife stopped. She took up her drink. She looked at the Theatre-sahib. Then she looked away. At the other end of the verandah, she saw that the young English girl and the young Bengali man had returned.

Khalid and Zeythi and the Minisahib turned out into the bamboo laneway at the side of the clubhouse.

Then the visitor said, 'Well, must be off. Expecting a telegram at the hotel. Thank you for the luncheon. I'll be in touch.'

The President watched him walk down the steps. Under a great almond the visitor stepped into a waiting car.

Then the President watched the Theatre-sahib walk down the steps and drive away. The President's wife ordered another drink. The President gazed through the clear tiers of the almonds. He looked through the big trees for a long time. After placing his spoon and fork together, he got up and went inside.

He walked calmly through the club. From the splayed lounge he took a short cut through the dining room. He turned into the library. He sat in his chair at the wall-to-wall window. This was the good perch, the small cliff which dropped away in two directions, one to the swimming pool beside the big tank, and the other to the last of the club grounds and then over a small rise out to the other side of town. This was his place, the library. Better than the office. Here he contemplated problems, found solutions. He silently began to wonder how his wife knew about the oven. This made him also wonder if she knew about the ayah.

The Chief Bearer arrived.

'You called, sahib?'

'I certainly did. I want to know about your cousin at the bazaar. How many ovens did we consign to him?'

'Four, sahib.'

'Only four?'

'Yes.'

'Why so few?'

'Let him work, sahib, make him put up the runs on the board.'

'Quite so. And what does he know?'

'He knows nothing.'

'Does he think it belongs to the cook?'

'No, sahib.'

There was a very long silence.

'You are certain.'

'He knows it is my tandoor, sahib,' Akram said with emphasis.

'All right, you may go.'

The Accident which was not really an Accident

They were off to the bazaar to create an accident. The Minisahib did not like the bazaar after he discovered that it sat under too many laws. But today he thought, Okay, Khalid's happy. And he decided with precision, Me too, I'll be happy.

Khalid sat back jiggling along in the rickshaw. Boomtime planning slap-bang came back into Khalid's eternal inner spring. Zeythi and the Minisahib seemed to be talking lively stuff, but Khalid was not listening. He was dreaming. So Khalid jittered along in the rickshaw considering what a lot of stuff the President had stolen. Khalid believed that to steal a thing was a weakness. You are weak in wanting it, he thought. You are weak in not being able to get another for yourself. And you are weak in thinking that it will make your status more luscious. But his memsahib did not respect him, no. Did it sound like respect? Khalid concluded, Maybe it is a weakness the sahib does not like of himself ... I know plenty of thieves, but they love themselves. All those bastards behind the village behind the bungalow. And that other thief who loves himself, Akram. And now Featherduster too. Mohendra. He loves himself too. Damn bastard, yah, he was taking too much interest in the tandoor, Khalid concluded.

The rickshaw turned a sharp corner, bumping over the potholes.

I knew the Chief Bearer. He was too bloated with himself for the liking of the other bearers. His natural lean was towards being admired. Although Akram was located at the top of the club's pecking order, he maybe knew, speaking deeply, that he was no man to lead others. But speaking shallowly, it is true to attach to his whites a badge that reflected his position over the levels of conflicting bearers. He gave out marks. Recorded nits of sloppy behaviour. Noted his toe lickers. Filtered from smokers out behind the kitchen a few thin conspiracies. Dished out lives through a roster and a day off. He loved it so strongly that he stirred his opinions into believing he was loved. This idea never left his side: he was a success at feeling loved. One of the cook's assistants liked him so much that the rest of them thought it must be some kind of hidden hatred. If you held out a samosa to Akram, it was no pastry and curry that he accepted: it was your obedience. Many times he didn't even bother eating the samosa. He would just toss it in the bin after you strolled back to work.

Khalid jingled along and thought cheerily that Akram was an idiot, a lost and foolish man.

'A fucking bloody idiot.'

'Hey!' Zeythi cried.

'What?'

'Filthy language!'

'What do you care?'

'The driver cares!'

'Driver!'

'Yes?'

'You know the Chief Bearer at the English club?'

'Oh yes.'

'You think it's fair to call him a fucking bloody idiot?'

'I don't like that language. If you were my son, I would beat you.'

The rickshaw slowed down and came to a stop outside the bazaar where hundreds of people hung in the baking hot dust. Khalid and the driver argued over the fare, and when it nearly came to fists three loitering men rushed to separate them. They held Khalid away, his legs spinning in the air. The driver was less bothered, he stood back and dusted down his shirt. A compromise was reached. The rickshaw-wallah rode away. He was pleased with his day so far. He was a cheery rickshaw-wallah in love with the body of the boom, not a grim-faced battler.

Khalid led Zeythi and the Minisahib into the bazaar. He said, 'Okay, let's go see the *cousin* of the fucking bloody idiot. Let's show him what for.'

Khalid walked high, with a donkey's kick in the foot. Zeythi walked high at his side. They walked past Lall Thankee the goatmeatwallah's stall. Lall waved and smiled. Khalid waved but kept walking past for the hardwarewallah.

The Minisahib fell behind. He was a smaller figure, short. But he had the kick of the donkey in him too, and maybe the thoughts of a donkey. She's rugged today, the Minisahib thought happily. I can see the shadow of her legs inside the loongie, and I can see her rugged bums. I'll just walk behind a bit, here, yes. I wonder if she would mind if I squeezed her bums out here in the open. Maybe Khalid would get nasty. I bet they're in love. Stinking grown-ups.

Khalid knew the place well. He knew the cunning positions to one day set up his own stall.

I lost count the number of times Khalid strolled in and out of the festering bazaar, to and from its rough and tattered beauty, a plan flapping from his hairline like a little curtain blocking his view.

When buying masalas Khalid would say to himself, 'The masala people are all right, how can a masala man cheat? Worst case is stale masala. Your nose can tell from ten feet. Doctored scales we know too. A rupee of this or that looks like this or that amount. The masala men get rich in such small bits, nobody minds. Besides, you can take hundred per cent, or masalas mixed up with garbage. If you are a cook you go to the pure masalas. If you are a cook from a restaurant or a hotel you take the mixed garbage. But both these masala men are damn all right. It is the hardware men. These scum should be shipped off to Dacca to wash the roads. Their pots that always get holes. Leaky hookahs. Rubbishy key holders. Stupid safe boxes that break like a stale paratha. Candles that never work, going fzzt fzzt.'

Khalid found that his musings fell from his mouth aloud. He found that Zeythi was smiling. They walked easily along the busy lane. Khalid thought he had the Minisahib on a good, tight leash.

'Where is the Minisahib?'

'Back there,' she said. 'Looking at my backside.'

'I'd be pondering it,' Khalid suggested.

'Yah, he is,' she said.

Khalid resumed the sturdy approach to the hardware stall. The stall boasted that it was the only place to stock the new engineered tandoor.

Engineered, Khalid thought. Look at his sign:

Engineered! I'll show him what is engineered.

Khalid prepared himself to stride right in with a boast of his own. He walked hard, kicking at the dirt, swerving through the crowd.

He thought again of the Chief Bearer. What a horrible bastard Akram has been. Looting the thing off to the President-sahib. Pushing aside the lives of the guys at the club for the President-sahib. Catching the beer thieves and sacking them for the President-sahib. How is it Akram has become so greedy? Maybe he feels lonely and alone. No girl ever talks with him. He tried to marry that stupid woman from Calcutta last month—even she told him to get lost.

A pity dampened the pungency from Khalid's donkey kick. He stopped. Zeythi and the Minisahib stopped. The rolling crowd fed round.

Khalid continued thinking. Why does Akram give everything to these foreigners? You don't give everything, you give only what they ask. The rest is then always yours. Akram would give his tongue if they asked. Well, he has. Tongueless twit. He's a true servant. The poor damn bastard. I'm all depressed now, Khalid thought.

But the tandoor loomed back into Khalid's mind. Whatever pity filtered into his purpose, was now again a thump in the base of the foot. Khalid walked the rest of the way up to the stall, and he stood at the entrance.

He announced with boldness, 'That is my tandoor, and your cousin stole it.'

'Yah, Khalid. We are going to bumble through this one more time?'

'These are my tandoors, and you are a thief.'

'These are not yours, and you stink—go away.'

'You want to ask Aranthi?'

'She copies one of these for you, and you dare to talk to me like that?'

'You want to ask the President-bastard's wife?'

'Yah? Let me ask my dog.'

'You are stocking my tandoor in your shop, and I am here to put a curse on you.'

'Dump a hundred curses upon me if it makes your smell go away. A thousand if you go with it.'

Khalid turned to Zeythi. 'Go ahead, do it,' he said.

From the folds of her loongie Zeythi produced the small green headband.

The hardwarewallah spat away a mouth of paan, and he quickly rose from his camel-skin stool. 'Hey! Wait one minute.'

Zeythi lifted the headband to her forehead and commenced casually to tie it at the back.

'I said hold it!'

Zeythi stood with a hip up high.

A crowd gathered, a small audience, for entertainment.

A guard in uniform strolled up, but when he saw the green headband he turned and walked quietly off. Then the crowd too fell away quickly into the bazaar. Zeythi moved her lips at the hardwarewallah. He began to escape back into the shop. He banged into pans, pots and tiffin tins as he stumbled backwards and then turned round for a full run through the goods. Khalid watched with disbelief.

The Minisahib was stunned by the hardwarewallah's panic. He was fumbling and thrashing through the narrow stall of hardware while Zeythi continued her noiseless mutterings.

He thrashed the dust off the floor, he thrashed at tin, aluminium and plastic, hitting his legs against bamboo shelves. He flung himself to the rear of the shop, heading for the small door at the back.

When Zeythi concluded the curse, he still thrashed, deep in the rear among the goods, unseen. Khalid could make out the hardwarewallah's leg far up in the shop protruding from a collapsed mound of goods. The foot pushed at the smooth tan of the floor, slipping each time it searched for stability. It would fall motionless a moment, move a little, and then make a push. The hardwarewallah lay exhausted, his foot convulsing.

Khalid turned to his tandoor. He brought his palm to his lips, and then put it down to the clay surface.

He leaned over to pick it up.

'What are you doing?' Zeythi hissed.

Khalid stopped. 'I am taking it.'

'Leave it! They'll get you for stealing!'

'The bastard has four of them. Come, we'll take this one.'

'Leave it,' Zeythi said quietly.

Khalid left it and he called the Minisahib into the open laneway. Zeythi followed. She removed the headband. As they walked away a dull clang of aluminium shot into the air.

He led Zeythi and the Minisahib down the lane. He knew it was now a clean matter of floating across the bazaar for household supplies. As they strolled, joined the crowd, he made a mental note. Rice vegetables. Garlic ginger. Mangos bananas. Matches salt ... and eggs. He felt fine to be thinking so clearly after such a harrowing spectacle.

'Iqbal?'
 'Yes?'

'Remember that day?'

'Yes.'

'What do you think?'

'It was long ago. I have nothing to say on it.'

'Even today, so many years later, you still believe it was a bad thing to do?'

'It is none of my business. But maybe you should tell who you are now.'

'Later, yes.'

One Ten Pound Pom to Another

It is fair to assume you are the only one who has arranged a curse today. Khalid strolling from the bazaar, picking his shirt from excited armpits as he walks head high, knew nothing.

Nowadays I can see things from a different angle, other curses. How could Khalid know that Shastri privately cursed Ayub Khan the very same day? And that Ayub Khan cursed Lyndon Johnson. Castro cursed Washington and spat on the Pentagon. The Dalai Lama curtly and cheerily cursed ignorance. Curses sprouted like quick shoots through cow dung. Chiang Kai Shek, at seventy-nine the cunning chess master of the revolution, cursed the mainland with his aeroplanes with cameras stuck to their bellies, that took snapshots of China's defences. The boss of the Joint Chiefs of Staff in Vietnam, General Earle Wheeler, cursed the enemy with the announcement 'Guerillas are like birds. They don't have skyhooks and they can't exist on air. They've got to light somewhere, and the place to get them is in their nests.'

But Mao saw it another way. He encouraged the guerillas 'to move like fish in water.'

Fish. Birds. What pointy curse can come next?

Harold Wilson, temples in a locked vice of frustration,

cursed a very slow country. Wilson was cursing the worst jobless figure in twenty-seven years. Half a million people had no work to buy the fish and chips or to pay for the lights. Definitely no Chittagong boom in England.

Worse, the shackled Prime Minister did not have the option of flinging them out of the country, for life, by using Australia's Assisted Passage Scheme. As one man had done in '57. The welder gleefully paid his ten pounds, agreeing, as he must, to stay for a full two years. Fair enough, he said and he swept up the fountain pen.

The Ten Pound Poms, the Consul said they were called. He said they were thought of by the 'sloganeers' as tough, happy, ready to take on the bottom half of the known world. And this was no cruise—one that sailed Port Out Starboard Home (POSH)—this was just the one direction. They went and they loved the beaches, burnt their pink cheeks, pushed rose cuttings into sandy beds in the garden, and set about beating the odds into spoons, tin roofs and motor cars.

Except one Ten Pound Pom. The thirty-seven-year-old welder 'took a quick look at what I'd lobbed into and thought, er, "bugger this for a joke" and slipped out on the next boat, see?'

He threw aside the official agreement, worked on a ship under a false name, enjoyed a grand adventure in Singapore, and finally left the ship at Calcutta. Much later he found himself flat out at the Chittagong club.

Sitting on a comfortable chair in the airy lounge, he sighed and thought, Here I can live the life of a real man. A thinking feller. Later in town I shall have a fuck. Then I'll eat a bit of biryani, and break open a coconut. There's more than enough work available. An air-conditioned restaurant here at the club. Stuff the ten quid. I'll set things up and send for the wife soonest.

And that was the President-bastard's first week in Chittagong. A strapping, fit welder, Australia behind his back, the world before his feet.

His father the sausage maker had always said, 'You want to be rich? Eh lad? Fine then. You'll want the effortless stamina of a smart bloke and the stupid stamina of the ox all running in your head in the one and every moment.'

True, at forty-seven the President had come a very long way from his days as the welder. But you wouldn't think the sausage-maker's son would take useless wisdom seriously. But then you wouldn't think an Englishman could become so easily comfortable in a place Mountbatten was once overheard calling 'a most curious patch of India'.

As the President contemplated the return of the ovens from the bazaar, he skimmed the pages of the *Guardian*. How could he know that his stockist at the bazaar had been cursed? In Chittagong these are not events that are mentioned. He turned from a report on the Red Army strife, to a report on the recession in England. Then to the scorched-earth policy in Vietnam. By the time the Australian Consul strolled into the library to meet him, he had taken a sip of cheer from comparing his situation to the grumblings of the outside international world. His friend Abdul the history teacher was fond of saying, 'Feeling low, yes? Here, read this crap. You will instantly feel better, takes a Chinese acupuncture needle to the toe.'

The President did not mind the returns so much as not knowing the reason. He decided there were too many invisible tricks in the air. He decided to cancel the small consignment at the bazaar and to postpone the larger job of distributing the tandoors around the country. He decided on London to see the restaurants there. He was pleased with the thought, a holiday. Returning fresh and with some success, he would start working on Dacca and Karachi.

The Consul, an Englishman who also migrated to Australia under the Assisted Passage Scheme, fell into a chesterfield opposite. He had chosen to become an Australian with a powerful, aggressive completeness. It was not possible to think he had been an Englishman. He produced an envelope from his jacket and handed it to the President. It was a list of Indian and Pakistani restaurants in Australia, arranged alphabetically with the name and address of the proprietor attached.

The President broke the seal and held the research in his lap.

'Is this a Sydney list?' The President asked.

'No. Australia.'

'Twelve? In the whole country?'

'Yep.'

'Not much of an export market then.'

I met the Consul once. His nose, he said, went to places inside people that were rejected potholes on the road to paradise. In these potholes he found the unofficial data, which he squeezed into personal opinion, which in turn made him a silent champion at his work. He regarded himself as an upmarket private investigator. He said there was only the one way to live two lives, and that was to trust the memory to twist things to the point where you can find yourself bullshitting yourself into remembering yourself as you were not. He was a bit drunk, but you took his general meaning. He said that this meant he would get nowhere, and he assumed everyone was the same in this way. Which meant to him that he would not look like he was getting nowhere since everyone was getting nowhere.

The Consul sat quietly. He felt useless today. Powers weak. If only I was, he thought, a more perceptive bloke today. If I could detect what the hell was wrong with Roger this afternoon.

'Ever been to Australia?' the Consul asked.

'Never,' the President lied.

'Well then. Buy a ticket and go there on a research-cum-holiday trip, mate.'

'It would be rather a pointless journey, don't you think?'

'Not really. What with all the crazy bullshit going on in the world today, Australia is like a haven of happiness and sunshine. Get out of this humidity at least.'

'Yes, the rains ... wish they would get on with it.'

'Go alone and go happy. Leave the wife behind.'

'She would not want to go there anyway. No offence.'

'Why not?'

'I do not want to go there either.'

'Why?'

'I'll go home for a bit, research the English market.'

'The market's no good. In fact, the pommy economy's wrecked right now. No offence.'

'Quite right. But you're forgetting that the upper-class urban markets are solid as rock. I'll go to England.'

'Yeah, good. Leave the wife here. Have a proper holiday.'

'Oh no. She would certainly come along. She would want to visit Devon.'

'Would she? I thought she was having a good time here lately.'

'Yes, well, she does like the pre-monsoon. Drama, see.'

'Does she? I thought she was having a good time at the theatre hall.'

'She is rather an actress herself, and she would like to see a show in the West End.'

'Is she? I thought she was having a good time getting a bit more tuition lately.'

The big library clock ticked with a slim metallic ping. Distant shrieks and shouts drifted uphill from the swimming pool. The President was disappointed by the fact that Australia contained twelve Indian restaurants. And by the returns from the bazaar, he remained mystified.

For the first time in all his years in Chittagong he suddenly formed the word in his mind: Retirement. It sounded foreign. Retire? To what? A gully in Devon? To pints and pots and eggs and scones? His mind leapt into abstract plans. Plans to die right here in Chittagong. Die. Divorce. Retire. Yorkshire pudding. Death. Re-birth. Die-vorce. Re-pud-shire. The words moved in their own way. Winter, Spring, Summer, Autumn. Sumring, Spinter, Auter, Wintumn. There was a smooth flow in his mind now. A good sign that all those things which were connected with retiring to England did not interest him in the slightest. A beautiful decision came to him. It was to never go back. He would set about planning to stay in Chittagong forever. He would be buried here, or burned, a finer detail at this time. He would arrange next week to purchase a Pakistani passport. If the goons in London wanted my British passport, he thought, they're welcome to it. And they were welcome to his British heart. His British head he would retain. And his British skin he would keep as well. These were survival tools, and he could arrange another two pleasurable working decades in Chittagong if he used them wisely.

The Consul, who was not the actual Consul but a middle official at the two-room consulate in the doctor's bungalow, broke into the President's reverie.

'Look here, matey, one old bastard to another, and confidentially, I retire next month. I'm going back to my beaut little place on the ocean estuary in a beautiful place called Mandurah after they've finished with my de-briefing in Canberra. I'll be fishing. I'll be drinking the beautiful tap water. I'll be spoiled at clean restaurants. I'll be watching good television. The phones work. You don't need generators. The only stink in the place will be the salty smell of the beautiful crabs we'll catch. And I'll down it with a crisp white at a quarter the price. So I don't much give a stuff what your problems are, see? So you can tell me, see?'

'Well, Consul,' replied the President, 'one old bastard to another, I hope scones and cream mixed with crab and wine doesn't make you vomit.'

'You poms crack me up.'

'Don't break before you reach the estuary.'

'I don't know what it is you reckon you're dealing with in this country—but I'll put one item up to your dizzy English mind. Things happen here that do not happen in normal countries.'

The President said nothing.

Then, one Ten Pound Pom to another, the Consul stood up, straightened his silk jacket, adjusted his tie—he wore a tie—and coolly dropped a curse at the President's feet.

'Yeah go root yourself. I only came up to ask if your wife would like to adopt my cactus collection.'

'My wife thinks cactus is a curse upon nature.'

'You wouldn't fuckun know what your wife thinks, matey.'

'No.'

Twitter and Biscuit

A rickshaw ride closer to the delta, the President's wife prepared to throw a paratha at the wall. She stared into the pan on the stove. She snarled at it.

There is no gain in filling your cheeks with anger, Khalid thought. If you cannot do a thing, then you cannot do it. No need not to smile. How wise Khalid could become when he was pleased as a parrot.

Khalid did not know that the President was making plans to take the tandoor to foreign places. But he did know he had an ally in the President's wife. And Zeythi had stopped the hardwarewallah selling the tandoor. So for the moment Khalid kept quiet and pleasantly did what he was told. He was happy.

She removed the failed paratha, and threw it against the wall, for instead of a paratha she had made another crispy biscuit. Khalid came forward to help, but she called out a warning to stay away. The other women laughed. It was a glorious afternoon; gin, tales, failures.

The biscuit broke into large pieces. It joined the other biscuits on the bench and floor. Khalid went forward with the broom to sweep it clean, but she stopped him. She wanted to use her failure as a vitalising whip of encouragement. One of the women made more gins, and in her laughing she poured it to the floor. The President's wife rolled out a fifth ball of dough.

The paratha—a good paratha—was her eternal favourite. For her, the paratha made the pancake seem shallow and drab.

She folded the sheet against itself and rolled it out once more. She smeared the flat circle with ghee, and again she folded it like a shirt. Then she rolled it out flat and plopped it onto the pan. It seared, sounded good.

A woman accidentally squirted lime into her eyes, and stumbled to the sink.

'Ladies, ladies!'

Khalid liked calling them ladies. His cooking class was the only chance to say it. When he rode the bicycle back from the bazaar to the cooking class, he would sing it. Lay-deez lay-deez, lay-de-de-de lay-deez …

One of the women started up a story. It was a quick story about the swimming pool. And about the new Dutchman and the university student.

Khalid: 'Ladies, please …'

'Be quiet Khalid!'

'Cook, yer ought ter juzz shut up!'

'Tell him bugger off!'

'He's the cook, he can't just piss off!'

The story continued. The student took him—'took!' they laughed—behind the change rooms, and there, in the long grass, the swimmer saw someone else and a local girl. The student and the Dutchman fled and never did see who they were, this mysterious pair.

'Fools!'

'Yes, fools!' they cried.

The rumour was told, and a fifth biscuit was made.

Khalid thought, Twitter twitter twitter and then? Biscuit.

Khalid saw Leila at the window. He went out and sat with her under the trees far down the back. Near the laundry, and today the laundry stank. It always stank, but today it was bad.

'I told you!' Leila whispered harshly.

'Told me what?'

'About Zeythi, I warned you did I not?'

Khalid drew back and sat on the low wall.

'You've heard,' he said.

'The whole place has heard!'

'The whole place? Yah, well good. Maybe we'll get somewhere now.'

'What reason has she to come to our town and do this to our friends!'

'She is helping me out.'

'She has no damn right to do this! She half destroyed the poor man. He has run off, and nobody can find him.'

'Don't put my tandoor in his shop without my permission, that's all.'

'I'm beginning to wonder if it is yours in the first place.'

At this Khalid stood up. He walked back up the compound.

'Khalid! Where are you going just like a bastard?'

He continued walking, disappeared into the cooking class where at least they were not calling him a bastard.

When he walked into the kitchen the President's wife picked up another paratha and hurled it to the floor.

Then a familiar voice behind him called out, 'What is going on in here?'

It was Abdul the history teacher. He had pulled up outside, parked, come in through the open front door of the house and wandered through, following the noise.

'We're making parathas,' said the President's wife, 'so go away.'

'Only she can't!' a woman called out and then bumped into the fridge.

'A paratha is very simple,' Abdul said.

'Then do tell, dear sir,' said the President's wife.

'Because,' he said, 'it's all too beige, too dull. It needs colour. When you slap it on the pan to get it going, you must shake your hips.'

'Shake the hips. Like so?'

'No no, a lot, shake them all over the place—dance. Colour, you need fistfuls of gladness and colour!' he cried out.

Abdul turned to the paratha teacher, 'Seen the Old Man, Khalid?'

'No sahib. But at four o'clock he will be at the club.'

'Thanks. Cheerio girls.'

The women called out after him as he left the kitchen, 'Ta-ta shorty!'

The President's wife looked down at the fifth biscuit. In a curious moment of silence, all the women dropped their eyes to it. Then she took her foot and ground it with the heel of her shoe.

The hour was up. Khalid put his hand out and led the group from the kitchen. The girls abused his mimicry of manners by slapping, sort of slapping, his shoulder as they walked out.

He must, he decided as he swept the floor, ask the memsahib to please cancel these cookery lessons. Please. What I mean is please please please. Yah, I'll say that.

I'll just keep saying please like a fat beggar and then she will shut them out.

His drinking friends insisted he was a weakling. Teahouse talk. Some of his angry friends, Spitting-bearer types, said the English were invaders. Some of his intelligent friends said he should read the newspapers and get an idea of the invasions done against freedoms and lands—fill your empty head.

Khalid would laugh and call out, 'Rubbish! You guys want some bastard to blame. Go blame your own lazy heads! Get off your flea-bitten backsides and do some using of brains.'

Khalid agreed they looked silly because they had no pigment, but, 'They drink water and they eat flour the same as you bastards.'

But his angry friends said that it was easy for him—he had a paying job with them so he liked them.

Khalid would be saying 'See you next week,' as he pushed on into the night. To get the last word he would call out, 'Blame blame blame ... same as twitter twitter twitter, you old hags!' And the angry friends would pick up stones and throw them after him. The teahouse. Vague disagreements leading nowhere. Always.

He finished off the sweeping. Now he looked forward to sitting in the cool shade. He filled his dented tin teapot, and waited for the water to boil. He sat on the bench and smoked. He tilted his head back and looked at the ceiling. He looked out the window. Leila had gone.

Shit, he thought. Will the sahib believe me? No. The memsahib? Same. I was hoping the President-bastard's memsahib stayed, I could have talked to her. She's a good type. She would tell them. I'll ask Razia. Queen Razia.

The President's wife had not left. She stood at the rear door. As she stood looking out over the afternoon, a recognition rose up. She took a deep breath. She thought maybe it was the gin. But, in looking into Zeythi's eye, she could not avoid the sensation.

Zeythi had just finished bathing. That was all. There was nothing more to it. She wore a comfortable cotton set of pants under a loose shirt. She stopped when she saw the President's wife standing up on the step. Zeythi thought, We never see them out here, sometimes the men pretend to be lost when they're looking for the toilets. But you never see them out here.

The President's wife swayed, and, sensing a memory, she would not remove her gaze from Zeythi.

Khalid appeared behind the woman, silently.

Zeythi moved aside again, but the woman's eyes followed Zeythi in two jerks sideways. She lifted her hand. The fingers ordered Zeythi to return to the doorway, waving twice for insistence.

Zeythi moved back, and she could see Khalid nod.

All that could be heard were two crows in the invisible distance exchange their dull panic over the oddness of the sky. Occasional traffic came to grate the far ear. And the paratha class had strapped itself into a contented knot of gin tongues too far to the front of the house to be heard.

It became so intensely quiet that Zeythi could catch the woman's coarse breathing.

'I am thoroughly shick of the making of parathas,' the woman said, growing irritable at the little flame.

Zeythi stepped backwards.

'In fact, I am shick of this afternoon entirely. I am shick of the weather too if you must know the full truth of it all. Why the innocent cloud you ask? Well it's like wearing your woollies in the summer, isn't it. You get itchy boobs. I could be shick any moment. But I'm too shick of everything to be shick.'

Zeythi fell back a few more steps.

'Where do you think you're going, I wonder?' the woman said. 'And where are you from? Are you from this house? You must be a new girl. But you can't be new. I've seen you somewhere.'

The woman fell to the doorframe with a sigh. She leaned against it and sighed once more and she untilted her head.

'And I am shirtainly shick of dreams, I'm having too many dreams, it's under this blasted cloud that does it. Oh what the hell, you probably think I'm an old bag all bleached away. That's what you think, I know. No colour, poor blasted albinos. Yep, I know that's what you think. Do you think I'm bitter and twisted? Well I'll tell you I'm not bitter and twisted. I'm bitter and twisted as the next person, and you can't go calling that being bitter and twisted. I'll tell you who is bitter and twisted. Want me to tell you? Well I won't.'

The Minisahib came running round, wearing wet shorts, hair stuck to his skull like a second skin. He had had a lot of fun bathing. While the rest of the world was being hammered to earth by curses, he came sailing into the back entrance high in the air.

In the ripple of his arrival the woman's head bobbed. It was no longer tilted, but it bobbed like a cork.

'And what have you been up to young master?'

'Swimming,' he replied.

'Swimmink?'

'Yes.'

'Around here? Where could a boy swim around here?'

The Minisahib paused. 'The pond,' he lied.

Curly Restraint, and
One Extra Secret

The President's wife stood at the top step. She felt the cloud might cause her to be sick.

Behind her, Khalid stood invisible and quiet.

To Zeythi, he seemed coiled, ready to pounce. Long before the women had arrived for the cooking lesson, Zeythi had had a talk with Khalid. It was a stern talk.

'Yes,' she had said, 'the tandoors were put back into the sahib's factory. It is a small success, yes. But now you must buckle your tongue to your teeth because it is too soon to make our next move.'

'It is never too soon!' Khalid had scowled.

'They will suspect who first? You! The Zakir Hussein Road cook will no longer be a cook, he will crawl on the road like another dog.'

'Pah! Some other bastard will take the tandoors from the factory. My moment will be lost forever. I will spend my life face to face with a Khalid Tandoor in every shop in the town and being every day arrested for throwing bricks at the beautiful things!'

She asked Khalid to promise he would wait. Do nothing, and wait. She then emphasised that the tandoors at the factory were safe because the incident at the bazaar would be well and truly off the tongues of every man and woman. Nobody would dare think about the tandoor, let alone consider stocking it.

This had made Khalid take a seat, and he squatted on the concrete. He worked at prising off a toenail. She watched the stained overhang peel away, and she convinced him.

She had said, 'If you do not wait, you will throw away the good fortune our goodluck kisses have sealed for you.'

He turned his head, and his eyes flew out of the doorframe, up through the cloud and onwards to a golden future. He gazed a long while. He knew that she was right. After some moments he stood up slowly and he had laid his promise at her feet.

But now, as he stood like a shadow behind the President's wife, it did not look good.

The President's wife and the Minisahib continued their small exchange.

The woman swayed and felt queasy.

Good, Zeythi thought, now I'll get rid of Khalid. With her eyes, she flicked the cook away.

But he stayed. And he stepped in closer.

Again she urged him off, and again he moved up behind the President's wife. He felt it was a perfect time, directly after the cooking class where his one chance to call out 'Ladies ladies!' had strummed his nerve strings.

Zeythi pressed further by stepping backwards down the stair. It was a good signal. It communicated to him: 'I shall destroy this, I shall leave it all to you.'

Khalid retreated into the dark corridor.

It was the reverse of what he wished. He wanted to use

the paratha class and the slippery gin to push the President's wife into informing the memsahib, more or less like the way she had listed off the stuff on the club verandah.

He also did not like to retreat because his cook's instinct was warm. Why had the President's memsahib been so angry at the cooking class? These are opportunities, he thought as he drew backwards into the dim recess; and a peculiar pinching which he seemed to feel in the balls of his footsteps, according to Khan the whining sabjantawallah, was the grazing of occurrence against ambition, the facts against a hope. At the end of the corridor Khalid vanished into the kitchen.

He began to clean the stove, and he thought, All very nice for the children to be having a cooling bath in the laundry, oh yes, all just like nothing has happened.

With Khalid safely away in the kitchen, Zeythi turned her attention to the President's wife high on the top step.

This woman is full of drink, Zeythi thought, like a bar-bearer.

The woman swung her head back to Zeythi. She saw that the face was striking, that the eyes were large dancing eyes.

'Do you have a boy?' she asked Zeythi. She added, 'A boyfriend?'

Zeythi did not answer.

'You're too young I suppose,' the woman sighed. 'One day you shall; one day you'll make a man particularly delighted.' She paused and then continued, 'I should warn you off taking a husband, though. Terrible business taking a man into your kitchen as a husband—one minute you have the city at your command, the next minute your life is finished. Bad business.'

The woman leaned to the left, and she breathed silently for a long stretch.

Then the woman suddenly asked, 'You say you have a boyfriend?'

She squeezed her drunken arms to herself, and she said as she swayed, 'I have a boyfriend.' She unfolded her arms and she began to clap her hands together, giving something, someone, a small but heartfelt applause.

The Minisahib watched the little applause. He sprang up the steps into the corridor, chanting as he skipped past Khalid in the kitchen, 'This old granny! ... what a dirty old lump!'

When he reached his room he jumped on the bed. He led a loud applause. To him it is a kind of idiotic act that lends a moment excitement: he did it quite a lot when by himself, and he joined in when others did it. At that moment, while he applauds with an imaginary crowd, he is filled by a great affection for the President's wife. He always did like the 'powder woman' as Zeythi called her, and now he felt he led the town into liking her.

But it would be wrong to think he is a special case. This I can nowadays say with certainty, for I can see far up and down the delta. In a downtown bar of punkahs and rattling air-conditioners a huddle of unwashed men applauded a win at the dogfight. Up in Dacca at a full-scale birthday production, applause crackled into the night for a hide-faced merchant as he blew air and saliva onto a cake of candles. In New Delhi at a ceremony, applause rose and fell as each graduate filed past the podium in the great hall. Around the world a ribbon of applause, ruffling the never-ending circle of congratulation, remained in progress every second of every year. It is not only Bengalis and the English who feel the urge. Shall I speak with you of the blackness prowling the unlit verandahs? Shall I speak with you of the dark elements of the delta? The sickness? The hunger? No, says the applause, I shall instead speak with you of humble deeds and of heroic ideals, and of momentary victory. And, in a natural kind of way, that, maybe, is what the Minisahib was doing as he bounced up and down on the squeaking springs like a twit with stuck hair.

Khalid appeared at the door, 'Your lunch is on the table.'

'What is it?'

'Paratha and dahl.'

'The cooking class ones?'

'My ones.'

Khalid stood in his way. 'What are you doing?' he asked the Minisahib.

'Clapping,' he replied.

'For what?'

'For the President's memsahib.'

He went out to the hall and across to the smaller dining room where he ate his lunch. A grumbling of thunder rattled a pane in the window.

Khalid appeared at the table: 'Why are you clapping for her?'

'She's got a secret boyfriend,' he said.

'Bullshit.'

'She told us.'

'Who is it?'

'She didn't say—what a dirty old woman!'

Ambition and Anarchy
Or, Paying Attention

Khalid could not see that he had an ally. He carried the newspaper clipping everywhere. He was a fool in those days, maybe a bit too much poking his eye into his ambition.

The President's wife was one of those who liked the little things, forgotten things, and for them she would slow down to a total stop. A new sprig of bougainvillea pouncing up the fence with pristine flowers was a key to a hundred doors.

'Pure joy ...' she would whisper slowly and bring her nose to the scentless flower.

It was not the peculiar redness, though this was itself a miracle. It might be more the smoothness. Or how the shoot stole food from the dusty earth. And those curves; if one danced like that, one would awake afloat on the warm breezes putting one's mouth where it must never be put.

Fuck, she would think, what is pure joy? Why do I say it, and what does it bloody mean?

Lately, she hit delicate contemplation with the fist of a demand. The President's wife felt tremors of change. She had begun an odd habit. She started to allow herself to side with people who believed that something as pretentious as a simple joy was a petty thing.

It would now be foolish to persuade her to contemplate the sound of a strange word like ignis.

'Ignis,' said the Theatre-sahib. He was playing with an evening of rhyme, some fancy.

'Ignis?' she repeated diffidently. 'What is that?'

Or the pleasure gained from the foolish-sounding pronunciation of fatuus.

She will not have been listening to him, and she'll say, 'Fattoos? What is that?'

He said it again for her, leaning very close to her ear, 'Ignis fatuus.' And he brought his head away so she could see the wide display of his smile.

But the President's wife was not aware of experiencing a moment of joy on hearing the quirky words. Had she been paying attention, her every worldly problem might have begun to dissolve. For if she realised that the phantom flame of recognition which she could not make out was the fugitive figure in the night who had driven messages deep into her dreams, she might have up and left the President for a new life in Bristol with her Theatre-sahib lover who respected her poets as profoundly as she did. Ignis fatuus she herself was about to embrace: a loose, erratic flame.

A lack of ambition to carry out a desire, though, to her, is not a bad thing. It is a point of graciousness—and more a choice than a shortcoming. She chose against a new life with her lover? I can say that she did not. Then what is it that is going wrong? From the laws of simple joys emerges a simple answer. She did not pay sufficient attention—she was too coagulated to the scars of others, to the scars of her century of disrespect.

The desire to fulfil an ambition. The ambition to fulfil a desire. To an erratic flame like the President's wife, these are one and the same. Besides, she did not want her ambition to deliver a desire as this would suggest the desire was not strong enough to be regarded as genuine. And a false desire is a ruined life, a wrecked century. Neither did she wish to allow her desires to realise an ambition as this would only suggest she was without talent in effortlessly assuming her destiny.

Defeat. Spiralling, grotty defeat. What caused it? She did not know, all she knew was that she was lately too given to thinking in unbreakable loops of lost boredom. Perhaps in this way her equanimity blinded her to the simple joys.

Then one day the whole thing snapped like a dry stick.

The ignis fatuus dwindled until it no longer flickered in the distance. Her desire to fulfil an ambition took flame, and her ambition to ignite a desire sank like mongoose claws into the flesh of her heart. She was with the Theatre-sahib after a long drive to the lake. Sitting on a blanket on the shore, a cool breeze arriving off the water's surface. A chilled bottle of champagne. That's when it began, her slide back into life. And the inevitable return to her joyous and beautiful selves simply went on and on without ever again pausing for breath.

'Now, please pay attention,' he whispered, smiling. 'You,' he began, 'are a bright, fierce, resplendent, scorching, dazzling, blazing furnace.'

'Oh nonsense,' she said leaning on her elbow and gazing at the lake. 'I'm beautiful, that's all.' She then turned her eyes to his, and smiled.

They lay back comfortably on the red dirt and sipped

lightly at the champagne. The lake glowed, and the invisible sun was now dropping quickly, bringing sultry colours to the burls of jungle curling into the shallow shore.

'And so is this,' she said lightly.

Then she added, 'It's pure joy, really, when you roll it about, don't you think?'

'Pure joy?'

'Yes.'

'Not impure joy?'

'No,' she said, 'pure joy.'

'Not rare joy?'

She smiled. 'No,' she insisted, 'pure joy.'

Yes, Khalid now had a real ally. Thanks in some small part to the visitor who did not care a stuff about her using baby talc. Or himself using ghee.

To Advise these Two

The Minisahib jumped into plenty of joy. The stone tub especially. It was a hidden spring of all pure joy. He could fall into an afternoon of aching boredom, and this was nothing unusual. This was the busy and bland day of a child. The true suspicion here is the secret joy, the real treasure. Reason maybe for a balanced interference. How much secrecy fills the bath is no riddle against how much salty revenge scums its walls like used ghee. No, these were not the children the household could say it knew. Nice little boy. Efficient little ayah. Very lovely.

Not that he pressed it to his forehead as a joy; he did not will apparitions of it to the skin of his experience. This he did not do. Adults generally did this, hoped to somehow force it. What he did was look forward to it knowing it was present all the time. There was an added sophistication to it nowadays. But he took it as it came. There was no curve of muscle at which he did not marvel. He would touch, or feel, or gently chew: he would lean over and place his hands and mouth to whatever he felt like putting his many mouths or hands.

She would assist him, and she would look upon herself where he touched her while he touched her. They wandered aimlessly in this way, and their sighs, their quickening breath and their muffled laughter were unnoticed pleasures. Eager biting from the young teeth added spice to the silent embracing. They could hear far-off shrieks from the paratha class in the kitchen. Nice extra cover. You always needed something else going on when you've got something going on yourself—this he learned in a vague way a long time ago, but he learned it solidly, sensing its truth to a point where he made it an ongoing rule. And she handled his peanut erection. Nice extra.

He became an immigrant in her cells, and she became an immigrant in his. They liked it slightly safe. But it was richer than safety: they became immigrants in one another's realms because they were empty of the notions of possession, or of belonging, in the manner in which these things are pressed into meaning within the dogma of citizenry. If they wished to fly somewhere, they went there. If they liked it, they'd stay. If they did not, they'd move on. In point of fact, she bathed the bony pink shoulders of an immigrant in her own country, and he slid the soap over the brown breast of an immigrant to his household.

I will never forget what the Old Man once announced on the front porch. It was the late afternoon, and a friend called in on the way home from the office. They sat and drank, discussed politics. It led to a single question: who will win the Vietnam war? The Old Man often had a good answer lurking up the back of his teeth.

He said, 'What can the winds of a hundred cities produce?'

What *do* the winds of a hundred worlds produce? I did not have answers then, and from Iqbal's brolly I do not have one today, but it does seem true that while you've got one dogma raising the standard, you'll have to offer another: a hundred fake worlds of phony freedoms. Revolutionaries who seethe with vision will maybe continue to stumble from deserts into palaces of the counterfeit worlds, or into a single world, and, not unlike the Englishman Oliver Cromwell, will demolish a fence in order to put up a wall.

At the end of the day, it takes a special kind of talent to conceal vitality. The whispers of Zeythi and the Minisahib in the cement tub behind the kitchen can produce the most precise and the most correct hearing of the thinnest, the most transparent, voice of another. And it can be true. Sometimes it can be untrue, but it can be true. While responsible adults insolently make and despatch bombs, these two make and despatch a burbling fart or two, make a touch or two, a kiss or two. Worlds and armies turn dogma into dogma, while two advisable young secret-keepers poke a knee up in a cool bath. The destruction and slaughter is done in the name of peace and freedoms. The soaping and touching, and the delicate listening, is not. It is not done in the name of anything. There is no cause in the stone tub. The triumph of physical contact over physical destruction. The ignorance in ten fingers. Of all the things that I could say I wished I knew back then.

Here, behind the last shadows of a rambling bungalow, sits a little shed containing a nil cause. It does not feed steam into illusions, it feeds steam into the afternoon air. As if the afternoon air of waiting Chittagong needed hot steam. Laced with stink. The two within, they have not heard of this man Cromwell; and Oliver Cromwell, some claim, had not heard of a bath. Advice? Surely advice is called for, at the least an intervention of some level kind.

Perhaps it is this: the revolutionary might attempt building a back shed. Here he could caress the breasts of his young friend, and she could handle his wild erection. This advice might even go some good distance in sorting out the Spitting-bearer. If Mahfouz didn't first eat the whole bath.

'Iqbal?'
　'Yes?'
　'What do you think?'
　'Seems like they were having a good time.'
　'What advice would you offer?'
　'I would suggest to that fellow who has never had a bath, quickly to have one. Shall we continue?'
　'Yes, my friend, let's continue.'

But advice is a famous game. A delicate game, bluntly played. Like gloating. And who might conduct advice at the young secret-keepers, those twisted spankables? Who would be so riddled by sensitivity as to be smart enough to clap hands on the special talents that conceal vitality? And hold still its vibrating code? Who would this be, this sophisticated player of the advice game? This level, mature adult who likes to give advice and who loves to gently gloat?

　In a far-flung, mostly forgotten place, it is taken for granted that there exist some things that still hold surprise. You lean lightly on the third ear. In Chittagong, a third ear is a very useful ear. Like Iqbal's. Where half the world is washed away, or half the traffic has broken down, or half of all walls fall to ruin behind lush frangipani, or along where you walk grows but does not grow, the world is unrecognisable as the present. So a third ear can be as essential as a second foot. The owner of a third ear might have advice aplenty on offer. Or he might choose to remain silent.

That afternoon, so many seasons ago, Khalid rode up to the turn-off to the club and stopped to buy a cigarette. Nearby, the letterwriter was taking a break. He sat on his three-inch cushioned stool, legs crossed comfortably. A sweet tea sat at his side.

'Busy today?' the cook's eternal inner spring asked cheerily.

The letterwriter rolled his head.

'Good jobs, juicy?'

He rolled his head.

'Anything embarrassing?'

He rolled his head.

'See you at the teahouse tonight?'

'Yah, good idea,' the letterwriter said.

The Invisible Cook

Khalid flew to the wall and jammed on the brakes to alight the bike in the jab it made. The teahouse, polytechnic, bazaar, he heaved the bike to a stop. It wore out the brakes, but he didn't care. He liked the bounce.

Khalid knew he was late, so he ran. When he appeared at the door, the teacher stopped the class to invite him inside. Khalid waited a moment, but the teacher invited him once again. He settled at a desk high in the corner. The newspaper article and sketches lay alive in his notebook.

The teacher resumed the class and progressed into the successful rise of Shamsudin the slave-king. The best thing, Khalid thought, was not this foolish history, though the stories did catch his interest. The best thing was the teacher's peculiar form of encouragement. Khalid responded to its idiocy, and its sincerity. It was also the small round man's interest in them as pupils. It was a strong type of encouragement, that he knew. It was like the sahib's. But lately the Old Man had turned lukewarm. Still, the teacher's sayings he liked, they stuck in his mind and revolved round his head even as he made meals, bought supplies at the bazaar or washed his loongie. They were sayings that exploded into the air.

'You lot must work like stink!'

Khalid would look around, embarrassed, for there were still only three of this 'lot'.

'You lot will have to pretend you've got elephant ears!'

'Bring out that dirty intelligence, right now this minute! Dirty? Yes! Downright filthy and unapologetic!'

Khalid liked these sparks, for where else in Chittagong did this sort of thing go on? The teahouse? The club? The bazaar? No, these were places where not even the fleas took an interest in your head.

'Give me your doubt to chuck into the rubbish basket! And, above all else, have the decency to say "Good Morning" to yourself!'

There was an army of good types about, yah, Khalid knew this as he knew Chittagong, and they meant well, okay, but they did not have the push, in real and day-to-day terms, to convert kindly smiles into prickly encouragement.

Khalid sat back. He waited patiently for a moment where he hoped to raise a talk about the tandoor. He knew waiting was what sahibs did. Waiting was good. After waiting, well there would be talk.

Khalid was off the mark by a long shot. I knew the teacher quite well. He was an ordinary Bengali good man, and a compassionate educator who could dislike his pupils settling into positions in Chittagong from where they would not ever be able to shift. One thing he did believe was genuinely ruining their chances was a celebrated government plan. He would cite Ayub Khan's policy of 'Functional Equality' and shout, 'What else is a history teacher supposed to do other than kick the buggers into some sort of achievement?'

He distrusted the useful trades. He bellowed, 'All they

accomplish is the slotting of a young man for the rest of his natural days!'

But he acknowledged a kind of respect for the fast usefulness. At least they were jobs. What he distrusted with a passion, was Ayub Khan's fancy idea.

Once, over a few drinks, I caught him banging away on the ear of his friend the club President-sahib.

'Yes! It is accepted that Ayub Khan will brandish a big word across the heavens—*equality!* Yah, why not? But *functional equality*? What does this suddenly mean? I'll tell you what it means. The foreign exchange is earned from jute. Who grows the stuff? Big plantations? The magnates in Karachi? Not on your nelly! The peasant grows it. He has two acres, that's all, a tiny little plot. Then he and his millions of fellow fools, like plenty of our students' parents, sell the harvest to the government for four American dollars per ton. Ayub Khan sells it on the international market for eight dollars. In comes "Functional" equality with the surplus money, oh indeed … Khan then ploughs this money at the projects owned by the big business of Karachi. He says it is they who will then develop the country's longer-term real wealth. They will then create factories, industry, jobs. Very funny.'

So it was against a backdrop of 'official theft!' that Abdul tended his students, even if present were only two this term, supplemented by a girl from boarding school in Yorkshire.

Concluding, the teacher announced that next week they would be starting on 'A new fellow, freedom-seeker by the name of Cromwell.'

'You told us that already,' Khalid said quietly.

'I'm telling you again to frighten you.'

'Sahib?'

'Reading, boy, you better start the reading. I gave you the book last time. By next week you lot will have read it.'

Over the next two weeks Cromwell came alive for the class, booming voice, rhetoric, passion and cunning. More staple stuff for the imaginations of the teacher's students.

At the end of the class the paanwallah's son and the English girl strolled off. They made an attempt not to go off together.

The teacher broke for lunch, packed up his case and left the room.

Khalid sat for a while. He had so hoped they might, somehow, have touched the subject of the tandoor, but no. He opened his notebook to the newspaper cutting.

'The bastards don't even say my name in it. What am I, see-through?'

Khalid spent many days dropping in and out of hopes. He was looking for someone who would jump all over the problem. He did hope Abdul the teacher would be the one.

A Visitor from Arabia

Khalid had another ally. But he didn't know it.

'What is that racket?' the ally shouted as she walked into the compound.

The sudden interruption made Khalid jump, but in a second he was bright as a torch. He smiled broadly and stood up wiping his hands. Here was the one memsahib no bastard could bully.

'It is my radio, Fatimah Westcott, memsahib!'

'It's a horrible jangle, do you like it truly?'

'Oh yes!'

'What instruments are they playing? I cannot even guess.'

'Tabla, sitar and pipes too, all mixed up.'

'And you,' she said to the Minisahib, 'what about you?'

'Yes, I like it.'

'Do you like any other music?'

'Sometimes.'

Fatimah Westcott sat down with the Minisahib a moment. Like most adults who ventured out to the back compound, she thought of him as a 'sweet and cute lad'. He stirred impulses for children of her own. Same kind of patting-off as the rest: nice boy, efficient ayah, very lovely. What a beautiful world.

'Want to hear a story about a mysterious instrument?' she asked a little awkwardly.

The Minisahib thought, No. But he said, 'Okay.'

'It is about Pan chasing a beautiful girl through the forest. You know Pan?'

'No.'

'He lived long ago and he had the feet of a goat to rule over the woods and the fields.'

Yeah, thought the Minisahib as he looked at her blankly. Sounds okay. Goat's feet but ... Wish I had wings.

'He was chasing the beautiful nymph Syrinx, and he was just about to put his arms around her ...'

She's telling me a dirty story! thought the Minisahib. He watched her huge red lips moving about. He could feel a buzzing in his pants.

'... but she changed herself into a bundle of reeds.'

'What are reeds?'

'Jute,' said Khalid.

'No, pond grasses. Only they are hollow like a straw. Pan sighed as he held the reeds in his arms, and his breath through the reeds made a whistling sound. Quickly Pan broke off the reeds and he tied them together. He learned to play tunes on this instrument, and he named it the syrinx in honour of his lost love.'

The Minisahib had thoughts about this Pan, just the fleeting and immediate reactions in a hot afternoon. Nothing too heavy to carry as he walked off into the house after Fatimah Westcott had left.

Pan ... dumb bugger, he reasoned in silence, when I hold Zeythi she doesn't turn into sticks. I like my girl better.

Khalid followed Fatimah Westcott up the side of the house to her scooter.

'Tell the memsahib I called by, Khalid. Let her know about dinner at my house next week.'

'Yes.'

He was about to launch into a plea, but Zeythi appeared on the front verandah. Khalid stood off and watched the trader ride up the drive.

Khalid tilted his head to the clouds and listened to the scooter buzz away on the dusty road. The sound of the scooter fading in the heat gave Khalid the definite feeling that a chance too was fading. No chance Fatimah Westcott could step in and help. But he was wrong.

He fetched his bicycle. He decided to visit the bazaar to ask his friend Lall Thankee to keep an eye on Mohendra the chickenwallah.

One Good Flavour Deserves Another

Lall Thankee the goatmeatwallah worked over the slab so that large steaks appeared, and bandages of fat fanned out from the thick layer of flies. His mouth was a perpetual smile. With too many Lalls about the place you would have thought, What is all this bulldust about misery? He folded the goat into a parcel of banana leaves, brushing at flies as he rolled. He held it out, and then accepted the cook's money with both hands. Hardly anybody bought old goat. It was tougher than anything that could have come out of the ground no matter how complicated.

'You might as well throw back ball bearings from an old bicycle wheel,' Mohendra the chickenwallah laughed from his stall next door. The gunnysack roof bounced in a quick breeze, and the featherdusters jumped about.

'Who takes any notice of what he says? He is a stinking liar,' Khalid stated blandly.

'Like your grandmother,' Mohendra said.

'Just like your stupid cousin Akram,' Khalid stated lazily.

Mohendra scoffed, 'You are nothing more than an Englishwoman's cook!'

'You are a dunderhead if you cannot see I am a man of many privileges.'

Khalid noted that Mohendra fell silent. Waiting I bet, thought Khalid, for this *privilege* to be explained.

Khalid leaned on the chopping block.

'It is a privilege to know the Minisahib—he is a fine young man, and one day, when you are nothing more than a featherduster, he will be a great young rooster. It is a privilege to know the young sorcerer, she is a clever and beautiful young woman. It is a privilege to know the sahib, he is the most honourable Karachi Pakistani I have ever met. It is a privilege to know the memsahib, she is a big-hearted soul with a sneaky laughter. And it is a privilege to know Lall here, your neighbour—so I suppose you do have some privilege—he is a wise and humble man, he is aware of the true value of a friendship, and he does not hide, like you do, the fact that he enjoys wanking.'

'What!' Mohendra cried out.

'Well? Do you enjoy it?' Khalid asked.

'You are a crass man!' Mohendra barked. 'Your mouth is a cesspit.'

'There it is,' Khalid stated. 'You are a smelly liar like your cousin. Forever pretending you are a decent man. You cannot even admit to an ordinary thing like a wank. It is no wonder to me that you have no sense of your privileges.'

'Please do not argue about it, guys,' Lall Thankee said from the eternal smile. 'Please, we are all friends.'

'Do not worry, Lall,' Mohendra said, 'people are entitled to hear his septic nonsense.'

Khalid strapped the parcel to the rack on his bicycle and rode down the lane into the bazaar past the empty hole that once flashed famously as the stall belonging to the hardwarewallah. Nobody had seen the hardware man; rumour said that he'd shot through to Dacca. For some time the stall would look like a big eye glowering darkly, unlettable. Memories would have to first fizz out like bad candles.

Khalid rode out of the bazaar allowing the slope to do the work. He removed his hat and ruffled breezes into his hair. Big almond trees flanked the copper-coloured road.

In the kitchen he sharpened his knife. Now he would become busy making mighty plans. Back outside, at the wooden block, he cubed the meat until he produced a large pile of diced pieces. He rolled the pile about, picking off bits which wanted a final trim. Then he rolled it round again, searching for escaped twigs of fat. Clean away the greasy stuff, he thought, and then it is fine to see what is what and who is who. It seemed good, so he whistled sharply out over the fence into the jungle. From the confusion of banana, frangipani and weed, the cat stepped between the broken glass of the concrete wall. He was a torn and scarred big cat, and his pitted, low voice was an instrument that sang, in broken notes, of wreckage. He stiffened and made a circle at Khalid's feet, brushing the ankle before moving out to make a start on another circle. Khalid watched him make the circle again, and he tossed a marble of meat out.

The cat snored as he chewed, and then a swallow.

'So what about you, little fellow? How do you say I

should catch these bastards, eh?'

Khalid picked up another marble and lobbed it at the cat.

The cat chewed and snored, then swallowed. Khalid took up the large clump of meat to the kitchen. He came outside to collect his transistor radio. He turned it on and danced to the tune as he went back to the kitchen. He hung the radio on a hook by the window and bounced around the kitchen working.

The meat was less than a pound now, looking fine. He was pleased with it. He brought out roughly the same amount in fist-sized brown onions, which he peeled. He thought, Get inside this bastard-mess no matter how many onion skins they've got around it. He placed a set of new goggles securely to his face, and proceeded to slice the onions into a mass of rings. Every cook was either tap-tapping on the memsahib, or putting away a rupee here and there for his own mask-and-snorkel outfit. You can only obtain it if somebody is coming from London, and Fatimah Westcott had done the deed.

He swept the onion off the board into the pot and said, 'And then just like this I will fry the bastards in hot ghee!' The ghee reacted loudly. Then, on a stir, it settled into a brisk frying, and he went on to mix the fresh masalas.

Into a bowl he splashed a quick whistle, a brawling hum, cardamom, turmeric, fennel, garam masala, cumin, coriander, five cloves, bay leaves, and, after he made a loose paste, he pounded garlic and ginger in the granite mortar. He attempted to drumbeat the pestle against the mortar, thumping along to the music, but today it was rock upon rock. On the happy night he found that his tandoor had worked, his garlic pounding sounded more like hip-shunting from the new Bombay movie. Today, he let the pestle hit the garlic flatly, and, to make it into an even paste, he retained an image of the Chief Bearer making a deal with the chickenwallah. When the onions arrived at their exact golden brown, he added the garlic and ginger paste, fried it in briefly until it too had browned.

He said aloud: 'Just like a suntan for the President-bastard.' Then he poured into the pot the masala, and took care with frying the paste before introducing the goat for a quick sealing brown. He salted the marbles of goat and then allowed the pot to arrive at a very low simmer with a cup of warm water. He flung five chillies into it, fresh, whole. Now it was done. After this, it was simply a series of cups of water over four hours on a flame no higher than the head of a match.

It was the sahib's favourite curry. Had a tenderness the teeth could burst, not the fall-away tenderness of good meat. It beat, Khalid knew, any goat curry the sahib had in any big hotel; Lahore, Karachi, or smelly Delhi—the Chittagong goat was the glory. 'Khalid's Goat Curry' … it was said with a peculiar important tone.

He spooned off a large, early serving into a plastic bowl. This he carefully wrapped and sealed so that it would not leak. He switched off the radio. He took the bowl outside and tied it to the raft on the bicycle.

He rode out into the late afternoon lightly through the town as it rose towards the evening. In town he saw the good Ajit Mookerjee smelling a cup of chai, so he pulled over.

'Where are you going?'

'To see Lall,' Khalid replied.

'I'll come with you, I need bones.'

'Okay, let's go.'

Ajit Mookerjee stopped a moment and took a long look at the cook.

'What is wrong?' Khalid asked as he swung his leg over the bicycle.

'You look like a donkey-driver has driven over you.'

'I was woken up badly, that's right.'

At the bazaar they came to Lall's stall next door to the hemline of featherdusters. The chickenwallah stood well behind his stall talking with the Chief Bearer. Their voices were low and grumbling, but in the tone was the pitch of caustic disagreement.

Khalid presented the plastic package to Lall, and the butcher thanked him warmly.

'Give me some bones,' the gardener said, 'those ones.'

Under his smile Lall rolled a stained yellow cluster of bloody bones into a banana leaf and tied it off.

'Thanks.'

'What are they saying?' Khalid whispered.

'I don't know,' the butcher said, 'they have been talking for a while.'

'Is it because of Zeythi's curse on the hardware guy?'

'I think so.'

'Good. Damn fucking good.'

Khalid stressed that the curry needed four more hours on a small flame. The tall old butcher said that he need not have brought such a fine gift. But he thanked Khalid again, and he accepted the cook's insistence on a favour requiring a favour.

'Especially,' Khalid said quietly, 'anything on the

Chief Bearer-bastard, okay?'

Lall rolled his head.

Ajit Mookerjee made a remark. In his quiet manner, he raised it as a simple observation. It caused a second disagreement.

'You put the foot into that hardware guy a bit too much, Khalid.'

'I didn't put it in enough!'

A heated exchange followed, and the gardener and the cook locked heads over the incident.

Mahfouz the Spitting-bearer rode up. He seemed in a fair mood, and he smiled as he watched the two friends go at it. He propped himself against the rusty frame and folded his arms. He enjoyed it. He thought, This is what they cause, these bastard foreigners.

When it ran out of steam, Khalid rode out of the bazaar to the giant almonds. Ajit Mookerjee rode off with his bones in the other direction. At the junction, where Khalid turned into the club road, he pulled over to buy a cigarette to calm himself. Then he rode up to the club. He was feeling settled. Lall would now listen out. A favour for a favour, he thought, that's how sahibs do it. Fuck this boom, better use it properly.

The butcher, with his hands resting on the fatty counter, shook his head and let it sink between his shoulders until he looked like he was filled by the dubious richness of sorrows. The 'smile' was still there.

'What is the matter?' asked Mahfouz. 'Those two guys having a quarrel has upset your gentle heart? Listen to me Lall—come to our meetings at the teahouse. Listen to me, I can eat fire.'

'No,' Lall replied, 'when Ajit and Khalid give a slapping match it is pure class because one has big respect for the other, great friends these two. But Mohendra and Akram—can you not hear it?—just rough and tatty.'

Changing Homes

The President came in from work. The house was quiet and empty. It was a good time to take a long, cool shower. To let the mind drift. Be at the club in an hour, he thought with satisfaction.

He thought idly of his wife. What are these dreams Catherine talks about? All she says is, 'I'm having strange dreams, so strange,' but she never offers the detail. Can't remember the last time we had a chat. Forget about Catherine, she hates it here. She never wanted to come in the first place.

The President remembered the telephone call he made to Exeter all those years ago.

'India? What's got into you?' she had asked with disbelief.

'Pakistan, not India. East Pakistan.'

'What happened to Australia?'

'I'm calling from Chittagong.'

'Where in the hell is that?'

'It's a beautiful place on the Bay of Bengal.'

'Well, this is Exeter, this is my home. I was born here, I bloody grew up here.'

Well, he thought as he reached for the shampoo, that was a long time ago.

He turned the tap high for a rinse. He shrugged as he held his head under the shower, I was born in Hackney. What's the difference? I grew up there. But now, this place is my home.

He shut his eyes to let the water run down the forehead. He enjoyed it.

Let the hands fall, he thought with the same satisfaction, and stand there doing fuck-all. That's how it works. You do fuck-all, and then it all comes clear. Will she leave? I bet she's dreaming of home.

But Khalid's ally had been dreaming of other matters.

The President then started to catch images of Hackney, himself as a boy.

He had always dreamed of being a soldier, of running over great hills, saving people from evil. He bought magazines for the pictures in which men ran over hills to rescue the world. By the time he was nineteen, when war was declared, he found he had no such dreams left in him. He spent his days in Hackney ducking the war.

He remembered the woman in the shop on the high street, her friendly smile. The boxes she asked him to carry, to store, to unpack, all that exotic stuff. Pickles, spices, tins of odd fruit. He could still remember the bareness of her chest as she leaned over. The fullness of the breasts, and the brownness. He remembered the day they came free when she shut the shop. She leaned against the boxes, unbuttoned the small pink shirt. What was it, was it a shirt? He helped her in the shop all through the start of the war.

'Hackney,' he said quietly, 'oh well.' The President rinsed off completely, and decided he would soon arrange tickets for the London journey. 'It won't be too bad. Catherine can go down to Exeter, and I can meet up with hotels and restaurants armed with my photos of the oven.'

He waited downstairs for the driver. The driver swung in, and the President climbed in.

'Club thank you, Rakesh.'

'Sahib.'

A Persistent Tapping of Trouble

Deep in the library the President lifted to his lips a brew of scalding tea. From the window the ground dropped away to the swimming pool. The pool bristled with shouts and laughter. He could see Zeythi. Probably, he thought, minding the boy. He put down the cup and saucer, and he picked up the binoculars. Yes, it's the girl. Standing at the pale green rectangle. The well-behaved ayah.

He put the binoculars down. He felt unsettled. A rattling tin of trouble rolled round. Well, doesn't matter, he decided, Catherine and I shall piss off to London for a week. He lifted the cup and saucer, and he sipped at the tea before he took up the paper.

The Americans had built fourteen runways, seven deep water ports, a fuel storage capacity of one million six hundred and sixty-six barrels, and eighty acres of paved and riveted pads for two hundred and ten thousand tons of ammunition. A new embassy; bypass roads for Saigon, Da-Nang and Gui Nhon; a bridge from Cam Ranh Bay peninsula to the mainland; and a sixteen-thousand acre American city at Long Binh outside Saigon. The President took a big series of rough sucks at the tea. Everyone already knew the build-up was a massive operation, but the article on his knee, for him, drew a clear picture of the effort. Must, he thought, keep this piece for Abdul.

Another statistic took his eye. Each of the four logistical islands of Saigon, Cam Ranh, Qui Nhon and Da-Nang orders, receives and disburses more than one hundred thousand different kinds of items from ammunition, tanks and jet fuel to fresh oranges, frozen meat, typewriters and air-conditioning units.

He read the next short paragraph, and the picture was complete. 'So well served is the US fighting man that helicopters bring him two hot meals a day out in the field. Many a soldier is able to sit down in the jungle minutes before going into combat and eat shrimp cocktail packed in ice.' He leaned back and poured another cup. He looked far out of the big window, a long gaze high above the pool.

Here at the Sundarbans the monsoon will disgorge its belly; and there, at Saigon, the rivers and seas would shunt upward to let loose more water than anyone thought the world could conceal.

He loved the monsoon because he felt it delivered ruin to everything that had no right to continue. He had once expressed this to his wife. When the words were spoken he knew immediately that there lay the exact moment, at the dresser as she tended her nose, as the powder popped into the bedroom air in little bursts, in which he no longer had her love, or even affection.

He hoped the monsoon might ruin the American building plan in Vietnam. It occurred to him that the war could count as history's first truly modern war. Shrimp cocktail minutes before combat? Now that's a ...'

The floorboards creaked. Footfalls approached up the

shelving. It was Abdul the history teacher.

'Greetings,' Abdul said as he strolled up.

The President invited him to sit for a tea, and he depressed a button on the edge of the window.

'It's a Chinese-and-Ceylonese blend he's made today,' said the President to his friend. 'Good brew to revive the spirit after flogging the day black and blue.'

'Do I look as bad as that?'

'You're not in possession of the brightest eye in Chittagong this afternoon.'

'Brightness perhaps not,' the teacher sighed comfortably, 'but mine was the quick and simple day today.'

'No miracles?'

'Absolutely not. All I did was loaf about.'

For a moment Abdul stood at the big window. He always did like the view, especially after work. He could feel the extreme quiet, and the way that it contrasted with the frenzy of activity outside.

The President recommended the paper to him for an essay on the American build-up.

'I already know about it,' Abdul said.

'Not like this, you don't. We are blasted with plain facts and figures: thousands of this, hundreds of thousands of that.'

'It's the same old thing—blow them to bits, then build a hospital. Fistfuls of lovely morality.'

'Take my word for it, there is not a skerrick of the moral tone in it, pure numbers only. I've never seen anything like it. The first truly modern war, shouldn't you say?'

'My dear friend,' Abdul smiled, 'you ought to know better. This is another burst boil on a buttockful of boils from long ago. The first disturbance was also a civil war, and that carried on for half a century. A sophisticated rage between the Trinh family at Hanoi, and the Nguyen family at Huè. The southern Nguyens blocked the plain north of Huè by means of two great walls—precisely where the demilitarised zone is located today. After fifty-four years, no clear victor sang into the skies. And do you know when this was?'

'No idea.'

'The 1670s. It was this neighbourly love that set the weave into the silk, my friend, for this north-south divide. Now *that* I would call "Functional Equality". Their languages began to drift apart too.'

'Ah, the new tea.'

'Very good. Three sugars and much milk please. Is the milk heated-up?'

'Yes, sahib,' said the bearer.

'After the Portuguese,' Abdul continued, 'the Jesuits arrived, and they wrote down the spoken sound in the Latin alphabet. What emerged? The Romanised system, quoc-ngu.

'It became the modern form of written Vietnamese. Officials resisted it and they kept the Chinese characters until early this century, but the Latin-soaked quoc-ngu became a groundswell of vernacular that took the southerners another shade away from the Mandarin north. From the French Jesuit Alexandre De Rhodes—who printed Christian works in quoc-ngu right up to this war—the north has been a Mandarin-flavoured place.'

'And today it's the Mandarin against the Californian orange,' the President said.

'Making shitty jokes so early in the evening—you have

223

had quite a good day I would say,' Abdul smiled. 'If we have Mao here,' he continued as he patted one big armrest and then the other, 'and LBJ there, each fellow selling his wares-and-why-fors, why not mess up somebody else's place who has already been at it hammer and tongs for generations?'

'Since you put it like that, seems about right.'

'Anyway, the Chinese have been mounting campaigns into North Vietnam since the T'ang Dynasty. The name the Chinese gave the north Vietnamese was An-nan, meaning the Pacified South. The north existed as a Chinese province much the same as we in Chittagong exist as the underwear compartment of shitty Karachi.'

'Who do you think will win this war?'

'The Americans,' Abdul said. 'And you?'

'Yes, the Americans.'

The door creaked, a long upward note.

The teacher turned in his chair. 'Who is there?'

There was no answer.

'Oh well,' Abdul sighed. With fresh satisfaction in his lungs, he returned to the conversation.

Only he and the President met here, usually on a Tuesday over tea and a samosa. Abdul liked it. A thread connected their varying interests.

'You and I have the beginnings of a pan-cultural type of thinking,' he always said.

But the President thought the phrase was stupid. He did not say so. He enjoyed Tuesdays anyway.

'Like a samosa?' the President asked.

Abdul lifted the triangle. A sharp corner crushed in his mouth of sprouting yellow teeth: 'Bloody hell! These are good today! Fistfuls of flavour!'

'Not as good as the shrimp cocktail.'

'We can have shrimp for dinner maybe.'

'The marines have it in the jungle.'

'And I am the chair of Bengali history at Cambridge.'

Abdul took another samosa to his papaya-sized head of stained teeth and began crushing it, sighing at its flavour.

'Mouthfuls of shrimp cocktail? Spoiled brats if you ask me. Did you see the big news yesterday?'

'The shrimp essay is all I've seen. Shrimp fucking cocktail. Did you ever wish to be a soldier when you were a kid?'

'My demonstrations at university in Dacca were quite enough. These samosas, they are top-flight I tell you.'

What's the big news you're talking about?'

'Muhammad Ali,' Abdul said. 'He got five years, bang! Plus a fine of ten thousand dollars. A fighter fighting against the fighting. Fistfuls of peace. And John Wayne?'

'Signing autographs for the marines, isn't he?'

'He is, oh yes. He is a central fellow in the Anti-Left Motion Picture Alliance for the Preservation of American Ideals. What a stinking mouthful. He has taken to referring to LBJ, climbing up a platform in his boots to the microphone, thunk, thunk, as "LSD".'

'Long way from Hollywood being infested with communists twenty years ago,' said the President.

'Have you seen the film studio the kids have made near the back toilets?'

The President looked blankly at his friend. What, he thought with sudden alarm, is this?

'No,' he replied casually, 'I have not.'

'They've put up a sign. In honour of Bollywood. "Pottywood". Kids have it lucky these days. Pretending to make films with Brownie cameras, very quaint. What films they are making at the toilets, who knows. But they have fun these days.'

The President enjoyed the library afternoons with his friend. But today had been a rattling tin lurking somewhere. He then gazed at the cloud. The clouds were Indian aggression, Abdul always claimed. The President barely heard the teacher talking. The lights came on at the swimming pool. Above, the low burls had taken some of the steel blue, and some of the orange and yellow, of a Chittagong evening. He could also see the place where Khalid had taken the photo at the big water tank.

Abdul continued in a far-off, cheery voice, 'Soon the Ganga plain will go under. Baths, kitchen sinks, laundry tubs, pots of last month's ghee, barbers' spittoons and the bazaar drains will arrive in one big rush at the coast. A thousand miles of the Ganga will transport a hundred million spits, pisses and excretions to our lovely delta … the Indians are coming, my friend.'

'The Indians are not coming,' the President said abruptly. 'But if they should, even their secret service will not find me.'

'Why so?'

'I shall be located elsewhere.'

'At the bar?'

'Quite so,' said the President. 'Quite so—and beyond suitable recognition.'

'And a good idea, too.'

The President folded the newspaper and returned it to the racks.

The teacher patted-off his lounge chair. 'We shall celebrate your exports of the tandoor,' he said.

'Oh, they're nothing yet. What about you? Anything to celebrate?'

'Between the loafing hours, yes, one modest miracle.

We placed a bright junior student into the polytechnic scholarship scheme. The boy is the son of a paanwallah from Cox's Bazaar—now, tell me, is that one for the books?'

'Congratulations, how did you manoeuvre that?'

'I jacked up his marks.'

'You'll get caught and sacked one of these days.'

'Maybe, but we mustn't tempt the dark forces by making mention of such a horrible thing, no.'

'Is he in fact a bright student?'

'Oh yes. Plus he is not shy of work.'

'Then why fiddle the results?'

'He has been sleeping with an English girl out for the holidays. Lucky chap, having earfuls of that kind of stuff. What would you have done in my situation?'

'I would have let them alone to make love.'

'And elevate his marks.'

'Yes.'

'Thank you, kind sir. Fistfuls of understanding; what a top wish for a petty world.'

'You think he might be prime minister one day?' the President quipped.

'No, he will be a scientist. It is the other fellow in my class who has the rogue quality for politics. The Zakir Hussein Road cook.'

'Oh that boy—not at all, he's a nice lad.'

'You are overly gracious,' Abdul said as he stood up, 'the dunderhead is still claiming that the tandoor is his own design. There's not a lot of hope for him. Yes, he will finish up in government telling the same old fistfuls of fibs only bigger and better. But who knows, maybe it can all work out in the washing as jollier than being a cook for life,' Abdul said with pleasant idleness as he gazed out the window to the pool.

'Shall we piss off to the bar?'

'I'll be ten minutes, I've seen the Australian Consul by the pool. I would like to ask him to join us.'

Good News at Last

Alone in the library, the President feels the room has shifted. The books do not help, he thinks, as he strolls the aisle to switch off the lights; they have strained off the presence of breathing. They cause him to feel a more stark emptiness. A room empty of books might be more the thing, but it is not important, and he flicks the last light switch. Then the darkness. He decides to follow the aisle back down the room to stand by the light of the big window.

The pool was alive with drinks and meals being served, and children taking running leaps; it looked to him a terrible place, shrill with screams and loud with orders which were unheeded. He could see Zeythi. She remained in the same spot.

He thought, How many are quietly urinating in that cash-drowning bath? Not to mention the dirty arseholes getting a rinsing. It'd be near as filthy as the damn river. I'll cast my vote and we'll fill in the wretched thing for tennis courts.

The room was once again filled by an even quiet, a velvet collar which touched the stiffness at the neck, removing all that had been drummed into the bone by the tin can of rattling events. And, to him, it had been a long day, bumpy, gnarled with the 'twisted sinew of puss-filled disturbances'.

Then the floor sounded with a footfall.

Deeply cushioned by the shelving, he caught it again.

He turned to the room, and a slow movement behind the spines, some sort of denser darkness moving along behind the slits, very slowly, like the final resting inches of a locomotive, caught his attention.

Khalid emerged.

The photos, thought the President, a good day after all.

The President invited the cook to sit in the armchair. Khalid did not move. The President indicated with his hand, and he nodded. But Khalid was nervous: he could not believe he had come into the library to see the President-bastard. Khalid was shaking in his bones, but during the last few days Khalid had also grown angry. He had fumbled from bitterness to frustration. Then he rose to a boldness that is born not of rightness and thinking things through, but of a constant anger. What he might say to the sahib, he did not know; but in a second he shot up from the step at the bungalow and flew down the road on his bike to the club.

The President nodded once more and Khalid felt his shaking bones coming to a stop. He thought, Okay, find out the fuss about these gigantic chairs. He sat in it and almost vanished, and then he shuffled and was seated comfortably. The bearers were right.

The President thought, How is it that such a dark day can transform into so bright a day? From a single moment, with a single gesture, your whole day can suddenly shine like a dance … it astounds me, I'm glad to be alive. This is becoming a day of dancing dimples. I shall get this matter out of the way and the boys and I will break the bar tonight, we'll just go ahead and break the bar.

The new cheer provided the President with the calm breath for: 'Dear boy, tell me your secret—how did you get a hold of the idea?'

Khalid remained silent.

'Let me say to you,' the President whispered, 'since time began, it has been a fat bulb, and you happen along to turn it into an hourglass—you have changed tandoori cuisine forever.'

Khalid thought, That's why we gave it a thousand kisses you bastard old thief. And you stink like dirty feet, it's all that cheese you people put in your guts.

'Well?' smiled the President.

Khalid recalled the lost afternoon he had been gazing out at the double hump of the Sleeping Camel Hills while Zeythi was bathing the Minisahib's bony back. And there it was. Not immediately. Though some days later, in the history class, the valleys appeared in his doodles.

But this I'm not telling him, Khalid thought.

'The ayah's waist,' Khalid said finally.

'The girl's figure?'

'Yes, sahib,' Khalid lied, rolling his head with finality.

'Do you realise the significance of that?'

'No, sahib.' And, Khalid thought, I do not care.

The President smiled widely and felt very good about the evening. We'll break that bar tonight, boys!

Khalid tried hard to resist, but, 'She is a pretty girl, sahib.'

The President immediately returned to the matter at hand, 'You have the photos?'

'Yes, sahib,' Khalid lied again. For he did not have the photos. And Zeythi had destroyed the film.

'Good fellow. Give the film and the photos to me, and perhaps I have a twenty on me.'

'Tomorrow, sahib,' Khalid stated with a light swagger. He was feeling better. 'First I would like to see the tandoors at the factory, sahib.'

'Oh? Why?'

'Maybe I will buy one,' Khalid said plainly, but he was shocked at his mouth working so smoothly to the spirit of boomtime bargaining. For a split second he could see himself as a sahib.

The President smiled. He felt a pleasant relief rising slowly from his feet. He began to see not a stale tin of problems but a plain, simple servant. Perspective has returned, he thought lightly. He then realised what a worried fool he had been. For goodness sake, Roger, he thought cheerfully, who'll listen to a servant, let alone believe him? Then he said to Khalid, with calm authority, 'Bring them tomorrow morning. I have to go to England the next day. On my return I shall give your sahib an oven.'

The bargaining made Khalid light-headed. Just talking with the President-bastard made him feel important beyond his dreams. He did not know exactly what he had achieved, but the bargaining banter made him feel drunk and powerful. In fact, Khalid had achieved nothing. But he decided he had successfully grabbed a bit of time on the subject of the lost photos. Then Khalid tried to stand up from the giant chair. His sandals slipped on the teak floor. He sunk back into the folds of the chair. He tried again. He stood up and he then proceeded to calmly leave the library.

He walked up the broad corridor to the rear of the clubrooms. He soon came to the storerooms, then a turn to the back door, then outside to the flight of iron stairs. Here he stopped a moment.

He could see down to a small group of bearers and kitchen people. They smoked and they drank iced drinks. The ice chimed in the heavy air. A young girl stood away from the group.

A bearer said to another bearer: 'She wants work.'

The other: 'Is she the Chief-bastard's sister?'

And another: 'I know her, she's the Chief-bastard's cousin's sister.'

Then another: 'No no. She's the Chief-bastard's cousin's uncle's sister.'

A fifth: 'Not one of you knows what he is talking about. She is the Chief-bastard's uncle's friend's sister. Hello little one, how's your sister?'

A small voice returned: 'Fine, thank you.'

'There is no work here.'

'No?'

'Go home.'

The young girl went away with small steps. She turned behind the dividing reef of bougainvillea that burned a deeper red from the lights of the narrow night.

Khalid climbed down to the rear entrance of the pool area. He decided he would locate Zeythi and the Minisahib. He would ride home alongside their rickshaw. And, he considered it, simply to tease Zeythi on such a fine night, he might sing his tune: *Oooh-ya-ya hot but wet! … Ooh ya-ya hot but wet!* Whatever she carried in her basket she would throw at him with force, but he would dodge bottles or shoes, and he would sing.

From the cool darkness of the library the President gazed at the cloud. It seemed to hang without movement. But it did roll over the low rises into the darkening distance. He'd heard the rains had already started up past Dacca, on the far side of the delta, at Jessore.

So, he thought, it's the cook's oven after all. He decided to stay with his plans to go to London.

Then he caught a big burst over the pool. The evening lights had come on. Much later in the night the pool would be settled and it would glow a shimmering emerald colour.

The girl, he thought, still there. A tiny pillar of obedience. Needless, needless. All this prim damn obedience. Right across the whole effing country. Oh well … let's up to the bar.

Reconnaissance of the Imitation

The President approached over the expanse of the lounge. From the distance it looked as though he skipped like a child with a rope.

At the bar the Sikh lawyer was shown an empty glass so he called the order for fresh drinks. The Sikh then performed an imitation of the President—'elbows only'.

The President noted that his friend was trotting in a tight circle, so he called out, 'You should take the ladies' waltzing hour!'

'It looks like you already did that!' the Sikh lawyer called back.

The Irishman said to the Sikh, 'If yer goin' ter decorate a man yer'd better get it right the first time. Let me show you what I mean.'

He threw his Irish nose high in the air, placed his elbows out like wings and skipped to the far end, repeating in imitation, 'Yikes! Close off the damn pool!'

Abdul said smugly, 'Do not forget. To imitate is to pay a compliment.'

The President arrived saying, as he walked up to the group, 'You bastards can denounce your leader as much as you like—tonight the drinks are on me.'

Abdul: 'Anyway, you Irish are too obvious.'

The Irishman smiled, 'If you witness a bloke imitate another, a strange peace has rained on the land. Acting only rises when peace falls strangely. When ordinary peace falls, no acting takes place, none.'

The President: 'That's enough bickering in the colonies—another round here!'

'I got a new round,' said the Sikh.

'Replace his round to my chit!'

Fatimah walked up to the bar. She called for the bearer.

'Where is my order?' she snapped.

'It is coming, memsahib.'

'We have been waiting on the verandah for twenty minutes, go and hurry it up you lazy nitwit.'

'Yes, memsahib.'

The Irishman called out, 'Hello Fatimah!'

'Hello Tom, what are you smelly children up to?'

'We're celebrating!'

'What is it tonight? A slaphappy divorce?' Fatimah Westcott's black eyes glowed, and her teeth gleamed in a smile powerful with intent, always with an intent of some puzzling kind.

Abdul forever wished it was intent aimed at him. He sat at the bar and lifted his glass to conceal himself as he looked her up and down. His determination was becoming so keen that his heart and head turned inwards at Fatimah's appearance.

The day before he had seen her in a small swimming suit at the pool. He quickly put on his sunglasses and proceeded to quietly feed on the firm bare fatness he so loved. Her gleaming smile he did not notice at all. In the warehouse Fatimah drew secret reactions from the smile:

'Did you hear that? What did she mean by that?'

Or, 'Do you think she's trying to tell me something?'

Or, 'That Fatimah Westcott, she's as crafty as a mongoose in a dusty corner.'

Or, 'She's a sly Cairo bitch who's never known what it's like to be on heat.'

None of it had any effect on her position within the higher rungs of the trading company. The boss once asked, after she had secured the biggest letter of credit the company had written, what mysterious forces she had conjured. It was during relaxed office drinks. Her answer?

'I came into this world,' she said with a wry smile, 'in Alexandria, and I proceeded to observe this world through the portholes of a ship called Jordan. Satisfied?'

'Join us!' the Irishman called out.

'I have better things to do.'

Abdul was greatly annoyed that the Irishman could be so easy with Fatimah.

The bearer returned. He said the order would be brought out immediately. Fatimah strolled out to the verandah to her table of friends.

The men at the bar returned to their party.

'So what's the celebration for?' the Irishman asked.

'Never you mind,' replied the President. 'Tonight, boys, we're going to break the bar!'

'Pulverise the ugly thing!' the Irishman sang out.

'And, bearer, bring out pakoras and Cornish pasties.'

'Englishman! Press Forth! We Shall Follow!' cried the Irishman.

The Sikh: 'But which one would it be wiser to follow? The English cooking, or an English future? Their sex I don't go for, it is too drab. Their girls I like a lot ... snowy white ... but to see the future in English eyes is a foolish glance. They are idiotically clever, whereas we ... we are wisely clever. We copy utterly nothing.'

'A speech!' said the President. 'A declaration of high repugnance and high love from the young lawyer himself!'

Abdul said, 'We copy nothing? What a barrage of poppycock. We copy everything. Our once-tremendous empire has been gobbling up whatever it is fed and it has fattened into a bumbling caricature of their empire. We *are* a copy.'

The Sikh to the Irishman: 'Abdul exerts a charm, don't you think so, through his pumping out of defective cant?'

The Irishman: 'Pulverise! Follow the English!'

The Sikh to Abdul, slowly: 'We *pretend* to copy them, Abdul.'

'Do you people not suffer any feelings of shame?' the President howled. 'Shitting on the English right before an Englishman?'

The Irishman: 'We do feel the shame, we are a shameful lot here at the bar, like it's a shame deeply embedded, you see.'

The Sikh: 'So don't be fooled.'

Abdul: 'I am fooled totally.'

The President: 'As is myself.'

The Irishman turned away: 'Well, look at this; what before our very eyes floats into the real world? The bossman of the Australia Bungalow, the fellow high-low Commissioner himself. Come on up you important bugger, join the festivities and help us destroy the bar tonight. Drinks are on el Presidente no less.'

'Celebrating the export order, are we? Great, we can also celebrate my retirement.'

'Pissing off home then?'

'Yep. Freshly caught mud crabs and cold beer, and you

girls can turn green in the gills.'

The Sikh: 'This is terrible news.'

'I might even write a memoir. Start with showing how thick all you idiots are, and how you try to cover it up by being opinionated and bombastic. But you know what? Yer just carnt conceal being a thickhead. Y'know why? Because yer always crapping on … Irish this … Pommie that … Bengali this … Sikh that … Erstraylian this … yers just can't help it 'cos yer ignorant, the lot of yuh.'

'The el Presidente's foreman, now there's a writing man, he's got himself his own stage work coming up next month at the dance hall did you know?'

'The bloke's written a play?'

'You'll be missing it.'

'That's real tough.' The Consul took a drink. 'What's it about?'

'It's about an Englishman who is the engineer in a Chittagong factory, but secret, illicit desires to become a playwright cause him to be a mighty sloppy engineer.'

'Oh beautiful, sounds like he's written a pamphlet on how to go off alone and have a quiet dribble.'

The Sikh: 'No, sounds like it is English drama.'

Abdul: 'No, Sikh drama. Fistfuls of original beauty.'

The Irishman: 'Sikh? Way too regional. He's written a Pakistani drama.'

The President: 'It's a Bristol drama, he's from Bristol.'

The Consul: 'Why don't you blokes get quietly rooted.'

The Sikh: 'We will not do that. Tonight we are all present to break the bar together. No crab-flesh sunset books, please, only silly Indian spies in Pakistan penning their reports for the Delhi dunderheads.'

The Irishman: 'Let the Consul alone; he's a distinguished feller and he's allowed a callous moment.

He's off home to publish his memoirs; what's more, they'll be Australian memoirs.'

At the bar they continued enjoying themselves. The bearers were attentive. The bar food was brought out fresh and hot. The air-conditioning was turned up high. Life ebbed away just nicely.

The Consul: 'Now ... where's my drink?'

'Don't you worry about a thing in the whole known world,' replied the Irishman, 'here it is, and, yes, we shall revel tonight in your going home. What's this other celebration, an export order you say?'

'Isn't that what you blokes are here for? The man's new ovens off to Pommieland?'

The Sikh: 'Is that so, Roger? Your new-fangled tandoor?'

'Yes,' said the President, 'I'll be meeting restaurateurs.'

The Sikh to Abdul: 'I rest my case.'

Abdul: 'Oh? Then explain the cook who copied it.'

The Consul: 'I heard a rumour that the cook did originally design the thing.'

One of the bearers, the senior Bengali, stepped away through the door behind the bar.

The Irishman: 'I heard a different rumour.'

The Consul: 'Yeah? What was that?'

'You dress up in the night-time like a private eye, but with pink apron akimbo.'

'An *informed* Irishman. What is it that they call that?'

The Irishman: 'Oxymoron they call it.'

'A boofhead, I call it.'

'What,' Abdul said with irritation, 'is this word "boofhead" you use all the time? What does it mean?'

The Sikh: 'Rumours? Geopolitical plates are crunching up with a force so violent that it ruptures whole nations and you carry on about his dressing up at night? And then you pester him about being a beefhead?'

'Boofhead, as in "boof".'

The President: 'The young repugnant lawyer has spoken!'

The Sikh: 'Seriously, how can one go on living a small, insignificant life, a life in miniature, what would we achieve?'

Abdul: 'One's life works because it is a small event. The door opens and closes with a click. When you turn it, your tap pours water. The bearer brings a whisky. Your Mini Minor ferries you to the office. If we lived truly gigantic lives, it would bring disaster—we would be sucked into the storms of who-knows-what, maybe a big star, and be tossed about the cosmos like fleas on a donkey's backside.'

'Let's talk about the oven,' the Consul said with a slur. He was swaying from drinking since lunchtime.

The President decided that the next round would be neat doubles. Whatever it takes, he thought, to stop this Consul's inquisitive itch. He called for another round. He casually changed each drink up and down the bar to a neat double whisky.

The Chief Bearer appeared. He stood away from the men, behind their noise and fire, so that he might remain unnoticed. The senior bearer returned, but the Chief Bearer sent him out again.

The Consul drank the double right away. 'Give me another drink. If I don't drink, I'll talk. Give me another drink.'

The President: 'Give the good man a drink.'

The Chief Bearer went to work. He worked under the bar, pouring a heavy whisky. He brought it to the Consul.

'Thanks,' the Consul said to the President.

'Will you still talk?' asked the Irishman.

'I reckon I will.'

'What about?'

'Since I'm the guy that's pissing off out of here it should be talk about you bastards. You're stuck here with your slack selves, with each other, with another day waiting for this bloody monsoon to burst over your heads, with broken air-conditioners. Any of youz had a fuck lately? No? But yer like the big war over there, don't ya? Lap it up every morning like a big wank. Yeah, I'll talk about you crumbling bastards right here in East Pakistan … living your *big lives*.'

Abdul: 'See how he still says 'Pack-e-Stan?'

The Sikh: 'He can't pronounce it correctly because he is not accustomed to the strange sounds. For Iraq, he says "Eye-Rack" even.'

The Consul mumbled, 'Least I don't call a boofhead a beefhead.'

The Irishman ignored him, and he continued, 'No, he cannot say it right because he is shy of sounding silly.'

The Sikh: 'It is not embarrassment; he cannot pronounce it as it is meant to be because his language is undernourished by the softer consonants.'

Abdul: 'No no … he cannot do it because he believes it is inherently inferior.'

The Irishman: 'So which one of us bastards will you encrust with your bile then I wonder?'

'Some of you in particular,' said the Consul slowly in order to get it exactly right, 'can be talked about to his face.'

'Yes?'

'But some of you others cannot be talked about to his face.'

'And which is which?'

'You bastards are all in it, all of you.'

'Is that your speech?'

The Consul smiled. 'Listen, that oven was done by the cook down the road.'

'Which road, a road, which road?'

'Get lost, just fuck off, I'm leaving this place intact, as a decent bloke. Look at these blokes—they've gone silent. You think they care? All that imitation bullshit? That caricature garbage? To them it's a way to get from night to night.'

'They are listening, and it is to you.'

'Is it that you guys want to pin the President to the wall? Or is it that you guys want to make him into a poster?'

'Do you realise what you are doing?'

'I had a big lunch in town, I got a telegram from Canberra, and I had a real good lunch this afternoon, a long, long lunch.'

'You are gradually slipping from the bar to the floor.'

'The cook did it.'

'How's the floor?'

'Fairly warm actually,' the Consul said.

The Sikh: 'Shall we pick him up? Let's put him on the couch.'

Abdul: 'No, push his legs over there.'

'But his leg is bent.'

'Straighten it.'

'How?'

'Kick it.'

'No thanks—you kick it.'

'I don't mean harmfully, I mean jostle it a bit. Settle it in.'

'It looks terribly painful.'

'Well, pull it straight.'

'You do it.'

Abdul: 'When Australian men are drunk they don't mind contortions, leave him alone.'

The Consul: 'Never seen Erstray-yan chicks, havvya, yey?'

'Is he finished?'

'He is finished.'

'Yerl my-sink-so. Yer-awl mysink um finisht, yeh.'

The Chief Bearer brought out a warm towel. He placed it gently on the Consul's forehead. He brought it to the nose. He patted the mouth and the chin. He wiped the man's nose again with the warm towel he had soaked in whisky.

The Sikh: 'When is he supposed to go?'

The President: 'He leaves on PIA Thursday afternoon. Is he asleep well?'

The Chief Bearer rolled his head with satisfaction.

The President returned to the bar. A deep internal relief, maybe as much as a sigh, joined the air-conditioning.

The Chief Bearer placed the cloth over the Consul's nose, and then he looked about to see if the place was safe. It was safe. He stood up. He gave the Consul a kick in the shoulder. He looked again. It was still safe. He gave the Consul another kick, but it was a sharp one.

The men at the bar continued to drink to the future of the delta. One proposed a marriage of the delta and China; another proposed the wedding of the Israelis and Arabs; another the wedding of himself and Fatimah Westcott; another the felling of all jute so that jute no longer attracted men of occultish power within the lifts of the great banks. Another suggested abolishing all countries—'Bugger the borders!' he bellowed from the end of the bar.

Then a funny thing happened.

The Consul burst into life. Eyes closed, his figure crumpled on the daisy-patterned couch, he barked, 'That's right! I'm outta here Thursday, but so's the Presidente, boys, he's off on Thursday too — to London—ask him … go on, ask him!'

The Consul then passed out again. Which was a pity, because after all the skirting around the edges, after so much prickly reconnaissance, nobody settled on which bastard imitated which bastard.

The London Meetings

The President gave the photographs of the tandoor to the proprietor before sitting down to the meal; they had conducted business in the alcove near the kitchen. He decided it had been a promising meeting. He and his wife then ate in the small restaurant.

After the meal he gazed through the curtains into the colourful life on the narrow cobbled laneway. His wife, too, looked out, but her gaze flew over the crowded lane and to the theatre.

At the theatre she felt a sudden excitement. She saw handsome men all over the place like a rash. Are they other actors along to see tonight's show? Beautiful women shuffled between hellos and shoulders. Oh fuck, she thought, smell your mouth Catherine. Curry breath. Why on earth did we eat at the Indian place? Oh well, can't complain—here it is: *An Inspector Calls* ... and at the Garrick Theatre. These women, my goodness, so much the grand slaves to something I too wish.

She felt an urge to smile, but held it firmly down the throat. I do know, she thought, it is the freedom of returning the meal into their noses.

'What is it, Catherine?' She heard the President ask.

'I'll just nip up the steps for a packet of peppermints,' she said. She said it with a perkiness, she was ready to make fun of herself. The night reminded her that she was outside of all this grand loveliness, that she was stuck in Chittagong.

The President: 'Shall we press on inside?'

'Not yet, shall be a petty little moment. Do you want chocolate peppermints or peppermint peppermints?'

'No peppermints for me.'

'Will you wait here till I bring them?'

'Exactly here?'

'Yes.'

'I might be over there.'

'There? Near the window?'

'No, over there, near the door.'

She felt good making fun of herself in private. She continued with the perky tone. 'You could be anywhere.'

'I could be anywhere, yes.'

'You would be back there in Chittagong if you could.'

'If I could be anywhere, yes, I would.'

'You are a cunning fool, and you are a charming fool, but you are not a wise and sensitive fool.'

'You were getting peppermints. Now you are placing your funny intelligence up against my ear. I brought us here to be in love in London, to drink a drink of the first murmur, and now your funny intelligence laughs at me.'

'I loathe that.'

'What do you loathe?'

'I loathe you calling my intellect funny. It's always been your silly warmth towards my intelligence. There you are dear, your funny intelligence. Ho ho ho. Har har.'

'You'd better go find the peppermints.'

'Will you be at the big golden door or the little purple window?'

'I'll not be at either. I'll be waiting here.'

'Here exactly?'

'Here precisely.'

'You are an odd man.'

'Yes.'

'I like being an odd one too.'

'Yes, I realise that.'

'I'm odder than you are.'

'Yes,' he said.

'I always liked you for that peculiar sting in your nature—I loved you for it. It was love, real love. With me it was a desperate telephone call each afternoon when the sun took bricks to the big golden town,' she whispered closer to his ear.

'Yes.'

'They turn gold in the later afternoon, lavish in dulled golden afternights.'

'Are you all right?'

'I am bringing little sweets.'

'But the show …?'

'The performance? My dear husband, the performance is this. It is ours.'

'Shall we go inside?'

'Yes,' she said, 'an Inspector Calls.'

They stayed in London meeting the proprietors of subcontinental restaurants. At the end of the week the President's wife took the train alone to Exeter, leaving the President to complete his run of the restaurants.

Early the next week they flew out in a silence in which she longed to tell her lover at the lake in Chittagong of the spicy mystery of the play. In the seat next to her, the longing was more general, a desire simply to return 'home'.

A lunch was wheeled down the aisle, and she asked for more wine to forget the twenty hours that she slept against a shoulder she did not want to sleep against. She kicked off her shoes to dream of a free walk with her lover on the shores of Rungamati Lake. Exhaustion gave a small lightness enough whim to become a free smile, and she slept.

It had been a resounding failure. Nobody had wanted to order the oven. The President was glad to be flying back. He quietly breathed it: 'H-o-m-e'. And he too rubbed his back into the seat and he let a smile tickle his nostrils.

Over India he tried to stay awake, but comfortable service and a vast continent sucked him towards sleep. It is indifferent to me, he thought, that whole continent, that large plateau of the world, he smiled, is absolutely indifferent to me. Drowsy repetitions continued. Totally indifferent ... happily vacant, to me and my piss-poor ambitions, empty, not even an acknowledgement.

Inside, the plane hummed. Outside, canine transparent men danced on the wings. They reached with yellow teeth up to the President's frozen window after successfully rolling clay ovens off the slope of the wing and, as one tandoor fell after the next over the edge of the wing into flat-faced India, his big frame slumped into sleep.

Arrivals and Departures

Dropping through the cloud they bounced with a violence that felt as if the wings might snap off. The rush of air from the vents competed with the grinding coming off the floor.

'Feels like the rivets could pop!' the President said.

She leaned closer: 'You'll have to speak up!'

'I said the wings, they're flapping all over the shop!'

'What did you say?'

'Never mind.'

For the descent they sat in silence, sharing the window by bringing their heads together to watch long streaks of Delhi appear. The view consisted of a carpet of miniature buildings, roads, vehicles, hilly burls, a flurry of scalloped gullies and veins of sharp ravines, and it looked very sweet—a false note of charm, and an incorrect sense of plenty. The plane banked along a cliff of massive cloud so large that in the distance another aircraft banking in the opposite direction, but right up close against the vertical side, looked the size of a hairclip lying flat at the base of a bed sheet. Up here, the unreal scale of these vapour-mountains of the monsoon became real.

The announcement came in Urdu and English. 'Ladies and gentlemen we have landed at Delhi International

Airport. For those of you disembarking, on behalf of the captain and the crew we hope you have enjoyed your flight with Pakistan International Airlines. We look forward to the pleasure of your company in the near future. For transit passengers, your boarding call for the onward flight to Dacca will be announced in approximately forty-five minutes. Please remain seated until the aircraft has come to a complete halt. Thank you.'

The passengers stood up straightaway. The President's wife stood in the aisle to let the President out. He recovered the hand luggage. The aisle was congested, and nobody could take a step. While the plane continued to the terminal everyone was stuck.

In the terminal the President located a coffee shop, and he cleared a table next to the busy walkway. They drank a pot of tea and ate from a small tray of cheese sandwiches. After sitting to watch the idle activity, the President's wife said she should search for a comfortable chair to read for a while. The President replied that he thought it seemed like a good idea.

'Do you have everything?' he said.

'Oh yes,' she replied. 'You?'

'I do.'

They stood fair to exchange a kiss on the cheek. She collected up her hand luggage. She then walked off in the direction of the transit lounges, and he walked off the other way, towards Arrivals.

After browsing a shop where she stole a small packet of expensive cigars, the President's wife found a quiet corner and a wide, cushioned chair. She sat down comfortably, and was about to open a Collected Keats she had purchased in Hackney. A woman in a dress of bright green and a pink hat walked on high heels down the centre of the thoroughfare. She walked tall and alone in the mixing crowd with a purposeful step, and she held a pink bag slung to her shoulder. She suddenly broke to a very slow walk. She then came to a stop, turned, and came back, stepping slowly. She came right up to the hand luggage.

She said, 'Excuse me, aren't you Elicia Pummeltongue?'

The President's wife looked up, and the pink hat took her by surprise.

'No,' she said.

'You're Mavis Pummeltongue!'

'No.'

'From Coventry?'

'No.'

'Your husband Jim—the restorer?'

'No.'

'Are you a Pummeltongue?'

'No.'

'Oh, well, thank goodness for that ... Elicia Pummeltongue, well she's a sort of "thinker". She started up what she declared a "School of Thought", but it was no such thing. So fetching, you know she was. Isn't it horribly annoying when you call a gaggle of opinions a little school of thought, don't you think?'

'I suppose so.'

'Well, sorry to bother you. Cheerio!'

'Goodbye.'

The President's wife went back to her book. Three hours later the boarding call was made and she found herself ascending the yellow Delhi air, bouncing through the thick cloud and then levelling out to a stable flight over the monsoon build-up. A lunch was served with sticky drinks.

In Dacca she boarded a Fokker-friendship, and two gnawing propellers swept her off the runway. They flew south-east down the delta. Now and then the flat silt shimmered into an explosion of light slicing through the Sundarbans' haze. It was not a long flight, and when they levelled out they were ready to commence the descent into little Chittagong, time up the sleeve for a Pimms.

Chittagong airport was once a simple cement building. Lazy brooms went here and there. Rickshaws and taxis loitered at the other side. Paanwallahs competed for the trade. The hawkers did well. Women with their tins or hands held out squatted against the wall under the shade.

She stepped down from the droning plane to the hot asphalt. This simple act flung her into a dark mood. Suddenly everything would irritate her. She muttered, 'I'm back.'

The Garrick Theatre seemed many days in the past. It had been a long journey, though she had slept well during most of it. She looked forward to escaping to the bungalow to step naked across the dry floor to a cool bath. She walked over the asphalt to the gate, to a big important sign, five-foot letters: ARRIVALS.

Looks ridiculous, she thought. Not charming, just silly.

She walked behind a man in a silver suit and a woman who wore a gold sari. She lingered on the back of the man's neck, and she felt there was something odd about its girth, or was it the furriness, or the sharp, level way his hairline stopped too far down, almost at the shoulder;

Whatever, she thought, it comes over as sordid.

She could clearly hear the man berate the woman.

'You should have remembered it!' he said.

'It is not mine, it is yours. You are the one who should have remembered to pick it up.'

'I asked you a hundred times!' said the sordid neck angrily.

'I didn't hear you.'

'You are deaf, that's why! Deaf and stupid!'

'Never mind, you can buy another one when we get into town.'

'Oh that's right, my back pocket is a blinking bank!'

'It's not costly, they're quite cheap.'

'Then I'll have two of the bloody things when we get back to Dacca—what do I want with two of them! Hah? Answer me that.'

The President's wife broke in and said firmly, 'You could stick one of them down your filthy neck.'

She hurried briskly around the pair and continued across the hot asphalt to Arrivals.

The President's wife was collecting her suitcase when she felt a tapping on the shoulder. She ignored it. The tapping again, firmer. She coaxed the suitcase halfway. Then a hand came round and lifted the case free.

'Madam?' he said, standing back, smiling.

He looked so fine, she thought. Fresh, and fenced-off from nothing at all. The big smile she had not before seen, not like the gleam riding his jaw.

'How did you know I was coming?' she said.

'This way,' he said, 'let's go outside first, get out of the way.'

He took her suitcase up to the customs bench, and

when that was done they walked side by side to the waiting car.

She said, 'What's all this?'

'What's all what?'

'The shorts, the Tahitian shirt, those loafers.'

'Ah. Like them? I'm taking the next two days off.'

'Who gave you the arrival details?'

'Roger sent a telegram from Delhi. Asked if I wouldn't mind seeing to it.'

'I don't like the shorts.'

'Why not? They're the latest thing.'

'They're rude. I prefer proper shorts.'

'Well that's all right, I've a proper pair in the car. You prefer proper shorts and I've proper shorts to wear. What a scheme.'

He drove out of the airport following the tight hibiscus bursting off the curve of the road. He weaved between a scooter rider and a rickshaw-wallah engaged in a conversation. He swept past a flock of bicycles. After town he turned into the outstation road.

'We're not going to the house?'

'No,' he said, 'we are off to the lake, to the lovely lake.'

'Do you suppose I've just gone halfway round the world?'

'But I do. That's why we have a chalet on the water; why the icebox is packed with roast chicken and cold champagne; why silk pillows await in a hammock dangling over the water by the jetty. Also Madam, you will find a small boat tied to the jetty.' He was talking with vigour and pleasure so he decided he might as well complete the list. 'And I brought along the Brylcreem and ghee.'

'Nice.'

'Yes, and the books too. Took them up yesterday.'

'Very nice.'

'Have a look in the glove box.'

She pulled down the wooden flap. 'Pimms.'

'Go ahead,' he said, 'there's iced lemonade in the box at your feet.'

'Oh it can wait,' she said. 'I've already had one or two on the leg from Dacca.'

She searched around in her handbag.

'Here, for you,' she said.

'Cigars?'

'Quality ones too.'

'Yes, they look it. A mighty pretty penny I'll bet.'

'No, they were free. I was looking in a little shop in the airport at Delhi, and the man was suggestive and impudent so I stole them.'

Secret Business at the Lake

The drive up the hills was not a long one, and pleasant views occupied the quiet passages. The coastal plain fell away in broad slices, and the juggernauts in the sky collected them up before they altogether fell away into the sea.

Halfway up to Kaptai, he pulled over at a fine-looking fruit stall and filled a basket with fresh mangos, bananas, lychees and two pineapples. The fruit had been displayed in the shade of a wetted awning of jute, so the produce was cool and he thought it would be good to eat a mango right away. He used his finger to puncture a deep orange mango, and he peeled away a large section of the skin. It came off easily, and he sat on the bonnet to concentrate on the cool flesh. The bonnet bonged under his weight, so he moved to the side, over the front wheel.

'Like a bit?' he asked as he chewed.

'No, I'd like to try a lychee. What's the mango like though?'

'Superior.'

'Superior?'

'Superior!' he called out.

She smiled. 'How superior then?'

'Exquisitely superior!'

'Only exquisitely?'

'Damagingly superior!'

'Could we recover from this "damage"?'

'Never!'

They were making a lot of noise now, and a small crowd gathered. They drove off, waving at the crowd as they joined the road.

The rest of the drive was fast. Late afternoon she climbed from the car. She went inside, found a bed and lay down. She could not sleep, so she got up and drank a Pimms on the jetty with him. The sun made the colours of the lake and the jungle look the same, and the tea redness of the small dirt beaches looked like paradise looks, she thought, on a postcard. She went inside to lie down for a minute.

She woke to a warm darkness. A doorway seemed very near. She got up and walked through to a room. She was on the open verandah. The lake lay in darkness. She sat in a chair with knees wide. She stretched her arms, yawned. She felt refreshed. There was a blur she could not account for, and she placed it as the mosquito gauze running round the verandah. She could see the glow of a house on the opposite shoreline, or was it the near glow of torchlight? She kept her eyes on it. The flickering gave it the appearance of progressing, but it remained in the same location. She ran a finger down her thigh and scratched it a bit, but then drew her nails up for a long scratch.

She looked for the position of the jetty. It could not be seen: an upright pole appeared to connect her shore and the jungle on the other shore, but the jetty she could not make out. The stillness was a coherent thing that lifted from the lake. It seemed to bear presence and have shape, and it seemed as if it were a type of stillness which would form, though invisible, solely for the late night and not for any other time. The lake was a kind of flat field, and the sky hanging over the jungle was a dark thing without dimension. She reclined further into the chair. On visits up here she had not been this far. They had always stopped sooner, the President and herself, at a shack near the centre of the village. But the lights had always burned late, hovered over the roadway winding off. Never had she felt this dark stillness making a silent ascent from the lake.

His footsteps came out to the porch. He took the other chair.

'Good sleep?' he asked quietly.

'Yes, very sound. You?'

'Yes.'

'What happened? I recall a Pimms on the jetty.'

He smiled in the darkness. 'You said you were going off to lie down.'

'Do you know what the time is?'

'Well after midnight I should think.'

'It's wonderful tonight.'

'Yes, it is different up here. And did you go home to Exeter as you promised to?' he said, yawning again.

'Yes.'

'To the house?'

'Yes.'

'By yourself?'

'Yes.'

He turned to look at her. But he could see nothing.

'A very sad day,' she said, 'as one should expect. Took

the train. Something happens to me when I take the train to Exeter. The new people hadn't tinkered with the house at all, even the flower beds were intact. Just like the pictures, the whole thing, just like the old pictures. I was distracted for the next day, utterly miserable. I should have stayed in London.'

'Easy to say.'

'Do you think?'

'Yes, it's always easy to say so.'

'But the play I adored! I do love the theatre. Don't you just adore the theatre?'

'No, I don't,' he said lightly and gently, 'I hated it in Bristol anyway.'

'I don't understand. But why?'

'For what it breeds,' he said quietly and contentedly, and he yawned. 'It breeds lies, not truth; people were endlessly bickering and running tedious battles over each other's patches; and it breeds mistrust,' he said in a plain voice. 'And it gives room to cowards who want to express their phony humility.'

'Then why are you still doing it, my love?'

'Oh, because it's different here,' he said yawning again. 'Here the theatre is uncomplicated by such stuff. Besides, it's amateur theatre out here. Yeah, not a pro for a hundred miles.'

'You are a professional, my love. Just because you're not situated inside a professional theatre it doesn't mean you're not as good as a professional.'

He smiled. 'I'm a dabbler. I like it; it's a thing to do, to dabble. Dabbling I learned from my uncle in Cardiff. He mucked about in all sorts of things including a curious system for making bricks. He thought you could supply all of England with bricks just by sending a man with a ladder and a diamond-studded saw off to a red mountain. Me too. I do think you can send a man off to a hall in Chittagong and get a good show from it.'

'The play's coming along then?'

'It's finished.'

'And is it a good play?'

'Yeah.'

'Not very humble then, tonight?'

'I'm not wetting the world at large, I'm mentioning it privately to you.'

'Well guess what I think? I think you're a conceited piece of work.'

He smiled in the darkness.

'No I don't,' she smiled, 'of course I do not.'

'Like a coffee?'

'I'll wait till breakfast,' she said. She fell quiet: she was *considering*. 'How about showing me what you do with the ghee?'

He sat for a while. Then, without saying anything, he went inside.

She wondered if she might add this to her tales with Fatimah. It was new: masturbating had been suggested by her poets, and she heard that an artist called Dali did it very much with his wife, but to her it was exciting and new. She decided she would lunch with Fatimah when she got back to Chittagong. She was now accustomed to the darkness and could see clearly an outline of the verandah and the shack.

She had a good show of his movements. He came outside and stood at the door. He moved next to her at the railing. He was naked. She didn't know what he was going to do next, so she moved away to watch. He moved closer. When he started to grease himself with the ghee she stood up and removed her clothing. She sat down again close to his waist. He went ahead and masturbated until he squirted onto the floor. They stayed up late into the night drinking champagne and talking and making love. She said she would like to do it all again and he agreed. He said he would get better at it over the next few weeks. They fell asleep in each other's arms.

The Wife's Dream of the Tandoor Prince

The morning was cool and fresh. They ate a bastard breakfast and then walked along the lake. Bastard breakfasts were those that put everything in—eggs, these things they call sausages, these tins they call mushrooms, more tins, pineapple, tomato, baked beans. What these sahibs and memsahibs squashed into the gut who knows. I never understood where it fitted. Everyone used to have bastard breakfasts, especially at the club. They even put in fried slices of pig. Please imagine it.

They took a swim, and they came to a small cove.

'What's that dog doing?' she said.

'Looks like it's sitting still.'

'No, he's champing at the bit. Something's in the jungle.'

'Let's take a look,' he suggested.

When they approached the dog the President's wife noticed a man squatting on a shelf in the undergrowth.

'Hello,' she said, 'are you the owner of the dog?'

'Yah.'

'Why is he sitting on the beach like that?'

'Why not?'

'It seems odd. Have you food for him?'

'No. He is the one who has food for me.'

'Then where is it?'

'He is waiting for my command,' the man said.

'What will he do?'

'You want to see? He can catch a fish with his teeth.'

'Show us.'

'When I give him the command, he will jump into the water of the lake. He will only return when he has taken a catfish.'

At the command the dog immediately broke his stance and bounded into the lake. He swam out and then disappeared under the surface. A while later he broke the surface with nothing in his jaw. He went under again, and they waited a long while. The dog emerged with a dark object in his jaw, and swam ashore. He came up the beach and deposited a mossy rock at the man's foot.

'He does not usually fail,' the man said.

'Do you sell the catch?'

'Sometimes. If he does very well, I have a daily catch to take into town. Not so well, it is a weekly catch. Sometimes we fish early, sometimes we fish late.'

She said goodbye and further down the beach they lay in the unseen sun. Later they strolled back. The dog owner had gone. They continued to the chalet.

That afternoon she took a rest, and she dreamed of the striking-looking dog owner, or she thought she did. There seemed to be only one of him sitting like a self-assured prince on a hillock, but he waved forward other princes who gradually appeared and disappeared, casually introducing themselves to her as they strolled around.

'Mister Early.'

'Mister Late.'

And then a prince darting down from the trees, 'Mr Sometimes.'

And another who wandered from the canopy of cool jungle, 'Mr Monthly.'

'Mr All The Time.'

They danced round a huge clay pot. Catfish jumped from the pot.

When she woke she took a cool shower. She joined her lover on the verandah. He had made a late lunch and laid it out on the wooden table in a display of fresh bread, fruit, a cold roast chicken and a bottle of champagne.

'Feels as if I've been away for months,' she said as she came to the table.

'Yes, it does,' he said. 'Did you enjoy it after recovering from Exeter?'

'Not at first. We visited every Indian place in Greater London. Finally, I put my foot down. He got a bit annoyed. Says a wife present lends the situation extra gravity. Him and his chips, his whole life is a bargaining chip. *Leverage*, he called me once.' She smiled.

'And was the oven received well?'

'As I say, I didn't keep up. In fact, I couldn't care less about his business.'

'You took a slight interest over lunch with the importer.'

'Did I?'

'Yes, you certainly did.'

'I can't remember.'

'You said Roger pinched it from the cook.'

'How would I know where he got it from?'

'That's what you said.'

'Well, I don't remember.'

But she had a flash of the dream. An image of men dancing around a giant tandoor gathered in her mind and fell away.

'Small matter anyway,' he said. 'What did you do in lovely London if you didn't accompany him to the business meetings?'

'Well, I did go to one of his meetings, but that was because we were off to the Garrick Theatre across the road straight after. He had the meeting in the back of the restaurant somewhere, and then we ate a meal and then we went to the play.'

'What did you see?'

'*An Inspector Calls.*'

'Oh nice,' he said with sudden excitement.

'Yes, it is so full of darkness, and decay, and puzzling contortions of time.'

'True.'

They sat comfortably in their loose clothing, and they made chicken sandwiches and poured the champagne. He lifted his tumbler. 'Welcome back.'

'Thank you,' she smiled.

They sat back to enjoy the lunch. The afternoon light made a pattern of shadows slide and slip on the tablecloth.

The dream again. But more detail. The catfish were skewered by the men to be dropped inside the pot, which was a furnace of glowing coals.

'What's the matter?' he said.

Then more detail. Khalid, seated back in the shadow of a rickshaw, flying slowly through a tunnel of deep green jungle.

Still further detail: she made out a man against a grey

cement wall. And a young girl at his belt.

Khalid arrived at the hillock in his rickshaw, and the men presented the catfish for his inspection.

'Catherine?' Brian said.

'Yes?'

'Another champagne?'

'Oh yes please.'

He poured out two tumblers. She sat back and took the chilled glass. She fell quiet and looked out over the lake for a while. A speedboat buzzed past. The skier flung herself out to one side to gain on the boat.

The invisible sun was warm. They drank, ate, spoke in patches, but they mostly looked out over the lake and took swims.

'Do you know,' she said after a swim, 'that oven ... it belongs to the cook. What's his name?'

'I don't know his name. I've never known his name.'

'He gives these cooking classes in Elanor's kitchen. It'll come in a second.'

'This is precisely what you said at the club.'

'Is it?'

'Yes,' he said getting up.

'Where are you going?'

'To make a note.'

'The play? Now?'

'Won't be long, just a few notes.'

He was inside for an hour. She picked absently at the lunch. She felt a mysterious calm. She didn't know what it was, nor did she know she was Khalid's ally and that the calm was more than rest and swimming.

Why a Cook should not Sit in a Kwali

Khalid was scrubbing the pot he liked for boiling the drinking water when Lall the goatmeatwallah walked into sight and stopped. Khalid invited him to come in; he kept an effort at the aluminium pot, but he called out to the butcher.

Lall strolled over. 'I have the news you wanted about Mohendra,' he said.

'Good, first let me hose down this elephant's earring.'

'Yah,' said Lall, perpetual smile, 'big pot.'

'I don't know why they bought it. What a stupid family. Can you bring the hose?'

'Yah.'

Khalid laid the kwali flat and then danced around it firing the hose, rolling his head and shunting his hip.

The butcher moved behind the tap.

Khalid hopped around the big pot, spraying the water against the inside skin. He danced around faster until it filled, and then he stepped into it. He sat down with his knees sticking into the yellow air.

'See? If you can fit a man into the stupid thing, how many goats can he cook in it?'

He stepped out. He rinsed it down and leaned it against the wooden block to dry. When he saw that his weight had dented the base he took a wet stick to it until he was satisfied.

'Like some chai?'

'Okay.'

Khalid went inside to the kitchen, his feet leaving wet prints. He came back out with his teapot, two tin cups and a separate tumbler of sugar. They sat in the shade of the mangosteen. Lall produced a small pouch of tepid pakoras.

'So what news about Featherduster?' Khalid said.

'Akram came to see him many times.'

'And?'

'You are right. Mohendra gave your design to Akram. Did you tell Mohendra about your design?'

'I told the bastard about it.'

'If you will forgive me for saying so, you are a mug. Everybody knows they are pocketing bucksheesh from the President-sahib.'

'Yah. What else?'

'What else is this. Both guys talked about what Zeythi did at the hardware place. That hardware man has not been found, everyone says he has shot through to Cox's Bazaar, some say to Dacca, some claim he's gone inside India, Calcutta—nobody knows. Nobody even talks about it anymore. But Akram and Mohendra, they were talking about it in the back, and, I tell you, they are two fellows in a lot of discomfort.'

'Really?'

'They are scared out of their wits.'

'Then it is all fixed.'

'How so?'

'Zeythi goes directly to Akram. She gives him the same treatment as that hardware-bastard.'

'Maybe,' Lall said.

'Not maybe, definitely. Oh sweet sweet Zeythi, you mongoose!'

'No, maybe.'

'Why?'

'Because of what they talked about next.'

'And?'

'They agreed to get protection.'

'Like fun. What can protect those two from Zeythi?'

'They agreed to spend a lot of money.'

'They want to give her bucksheesh?'

'No, they agreed to get a powerful old witch.'

'What old witch?'

'I do not know, but they say she is famous. She is from Kutubdia.'

'From the island?'

'Yes.'

'Oh shit.'

'That's what I mean.'

Khalid chewed on a cold pakora. Chew need. Sometimes you have to chew. Nothing you can do. Chew, look, chew, look. They were soggy from travelling in the paper bag, but he chewed heavily anyway. The taste was sharp and spritely, so he took another. They drank more tea together. A work-mouth silence went by. Chew chew. The music pinged at the quiet compound. The air was cool. No breeze, but a gust from under cool shade stirred the dust now and then.

'Are you purposely trying to mislead me?' Khalid finally asked.

The butcher looked across without expression. The

perpetual smile for once fell to a flat line.

'Khalid,' Lall said, 'please don't be so stupid. You have become a different fellow, somebody should tell you that. I am telling you that.'

'Sorry.'

'You do not have to be sorry, I realise that this whole mess has broken your heart.'

'When is she coming?'

'Very soon, they talked about getting her straightaway.'

'Did they talk about anything else?'

'No.'

'Nothing?'

'Nothing.'

Another work-mouth silence passed them by. Pigeons fell past the far side of the tree.

'What else did they say?'

'Okay, but you must promise to be calm.'

'Me? You know me and my calm.'

'Yes, I do.'

'Yah, I'll be calm.'

'They are going to bring her to Zakir Hussein Road.'

'Right here?'

'To find this particular man, you, yes.'

'What does she want with me?'

'What do you think?'

'Oh shit, oh shit. I knew that thing was right.'

'What thing?'

'A thing which I felt. It was very strange. Like a premonition.'

'Really?' Lall said suddenly.

'Yah, some time back.'

'You know, Khalid, you better tell Zeythi about this.'

'What can she do against an old bitch from the island?'

'That's why. She is a very nice girl, Khalid. You should tell her to chuck it in, go back to the hills. She is young, she has a future tumbling inside her toes.'

'Fuck fuck fuck.'

'My friend.'

'What?'

'You asked me to do this for you remember.'

'Yes, I did.'

'As long as you know.'

They drank the tea and sat quietly.

'Do you have an idea of what to do?' Lall asked.

'No, I'll go to Dacca. I'll get on the bus like every other beaten bastard.'

'I have an idea.'

'I am very glad.'

'Listen for once.'

'Okay, what.'

'The Kutubdia witch will not be here for two days, right?'

'Maybe.'

'Take Zeythi quickly to Mohendra and Akram, get the whole thing out of the two buggers before anyone can say "nice day".'

'That is not a good idea.'

'Try it.'

'No, I'll think of something else.'

After dinner Khalid boiled a pot of drinking water. If he needed to think he put a pot of water on because water had nothing in it to take the shine from your need to think. He went to his quarters. He was tired. Overnight, he considered other options. Nothing seemed to leap from the tangled mess. It remained a haze of half-considered ideas, plans with no backbone. As he drifted into a bad sleep, he decided to tell Zeythi they must expect a visitor.

Finding the Chief Bearer

'You do not know this old thing?' Khalid insisted.

'No,' Zeythi said.

'Be definite. From Kutubdia?'

'How would I know of someone from the island? But, if Lall is saying no bullshit, then we are in trouble.'

'Lall never tells bullshit. Come, let's go to the club to catch the Chief Bearer. Featherduster too.'

'Featherduster has gone to Cox's Bazaar.'

'How do you know that?'

'I have a friend now, you don't have to be a sahib around me nowadays.'

'Why has he gone there?'

'Maybe chicken business. And then he is collecting the woman from Kutubdia maybe. How must I know?'

'Okay yah yah okay. We go straight to Chief Bearer-bastard first. And remember, don't let him talk you out of it.'

Khalid took to his things. He put on a new shirt, and he threw off the sandals in favour of shining shoes.

'He will talk you out of it before he will talk me out of it,' she said as she watched him.

'No he won't,' Khalid said. 'He already knows what I think of him. But you, he'll go first straightaway to your high rubbish. He'll put on airs and you will feel like you must try to behave all like a memsahib, and not like yourself.'

'You are the one who carries on about being a servant.'

'Just don't let him do it.'

'Yah,' she said calmly.

'I know this guy, you do not. If he starts talking about how nice you look and give his regards to your umma and what a talent you've got, don't get sidetracked.'

'Yah.'

'He plays this servant bulldust to get around people like you all the time, that's what he does for a job, day in day out he just walks around with his dangling arms.'

'Yah, okay.'

Khalid looked at her directly for a moment. He said, 'You are not a servant, okay?'

'But I am a servant.'

'You are not the kind of servant he wants you to think. He will start talking about how sad it is that a Bengali servant behaves all jungly, and that this is their downfall and so on and so on. He will try to make you think that being foul and jungly is the same thing as being inferior. Ignore all that. If you want to be foul and jungly to him, then go ahead. No, be *very* foul and jungly.'

'He is a two-faced man, I already know that,' she said, keeping to herself that she was a Chakma and not a Bengali.

'Yes,' Khalid said, 'he is a show-off pig.'

'Are you ready?'

'Not yet.'

Khalid went inside to see the memsahib to add final items to his list. He suggested the ayah come along to assist, and he also suggested the load might be too big for his bicycle.

'And buy two ducks,' the memsahib said.

'Ducks?'

'Ducks—what am I talking, Chinese?'

'No, memsahib.'

He and Zeythi walked out and signalled a rickshaw. They rode into town and then turned left for the Club Road. The rickshaw put them under the big almond trees of the club, and they walked round the back.

She stood at the top of the slope that fell away to the big cement water tank. She looked into the grove and it came back, the memory of pulling at the President's pants.

Khalid stood on the top step, at the kitchen door, talking to a bearer who was bringing out two heavy bags of garbage.

'Khalid. Damn, how are you?'

'Fine fine. Is the Bastard around?'

'Chief Bearer is very busy in the Gentlemen's Bar.'

'Do me a favour, tell him I am here.'

'Okay, hold on, I'll try, I'm very busy.' The bearer called into the building, 'Rahim!'

'Yah?'

'Go tell Chief-bastard Khalid is here!'

'I am busy!'

'Go tell him or I'll tell him myself what you are doing with his ugly and pathetic sister!'

'*Okay okay*, hold on.'

He turned back to Khalid on the lower step. 'Okay?'

'Thanks,' Khalid said. Then he added, 'What has Rahim been up to with Bastard's sister?'

'Nothing.'

The bearer continued down the steps to offload the garbage and then returned.

'So how's your schooling, Khalid?'

'Good.'

'Can you get me into some kind of chef class?'

'I don't think they have cooking class.'

'You are in a chef's class, no?'

'What do I need to be in a cooking class for?'

'True. Well I better get going or get a hiding.'

The bearer hit the screen door and whipped himself back inside to work.

Khalid waited. He kicked the iron rail and it gonged. He put out his hand to lean against the red brick wall. When he had waited more than he thought were ten long minutes, he walked down the steps.

Khalid and Zeythi strolled far down the slope, to the end of the club's grounds. On this side the slope was rich and green, and the clear descent of grass was surrounded by trees so big it seemed like you were sunk in a crater in the centre of a jungle. The gigantic mangosteen, almond and flame trees rose in abundance, and the other, smaller trees followed their lead, though not with the same Shamsudin success.

The bench was the centre of a comfortable corner. Most of the staff took their rest here. Constant jars of pickles and chutneys littered the table. Shallow bowls of flaking peanuts, smooth chickpeas and salty dahl mooth were forever present. Permanent tumblers stood up and down the scarred wooden surface. A big basket of implements eternally occupied the business end of the table. And a series of cut-away tins carried the immortal candles. Bring your appetite down here morning day or night and the table will be ready. Its bench awaiting in perpetuity your weary legs.

But with the monsoon these everlasting features would vanish. They would reappear in the stuffy room underneath the kitchen floor. Outside, the big table and the hefty bench would be brushed with a coat of paint, and the sky would unleash the battering over the long day and night of the new season.

Khalid sat down beside Zeythi.

'Are you all right?' he asked. 'You look worried.'

'I'm all right.'

'You are scared?'

'I said I am all right.'

'He's here!' Khalid said with a sudden jerk of the shoulder. 'You have the headband?'

'Yah.'

'Remember, he will act like nothing has happened. Cool as a dead fish, don't forget it.'

The Chief Bearer wore stained whites. His figure gleamed like a cloud catching direct sunlight. From the small distance he smiled, and he waved lightly. Then he walked casually across the slope.

'Pooh,' he said, 'what a busy day. But never mind about me.'

He then sat at the table. He placed his elbows on the wooden top and folded his hands.

But according to Khan the sabjantawallah, the Chief Bearer was thinking: Damn, does this pesky cook know I gave his tandoor to the President-bastard? Or does he not know? I don't think he knows, Mohendra says he doesn't know. But show-off Mohendra, he has a big stupid mouth. Never mind, the Kutubdia woman will take care of it.

'Hello Khalid, hello Zeythi, how are you today?'

'We are fine,' Khalid said.

'I am fine thank you,' said Zeythi.

'We have a proposition for you,' Khalid said.

'A proposition?' the Chief Bearer smiled. 'I am holding so many propositions in my head today, I do not know what to do with them. One outstation club member wants me to travel to Calcutta to manage his restaurant. Another member this morning asked me to oversee his daughter's wedding. Another sahib said I should work for him at a big hotel in Dacca. This boom is too much.'

'Hear me out,' Khalid said without concealing a small grin.

'No, I cannot consider another proposition. But thank you just the same.'

'If you refuse my proposition,' Khalid said quietly, 'you will desire to go far beyond Calcutta.' Khalid leaned forward. 'Know what I mean?'

'Sorry,' said the Chief Bearer as he stretched his arms, 'I do not.'

A bearer appeared at the end of the table. He held a large tray.

Khalid eased back. He unfolded his arms and took a glance at Zeythi.

The bearer arranged a jug and a plate on the table.

'Iced lychee juice,' he said. 'Also,' he said, 'roast chicken sandwiches, pakoras and hot samosas.' He then looked at the Chief Bearer, who rolled his head in satisfaction, and the young assistant dragged his sandals back up the slope with the tray swinging from his hand.

'Like to have a drink and something to eat? Khalid, give me your opinion on the samosas especially, new recipe from a new cook.'

Khalid did not turn to look at the food. Nor did Zeythi.

The Chief Bearer looked up at the trees.

'They say this will be a bad one,' he said.

'Mostly for you,' Khalid said.

'No. For everybody.'

'No, especially for you.'

The Chief Bearer brought himself back to the table.

'Khalid, I have known you for a long time. But this paddling in the river of your riddles. Be careful my friend, one day you will paddle too far and you might never find your way back to us.'

'Your monsoon, it starts this very minute. Go ahead,' Khalid said to Zeythi.

Zeythi produced the headband and began to turn it into neat folds. Her hands were unsteady, but she continued to make the slender folds.

The Chief Bearer then addressed Zeythi. 'Maybe, Zeythi, you have not been informed.'

Nothing was said.

'Has anyone told you of a woman from Kutubdia? No? A strong, fearful one? No? What a pity.'

Zeythi's hands, uncertain, made another fold. She remained silent, attending the rough material as slowly as she could.

'Nobody told you? Then let me. She is coming here, to Chittagong, to Zakir Hussein Road. No? What a pity. And nobody told you more? She is searching for nothing else than a young upstart. No? What a pity.'

Khalid then made an attempt to bring a bit of bargaining power back to him and Zeythi.

'Well? You want to hear the proposition?'

What a way to try for more bargaining power.

The Chief Bearer sat comfortably, saying nothing. He examined his nails, which he regularly shaped to emphasise his station.

Khalid decided to say it out straight. 'I'll give you some advice—you go and tell my sahib everything. Tell him the thing is mine, tell him Featherduster gave it to you, and you gave it to the President-sahib.'

The Chief Bearer ignored Khalid. He addressed Zeythi.

'And did anyone tell you the worst part of it? No? Then let me. She can catch a girl by the neck from a hundred paces. She can be sitting down to chai just like we are now. Then? Gripped for good, no hands. Nobody told you that Zeythi? Nobody told you she is the most powerful terror in all the south? What a shame. Somebody should have told you, because you would have not bothered to come here today with this failure of a cook. Instead you would have your things packed and you would be off home to, whereabouts in the hills? Barkal is it?'

Zeythi sat with a poise, folding, wresting drips of concentration from the material, though she now felt the folding tighten into a wringing.

'It is up to you,' the Chief Bearer said.

She continued folding.

'If you do anything stupid just now, what do you suppose will happen to you tomorrow? Come to think of it, she might arrive tonight. Can you think for a second what it will be like, that whipping you gave Aziz—only a hundred times worse? Can your little gifts imagine it?'

She ceased folding the green headband and sat very still.

'Of course you can.'

The Chief Bearer lifted his leg over the bench and stood up.

'My bearers are waiting. Why don't you stay a while and enjoy the roast chicken? It is a fine day for samosas too.'

He strolled loosely to the slope, bringing his dangling hand up to dust off his shirt, a light flick with the back of his finger. He climbed the steps, and his dirty whites vanished into the screen door. He never liked washing.

Khalid sat gazing at the flyscreen. Sometimes, he thought, a day can come when you want to say nothing. You don't want to say 'Trouble?'

He got up silently and nodded at Zeythi. They walked up the slope and up the side of the old red bungalow to the car park. Under the giant almonds he unpacked a small paan and sat on the broken bitumen but re-arranged himself back a bit, against a trunk.

'What are you doing?' she asked.

'Eating,' he said flatly.

'We must have a rickshaw, we're going to the bazaar,' she said. These orders felt strange. She was always ordering him around.

'We'll get one here,' Khalid said with no life.

'They don't come in here.'

'I asked him to check it out once in a while.'

After some time the same rickshaw stumbled in and they rode off down the long laneway and then across town to the bazaar. Khalid daydreamed recurringly of a Dacca he had never been to, an endless city, bigger than fifty cities. One can disappear there. They say. Shitty cooks can.

Finding the Featherduster

At the bazaar a stallkeeper held out to Zeythi a gift plucked directly off the racks. She declined, but the stallkeeper edged out the object with a bounce of the wrist, and she reluctantly accepted. She also collected vegetables, sandals, glass bangles and a perfume.

Khalid did not talk. Without real interest, he took the list from his pocket, and then realised he had forgotten the goat. He walked back round the outer edge of the bazaar. At Lall's stall he took a good pound of goatmeat.

'This bit?'

'That'll do.'

'Or this chunk?'

'You are confusing me.'

'Khalid. Which bit do you want me to chop up?'

'That one.'

Standing high under the rim of the shop next door, Mohendra the chickenwallah tended a customer. The featherdusters shook when his thigh hit the counter.

When he felt done with the transaction he called out, 'Zeythi! Hello!' And then, 'Damn pretty today! I have a present for you. Imported, this one, special. From Kutubdia. Organised it myself yesterday when I went to Cox's Bazaar.'

Khalid took no notice, but he then put his eye sideways. He looks like a chicken, Khalid thought. The dunderhead wants to be one maybe. Why is it that guys like this go getting away with things like this? I'm going straight to the Teacher-sahib, and I'm just putting it on his desk—everything. This guy who wants to be a chicken. Akram who wants to be an Englishman. That Englishman who wants to be a Bengali. I'm going to tell Abdul-sahib all of this kooky stuff. I tell the teacher, *or* I go to Dacca.

Khalid glanced quickly at Zeythi. She stood unaffected. Without concern she held the day's goods at her feet, and she watched Lall work his way around the pound of meat. Flies made a crust on it, and when he shifted to re-make an angle into the side, the flies buzzed into the air but then settled again as he sliced the meat.

Lall packaged everything up and Khalid walked down the lane remembering ducks.

'Go back and get two ducks,' he said to Zeythi.

'Me?'

'Then?'

She went up the lane. At the chickenwallah's stall she asked for the duck.

'Zeythi! You say two? This means you can take my featherduster!'

'I do not want a featherduster.'

He squeezed a duster between the ducks, took the money with a big smile, and gave out the change. He whistled after her and called out loudly, 'My darling! It was beautiful last night with you!'

She continued walking.

They took a rickshaw to the bungalow. Sometimes,

Khalid thought, there are those moments. Say nothing. Do nothing. Try to think nothing.

When they reached the house, after they had put away the shopping, and after Khalid had given the change to the memsahib, which she told him to keep, after he kicked off his shining shoes, the say-nothing do-nothing silence cracked like a plate. First the Minisahib came trotting out of the path from the jungle with first-rate lengths of green bamboo he had taken from the gully behind the pond. He came up and he flung their bounce to the ground. He was in a very good mood. Pure joy aplenty.

'How was the bazaar? Did you see chickenman?'

'Leave us alone for a minute,' Khalid said.

'I'm going to the lake with the Smiths!' the Minisahib announced happily.

Then the say-nothing calm broke.

'*Get lost!*' Khalid barked.

The Minisahib kicked the bamboo, and went inside.

Then Khalid turned to Zeythi. 'I told you! I told you not to be sidetracked!'

'I wasn't.'

'Then why did you stop?'

'It was something else.'

'What then?'

'It was something else.'

'What bloody else?'

'That woman,' Zeythi said quietly, 'she is too dangerous.'

'Nonsense! If you didn't stop, Bastardhead would have been on his knees begging. He won, the Bastard won! Akram climbed all over you!'

'Khalid. Be silent,' she said. She got up and began to leave.

'Where are you going?'

'I am going out.'

'*Out?* Where?'

'To see a friend, what do you care? I need a lazy night.'

'Oh? One of these new friends you've got somewhere?'

'Yah,' she said over her shoulder. But they were not friends. They were one or two small-time hawkers and useless thieves near the post office. They knew what she had done to the important hardwarewallah at the bazaar, so they gave her enough respect for her to not worry. She went outside and walked across the compound and up the side of the house. On the roadside she stopped a moment. Then she walked into the sudden dusk.

Khalid sat numbly on the step outside the kitchen. Yah, he thought, I am going to tell the Teacher-sahib everything—that idiot who wants to be a chicken, the Englishman who wants to be a Bengali, the Bengali who wants to be an Englishman, all this kooky stuff, all of it. What else but just tell Abdul-sahib?

The Persistence of the
Compassionate Overview

Khalid did the right thing. He took it all to the polytechnic. He was determined to walk in and tell it all to Abdul-sahib.

I met plenty of compassionate types in that time. They had principles. Never let slip the determination to bring decency to the doorstep. Weave a path of grumbling complaints to the paunch-bellied overlords in Karachi. Even the all-but-forgotten English remained worthy of the efforts of a sharp tongue. In his own circle of friends Abdul-sahib led the way. His was the voice that railed against the 'caricature we have become of the English nap'. It was on his insistence that Ayub Khan's policy of 'Functional Equality' was subjected to cold scrutiny at fitful dinners. Abdul-sahib was a champion. A fair champion with a big mouth that slung out even bigger bruises. He could tell, declared true friends, facts from fun.

Khalid would not have expressed it in this way back then, but I do know he felt that the teacher was worth special considerations, and some of these seemed to cross Khalid's mind in the form of simple gratitude. Firstly, the cook was grateful for the ongoing story of Shamsudin the slave-king. The inspiration it bestowed on him came in instalments, which was, to his inner spring, like accepting a different gift on a regular basis. When he left the polytechnic grounds, swinging out the gate on his bicycle, his head would buzz with flight and his heart would flutter with excitement. And he was happy with the encouragement. Plenty. That was Abdul's gift.

When the class had concluded, the teacher patted down his forehead. He sat at his desk to rest a moment.

The paanwallah's son and English girl left the room obeying laws adults and bigots knew nothing about.

Khalid sat and waited. He approached when it seemed the moment's rest was done. Rest rest rest, he thought and then just stood up. He asked politely if the teacher could give him advice.

'Urgent problem.'

'Certainly Khalid, certainly.'

'My friend is a stallkeeper at the bazaar, the chicken-butcher.'

'Good for him. Is he happy?'

'Is he happy? What do you mean, sahib?'

'What I mean is, what has your friend got to do with my history class?'

'Well, his friend is the Chief Bearer at the club.'

'And so?'

'The chickenbutcher sold my drawings of the tandoor. To the Chief Bearer.'

'Your drawings?'

'Yes.'

'Khalid. Come here, sit down. Here here, just here.'

Khalid took a seat in the front row.

The teacher rubbed his toes.

'What,' Abdul asked, 'can the Chief Bearer do with these drawings?'

'He can give them to the President-sahib.'

'Really? Why can he do this?'

'He did this for bucksheesh, big bucksheesh.'

'For a few rupees?'

'Few nothing, sahib, fantastic amounts, sahib.'

'Fantastic loads of rupees.'

Khalid rolled his head with a smile of satisfaction. He was excited that he had made the decision to talk to the teacher.

'Khalid, you want to know something?'

'Sahib?'

'Let me tell you something tremendous. You are a bright young man. You have zip, you have get up and go. You have a job that is a stepping stone. One day, you might be a chef in a big hotel. You are one of the guys of Chittagong who can lift himself. But you know what?'

'Sahib?'

'You must promise me one thing.'

Khalid rolled his head with great pleasure.

The teacher spoke quietly, bringing his voice down to a whisper.

'You must do it with a sense of confidence.' Then he added, slowly, 'You must not copy the English.'

'Sahib?'

'There are plenty of things to accomplish, you do not have to copy the foreigners. We are just as good as them, maybe better in a lot of things. When we copy them, we are submitting to the very thing they want.'

'Sahib, it is my tandoor, I did the drawings in this classroom. Please, you must tell my sahib to talk to the President-bastard.'

'Hah?'

'The President-sahib.'

'And let me tell you something else, my boy. Your employment at Zakir Hussein Road is a very lucky situation for you. Your sahib is a good man, he pays you well, and he sends you here to lift up your station. A world of problems exist, Khalid. You must one day understand this fact. These are troubling times. The Prime Minister's rubbishy "Functional Equality", it is a government-designed theft. Against who-all? You-all, guys like you, against your jute-farming friends.'

Khalid thought, I do not have any jute-farming friends. It was a plain and sensible thing to think.

'And you know what else? Over those hills? You know a place called Vietnam?'

'I have heard of it, sahib.'

'You and I are sitting here having a chitchat about invisible bucksheesh, and they are not chatting one bit: they are having a war.'

Abdul paused. It was Tuesday, the day he and the President met in the library over a tea to enjoy their exchanges. The 'pan-continental pleasure of real equality'. He thought fondly of the real contempt he could freely express for Ayub Khan, the unconcealed contempt he expressed for the dark excesses of English interference, the rolling and endless contempt he had of the Vietnam war, and the secret contempt which he held for history's ugly tricks and surprises. They were invigorating afternoons, though no more than his real work of lifting the kids—his students—from the pall of stagnant lives.

But today he would miss it. The President was in Delhi. When would the President return, he wondered idly. Perhaps this week, he thought, after some success with the big Delhi restaurants. Yes, after some success with the tandoor.

Khalid sat silently.

When he rode from the gates there was no buzzing and fluttering. He rode recklessly, though not quickly. A sweeper lurched from his path, stumbling into a frangipani at the roadside. The sweeper shouted abuse after Khalid.

A cook like Khalid becomes fifty empty cooks if his future is taken away. He heard nothing and he rode away and he thought nothing.

Who are these New Friends?

'Make it mingle a bit more, you have to make it mix and mingle otherwise you will get a bitter shock and it won't be liked and nobody will want it,' Khalid said.

'My friends won't mind—don't be bossy,' Zeythi said.

'You asked me to show you.'

'Okay, but throw away your temper, I am not the one who stole your stupid tandoor!'

'My stupid tandoor? Last week it was a troublesome one. Now it is a stupid one? You want me to show you this mulligatawny soup?'

'Yah. But shift to that side, your armpit stinks.'

Khalid sniffed at his armpit and then he moved round.

The Minisahib sat on the stone slab of the laundry. He watched the blue tails turn orange when they licked the sides of the pot. The small gas cooker roared. Khalid used it outside when he made nose-curdling Burmese balachong with its mixture of shrimp, garlic and chilli, or other favourites which he fried so hard they choked the house with an acrid smoke that caused coughing and the death of spiders. Cooking outside felt fine, and its novelty was renewed each time. Sometimes he fried a mixture of dried fish, green mango and broken garlic. Other times he would sear trumpets of spring onions until they turned black, and he used these as an additive in his own especial korma paste. But there was no reason to make mulligatawny soup outside. Other than to have a good time.

Zeythi stirred the auburn soup until it arrived at the boil, and then Khalid lowered the flame.

'And there it is,' he concluded.

Zeythi ladled a good portion into the small bowls of a tiffin carrier. She fixed the bowls into their places and then went to her quarters where she collected a pair of sandals. When she came out she crumpled her wrist goodbye to Khalid and the Minisahib.

Khalid came alive for a moment. He stood by the rough laundry ledge.

'You know these new people?'

'No,' the Minisahib replied.

'You have not met them? Are they guys?'

'I don't know. Want this lychee juice?'

The Minisahib handed him the glass and Khalid drank from it heavily.

'What is all that grass in your hair?'

'We were playing.'

'Playing.'

'Yeah.'

'You want some soup?'

'No thanks,' the Minisahib said.

'Not hungry?'

'I had two mangos and three samosas when me and the Smiths came back from the lake at lunchtime.'

'Nice time?'

'Yeah, we went fishing.'

'Where? Kaptai? Catch anything?'

'We caught catfish only. There's a man who catches the catfish with his dogs.'

'You can't catch fish with dogs.'

'He says he can.'

'You cannot catch a fish with a dog. Did you go in a boat? Have some fun?'

'Yeah. Swimming as well. And I know who is the President-memsahib's boyfriend.'

'Who told you, somebody telling bullshit.'

'I saw it.'

'Yah? Who is he?'

'The tall man with the big pink nose.'

'Every English guy is tall with a big pink nose.'

'The one who always wears those shirts.'

'I can tell all stinking bulldust from a shirt. What is his name?'

'They call him something. But I can never hear it.'

'You are a lazy bastard. Mister something? You didn't hang around when everyone was meeting up drinking?'

'Nobody met up for drinks, I saw them coming out from the shop and they drove away. He's got a jeep.'

'They all have a jeep.'

'I'll show him to you at the club.'

'Has he got yellow hair, red hair, black hair?'

'Yeah, yellow.'

'Sounds like the President-bastard's factory sahib. You say he is tall?'

'He ducks punkahs. Ducks in any door, he puts his head …'

'Okay yah yah okay … Tall and a big bugger, or tall and like a rope?'

'Skinny.'

'Factory-bastard.'

That evening Khalid slept and rested better than he had done for many nights. Fifty empty Khalids merged again into one that had blood and bone. He took the pleasure of a long, cool bath, working up a thick soap and then sending it off with a pleasant smile under the open tap. He rinsed off with fresh water running from the high pipe, and he slept with fresh armpits. He did not linger at the open window thinking of a naked Leila Ghosh grunting like a demon Razia Iltutmish. He fell into a happy slumber.

Later that night Zeythi returned. The house lay in darkness. The lights at the front verandah rubbed against the night, a double-handed worry about the monsoon. She felt her feet lift to accept the precious dirt memories of the day. She lay awake. The rain, like a filthy whisper, promised so soon to arrive, you could smell it sometimes this late. Like a small clean snarl, the rain asked too openly for a place it could spoil. She was too tired to keep thinking and fell asleep with her hand under her cheekbone.

An Invitation

A hawker came strolling into the compound. Khalid was busy.

'What do you want?' Khalid called out.

'I have a message,' the hawker said without care.

'And who are you?'

'I am nobody, don't worry.'

'Come on inside!'

'It is for Zeythi,' the hawker said flatly.

'Who is it from?'

'Some guy in town.'

'Oh? I'll take the damn message. What is it?'

'This.'

He produced the small skull of a perch.

'What is this?'

'It is the head of a fish, what does it look like?'

'Be funny and I'll slap your head.'

Khalid received the skull into his hand. It felt smooth as a river stone. He examined the cavity, and then felt it with the tip of his finger and found that it had been as closely polished as the outer bone. For eyes the sockets glinted with a pebble of brass. It seemed to him to be a clever piece of jewellery. When he had finished inspecting it he looked up, but the compound was empty.

Zeythi came outside carrying a basket of clothing.

'Here,' he called out, 'a present for you.'

'What is it?'

Khalid took it over to the clothes line. He held it out.

Zeythi was singing into the morning. To Khalid it seemed like she was pleased with something, but he didn't hear it right. It was a melancholy sound. On seeing the skull she fell silent.

'What is the matter?' he asked.

She took the skull to her quarters.

He followed. 'What is it? New friend? The son of a rich fisherman? Eh?'

'Never mind. Just never mind.'

'Tell me what it is.'

'Go away!'

He stopped, and let her vanish into the door. He heard the wire fiddle into place and then a click, and he walked back into the kitchen to look at the extent of the preparations for dinner. He walked around the bench to go to it, but while looking into the floor at the image of the small skull he forgot the work.

That night Zeythi crossed the jungle and then took the village road, a short cut. In town the lights of the night were like fingers they were so yellow. Dust hung over the roads, and kerosene lamps hissed like sick cats calling to other sick cats.

She found the shop and went on inside to a thin corridor which led darkly to a narrow staircase. She climbed the stairs.

'What do you want?' said a man crumpled over and looking at the step.

'I have come to see the Kutubdia woman.'

'Yah? And who is this "Kutubdia woman"?' he said to the top step.

Zeythi held out the skull.

'Stealing from the fish shop today, little one?'

'Please move aside, she has sent for me.'

'And I am Vishnu's gatekeeper, get lost.'

'Be warned: I am Zeythi of the bazaar incident.'

'Oh you are, are you? Listen, go home to your umma before I stand up and kick you in the backside for free.'

A long hand emerged from around the man's neck and took a hold of his rough beard. It hauled him off to the side, where he was pushed down the darkened, narrow corridor. A double thump, another small thump, and a moan.

'Come inside,' the tall woman said with a murmur. She had a long, uncluttered face of plain simplicity, and prominent eyes. As she walked away her hand came up into the air like a feather on a warm breeze. 'This way,' she said.

She led Zeythi up the other corridor. Inside a bare room where a dim bulb burned from the ceiling she turned round. 'Sit down,' she murmured.

Zeythi took a small chair on the wooden floor.

'So. We meet.'

Zeythi said nothing.

The woman lit a thin cigarette.

'Move into the light where I can see you better.'

Zeythi lifted the chair and sat down again.

'Ah, not such a small girl after all.'

The woman smoked leisurely, and she took a sip of a drink.

'Look at that beautiful face,' she said at last. 'Not so small at all, no. Have you ever smiled? In your short life has that face ever smiled? No? Ah but you will not be letting on to a stranger with no mercy up her sleeve.'

The woman paused and took up her glass.

'So you are from the hills.'

'Yes.'

'Where exactly?'

'Near Barkal.'

'A Barkal face, well there we have the reason. These Barkal faces with their strong, fine features ... you know, the boys down here on the coast do not know where to look or what to do next with a Barkal face. Do you agree?'

'I do not know many people yet, I am new here.'

'You keep to the household I suppose.'

'Yes.'

'This is your first lie. So soon. Not very good manners in such company.'

'I apologise.'

'Yes, some boys would be very pleased with such a face.'

'Yes.'

'And then other boys ... types who would simply run for a hundred seasons, no?'

'Maybe.'

'Terrified types.'

'Maybe.'

'Do you know where that terrified hardware man from the bazaar is these days? I will tell you. He lives on my island.'

'I did not know that.'

'Yes, on the mainland side. He is a broken-down mess. He lives by himself in a joke of a hut. He talks to not a soul. His pathetic hut will not come through this monsoon. It will be washed into the bay.'

There was a long silence. The woman emptied her glass.

'Anyway, I do not have time for this,' the woman said abruptly. 'I knew your mother well.'

Zeythi was startled. 'I did not know that.'

'Before you were born. I remember she had a fat little belly. Perhaps it was you. Well she certainly gave birth to a very beautiful girl, though I do not know what you young things see in Chittagong. Are you in love here?'

'No, no.'

'This is your second lie.'

'I apologise.'

'No need. If you do not want to say who you are in love with, that is your business. The real business is this. These two I'm working for, they can go take a running leap into the festering river. I am returning to the island. This mainland, I hate it. It stinks like a hundred forgotten perch. I have a good house on Kutubdia, come visit sometime. Ask for me, they'll show you the way. You can stay a while and rest from your work. It is a peaceful place, a beautiful island, not like this toilet.'

She poured a fresh drink. The aroma filled the room and it resembled coffee.

'One more thing. The chickenwallah and his cousin have been falling over thin air to pay me. They have paid me very well. Under your cushion there is a hundred rupees. Send it to your mother. Long time ago she helped me when I needed it.'

Zeythi could say nothing.

'One last thing, and this is between you and I. The skull of the fish: keep it safe. If you come to the island, show it around. It will bring you to my place.'

Zeythi did not know what to say.

'Well?'

'Yes, thank you. I will value the invitation.'

'Good. Then that's it.'

'You are leaving? Tonight?'

'You are observant. One day you will be humble.'

'But did you not arrive yesterday? What about your work for the two men?'

'I have done it. Here, tonight. Did you not hear what I told you about the hardware man?'

'Oh. Yes, yes I did.'

'And? You want those two bhainchodths to finish up the same?'

'They are crooks.'

'Then take them to the police.'

'We cannot, it is not that simple, and we have no proof.'

'You will work something out.'

The woman stood up and cleared the small table of the cup and the tie of cigarettes.

Zeythi protested. 'But there is only one way—for me to force them …'

'Force these idiots? To do what?'

'To admit they stole the tandoor.'

'You will not be able to force either one of these swine to do anything.'

Zeythi fell silent. Then she said, 'You have made them safe.'

'You are a very observant young woman.'

'But why? For filthy money?'

'No, not for the money. As a favour … to an old friend.'

'I do not understand.'

'Tough. Someday you will. Have you ever seen the bay

at Kutubdia, mountain girl? It sparkles.'

The woman stepped quietly from the room to the corridor, and she was gone.

Leila's Words of Advice

Khalid turned down the flame to simmer the pot of mutton. He was about to start on the chicken when he heard a tapping on the door. Through the gauze Leila's face caught the light of the afternoon. They sat outside under the shade of the mangosteen tree.

Khalid's dream of Dacca was straightforward, like riding into the teahouse: he assumed he would swing his bicycle into the city, climb off, park, walk up, say hi, all in one smooth action. And it was true, partly. The place cast beautiful stories out over the delta. Rumours of easy riches tore into eardrums. Whole villages of guys like Khalid poured into Dacca.

Leila remembered Khalid's early excitement for the place. How he asked about it over and over with serious eagerness. But now she saw only the results of what Mohendra and Akram had done and what had happened to the tandoor. She didn't mention it.

Leila gave him clear directions for a good place to start when he arrived. At the bus station he was to follow Sayedabad Road for a mile and then at the train station turn left into town. Find Topkhana Road. Here the sahib hotels are small and old, better chances for a cook like him. She also told him about places along the Buriganga in Old Dacca. On the river lay creaky old boats. These baras, floating eating houses for the poor, were good places to find work.

'Dacca is not like Chittagong,' she said. 'Everyone is a thief, the whole place is a foul smell. In Chittagong only people like Zeythi are thieves and everything is clean.'

Khalid was called into the house, and Leila left for the bazaar.

Thunder

Khalid reached a big decision. But he sat heavily, saying nothing. Zeythi was shaking from a lack of confidence in her efforts with him, and she could not make out if she had succeeded or failed. A quiet, lazy morning, and they sat at the table under the shade at Khalid's quarters, though shade was hardly needed as everything was soaked in a cloud cover big as his private pledge. The cat made crescents at his feet. Khalid tossed a marble of goatmeat into the rotating air. Only one remark provoked his reaction, and he again fell into saying nothing.

'You look tired,' he began. 'Good time at the new friend's place again last night?'

'No, I went to town.'

'You all went?'

'Only me.'

'Alone? Into town? What for?'

'I went to see the Kutubdia lady.'

'Yah?' Khalid said with a sudden shock. 'What happened?'

'Nothing. She has protected the guys, and she has gone back to Kutubdia.'

'Just like that?'

'Just like that.'

'She is not coming to the house?'

'No.'

Reaction spent, Khalid went inside to get the chai. Zeythi stayed under the shade. She tossed meat to the cat.

'Thank you,' Zeythi said.

The cat chewed with a rough snoring sound and then swallowed. He then started making a circle of encouragement at her feet. She tossed out another piece.

'Thank you,' she said again and gave the cat's head a slap.

Khalid returned with the teapot on a big tray. Sugar, milk, mugs, pakoras, a paratha, a couple of guavas; the known world. He set the tray on the hard dirt. He filled the tin mugs, and the teapot released a plume of steam.

Khalid then talked. He began quietly and he hesitated. He had an elbow on his knee and faced the cat. Zeythi sat beside him. The cat put his paws together and looked at them one at a time. There was no blink from one to the next. But when they ignored him to talk, he walked off over the compound.

'To you I will give my mirror and my transistor radio,' Khalid said. 'I know you like the transistor, but you must keep it clean, dust it with a good brush, and keep it out of the rain because a transistor will not work if it gets wet. The goggles I will keep.'

She found it difficult to speak. She was shaking.

'Have you told the Minisahib?'

'No,' he said.

'Have you told the sahib?'

'Not yet, but he will be fine. Memsahib too. They all will be fine with the decision. They will understand that I must rise.'

Zeythi sat quietly. She did not know if Khalid was still in the experiment of trying to convince himself, though she sensed a boldness.

'Dacca,' Khalid said quietly. 'Full of jobs and full of exciting days. A big, lucky place. Chittagong cannot be forever. I wanted to be working in Dacca from day dot. And the rain is nearly here. Every year I say it and every year I miss it. "Let's go before the rain, let's get going. Go check out the bus, go get some information, go take a look at the other bastards stepping on, stand back and take a look only. Go tempt it. It might help to tempt it." Every year is the same. So now, it is to be different. And anyway everybody goes to Dacca.'

He gave a ball of the sticky meat to the distant cat, flicking it hard with his long, dull thumb at the laundry wall. It stuck waist high to the cool cement. The cat strolled over, his big shoulders alternately rising and dropping. He sat under the meat and let out a croak; but he then sprung up and removed it.

'I will go before the floods to find a place to stay. If I go quickly I'll be able to get a good high spot. This is a boom.'

Khalid knew he was overtalking it.

Zeythi lifted her sleeve to wipe an eye, and quickly set it down again. Then she caught a curious thing. Her eye followed the rumbling money plant and then it fled into the thick cloud. The cloud gave her no anchor and so she swam with the rolls for a few moments until the vague sense broke into an exact sense. She realised Khalid was purposely looking away.

Then a second curious thing. She felt a relief. It was new to her, this selfish feeling, but at least she now knew the difficulty was as well for her. It was a sign for which she was thankful.

'I am not making a sudden leap,' he said quietly. 'A guy has to decide if he wants to reach a better station in life. The sahib is an important man and even though he cannot believe the tandoor is mine, he still counts me as a damn fine cook and so I hope he will give me a damn fine letter to take with me. The Teacher-sahib maybe as well. I'll find good work.'

Her heart slid to her small bare foot. Another thing taken. It was less like a direct removal, and more like what she had grown to know as reality. This gets taken away, that gets taken away. She didn't even, not really, want to leave the hills, but she took herself away to Chittagong. There was no normal sadness, no normal frustration or resentment, just a staring.

One small difference had touched the skin of her life: she was happy here. She had been deeply grateful for the Minisahib. And for Khalid. She was almost too frightened to think too long on the cook. So much he had given. So much he had shown her. She reached out and took a swipe at a mosquito circling Khalid's shoulder, then a clap, but missed.

'That is not a mosquito,' he said.

'It is.'

'No, it is not.'

'You are always saying that. How can you tell if it is not a mosquito?'

'By how it flies. A mosquito flies smoothly, like silk in a wind, with sudden turns, sharp turns. Smooth and definite.'

It returned and she got it. She opened her palm.

'I told you,' he said leaning over and looking.

She sat with him. But not for long. She sprang up and went away into the house.

Who was this Stranger?

Zeythi did a very odd thing. It flung the living daylights from the Minisahib. First he trekked back from the pond at the usual time. He found her dusting the air in a bedroom. She turned round and followed him outside. They strolled up the side of the jungle and then slipped into the concealed path and went winding into the cool green clearing of the banana grove.

Inside the grove she immediately removed her shirt. She looked beautiful. He liked the heat of these secret moments that would burn his throat with hot air and set his face on fire.

She seized him by the arms. That was a bit odd, he thought.

She pulled him close and thrust her chest at his mouth.

With one hand clutching the back of his springy head she consumed the moments. Her other hand gripped his arm.

'What are you doing?' he hissed.

'Be quiet!'

She pushed him back until he fell to the soft grass. She climbed on him and put her mouth to his. It was a hard crush. Their teeth collided.

For him they were strange moments.

She bit his neck, and she rubbed her thigh roughly against his pants.

Then she simply frightened him: she cursed through clenched teeth, and let rip a terrible scream.

He managed to slip out from under her weight, but he needn't have done so, for she fled from the grove and vanished into the deeper jungle, screaming as she went.

He was shaking. He ran out to the field and then fell breathless to the long grasses by the stream. His heart was beating wildly, and he thought the sky had caved in. It was a long time before he got up. When he made his way slowly back to the bungalow, bats were wiping at the dark night.

An Explosion

Then there was something else, and it was bad stuff. It happened while Khalid cleaned his room. He lifted the jute bed frame outside and placed it against the laundry wall. And though there was no actual sun to speak of, he thought daylight would do the bedding good. He had not given the memsahib his decision, but he went ahead shaking out his quarters.

He felt a shudder run up the spine. He stopped. He put everything down and took a long look around the compound.

He picked up the mattress. He threw it into the air across two clothes lines. He then picked up a green bamboo pole.

'What are you going to do with that?' Lall Thankee blurted.

'I am going to box its ears.'

The goatmeatwallah sat saddened by Khalid's decision. He did not disapprove. He was simply saddened. He had his perpetual smile to show.

'You are not taking it with you? Roll it up like a flap of gut, and tie it off, simple as carting a small bolster under your arm. You'll be thankful for something to put under your aching bones,' he said smiling.

'Maybe. But it is not mine. It belongs to the house.'

Khalid struck the thin mattress twice to test that it lay secure on the lines, and he then arranged his feet to launch into it. The mattress danced about, heavy in the dense air.

He went inside to the fridge. He called out to Lall, and the goatmeatwallah strolled inside to the kitchen. Khalid swung open the fridge.

'Look at this,' Khalid said with large approval.

'Lot of stuff. Only one other sahib's icebox I have looked inside—Ajit's Mayor-sahib. Same, damn lot of stuff ...'

'This, I mean this.'

'What ... that thing?'

'Yah.'

'What is it?'

'It is a jug of juice. Plenty of ice too. Want some?' Khalid reached in and took out the jug. He gave it to Lall.

Lall lifted it to his mouth. Then he pulled a face.

'What's wrong?' Khalid said.

'What is it?'

'Lychee juice. And whisky.'

'Whisky? You are taking whisky? What has gone wrong with you, Khalid?'

They went out and sat on the steps with the jug. Khalid sweated heavily. His forearm glittered with a fine dust.

'Want some more?'

'No, you have it.'

'It's nice, mixed up with ice.'

'Looks good, you take it.'

They sat quietly for a while. Khalid looked off at the double hump of the hills. Then he caught a movement at the corner of the house. He got up to inspect the entrance.

'Expecting someone?'

'No. But I've got that feeling.'

'"Feeling"? What feeling?'

'That strange thing I told you about.'

'It's not the whisky?'

'No.'

'Any more cleaning left to do?'

'Quite a bit.'

'Want some help?'

'No, it's okay. Thanks.'

'When are you going?'

'Soon.'

'Well I better take off. See you maybe tomorrow?' Lall suggested.

'Yah.'

Khalid accompanied Lall as he walked his bicycle up the slope to the dusty shoulder of Zakir Hussein Road. They shook hands and he rode off.

Khalid returned to the compound and continued taking a rest on the steps. He surveyed the things that lay between the laundry and his quarters. The bed frame. The mattress. Two chairs. The box of torn hinges. A wooden rack on which his clothing hung. The oven sketches, weighted by the Brownie camera on a table of two drawers. A pair of shining black shoes failing to appreciate a pair of worn sandals. And calling to be washed, a clump of smelling loongies. To him the clutter seemed like a jumbled list of the luck that had been thrown to his feet.

He took a mouthful from the jug, and some of the whisky ran down his chin. He wiped his neck, and he took another swig to balance the mistake. He continued to take a stock of events.

He whispered, 'Kissed by the luck of the stinking camel driver!'

The cook gazed in ignorance of a golden rule; but I now know it is never a good idea to sit back and fall into contemplating your bad luck.

'Is this not so, Iqbal?'

'Yes, in my opinion that is wise.'

'Especially when drinking whisky.'

'I never take whisky, so I cannot say anything about that.'

'And no matter how much bad luck one holds in the palm of his hand.'

'No matter how much, that is true.'

'Never a good idea. Because something will happen.'

'Yes. Shall we continue?'

'Yes.'

But something happened for which I cannot blame the cook. It started quietly. Behind him the house lay empty. It was a perfectly good bungalow popping with windows, but it seemed to curve down in obeisance to the cloud; and it was a porous thing. The walls held a light sweat running into the green-black cracks. The memsahib was out. Her grown-up children were at work. The Minisahib and Zeythi were at the club with the sahib, where after dark Zeythi would reward herself and slip into the emerald.

The emptiness improved Khalid's reflection. It is rare that he is alone in the house. Quiet would bring bad stuff. And Khalid was not ignorant of a clear glimpse. Look at his keen sense of the strangeness lurking in the days before the exploding sky. He knew another year, at this time, would bring a sweet tendency to the air, and he also knew that there was nothing sweet about it. Riddles fill the afternoons, and you are a fool to cast away time trying to catch them. You simply do not waste your brain thinking about it. All you did was to accept the change and keep the nose to the grindstone. But Khalid was clear that this was the exact time of year for strange things. This he knew. Just don't think about it.

Counting off his strewn bits of rotten luck, he took a swig. He went over to get the hose. He took hold of a bucket of water. With a firm floor brush he scrubbed the bed frame, and the textured jute foamed up. The brushing he overdid; it was a harsh, resentful forwards backwards crush-a-crush movement with all his bitter strength and more.

He came up and stopped for air. Then he went to the steps and lifted the jug high for a large mouthful. Just as he brought the jug back down, he saw the figure.

Set under the low hang of the mangosteen, the figure stood facing the cook.

Khalid held the jug below his chin, but he did not move.

The figure made a small shift of his foot, and this gave him an angle to lean on the tree. He folded his arms. Now the posture looked insolent all over again.

Khalid curled his lip and bared his teeth. With a sudden leap, he released the jug, which smashed on the steps, and he bolted across the compound. His throat made deep grunts, but exploded in a snarl into the quiet air.

The figure stumbled backwards and then dissolved into the deeper shade.

Khalid flew into the shade and caught the long, sharp grasses. On his arms he felt quick stings and sudden cuts. He could see the figure slip out through the break in the wall and flow further away into the undergrowth. The figure ran very well, not fast, but with a measure which avoided the catching of grass.

A whip caught Khalid under the eye, a thin new branch of sap, and the effect it had was to heat up his temper. He flung himself faster down the slope. The figure broke into the overcast afternoon on the field. When it came Khalid's turn to break into the open, the figure was not too far off and this brought to Khalid's legs a new burst of strength.

The figure made a direct line for the gully between the hill and the road. He turned and disappeared into the curve.

When Khalid turned into the curve he saw the figure leap easily away in the shallow stream.

Khalid found a sandbank and he used it to make up ground. His feet punctured holes in the shallow flow. The figure seemed far ahead, but he was now straining in a stretch that came up to the thighs. The start of the open river sounded quiet, and the road descended to the river's bank so that they ran alongside a rickshaw. The figure was struggling in the deep stretch and Khalid was now bounding over the sandbank.

The road veered away from the river to avoid the cemetery. This was the grove of guava trees. The figure climbed out and vanished over a small boulder. Khalid ran along a ridge above the river bank, headstones flying past his shoulder, to the gap where he saw the figure disappear. He stopped. He clasped a solid guava branch. With the flow of the river directly behind his back, he held the branch. Dangling with one arm, he looked through the plateau of wood and headstones. He sunk his head low under the leaves to survey gaps and broken rows.

Suddenly the chase of crashing water had fallen silent. Beyond the cemetery the distant buzz of a scooter rose and fell away.

He released the guava branch. As he moved into the cemetery he was able to walk with a soundless step on the fine grass. The headstones were etched with dark mosses. The name of the cemetery sprung to his mind, not the proper name, but a name used. The Place of Many Guavas. He moved along an open courseway. This gave him a clearer sweep of the stillness. He kept himself down and made good progress into the small plateau. The clear, sweet sound of the river grew thinner. Guavas hung everywhere, and patches of lemons appeared and vanished in the distant leaves. He came to a shallow gully. He followed its ledge across the cemetery. When the gully became a drain he finally sat at the roadside.

He took a running leap over the monsoon drain and started to walk to the teahouse. He stopped for a look down the curving line of the road, giving attention to the edges where he thought the figure might be using the cover of the drain.

He walked until he came to the teahouse. He paused to see if he would go inside for a beer, but then continued. Instead of proceeding along the pathway, he used the bitumen proper. A scooter buzzed up and swung by too close and Khalid swore loudly. Ahead, the scooter pulled over. It suddenly buzzed around and came back up the road. When it stopped the rider removed the helmet.

'Foul mouth today young man! ... Khalid?'

'Yes, Fatimah Westcott memsahib.'

'What has happened to your face?'

'I was just at the teahouse with friends.'

'Fighting?'

'No, just fooling around.'

'One day we wiser people will close down that notorious place from under your noses, squalid dump that it is. Where is your bicycle?'

'I left it at the house.'

'You're going there now? Jump on, I'll give you a lift.'

'Thank you, no.'

'This is my new scooter, Khalid, take a ride. Get on, I have to pass the house.'

They swung down the road and she dropped him at the front gate. Then she rode off.

When Khalid walked down the side of the house and out into the compound he was surprised to see the Minisahib sitting on the wall. He was sunk in the dense vines of the money plant.

'How come you're not at the pool?'

The Minisahib did not respond.

Then Zeythi emerged from her quarters, flinging back her wet hair. She sat with Khalid at the back steps.

'I cleaned up the broken jug for you,' she said.

'Yah.'

'What happened?'

'I stumbled and what-not. What's the matter with him?'

'He heard them talking. They're sending him to a different school.'

'So? It's time for a big school.'

'In England.'

'Hey? When?'

'Don't know.'

'Have you told him about me?'

'No.'

'Good, don't say anything just now. I will ask the memsahib for my pay tomorrow and then see when she will let me go.'

'Who will replace you?'

'She will get someone.'

Export Success

It is right, in the scheme of things, that an Information Minister should be a straight-faced fibber, but in Sunny J Fernandez's case every time he uttered a fib his left eye twitched. Not the eyeball, not the eyebrow, only the top lid. It flung itself partway down the eye and then fluttered like the wing of a butterfly. No way known Sunny J could keep a straight face. When making an address to a visiting dignitary, it was good to watch him announce, say, India's 'vast indebtedness to the British legacy'. At a moment like that his lid would do more than twitch, it would flap and bounce like the wing of a bat until it looked like it would fly clear off his head. But Sunny J dismissed the tick as a petty hereditary flaw of no consequence or meaning.

Sunny J's assistant was an altogether different sort. Ministry workers had him down pat. Ask anyone and they'd say the assistant is a 'moribund, humourless fellow'. More than that. 'He is a blunt guy. Serious, grim.' But he was openly proud of these traits. To his way of looking at 'the equation', these features simply constituted honesty. I'm an honest man, he'd declare after a meeting. If you can't hack it then bad luck. He had spent his undergraduate years in Accra. In his time it was still the Gold Coast, which had later become Ghana after violent freedom struggles. They say the experience had set his stern mouth forever. So they made an operational pair, Sunny J and his smileless number two. The fibbing minister and the honest assistant.

More captivating, though, to observe Number One, Sunny J, as he spoke with the Chittagong club President in the serene main lounge of the Delhi club. Outside lay a warm Sunday afternoon with the dusty ramparts of Delhi as hummingly quiet as they ever could become. Pretty big thing, the President-sahib from the Chittagong club chit-chatting away with India's Info-sahib. It was a 'chance accident' that they did meet, through a mutual acquaintance, Fatimah Westcott's husband, and the moments expanded with the medium temperature of importance.

Sunny J and the President chatted amiably on the prospect of importing the ovens to Delhi. Well, the President chatted on the subject. Sunny J sat back with his arm outstretched over the lounge chair and listened.

The President's meetings at important restaurants and big hotels round Delhi had been effortless. Though, truthfully, what had done the hard slog was the album full of photographs he had taken at the factory.

The President opened the album.

Sunny J looked down. Then he moved forward. He turned a page.

'This tandoor actually works?'

'Oh yes, very very well,' said the President.

Since Sunny J was a mellow bloke, the President sat back in a comfortable manner too. All round, thought the President, it was an enjoyable afternoon. He was glad he had come to the club. The Minister asked politely after his business, and he also promised a small token of good advice.

The President's confidence afloat, he gave the tandoor a bit of high praise.

'An ingenious invention,' the President said. 'Quite stunning. Our premises might manufacture in the order of dozens each month ...'

But Number Two interrupted. He said, without expression, 'You must remember, there were one hundred thousand people present at the Red Fort alone on the morning of April 14th 1947.'

'Independence Day,' said the President, 'a very happy occasion.'

'Yes, down came your flag and up went our flag.'

The President was unsure what the assistant was getting at, but he weighed in anyway.

'Indeed, and a beautiful flag it is too.'

The assistant continued. 'Independence rose up from slumber. It is just as Nasser said ten years ago, "All over the world peoples are wanting their sovereignty, their freedom." One can see it still in progress today.'

He continued in a stoic tone, 'But that is only to talk abstractly of peoples and borders and nations. Once they secure the freedom, other tensions will rise from under their feet, just like we have in India today. Rolling tensions are nothing new.'

Then Sunny J spoke a word, 'Sudeep, we can chat on this subject perhaps later.'

'Yes, Sir.'

But Number Two proceeded, addressing the President directly.

'One day the world will consist in four thousand

countries, maybe more. At this time the world will require a superstate, and it will be us, India. Look at Senegal, Ghana, Nigeria, Zaire; all these places might break down even further. Harold Macmillan and his "winds of change", he's a smart man. I myself saw the independence celebrations in Accra, the fireworks and the dancing in the streets. It was a night of profound portent.'

The President sat quietly. Carrying on like a mutton chop, he thought.

But it was the mellow Minister that spoke again.

'Sudeep.'

'Sir?'

'That's enough,' the Minister said quietly.

'Sorry Minister.'

The President smiled and brushed off the interruption, and continued praising his factory's capabilities. He felt a small pleasure in informing the Minister, and looked forward to his token piece of advice. Here a token morsel of advice, the President of the Chittagong club knew full well, would be worth its weight in the gold braiding of a whole wedding party.

But the assistant continued.

'Nkrumah the hero, Ghana's first prime minister. But he turned into an autocrat. Arresting people for no reason. So just last year Nkrumah was removed by the army. But it is fragile, democracy. Today you can see Ghana is a dark military state, full circle in only ten years. That is a shame of course, but it is fragile, democracy.'

'Sudeep, that's enough now, please.'

'The flow of capital dried up, national projects turned to regional cobwebs. Mobutu in the Congo. Uganda another dark tyranny. Since the dancing and fireworks Ghana has had fourteen coups, or tried-out ones. And when the world is a juggling giant of thousands of countries? Then it will call out for a superstate. And it will be India.'

'Sudeep, what is up with you today? Please go home now.'

'So we do not need to talk about your novelty tandoor from your factory in your patronising tone. India is the only one to have successfully sustained a democracy.'

'That's it Sudeep, leave now, I'll speak to you later.'

The assistant stood up and politely said his farewell, and walked off through the cool lounge.

'I do apologise for the lad. Sometimes he can be a touch mystifying.'

'Oh, it's just confidence. Sounds like a very informed young man.'

'Yes, he was there at the riots in Ghana so it seems to be the fount of most of his theorising.'

'Has he worked for you a long time?'

'No, not so long. So to which club did you say you belong?'

'Chittagong.'

'Oh lovely place, very nice.'

They finished off and Sunny J advised the President that it would be best if he followed the formal routes into the Indian marketplace, and that this was also the opinion of his cousin who worked in the Department of Foreign Trade. Business with Pakistan was a bit tricky just now, he said.

'Team up with a reputable trading firm,' Sunny J said, and then excused himself to lunch with his associates.

The President watched the group walk off. He then decided that when he returned to Chittagong he would meet with Fatimah Westcott.

Not One to Waste a Moment

Fresh from a good night's rest, the President stepped out of the twin-propeller Fokker with an eager spring in his step. He paused briefly on the top step to give the airport a once-over.

Good to be back, he thought. Home.

Delhi to Dacca had been a pleasure of planning, and Dacca to Chittagong was highlighted by a cheery sense of the last leg home. Rakesh the driver waited out front, and in a short while the President was at the house and on the telephone. The hostile world behind him, he picked up the black cradle with a level glee and dialled away.

'Fatimah Westcott is not available,' said the secretary, 'just for the moment, she is on another call.'

It was with the President's wife. They were talking about their lovers, enjoying the detail. The President's wife was describing the Theatre-sahib masturbating.

Waiting, the President picked up a green guava from the fruit bowl, and sat down to press a good bite to it. A big chunk came away, and the firm, chalky flesh gave off the customary tang he liked.

By the vase lay an envelope carrying his name. He took it up to examine the underside, but set it back on the table as Fatimah Westcott came to the telephone.

They agreed to meet for a discussion after work.

'The club at five then,' she said pleasantly to cap off the short exchange.

He crossed the big living room and bounded up the staircase. He was surprised by the vigour he displayed so directly after the flight. After a brisk shower he wore his favourite loose 'Chittagong' clothing: a short-sleeved shirt and a pair of billowy trousers of 'stunning cotton coolth'. In London, he thought, you might want warmth. But in Chittagong you want coolth.

Downstairs he made a survey of the living room to be certain he had forgotten nothing, and then went outside and took a seat behind the clear windows of the car. Cheer. No question where to place the hand. Up along the top of the back seat, a happy splay. In town he remembered the envelope, and they turned round. Annoyed. At the bungalow he picked up the envelope. Then he snapped his teeth at the driver. At this, Rakesh put his foot on the petrol. He weaved through the Chittagong traffic like a magician. He brought the wheel down with force, he lifted the wheel with effort. He used the car to remove obstacles, hooting at the road of dust and smells. He yanked the thing from one side to the other like a head of hair is tossed around by movie stars in better Bombay. He made the world move aside. Make no mistake, he liked it when the President-bastard snapped his yellow teeth. Rakesh was no friend of the Chief Bearer's, and to Khalid he was no friend either. Neutral. But to speed, he was an old friend. Finally, he slowed the speeding wheels up to the bursting tar in the car park, and the whole bumbling metal invention bounced like a boat on the root-ruptured road, until he placed its tilted nose to a big almond tree.

'Sahib,' the low-headed driver said comfortably.

In the lounge the President found a corner table. A bearer walked up with a saunter, but got the shock of his life when he saw it was the President. He picked up his pace, filled the order, brought out a bowl of mixed dhal mooth and chickpeas, and hurried to inform the Chief Bearer.

Akram came to the lounge. He greeted the President, welcomed him back, and the President said it was bloody good to be back. Akram went off to attend to other things, saying he would return soon to check if anything was needed.

But Khan the sabjantawallah says Akram was grumbling inside: Bastard. Useless rich bastard. Oh! Goodtobeback! Goodtobeback!

The junior bearer stood by. The President gave him a glance, and he moved back a step.

The President sipped at the gin and tonic, and he produced the note from his shirt pocket. He tore open the envelope.

Received your telegram with the arrival details. Unfortunately had to assist at the rehearsals this afternoon, as they open very very soon and all is pandemonium with plea after plea for all the helping hands they can gather. Hope Delhi was perfectly useful. I shall be home round ten o'clock tonight or thereabouts.
　　　　Catherine.

So she's here, he thought, in the hall. Well good. Well very good.

When Fatimah Westcott walked up to the table he stood

to greet her by the hand and they settled easily into pleasant chatter. It did not take long to outline the procedures involved in bringing a consignment to the firm's Delhi operations. The President mentioned his meeting with the Information Minister.

'Sunny Fernandez?' Fatimah Westcott asked to be certain.

'Yes.'

'Forget about dear old Sunny J quickly as you can.'

'He seems a reasonable fellow.'

'No argument, but consider: he holds little connection with trade. Darling old Sunny J is a PR man. He drips with charm and only ever makes a fist at the cricket. Besides, Sunny J is not the minister, he is one of the minions. Indira Gandhi is the Information Minister. Would you like to dine?'

'Good idea.'

The bearer stepped forward. They ordered another round of drinks, and decided, on the President's suggestion, to share in a large boat of goat curry with side serves of biryani and dhal.

'And put some green chillies please on a clean plate,' she said pleasantly to the bearer.

With a small drop of the head and a faint smile the bearer slid away.

The Irishman walked past. 'Hill-o there Fatimah!'

'Hello Tom—what's this overdoing the Irish today?'

'Exhaustion,' he replied. He stood at the table a minute, leaning on the back of a bamboo chair.

'Exhaustion?'

'Yes. Had a meeting with the Mayor this afternoon.'

'The Ring Road Bridge?'

'To be bloody sure.'

'Long meeting?'

'Not at all—the bridge was like a slap. Then I had to sit about and listen to his valuations of himself, the dear soul. Fella genuinely takes some kind of stock in the notion he's "an affront' to the fellows in Parliament. "Still here after all these years!" he says, cackling away.'

'An affront?'

'Yep. And he actually believes it. Poor sod.'

'Never mind, join us for a drink.'

'No thanks, I'll just be up at the bar for a minute. Hello there el Presidente, how did your trip to London go off?'

'Really very good, Tom. Sorry to hear about your rotten day.'

'Thanks. Coming to the bar later on?'

'Might do, just might do.'

'Fatimah?'

'Very probable,' she smiled.

'See you shortly.'

The Irishman walked off, calling out his drink to the bearer before he reached the bar.

Fatimah and the President sorted out the remaining details of the first shipment. The President said the factory might have made around thirty of the ovens by the end of the month.

The Mayor walked in and he made a few strides up to the table.

'Here's a spoiled pair! How was old London town?'

'Oh fine thank you, Mahmood, fine.'

'England still afloat, eh?'

'Oh yes.'

'All great things remain afloat, don't you think so?'

'All good things great and small, yes indeed.'

'Then you are up to a game of snooker tonight?'

'Best of five.'

'A tournament! Look what London has done to you! Shabash—let me show you what a better man can do!'

'Eight o'clock then.'

'Very good. How are you Fatimah?'

'Afloat Mahmood, afloat.'

The Mayor laughed and then walked off.

When the meal arrived they ate without pleasure.

'This goat is tremendous.'

'Didn't I tell you?'

'Oh you did, you did. Pass me the pickles.'

After the meal they joined the Irishman at the bar.

Abdul the teacher arrived, and the evening got off to a good start. The President smiled widely, appreciating his home, his friends. Abdul said it was good to see the old boy back again. He raised his foot to the railing and brought his elbow up to the padding.

'How was London? Good?'

'London'll never alter.'

'Oh?'

'It continues to think of itself as the centre of the country, but, let's own up to the fact, it's not much more than a provincial town. Chittagong any day please.'

'Dear me.'

'Not at all,' said the President as he smiled.

Dacca or No

Khalid sat alone with his decision. He gazed over the teahouse balcony at the stream. Sharp sparkles were smoothed over by sunlight making a creamy haze that offered nowhere to fasten the eye or the decision. The stream appeared to stand still, though the shine made a mass of exploding pins and bolts. Khalid thought of it numbly as a thousand torches stuck to a fat python. Somehow, running along it, the figure had been too smart for him.

Mookerjee the gardener came outside.

'Waiting for the girls to remove their loongies?'

'Ajit. Hi. Which girls?'

'Down there at the stream.'

'Oh. Yah, they look fine today.'

'You might get lucky, but first they'll have to finish the washing before someone takes a dip. Maybe a drink while we wait? Another one of those?'

'Yah.'

Khalid shifted his chair to watch the women beat the clothing on the rocks. They made trails that looped high and gleamed brightly. The rhythmic movement gave his eyelids a sensation of weight, but it was the golden haze steaming off the lazy stream which made him feel the afternoon's heat. In a vague way he wondered what had brought Ajit out.

Mookerjee returned carrying two drinks. He placed them on the table and sat down.

'What are you doing here so early in the afternoon?' he asked.

'I can ask you the same question. Your sahib is the Mayor, he is more strict than mine.'

'The sahib is in bed with a bad head. Anyway, first I went to your place. Zeythi told me you were here.'

'She doesn't know where I am.'

'She does, she followed you.'

'Did she? Why?'

'What am I? A fig in her pocket? All I know is you are a lucky fellow to have that little woman as your friend.'

The 'little woman' was more than the cook's friend, Mookerjee knew that but he let it rest because he could see Khalid did not know it.

Khalid smiled and took his eyes off the glittering stream to join Ajit at the table. They raised their glasses.

'Guess who is back in town,' the gardener said.

Khalid did not respond.

'That's why I came to find you. My sahib saw him. They played snooker and drank all night like dogs. Betting and playing and betting. So much money was floating around that one of the junior guys estimated Chief-bastard was given about a hundred rupees. That Chief-bastard, he is no fool, and he will keep on taking their money until he will be a richer man by the end of the rains than you and I put together when we are tapping a walking stick on this balcony.'

'He wants the money to lure the Calcutta woman,' Khalid said flatly.

'No, he has given her the flick.'

'Akram give a rich man's daughter the flick? No, what the mongrel wants is for her to come back.'

'Khalid, you are wrong. Iqbal told me.'

'Iqbal?'

'Yes. What is wrong? You don't trust Iqbal?'

'Iqbal showed you his work?'

'He and I have been friends for a long time, since before you came here.'

They looked down to the lazy stream for a while.

'Can you remember telling Featherduster about your oven?'

'Yes, I am an idiot.'

'Clumsy maybe. Don't call yourself an idiot, never call yourself names. Anyway, you are a very smart guy. You have schooling, and you know how to live.'

'I remember telling Mohendra, I showed him the sketches when he took me to Aranthi at the bazaar.'

'So then it is true what Iqbal and I suspect. It was Featherduster who stole your oven.'

'That is how it looks.'

They sat at the table in silence, watching the women at the riverbank flail the clothing in the golden light. The still water gave the impression that there had never existed any such thing as the monsoon.

'Iqbal?'

'Yes?'

'Remember that?'

'Oh yes. It took me many nights to tell Ajit Mookerjee. But sometimes a decision has to be taken. The Featherduster made it easier for me by his gloating attitude, but still I tumbled inside many empty nights to reach that decision to dishonour my code.'

'Did you feel bad?'

'I expected to feel very low, yes. But I didn't. I remember actually I felt quite good. Shall we continue?'

'Yes.'

Khalid took a large mouthful of his drink. He was pleased—in one way. His vague notions were made into fact. He thought that he should go to sit with the President-sahib again, nut out a visit to the factory to see the tandoors. But he didn't care any more. So the bastard has come back, he thought. So? It's like this damn boom, what does it mean? All it means is everyone gets excited and screws everyone else for whatever they can get.

Khalid then recalled what Mahfouz the Spitting-bearer had told him the morning after the newspaper story was passed around. Shouted was more like it. Shouting about independence.

'See what I mean?' Mahfouz had growled as he hit the paper with the back of his hand. 'This is the cunning sweetness these people rub in our faces! You, with all your stupid feelings—you should have feelings for yourself this time! If you come to our meetings you'll see what is happening these days. My uncle will tell it. He says even the Karachi bastards have to be kicked out ... do you know what that is called? You do not even know! It is called yandee-pandence! This teahouse, it is ours. That river? Ours! Those hills? You are just like everyone else who thinks these people are all right. This bastard has stolen your tandoor, and you are lying down like a dog waiting to be washed away into the drains and out to the sea!'

A boy wiping up tables came along. Khalid asked him

to run downstairs and fetch two drinks. He gave the boy a note and told him to keep the change.

Then Khalid continued. 'They made a damn smart ploy to pass it on to the President-bastard.'

In his quiet way Ajit Mookerjee agreed. He accepted that their slinging of a sahib such as the President into the plan had made things difficult. If they had taken it by themselves, the matter might have been dealt with in a single night.

Mookerjee then said, 'Zeythi is talking like a mynah bird.'

'What do you mean?'

'You are planning to break into the factory. Is this true?'

'No, it is not. You think I'm stupid?'

'If you do that, you will be ridiculed and finished by everybody—if that gigantic Karachi chowkeedar doesn't hammer you first.'

'I am not thinking any such thing. I am going to Dacca, that's all.'

'That's another worry. I know Dacca ... it is a cesspool,' the gardener said gently.

'How can you say such a thing? You were born there, no?'

'Yah, but that morning made no difference to it.'

'Dacca is a city of opportunity, the boom is better there.'

The gardener then felt he ought to give Khalid a small picture of Dacca. In a measured, relaxed way he described the city.

'You will find nothing there but the biggest jungle of all. Inside Dacca, outside Dacca, around Dacca, you cannot escape. To eat you will pay three times as much.

Sleep you will take on the roadside in a wooden box. Nothing like the luxury of your quarters at the house.'

'My place? My place is not good.'

'Your place is very good. Wait and see.'

'Well, the sahib will give me references to the Dacca sahibs.'

'Yah he will, he is a good man. But in Dacca for every fellow like you there are another thousand. They come from everywhere. From far, far places. Right in the north as far as Rangpur, and right in the south from Patuakhali and further past us down in Cox's Bazaar. There are guys in Dacca from inside India too. Calcutta and places like that, big damn places. You know of Varanasi?'

'I have heard of it.'

'One hundred Chittagongs. Patna?'

'Yah.'

'Also damn big. There are guys from Bhutan and even Nepal. All why? All chasing the boom Khalid, like you. The place is crawling with guys looking looking. Searching for gold. And with the rains coming any minute, Dacca, well, you don't want to know. These guys are not travelling to a new beginning, they are walking to the oldest khuttum. Every year, same thing, thousands.'

Then he thought he would offer Khalid an alternative, rather than simply blocking the cook's urges.

'If you have to leave us behind for the boom, then Karachi is the place. Karachi is a big filthy mess too, but most of the money gets thrown at it. That is what my sahib says all the time, and we should take his word for it.'

'How can I afford to go to Karachi?'

'Stay here a while more, until after the monsoon, and save up. Then the sahib can tip some in. Maybe me and

Iqbal can put in a bit more. Have you ever been in the sky in an aeroplane?'

'Yah, that time to Lahore with the memsahib.'

'Then?'

'It is too costly.'

'Consider this,' Mookerjee insisted gently, 'it is Dacca that is too costly.'

Khalid remained silent. He cast his gaze at the young women lashing the clothing. Under the absent sun their figures were wet and shining.

'Let us make a wager,' the gardener started afresh. 'If one of them removes her clothes to take a wash, Iqbal and I will help you go to Dacca.'

Khalid looked into the gardener's eyes and gave him an empty smile.

The boy returned with the drinks and then continued hitting tables with a cloth.

They sat in quiet in the vague sun. It was a stupid idea for a wager on the subject, that Mookerjee admitted to himself right away, though he made it to attempt to brighten the afternoon. They never remove their things down there, ever. Though the opposite is true too, in a sense. With the first rain, he knew, comes the crushing jumping up and down, the joy, the happiness, the carefree abandon with the closing of schools and offices. And then, Mookerjee thought, as it is every season, lovers take to their beds; maybe people *want* to fling off their clothes outside. With extended reasoning, Mookerjee also thought that if Khalid took the wager loosely, like a warm wind high on a mango tree, the monsoon would arrive before he could depart.

But on the subject of his mission, which he did just as much for himself as he did at Zeythi's pleading,

Mookerjee was uncertain if he had failed or succeeded. Well, he'd given it a try. And Khalid was, after all, Khalid. Stubborn. Maybe, thought the older young man, just maybe, one day the guy will learn. Iqbal is right. It will not succeed, this attempt at holding back the mountain goat. Still, what a terrific idea, that tandoor. It'll catch on like paan, so how to blame the guy for his frustration? Make the curves go inward. Damn nifty. Who the heck would have thought such a thing? The ayah will be disappointed. More disappointed than this guy realises. He will find out for himself. Who am I to tell him?

The sabjantawallah shuffled along, and with a humming sound he said, 'Dacca will finish many men … khuttum khuttum.'

Mookerjee then suggested a plate of biryani to share. Khalid agreed, and they sat a while longer, making forecasts on the arrival of the rains. The light of the afternoon ruffled on the slow water below the balcony, and the women lashed the washing against the golden boulders.

Letters in the Wind

Zeythi swept the last of it clean. The dust found the black shine of her hair. She then emptied a bucket of water across the steps.

'Yah thank you,' Khalid said as it wet the legs of his shalwar kameez.

'What are you doing standing there like a ghost? Ajit is looking for you.'

'I have just seen him.'

'Iqbal is looking for you also.'

'That is what I want to talk about,' Khalid said. 'Come, let's sit under the trees.'

'We can sit here,' she said dismissively.

'It is wet.'

'Okay, we can stand.'

Khalid did not move. He looked at her a long while. What had done it he did not know, but she no longer looked like the gangly girl who stood on the step that first day. The hotel of moans in the night, he thought. He liked it, that clear and direct sense. But now look at the legs. And the swelling breasts. She is beautiful. Very beautiful.

'Well?' she said, head tilted, one eye shut.

'I am arranging something with Iqbal.'

'You have been arranging things for many days, I do not know what is left to arrange.'

'I want him to let you and me send as many letters as we want.'

'I do not want to send any letters.'

'Yes, I thought you might say such a thing. So there is another arrangement.'

'You will miss all this arranging.'

'I want him to let you send as many letters as you want to your umma.'

She immediately fell silent and walked off.

'Zeythi!' Khalid called quietly.

She continued to the back gate.

'Zeythi! What is wrong?' He caught up with her and he held her arm.

There was a strange gaze in her eye. And the beauty, he suddenly realised, had vanished. It was a void he was looking into.

'Zeythi?'

'What,' she said. She gazed past him. Through the braiding of the shalwar kameez at his chest.

'You want to send your umma these letters? Iqbal is saying he will do them any time, for no charge.'

'My umma died.'

Khalid stood still a while.

'When?'

'Before I came here,' she stated.

Khalid stumbled backwards. It took a few seconds, but he collapsed on the hard dirt.

She gazed at him as he lay on the dirt. She carried the bucket to the laundry and filled it again in order to clean the steps at the front verandah.

'Iqbal?'

'Yes?'

'Do you remember that?'

'Yes. But I only found out much later. If I knew, maybe I could have helped, but she was just putting those letters all summer into the postbox. Putting enough to make somebody sick of putting.'

Plastic Boots

In my position you do not suggest what might have been. Looking back into those hollow days I see endless fingers twitching back and forth like a march of so many teachers telling us more stuff we already know. Too late, we sigh.

But it's true enough; consider the regrets. Recall the warm, open face of that dear friend at your side. And what about the many times the upturned palm of trust was held out? I am tight-lipped about these easy contrivances, for they comfort nobody and annoy almost everybody.

Every mistake is put back and put right by the invisible hand of hindsight. Name it. The teahouse, now a relic held up only by vines, 'should' have been built properly at the start. This is a place of terrible monsoons. The builder, the Athenian, though he knew how to grease the pockets of councillors, was maybe short on the techniques of raising a stable bungalow of two storeys on the bank of the stream along which Khalid chased the figure into the guava grove of headstones.

Or take the tandoor. Khalid 'should' never have shown it to Mohendra the chickenwallah.

See? Easy as pakoras, is it not? Chuck them in with your eyes closed, they come up golden.

Or take the President. He 'should' have avoided the bushes behind the big cement water tank.

Or take Zeythi, beautiful Zeythi; what happened in the banana grove when she screamed on the high, dusty air and bit the Minisahib's shoulder, growled, ran deep into the jungle at the back of the house—sending his heart into a wild panic? What 'should' she have Not Done?

She liked the Minisahib, he was fun and games. But her feelings for Khalid were different. And did she finally tell her mother in those letters that went nowhere?

It is too convenient, this petty insight. Hindsight insight. So my apologies, but there is one remark I cannot avoid. It is this. Khalid should never have got on that bus. And that's the damn truth of it. I don't care how slackly simple it is to say in hindsight.

Khalid fastened his bicycle to the roof of the small bus, took a seat up the back for which he paid good money, jammed the plastic boots securely between the metal skin and the torn seat, and felt the exhaust under his feet shudder and roar to life. Through the window the faces of Iqbal, Ajit Mookerjee, Lall Thankee, Leila Ghosh and Aranthi the potterywallah slid away. Faces only, no twiddling fingers.

The hands belonging to these friends had done the opposite. Iqbal had smiled and held out to him the whereabouts of a letterwriter who would not charge the full price; inside the envelope Iqbal had also placed a few rupees.

'Let us know how you get along,' he said. He smiled and stepped backwards.

Ajit Mookerjee had given him a new shirt 'for presenting' himself. Lall handed him a watch. Aranthi had wanted to give him a fresh tandoor she had made, and she lugged it to the bus, but Khalid declined, as wistful Mookerjee said he would, so she gave him the backup, a hefty lock for his bicycle. And Leila Ghosh presented him with a pair of black plastic boots.

'In Dacca,' she said, 'with the rains, you will see these are very useful.'

'I will look stupid,' he protested.

She said, 'In Dacca everybody looks stupid and nobody will notice.'

These last moments, the giving of thoughtful gifts, were the bumbling expression of inevitability. Nobody at the bus would mention them. Not for a while, not until some work had been done, when their hands had helped them to forget.

At the house the Minisahib had asked the simplest of questions. 'Is he going for a long time?'

'Yah,' Zeythi said from a dry throat.

Khalid tied off the bundle of clothing to the raft. The Minisahib and Zeythi looked like a pair of monkeys on the laundry wall. Big-eyed confusion. Above their heads the mangosteen swayed in the breeze. The tap by their dangling feet dripped its warm spit to the thirsty dirt.

'How long?' the Minisahib persisted, 'forever?'

'Yah,' she said with a vacant gaze. She would have said yes to anything this afternoon, it was the easiest automatic no-thinking thing to utter.

This was the afternoon where everything changed, and she knew it had. This time there was no knowing.

Perhaps she was saying, 'Take another thing away. Yes, take.'

Khalid continued to exert himself with the rope,

strangling the bundle. It was like he was wrestling the bicycle, the raft, the clothes and the rope as a single beast. The cleaning he applied to his quarters too had been a battle. The hollow shell containing just the jute-slung bed frame with the mattress rolled at the end. The window where he had many times wiped his hands after thinking of naked Leilas. The washed and scrubbed cement floor. These were the exertions of a resisting heart. A counteracting will. And the friction, it left no visible trace. The markless surfaces of unseen arrivals and forgotten departures.

The household was taken by surprise. In a typically busy day they came and went from the kitchen to see him off, bringing good wishes and strings of good advice. Towards the conclusion of the morning, the memsahib presented him with an envelope, and for a moment she held the young man in a warm embrace. She then asked him to go to the front verandah. Go. Often it was used: go; people said it like others say hello. It was not any kind of badness. She remained in the kitchen, staring with moist eyes from the window. It was bullshit. Go really did mean go. She began to shake, and she went to the door and closed it.

The Old Man, Khalid thought, comfortable on his bamboo lounge chair of worn green cushions.

He sat tapping a finger on the polished curve of the armrest. It was a known habit. Household legend insisted he sang a tune. Sinatra, Jones too he didn't mind. Khalid hadn't heard of Frank Sinatra or Tom Jones, but he was sly enough to know that the Old Man was not following a tune. No fool, was the Old Man.

Khalid knew the Old Man was thinking serious things. Matters to push the future. Just like a sneaky sage, Khalid thought, like that other sage, Zeythi.

In the old days, nobody had imagined for a second that the new cook had a small number on the Old Man, but he did. Khalid came to know the sahib better than most. Tune like hell, Khalid thought, the Old Man's got something to say.

The finger bones under the skin of crinkled yarns and snooker shots. Seeking rhythms. And hopes for the country. 'The country?' the Old Man would say at discussions at the club. 'You ask about this place? Very simple,' he'd reply at the card table. 'A time to bring our people to the table where they can shuffle the cards and choose the aces. Jute. Fish. Hydro-electric. Rice. Whatever. Just bring them to the table.'

Three monsoons past, when Khalid had first arrived at the house fresh, like Zeythi, the Old Man had put him to tasks that had no bearing on matters cooking. Initially, sheer bemusement. Extremely busy with the new job, but confused okay.

The cook would think, For what am I measuring the kitchen floor?

The Old Man would return a few minutes later, 'So, how big is the kitchen?'

'Two hundred square feet, sahib.'

And, for what am I counting these mangos on this damn tree?

'So? How much for the lot?'

'Ten rupees, sahib.'

It went on and on, all manner of puzzles and calculations, a riddle, local geography, and it had only ceased weeks later when the Old Man had secured the cook a place in the polytechnic the following term.

But that had been many seasons in the past.

Khalid emerged on the verandah. The Old Man's eyes were shut, head was laid back, crinkled fingers tapped the polished bamboo.

Then a sudden cry from the road, so loud it was a scream. But it was wild sarcasm.

The Spitting-bearer riding past: 'K-H-A-L-I-D! FILTHY DOG! RUN FAR …!'

And his voice trailed off as he rode on.

The Old Man opened his eyes. The fingers tapped to a stop.

'Who was that?'

'Nobody, sahib.'

'He tries that one more time—you tell him—he will actually be a nobody.'

'Yes, sahib.'

'Well then. Take a seat.'

'Thank you.'

'Now listen. I cannot stop you from going. Dacca is a very important place for a young man. It is full of opportunity. You will meet new friends. Sometimes you can even meet worthwhile buggers who can show you how to make progress into the world. You can meet these types by working at pukka hotels, restaurants, even at some of the big roadside eating houses. But there is one thing you are doing that is not right. I have been thinking about this since the day you gave memsahib your notice. Do you know what it is?'

'Yes.'

'Good. What are you going to do about it?'

'I can maybe take more schooling some other time.'

'Some other time never comes. When it comes, you will say "some other time, soon".'

'Then maybe,' Khalid said with lame reasoning, 'I can

find a polytechnic.'

'And then? When you find this polytechnic?'

'Then classes.'

'Just like that.'

'No, first I'll ask them.'

'Here … I have a reference for you. Two actually. One is for the hotels and one is for my friend, who might be able to offer you work from his friends. What is wrong? Take it.'

'Thank you, sahib.'

'And this. It contains your results from the past year. Go to the Dacca Polytechnic—here is the address—and give it to the main office. Tell them you studied at the Chittagong Polytechnic, tell them this when you give them the letter otherwise the dumb bastard in the main office will just let it sit on a shelf for the whole year collecting a touch and a look every month.'

The Old Man settled into the comfortable lounge chair. He looked out over the garden and at the mango tree in the corner near the road. He saw the day he had the cook counting the fruit. Bright new whites under the shade. Peering into the tree. Had the boy really counted the mangos? he wondered. Probably. Knowing him now, his fastidiousness, it would seem right that he missed not a single mango.

It suddenly seemed to the Old Man so very long ago, and it seemed like last week too. He then took a moment to consider the cook. Rambling thoughts on the hot verandah. From the kitchen, he thought, out came the boy's peculiar cheer. And his radio, that stupid bloody radio. Very good. His intelligence was a promising glow to behold. Also, he is a damn okay cook. And on top of all that, he is honest, generally—well, except the embarrassing copy of Reid's new tandoor. Though, that's an ugly problem? Not at all, it's just the sort of caper you put down to youthful exuberance; and that stung long ago, forgotten. Plus he has learned a good lesson from it. Besides, he'll need all of that exuberance and more if he's to get along in Dacca. The Stevensons will probably help him out when they see my letter. Hope so. Stevenson owes me a couple of favours if he hasn't gone off into a gin bottle and forgotten. Mind you, this young bastard is a resourceful piece of work, so if he gets a hand from Stevenson, it's a bonus. Shitty old Dacca, eh? What these young people see in the place, I have no idea. We shall miss this fine young man. I will at least. And Elanor will too, very much.

Khalid and the Old Man talked about the way the sky was turning today, and the good breeze that had come up from the bay. Soon the frogs would be out in great numbers, and the geckos too, which would fatten on the insects into a white finger.

But it was the Minisahib and Zeythi who were like belly-up guppies. They said nothing. Did nothing. The Minisahib didn't know if he should stun the pond for a short while. Or walk into the grove. Or get on the bike and cross the field to the cows. He had to stay and wait, but staying made him feel agitated.

Zeythi simply sat on the laundry wall looking at the hills. The bicycle, packed, ready, leaned against the trunk of the mangosteen, didn't bear looking at any longer.

'Where is he?' the Minisahib asked.

'He is still at the front.'

'What is he doing?'

'Why don't you go and see,' Zeythi said flatly.

The Minisahib sat annoyed. He dropped from the low

wall and crossed the dry compound. He climbed the money plant to the wall where he sat to get a better view of things. There was nothing to view, he discovered, but he sat in the leaves anyway. Beside him lay an empty bottle. He tossed it up in the air and wondered if it would come down on one of the cows.

Khalid collected the bicycle. He took hold of the bundle on the handlebars, gave it a shake and then walked the handlebars across the compound.

The Minisahib and Zeythi followed him up the side of the house to the driveway.

The Old Man and the Old Woman stood on the verandah with two daughters and a son. The others were at work. One tended business in Karachi. A daughter and the son came out to stand on the lawn.

Up on the road Khalid swung his leg over the bike and rode off.

The Minisahib waved. He became very quiet and started trembling. Zeythi stood beside the Minisahib.

Khalid rode along the fence, made a wave to the verandah, and he then stood up to get the pedals going. When he was a long way off, a fleck, the Minisahib waved again.

That night the Minisahib followed his mother around the house. Finally, he fell asleep in her bed by the broken pane.

The Biggest Hand in the World

Khalid should not have gone. The bus was an old fly trap that had been riding up and down the delta for more years than anyone could remember. It would climb the country along the coast and then cut across the eastern section of the delta rattling dangerous bridges at every turn, and then start a final run up the estuary where it would roll into Dacca along the last leg of a northern loop of great hope.

Salt had fed on the skin, etching holes up the wheels. The roof-rack, stuck as it was to this net of rust, swung heavily from side to side. New joins met old joins, and new skin met old skin over the surface thanks to the owner-driver's skill with an antique oxywelder. Before him, his father had operated the old Leyland. One was an optimist, the other a pessimist. That's how they were known back in my time, the Laugher and the Lamenter. So with both ends of life taken care of, there was no way the bus would be given up on a whim. What can be fixed will be fixed and refixed. What must be fixed must be fixed and refixed. Twice they remade the motor. All kinds of things had once snapped, including the crankshaft, and he and his father, along with labouring help, took the thing apart, had a new crankshaft machined at the polytechnic, cleaned everything else, new piston rings while they were at it, tappets too, and put it back together.

'Missed two journeys only,' claimed the Laugher.

'Lost two whole damn journeys,' claimed the Lamenter.

The bus station, to look at it, implied plenty. An overflow of hawkers spilled from the iron uprights to the surrounding clearing. With the season soon, this would be one of the last remaining journeys considered reliable.

Smart people are smart people. Tickets were changing hands many times. Iqbal knew the driver, and so Khalid had no trouble. He climbed down from the roof where he tied off his bicycle.

He stood with Leila and the others. They embraced, shook hands; Leila placed a soft kiss to his cheek, and her neck grew hotter than she'd known it could go, and then Khalid was sitting up the back with the plastic boots. The kiss had gone straight to his groin, and it was still there, not soft, as he sat watching her eyes slide away.

It was a ship of men with a destination. Family men in pursuit of work, and single men in search of the glittering future the whole country talked about, and men who knew nothing. Thin, snaking roads full of holes, that's all. Fairways that were entrances to something new.

When the bus began to move away, the crowd stirred. Children in the arms of their mothers, young women with set, stern faces, unbelieving; others hoping. A small group of roaming boys began to cheer and give dust-bursting chase. One caught hold of a window as he lifted powdered legs into the air. Men whooped high calls of triumph. Other men rolled sober heads from side to side. Four men slipped from the corrugated roof down to the load on the bus. One fell over the side to the hard dirt road.

Khalid took no real notice of the commotion. On a seat nearby, a man clutched his hands in his knees and sobbed.

Khalid gazed out the window; he thought nothing, or thought too many things so that they cancelled out and gave him a deep numbness. Not even the word 'Dacca' entered his oiled head. He sat in a stagnant heap, tired from the effort of the last few days, the plans, and, say it, the sadness. He just sat. Leaned against the black boots. Leila that damn beautiful.

But with no warning, with a sudden blink, he caught sight of the figure. Over the top of the moving crowd, clear on an oil drum at the last rusting post, the figure stood leaning against the iron. Khalid made a quick effort to get up, but the wall of hope, and the man who sobbed, could not be moved aside.

The figure's head turned on Khalid's window. As the bus moved off, his insolent arms were motionless, casually folded. But the invisible gaze, it moved to stay fixed on Khalid's.

The bus was away. Clattering and belching over the hard dirt and then joining the road. Destination: that vast hand gripping the shifting delta. Dacca.

He settled back into the seat. He felt something pressing into his side at the shirt pocket. He twisted round and was able to draw it out to the bad light.

Her big, dark eyes full of life and laughter. The silver ring glinting at her nose. Sitting with her hands flat by her side, the golden fingers telling the cement what a shit dull dead thing it is. And there was himself, sitting on the laundry wall beside her shoulder. The early days, before the swimming pool. It was the one photo she must have saved. She must have taken this plastic ache around all the time. She must have slipped it into his shirt that morning, when he laid the shalwar kameez on the empty jute.

All this time she has been sending those letters to nobody? This, thought the cook, cannot be so. The bus broke a flock of chickens in two. It ploughed up the hill and into the dusty distance.

The cook was now hollow.

He felt tired. In his hand, she kept him awake. Hollow Khalid as he played with that photo. He didn't know anything. He was alive. But what did the guy know?

He slept for the first time in many years like a baby boy. Here he was, a young man, embarking on a journey. He dreamed of Zeythi. He loved her and she loved him. He made love to her like a film star makes love.

Rain

The Minisahib was feeding guppies and his ear caught a light pit! pit-pit! on the dust. Inside two simple minutes it fell so hard that he couldn't see the kitchen windows.

Fish're dry, he thought in a satisfied way. They were dry because he placed a small table over the tank. It was like a roof past the edges. His 'friend and guide' had reminded him about the table and the roof.

Last year, the Minisahib had forgotten altogether. It had not been the decay of the summer heat—all things wore the crease of neglect. It was something much simpler: he had half reasoned that fish and water go together. But the open tank had filled, taken a pounding, and in the overflow he lost the guppies.

He stood on the top step, in the worn curve of cement, and looked in amazement down to his toe.

'Got me good and proper,' he murmured. The new shoes he'd worn into town, the shirt, everything.

He decided: 'But the table's sitting over the tank now.'

He looked up. The drumming of it was furious. Hitting the house, it seemed like stones. Lashing the invisible trees, it seemed like the hissing of uncountable cobras.

Halfway down the compound he could barely see Khalid's quarters. Although it was no longer

Khalid's—was now occupied by another guy—he still called it Khalid's place.

Streams formed immediately and they flowed away from the house.

In the bedroom he found a pair of dry shorts and a shirt. He jumped onto the bed to applaud, but a burst of wind hit the window, clapping shut a pane so that it smashed to the floor of the room.

Then he heard shouts on the road. He jumped off the bed and ran to the front verandah.

Half the household was there. He had to push aside their fat thighs. He could see only the gauze of rain, but behind the hissing he could hear high screams. Invisible voices in the downpour. Thin voices that arrived across the rain to seem like far-away children. They were on their way to the teahouse. Revellers; downstairs, upstairs, and the teahouse balcony would tilt under the weight. From the two holes, the water would pour in long curves to the stream.

An invisible voice called out, 'Hoi …!'

'What?'

'Come and dance!'

'Get your filthy hands off my bicycle!'

'Don't be a fool—come and dance with us!'

'Let him go—he's got all that stuff on his bike!'

Rejoicing the rain. Strangers shouting the miracle of the monsoon.

Then, from the gateposts, a faint figure emerged on a bicycle, and he coasted down the driveway with a load from the bazaar. The new cook rode past the verandah down the side of the house.

It would not be long before the abatement. A lull. Dormant summer corners would bring out peacocks and scorpions. Snakes and frogs would emerge. Mosquitoes would whine at the ear only to feed on the ankle, replace the summer dust. The first rain would stop for quick outings and picnics. Up to the hills maybe, to the lake, or to the flattened beach. And the compound never shifted.

To look upon it now, I see beyond the compound. I see the peaks shifting, like Everest.

On the plains, after the early-summer flowering of the flame of the forest, the silk cotton, the grand gulmohur and then the bright gold of the laburnum, after the bloom, their bare wrists reach for the peaks. Then the summer sun ignites the scrub, and fires lick valleys and thirsty jungle burns the fingers from hands of so-called ignorance. The children, playing, are stung into the newspaper as charred sticks. One American newspaper-wallah went back to his bungalow in a place called Long Island—what a pathetic thing to call any island—and showed his friends his snapshots and told them stories of the dead children. He became a hero. Even after the fires expire, the heat of the summer continues, shifting the peaks. Bringing the melt down Bhutan's seated knees, along the Amo river, the Sankosh and the Manas. If I meander back up the Brahmaputra into China and then into Lhasa in Tibet and beyond, there I shall find the summer sun working on the peaks. Shifting the sharp edges. And up behind Darjeeling there's the melt into the purple Tista. There are thousands of peaks. Shifting into a net of streams. They join at the Ganga and the Jamuna to again disperse over the delta. Remaking the Sundarbans into yet another bold and sparkling image of itself.

If Iqbal worked in Lhasa, he could put a letter in a cigarette tin and glue the lid tight. Out strolling one evening at late sunset, he could place it in clear shallows at the bank of the stream. To the inch, so that the glow of the stones and the shine of the small fish that hover, seize his attention for a moment. The tin would then journey into the Brahmaputra and curl across the upper plateau, veering down into India and then into the Jamuna in East Pakistan where it later roams the churning whirlpools of the Padma. By now it would be filtering through the great float of many other objects, and it would slide up on a wash and scrape to the beach at Kaptai, and Ramza the squid catcher could have carried it to Khalid before he left. On the cracking teahouse balcony the cook would cut open the set glue. When he lifted the lid, the tin would reveal a folded note, crisp as it once was in the dry air of Tibet. It would read:

Hello Khalid,

What are you up to these days? Still trying to invent that new tandoor you dream of? I know one day it will bring you great happiness. But if you are not too busy sorting it out, come up for a drink. Summertime is best up here.

Your friend,
Iqbal.

It is not too fanciful. The ink from Iqbal's pen has travelled far. He once posted a customer's letter to a Pakistani worker in Johannesburg. Another to Entebbe in Uganda. Unlikely towns in which to find an industrious Pakistani. But the letters were to distant relatives rumoured to be doing very salty capers in their new lands, mainly with vibrant shops.

Tumbling harmlessly over glowing stones, and then

crashing down the rugged slopes over boulders to seek the roaming plains, the shifting peaks bring quiet messages and invitations.

The baking summer brings the shifting snows; and then the monsoon brings the rain of twenty worlds.

The Transistor Radio

Zeythi felt lonely. She searched for something to do that might cause the ache to go away, but she finished up doing the same thing she always did when she felt the dull pain: she went to find a window to check on the rumour about grunting less hard. Why did she always do this? Maybe it handed back the days when her mother and father were alive and grunting in the next room. Iqbal says he has heard of a German sabjantawallah, someone called Froyd, who would give the opinion that there is nothing unusual in Zeythi's habit.

She drew out Khalid's radio from under the bed. She flicked the switch, but she could hear only a scratching sound behind the hammering rain on the tin roof. She turned off the radio and placed it on the sheet. She moved away from it.

She brought out the fish skull. The brass eyes had turned the colour of an old shirt. She decided to use the Brasso tomorrow to shine them up.

She sat up for an hour under the fall of rain. Kutubdia, she decided, I will go to the island.

The drumming of the rain softened. Darkness was filling the compound, so she walked up the road to the President-sahib's bungalow to see if she could find the

President's wife and the Theatre-sahib.

At the bungalow she waited under the window for a long while. When they came in Zeythi heard the clinking of glass. Zeythi edged up to the sill. They had brought in wine and food. They discarded these on the floor near the bed and started to undress. The sahib stood by the bed naked. The memsahib sat on the bed. She scooped up a blob from a tin of ghee and started to slide her hand over the sahib's penis. At first the low breathing and the noiseless movements told Zeythi the same thing as always: they grunt like they live; soft, fine, smooth, pukka, useless. But when the noise started it gave Zeythi a fright. He started to grunt like a big dog. Then huge sounds burst from him. Then he was shouting. 'Arh! ... A rggh! ... fa ... fa ... faaack, ack, ack!'

Zeythi quickly hid under the window, her eyes popped from her head like marbles. She was breathing heavily and scared that the town would appear from round the corners of the bungalow. She lowered herself into the hibiscus and lay on the wet ground very still. She then heard quiet words.

'What happened?' the sahib said.

'You squirted into the samosas,' the President's wife said.

Zeythi crawled away and then ran off. Yah, she thought as she ran into the night, the stupid rumour is false.

Rehearsal

In the club hall the President's wife and the Theatre-sahib took a short break.

'I'm worried!' she whispered urgently.

'Let's talk outside,' he said.

He was burning with a kind of heat. She put it down to the rehearsal, but he burned with a dark determination.

'I'm very worried,' she insisted. 'I had no idea you were putting on this damn oven business. You told me it was a play about a frustrated engineer!'

'I thought you didn't care what the boss thinks,' he said without altering his walk.

They crossed into the corridor to the front verandah. They passed by Fatimah Westcott sitting comfortably at a table with hopeful Abdul and others. Fatimah's arms flowed over the clammy imagination of the whole table, but she loved the warmth of the night rain.

'Hello Catherine,' she called with confidence. Fatimah and the President's wife had talked the previous night plenty about their lovers. Exchanging notes without the slightest care.

'Hello Fatimah.'

'How's the play coming along, Brian?' Abdul asked.

'Very well thanks.'

'Opening tomorrow night still?' Abdul asked.

'Yes, we open tomorrow night.'

'Terrific, I look forward to it,' Abdul said.

They continued down the verandah and found an isolated table around the corner.

'Don't worry,' he said finally. 'All that I've done is to include what you told me at the lake.'

'But they were just dreams.'

'Then why worry?'

'Tomorrow night he will dutifully come along, watch the damn thing, and the next day he will quietly sack you. I don't know where you have put your mind.'

'That doesn't matter anymore. I resigned, it's all finished. After the show, we clean things up and then we're off.'

'Oh lovely, a little visit to the lake.'

'No. To Bristol. I collected the tickets this afternoon.'

A bearer appeared, and the Theatre-sahib ordered a light supper of sandwiches.

'Cheese and chicken?' he asked his baby-talc lover.

'I don't feel like eating.'

'One cheese and chicken please. And one gin and tonic.'

The bearer tilted his head and moved off. His eye remained for a minute, but he moved off.

The President's wife looked into the almond trees. The rain had returned a deep shine to the leaves, and they looked healthy.

If the Rain carries Whispers

Abdul was always proud to introduce himself as 'A Bengali yes, but a Bengali who possesses an international backside. I don't mind where I sit as long as I can watch the world go by and take a gin and tonic, see?'

'Have you heard,' he muttered, 'what the cabinet in Karachi is proposing for flood plans?'

'No, I haven't,' said Fatimah Westcott.

'I can't stand these people,' Abdul said. 'Running the country from their spooky little corridors in government house. Buggers. In fact, I hate their guts totally.'

'I did too, once. A long time ago.'

'And what is your opinion now?'

'My feeling is pity.'

'Pity? You exaggerate,' Abdul scoffed good-naturedly, and he finished his drink.

'No, I do not. Consider: do they live their lives in the world? They miss out on the ragged detail of actual people going about their ordinary business. They see a kind of country, but a textureless country. They fail to sight a hawker handing a fellow his paan and receiving his due annas for it. Or some poor damn cook who makes a new tandoor.'

'That boy is my student, he simply copied it from

Roger's factory. Let's get back to these dogs in Karachi—Fatimah, I had no idea you are innocent to this extent. Foolish, foolish.'

'Yes,' she said with a smile, 'to be entering into formless generalising with you up here, when I could be relaxing by the pool being waited upon by that delicious bearer. Very foolish.'

'Take me seriously, please. It has become a terrible world. What happened to the days when it was a life's work to aspire to the condition of truth? Nowadays all we get are these greasy buggers aspiring to the condition of corporation.'

'I'll let you on to something, Abdul. No man is more given to generalising than a teacher, how's that for a useless generalisation?'

'You want a proper generalisation? A true one? All Karachi people smell of carbon-copy paper. In fact, all Karachi people simply smell.' The teacher paused a moment. 'Stinking buggers.' He paused again. 'Especially this guy.'

'Which guy?'

'This flood-plan fellow.'

'Him? Oh he just talks a lot of rot.'

'I hope he rots in his own ignorance.'

'It is not ignorance which he has. I've met him. He is full of hatred.'

'Yah, I hope he rots in hatred too. Like another drink?'

'No, thanks. I'll be off now to take a swim.'

'But it's raining.'

'Yes.'

'I must admit, Fatimah,' Abdul said with a sudden secrecy, 'if you do not mind, I quite like you.'

'Yes, it certainly sounds like you do.'

'What about me? What will I do?'

'Work, Abdul, a bit of work. Work inspires me to the pool—it'll make you wish to swim also.'

Fatimah Westcott stood, giving the chair a natural heave with an easy movement.

'You are deserting me?'

'I am letting you go, yes.' She smiled and walked off down the verandah. Everything she wore swayed in the wet breeze.

'See you at the play!' he called.

She waved and continued walking.

He looked on, and when she was far enough away, he said quietly, 'I am a Bengali, with an international pung-goo.'

He sighed and looked back down to the paper.

The Play

It put a scent up Fatimah Westcott's nose. What to do?

Over many monsoons the sahibs played in the club hall a lot. They played cards, they danced and they sat to watch plays. But if you came in from Karachi and you went bounding round the club looking for excitement, and nothing was on, you'd stand at the door looking into a dowdy brown box. A sparrow might flick from the beams, and you'd sigh: 'This rotten damn Chittagong … what a dump.'

The plays were done by a loyal group of amateurs. For the love of it alone. Any play, it didn't really matter. The cards and the dances could get lost, it was the play that counted.

But Fatimah Westcott? She kept a distance, she was never dipping her nose into a play. Though this time the scent was too sharp. Reminiscent.

For the loyal few, it was the involvement, the complexity, the excitement as it drew nearer—loomed, like a one-eyed monster. The jiggery-pokery put an edge on the dull days. They tasted a hint of danger, a pleasurable kind of safe danger. Which they all liked, especially the stage manager.

Some years the vigour would fade. The enthusiasts

had to settle for one production, other years the hall would creak with two. In their shared confidence, the loyal knot took it for granted that everyone in the club looked forward to opening night, and mostly the shows were said to be fine and intelligent.

Not everyone went to the Theatre-sahib's show, but then not everyone took a dip in the pool either. The stage manager didn't care. Most of her toughness was located in her thin blue lips and big grey eyes. At the opening of the Theatre-sahib's play, a visiting soccer team jammed the front bar, and the captain was invited to the show by the stage manager, but his team declined and laughed, and they were dismissed as louts.

'To be left at the bar,' the stage manager declared to the cast and crew.

'Not even one?' the Theatre-sahib said.

'Beggars,' she snapped. Her brittle lips said it with a puff.

'They're just going to drink at the bloody bar all night?'

'Filthy Birmingham beggars,' the stage manager said. And she called curtain. She had a thundering voice.

The audience began to arrive at the door, a trickle. And then a good number began to appear, a promising start.

Abdul arrived in good spirits. He had closed the class because of the downpour. Fatimah Westcott wore a brightly coloured sari and flat slippers. The Old Man and Old Woman took a seat three rows from the stage. The President and his wife took good seats. The Irishman, the Sikh, and the Mayor with his wife also showed up. Everyone was cheerful. Small talk revolved round the power of the first rain. The Australian Consul had long since departed for his home town of Mandurah. A pity.

The only bastard who tried hard to lay down the truth about the tandoor.

But there was still Khalid's ally sitting in the chair next to her husband, and the fiddling with her dreams of innocence. And the scent up Fatimah's nose.

The lights were brought down, and the Theatre-sahib took a position on the stage before the curtain went up. Standing in a circle of light, he offered the audience a word of introduction.

'Good evening ladies and gentlemen. This play is about virtues, about their delicate nature, and about how easy it is to convince your friends that anything is a virtue, anything at all. I began work on the text weeks ago and completed it on a break from the office during a peaceful sojourn at the lake. It was a very enjoyable play to write. I hope you enjoy it too. The cast has worked hard to bring the characters to life for us tonight, so please offer them a big hand—and I bid you welcome to *A Valuable Virtue*.'

As the hall dropped into darkness the audience erupted in applause.

Fatimah Westcott found a good seat alone. Nil obstruction, set apart, at the back. This promises interest, she decided. She crossed her legs, scratched the bridge of her nose, and placed her chin into the heel of her hand. Sounds like a lot of work but it's natural if you look at it: a large settle-to which the Jordanian trader always liked. Talk to her, she did the same thing more or less. Give her a smile, she undid all that. Be suggestive, she slapped you hard, twice. International pung-goo or no. Even if you were joking, which you were not; not Abdul anyway. French husband. In Paris slaps are like kisses, she'd say with a languid wipe of her mouth.

When the lights came on, a Bengali cook stirred a pot on a stove. He was played by the Yorkshire doctor who also helped out with inoculations at the small premises of the World Health Organisation. He whistled as he stirred the pot. He poured a bit more imaginary water into the pot, and continued stirring.

Iqbal saw the play. He called in a favour from one of the bearers, and he stood quietly up the back in the humid darkness, far behind Fatimah Westcott. He informed me it did not display anything about the tandoor he did not already know. He said it was a bit stupid, and that there was no mistaking it came from the hand of a concerned foreigner. In parts he found it amusing.

'Staggering dumbness,' he said to me. 'If you like it,' he added, 'nothing wrong.'

The cook designs a tandoori oven shaped in the 'wrong' way. Yet it produces so fine a result that he and his friends dance round it, holding hands in a bumbling circle, yelling joy, smelling happiness.

A resident Englishman claims the cook simply imitated a prototype being produced at his factory. This news he announces with warm affection, and he does not intend to pursue the matter. A fair man.

The township, a passive place where the prevailing attitude assumes that the creative spark exists in England and not in Bengal, forgets the incident and returns to an existence of featureless waiting. The monsoon breaks, bringing with it explosive forces of bottled-up beauty.

With the first act concluded, the lights went up. A small applause, brief and dubious, lifted into the big, humid hall.

For a moment nobody moved. A shuffling of the feet,

though no one actually got up. Just yet.

But then a drunken man stumbled into the entrance. He was one of the soccer players. Swaying wildly. He called out, 'Anyone here by the name of Dick?'

The audience turned round, but sat silently.

'Anyone Virginia?'

The hall was silent.

He stumbled back out the door and was gone, for a moment, but then he stumbled back inside.

'Their driver is waiting ... anyone? Dick? Vagina?'

He began to laugh at his joke, with harshness, and he fell against the doorframe, knocking his head badly.

He lay on the floor.

The hall sat like it was empty.

After some time, they began to disperse. They walked around his crumpled form on the parquet floor.

The Old Man went to the bar. The soccer team dominated the place. He tapped a shoulder.

'One of your fellows has passed out.'

'Really? Where?'

'Just down the corridor.'

'Thanks old feller.'

Two men stumbled away to the corridor.

'I'll give the bastard "old feller" ... Bearer!' the Old Man called sharply.

'Sahib?'

'See those two? When they come back, give them a drink on my chit. Them both.'

'Yes sahib.'

'Gin, whisky, Pimms, Cinzano, double shots all mixed in one glass each. Put beer in also.'

The bearer looked at him.

'Well?'

'Yes sahib.'

The Old Man then ordered a gin and tonic, and a sherry. He then walked into the lounge and sat with the Old Woman. He gave the Old Woman the sherry, and kissed her on the cheek.

Fatimah Westcott joined them.

They talked pleasantly, and the lounge was busier than usual. The club seemed like a small, vibrant hotel, and Abdul emerged from the crowd. He stood at the table with a contented smile.

'What are you grinning at?' Fatimah asked.

'The smell of the rain,' Abdul lied.

Khan the sabjantawallah says Abdul was grinning because he could see Fatimah naked in the pool. Abdul organised a poolside dinner for two for the following night, and he intended to ask her after the play.

Beyond the verandah the rain absorbed the world. It stirred the sleepy club. It had shown up leaks in the roof, and these had been attended to. Since the first downpour, the place resettled into a hubbub of familiar faces and laughter.

Nobody took much notice of the play. Others arrived from the hall and they chatted and discussed the rain, the flood contingency plans, holidays. They talked about closing the office for a few days, and they ordered drinks.

The Irishman walked up smiling, 'All right play?'

The Old Man said, 'It's all the tandoor nonsense—long ago, and irrelevant.'

Fatimah said, 'I heard that the second act develops into a big metaphor for British colonialism.'

The Old Man said, 'Brian should check his diary. It is 1967, a bit late for all this dribble we've seen before.'

The Irishman cheerily agreed: 'We can't escape. Forever

the same with these new boys. Bash the English. Particularly when they're from the old country themselves, haven't you noticed?'

Abdul: 'I might talk to him. I think the play should be about those other colonial rodents, in Karachi.'

The second act lifted the story to what the Theatre-sahib regarded as a higher plane. Towards the end, a wave of chanting by a chorus of Bengali workers, played by club members, gave the story a foot-stamping conclusion to the metaphors for freedom and domination.

A big woollen sock placed over the head down to the neck, was domination.

Each actor in the chorus, one by one, removed the cover from the head and placed it beneath the feet, saying this was a lake. They fell suddenly still and silent. The imaginary lake remained silent with voices: the paradox of unseen, drowned voices.

They commenced chanting to a rhythm, and as they chanted they also trampled the socks. This was freedom.

In the final moments, the actors were jumping on the socks in unison, chanting gleefully and wildly.

When the lights came up, a weak applause echoed around the hall. The players in a jumble appeared once more. They went off, then came on again. Then they encouraged the Theatre-sahib on to the stage, and a small applause lifted into the damp punkah air.

Fatimah follows the Powerful Scent

Fatimah Westcott wandered down the crowded, buzzing verandah with a drink in her hand. The scent in her nose was now a distinct smell.

Striding comfortably past a table of four Bengalis—two lawyers and their wives—she overheard a remark made by one of the women. It was an exhausted, gentle tone. 'My goodness what a damn boring play.'

Fatimah stood at the railing a moment.

The second wife disagreed: 'I like it. After all, it is a story about our people and our place. I find that a refreshing change to all these blasted West End things.'

One of the lawyers disagreed again. 'No, that doesn't help, it makes it worse—it propels our provincial attitude to even more insular depths. If that is possible.'

The second lawyer said, 'Not only that—the idea is childish.'

But the second wife continued: 'What was the valuable virtue supposed to be?'

'Who knows,' said a lawyer, 'maybe my tranquillity under sufferance.'

'Anyone like to have dinner?'

'Good idea.'

Fatimah Westcott then turned away and followed the scent. She strolled down the verandah, took the corner and walked up the side. The Theatre-sahib and the President's wife sat at the last table.

'Congratulations Brian,' Fatimah said warmly.

'Thanks,' he smiled.

'Feeling a sense of relief?'

'Oh not at all.'

'Exhausted?'

'Not a bit.'

'A man of boundless energy, very good,' Fatimah said and gave the President's wife a smile.

Fatimah continued into the building to search the lounge. Then she looked into the snooker room. After the big green room, she finally located the President.

At the far end of the library, the back of his head was visible over the chair. The big window glowed from the lights at the pool.

Fatimah placed her drink on the windowsill, and fell into a chesterfield.

The President gazed into the rain. 'Hello Fatimah,' he said flatly.

The greeting was the dullest she had heard in a long time.

'You didn't enjoy the play?' Fatimah asked.

'Oh yes; just drained from the day's effort. Getting things off the floor at work, big job too. Pandemonium actually. And you?'

'I'm afraid it was fluffy waffle.'

The President made a snort, a laugh. But he asked, 'What do you mean?'

'Consider: it is a complicated subject, and your

foreman playwright has mangled it into a tender pantomime. Guys like him are all the same. They used to flock to Alexandria in the fifties and put on the same dreary squeals of petulant shock.'

The President took a glance sideways at Fatimah.

She was sitting low, gazing out the window. They spoke like that, looking ahead, weary from a long day.

'Roger, I don't intend to interfere.'

A small silence roamed the alcove. The hiss of the rain was distant.

'Do you like it here?' the President asked finally.

'In Chittagong? It's all right. It is not Alexandria, but one takes the work.'

'I adore it here.'

'Yes, I know. We all know that. Even my ayah knows that. She knows something else as well.'

'The servants are forever picking up bits. It's their job, our festering linen. Our dirty washing. They know everything about us, feeding habits, ablution habits, drinking habits.'

'Understand me, Roger. I never interfere. I get on with my work. I shift goods around the oceans. I ride my scooter. When I'm invited, I go on a picnic to Cox's Bazaar and take a swim. I play tennis. Now and then I go to Delhi …'

'Delhi, yes. Guillaume. How is he?'

'I have no idea. Are you all right Roger?'

'Oh yeah, fine, just dog-tired.'

The Chief Bearer came in with a tray. As he lowered it to the small table, Fatimah glanced up. She caught him staring.

He set the tray down. He was about to go.

'Bearer,' Fatimah looked at him squarely. It seemed like

a long time. 'Do you know my ayah?'

'No, memsahib.'

'Leila Ghosh.'

'Leila Ghosh? No, memsahib.'

'You may go.'

'Thank you, memsahib.'

'That is a sinister man. And a liar.'

'Oh he's all right.'

'My ayah says different.'

'Your ayah is probably having you on.'

'Leila is a very good sort.'

The President took a samosa and a fresh drink from the tray, and he continued: 'They are all good. That's exactly what folk like you do not understand, Fatimah. They are all good people. In this part of the world all people are good people. I welcome the world to a place like this. But you, folk like you warn them off. You pour your boredom on the place, your irony, your spite even.'

Fatimah now moved her feet. She waited a moment and listened to the rain, but then she spoke.

'Well, I do not say to inquisitive parties, "Yes, you're welcome here, please come in, make yourself comfortable." I've never had that saunter in me. Not when I lived in Paris, not in Amman, and not even when I put my feet up in my beloved Alexandria. That kind of swagger I leave to others. And I know that you, also, leave it to others.'

'Your ayah is lying.'

'As I say, I do not interfere. My ayah has told me that back in the last days of summer the cook had been fiddling around with the idea for a long time, that he made all kinds of sketches, that a potterywallah at the bazaar made the first tandoor shortly after my ayah returned from Dacca; all this detail, Roger, where would it come from?'

'How old are you?'

'What's that got to do with the price of jute?'

'You still fail to open your eyes. It's this place, the delta, it exudes detail, oozes.'

'Is that all you will ever do? Roll around in sorrow? "This place this place." All right then, consider: where did *Brian* get the detail for the play?'

'He made it up, I should think.'

'You confuse me. Of all the lizards in this place, why on earth would a successful man like you want to pick a cook's pocket? I do not understand it.'

'You want to watch what you are saying, young lady.'

'I'm here to tell you, privately, that I now know where that tandoor came from. That is all. That is all I want to say. The rest is up to you. I cannot, and will not, handle any shipments of the tandoor. I'm sorry.'

Fatimah Westcott stood up and held out her hand. 'No bad feelings?' she asked with a smile.

'Why should there be?'

'Well, whatever. I hope you work something out.'

The President stood and shook her hand.

Fatimah Westcott strolled through the crowded club with her drink. At the verandah she searched for the President's wife and the Theatre-sahib but could not find them. She joined a table of friends to enjoy the closeness of the rain and a late meal. Her sari flowed as she walked, and she liked taking the tour.

Starting with the bearers, the play caused a low stir. Then it moved among the kitchen staff, pool staff, and inside a day the entire club was buzzing with friction.

The Chief Bearer did not, like Iqbal, see the play. Why should he? But it was like a growing hum. The rumours robbed the Chief Bearer of an ounce of his authority.

Mahfouz the Spitting-bearer and his gang believed the President was to blame; other bearers had heard that Ajit Mookerjee was quietly pointing at the Chief Bearer and Mohendra the chickenwallah.

'Ajit Mookerjee said so?'

'Yah.'

'Then it must be true.'

But the Spitting-bearer's gang had other ideas, and they took every opportunity to smear their rags on the President's head.

'Yah, but don't forget, President-bastard is cunning. Like all of them.'

'No, the President-sahib is okay. He is a man who likes it here, and he likes us.'

'Rubbish. He doesn't care for any people. Do you know he has thrown his wife to his foreman?'

'Truly?!'

'Yah.'

The bearers talked endlessly about the whole thing. While some hoped it might get the Chief Bearer the sack, others sipped warm chai saying that nothing had changed. Iqbal heard it all.

Fatimah Westcott's Drooler

The President was pleased to reclaim the room.

Soon Abdul walked in. He was bright and cheerful at first. 'That Fatimah Westcott, what a gorgeous woman, a real temperature I get only from setting eyes on her. Let me tell you something, it is a damn deep secret so keep it to yourself—I am at last going to try my best to have a fuck with her, I'm going to arrange candles and dinner down at the pool. What say you, good fellow? Handfuls and mouthfuls of Fatimah!'

'She's too young for you.'

'What are you talking like a schoolteacher for? She's thirty-thereabouts.'

'Fair enough. But she doesn't go in for academics, my friend.'

'Perfect. I am a tutor at a pathetic polytechnic.'

'Anyhow, she's married.'

The teacher's cheer dropped away. He took a whisky soda from the tray.

'Convinced?' the President said flatly.

'Fatimah is as married as my big toe; no, it is something else.'

'What's the problem? You don't go in for Arab traders? Bit rough and rugged?'

'Don't be funny. What did you think of the play?'

'Oh it's all right. You?'

'When did you employ that guy?'

'I can't remember. Last summer I suppose.'

'Has he done many plays?'

'How should I know? Perhaps. Maybe he did lots back in Bristol.'

'He is a snake. I don't like these smooth stage guys, they're always up to something or the other. Piss-farting around like nobody's business, as if the world was made only to piss-fart around in.'

'It's the man's hobby. Do you not have a hobby?'

For long moments Abdul remained silent. He sipped at the drink he held with both hands, and then replaced it to the windowsill. His cheer had vanished.

'This is bad for me, Roger.'

'What's the matter?'

'You see, I want my students to be given a potent chance at life, that is what I teach the buggers. I don't show them plain history, I show them they must not totally emulate foreigners, that they can do things for themselves ... I am very vocal on the idea of laying one's hand on the table, yet here I sit, stuck for words.'

'Abdul, we are friends. "Pan-continental" twits, remember?'

The teacher did not laugh.

The President emptied the last of the bottle for himself.

'It is a delicate matter. Aah, I don't know ... where are my teaching talents when I need them? I pride myself on openness, and look at me.'

'You were flashing with excitement when you walked in.'

'I was bullshitting.'

'About Fatimah?'

'No no, not Fatimah. Let's get another drink.'

The President depressed the buzzer.

After a while the Chief Bearer arrived with a tray and then left the room.

'Okay, I'll tell you what it is about. It is about Catherine.'

'Is she making a scene out there?'

'Roger, are you having me on?'

'Not at all. You know how she makes a scene.'

'She has been sleeping with Brian. Well, I am assuming. I have not watched them at it, but I am certain they are lovers. Give me a whisky.'

The President poured the drink with a beautiful flow of relief. A calm subsided in his stomach. It percolated to his legs, and he stood to give the teacher the glass.

'Thank you. Let me sit down.'

'Are you all right now?' the President asked.

'No, I am not all right. This is precisely the kind of thing that happens around here. Ever since I marched as a student in '52. The same damn thing again and again. Year after year. Some fellow comes out here with his nice wife and the next thing she is off with an itinerant. No I am not all right. I have seen friends come and go, broken broken broken. Here, give me a whisky.'

The President poured another and handed back the glass.

'Thanks. What about you? Are you all right?' Abdul asked with concern.

'I'm okay, don't worry about me.'

Abdul put down the drink, and his hands were fretting in the air as he talked.

'They say that, all of them say that, "I am okay".'

'Truly, I am all right.'

'Right, what else can you say?'

'I am fine.'

'You know what? It is always after the damn rains. Never fails. Next step is that they pack up and go home to heal and assuage and fix and rekindle. But it never works. A slow dawn rises, cold and misty, over the little fence and they are lost in it. Shopping around the high street healing one another. It never works because …'

'Abdul …'

'… because the dawn soon swallows the fog, and all he sees is the face of an older, altered wife.'

'Abdul …'

'… and she too, just some older, changed husband. For some dumb reason there is no such harsh dawn here in Chittagong.'

'Abdul!'

'What?'

'I am not going back to England.'

'Well you cannot stay here. What a shocking thing all this rigmarole can be, I hate it.'

'Catherine is.'

'With that bastard?'

'With whoever. She has been leaving Chittagong for some time.'

'You have known about this? All along?'

'Not really. Not anything as grubby as a name. But I do know that only her limbs remain here.'

'Truly?'

'She is very unhappy. Her heart and head and spirit long ago went to Exeter, and she has been suffering vacant nightmares ever since, as far as I can tell.'

Abdul's hands came to a rest on the arms of the chesterfield. He sat up.

'You actually intend to stay?'

'I shall take a clear look at the possibility, yes. What is it but paperwork?'

'And you'll send the old girl home?'

'We can sort things out very amicably, yes. She is hardly old, by the way.'

'I meant it affectionately, sorry.'

They were silent for a while.

'Do you feel better?' the President asked.

'Well, you know me: I hate it when marriages go to pieces. They prevent this molten world from just going off and dissolving into the ether.'

'Like a fresh one?'

'Why not. Well, though he is a sleazy dung, I think the idea of his play was pretty healthy. Overall. The less we copy foreigners, the more we will turn the key. Though I still cannot figure out what was that "valuable virtue". What do you think he means?'

'Education.'

'Oh please don't be funny.'

'All right. How about persistence? If you persist, you can be free.'

'Could he be making such a sweet point?'

'He could. He's a very moralistic kind of a bloke is Brian.'

The President's Plan

Persist and then be free. The President depressed the buzzer. He sat back and watched the rain lash against the window.

Akram the Chief Bearer entered. He looked tired, and his whites were dirty.

'Sahib.'

'Come in, sit down.'

'Sahib?'

'Sit down.'

Akram sat in the big armchair as he had done many times, though not with the President.

'How is your friend the cook?'

'Which one, sahib?'

'The fellow from whom you stole the tandoor.'

Akram had heard the club creaking with the news, but he did not care.

'Sahib, I did not steal it, you did,' he said without concern.

'That's what they think, you're quite right. You can go now.'

After Akram left the library, the President stared from the window. Making plans. Persisting.

Drowning in Loneliness

There came the break in the rain. Sheets of half-sun appeared. The Minisahib lay flat, and the boulder warmed his back and his legs. He tried to stick his arms to the rock, but he knew arms are shaped in all the wrong ways to get the heat from a good rock like this.

The pond overflowed the colour of milky tea into a small gully. The flow might be a good place to net a catfish over the clay bank, and when he had suggested this to Zeythi she had said nothing.

He lay on the curving surface of the rock and pretended he was flying through the clouds. He gave that up and turned his head to the side, but there was no movement from Zeythi. She was not half naked. She was never half naked anymore. She wore a shirt and a light loongie. He felt warm, and he jumped off the boulder to stun the pond.

Zeythi lifted her knees and sat upright. She looked out over the pond for the Minisahib, but he was still under. She felt the heat in her foot as she stood and said, 'I Do Not Care Anymore.' Her feet were becoming warmer, and she kept on saying to herself that she did not care. It developed into a humming kind of ballad in her throat. Khalid made songs out of anything going. He could be at the teahouse calling *get to work you filthy scum* and he'd keep walking, repeating the words into a stupid song. And here she was, in imitation.

Embracing him.

Yesterday, Ajit Mookerjee had called round.

'Have you heard from Khalid?'

'No,' she had said. 'You?'

'No. Never mind, he will send a letter soon—Iqbal told him to use a letterwriter up there who will be a friend. He can write fine, but Iqbal's friend will make it easier.'

'I don't mind,' she had said.

Ajit looked her in the eye, and he smiled to say, 'It's all right,' and then walked up the side of the house. He thought as he walked off, Zeythi who has no mother, no father, what is she going to do saying 'I don't mind'?

Now, on the boulder, she felt an echoing hollow as the sound rolled. 'I Do Not Care Anymore.' She had begun to lately think about leaving Zakir Hussein Road. Here, all things were now empty and broken. The compound of paradise was full of rain, but the place was empty. Take up the invitation, she thought. Stay with the Kutubdia woman.

When she walked to the house the memory took hold. It would be a simple thing to do. Two steps, that's all. First, take a bus down the coast. Then, show someone the skull of the fish. 'Show it to anyone,' the woman had said. 'They will lift you on a boat to my place. Stay as long as you want. You can learn from me. The food is fresh and plenty. The air is cool and every morning it is new. The sand at the water is golden and every night it is silver. Can you swim, mountain girl?'

'Yes I can swim,' she had replied. Zeythi's whole lonely life had been lived in river or lake.

As Zeythi walked along the twisting path she heard the Minisahib call out. He was not visible, and the call was slight, but he was close. He must be running.

When they arrived at the house it was already mid-morning. There was plenty of work to tend, so she went about the place with an empty attention to one task after the next. It was automatic and blank.

That's how it had been the past two weeks. She grew more remote, and the Minisahib did not know what to do about it. He climbed the money plant and sat on the wall. But he climbed down the other side and began to stroll across the wet field. The water was ankle deep, and the mud oozed between his bare toes. He walked with his head down, keeping an eye out for frogs, but there was nothing much in his mind. That he was soon to go away to school floated across his concentration. England. He had a vague memory of it. The houses were stuck to one another. And it was like standing at the icebox.

Zeythi had worked up to the living room. The house was empty. That's the way she liked it, restful and noiseless. Ibrahim the cook had gone out, and none of the others were home. The room was untidy, but nothing much else.

She straightened things up, and a knocking came from the front door.

She opened the door, and she quickly stumbled backwards and came to a stop at the credenza.

He stepped into the doorway.

He then came in proper, where he stopped to view the room. He looked up the corridor. He went walking into the dining room. Then he searched around the house, calling out for his friends, disappearing into doorways. There was no reply, so he came back up.

Zeythi pressed her back against the credenza.

'Is nobody home?' the President asked.

'Yes,' she lied, 'memsahib is asleep, sahib.'

'Where is Khalid?' the President asked.

'He is gone.'

'What do you mean?'

'Dacca.'

'Dacca? Is he returning?'

'No, sahib.'

The President was not yet satisfied. One last question would fix it.

'Does Khalid work here?'

'No, sahib.'

This cannot be right. One final question.

'What is the name of the new cook?'

'Ibrahim.'

Well. Must be true. He turned and looked down the corridor. Then he turned back.

'Where are the photos?'

'Khalid has taken them,' she said. She felt herself shaking, and her voice giving, but she hoped it did not show.

The President strolled outside and stood on the verandah. He came inside and walked down to the kitchen. He came back up, went outside to the driveway, and stepped into the waiting car.

She was still shaking as she watched the top of the car glide along behind the hedge of bougainvillea.

Maybe Zeythi did not know it, or understand it fully, or perhaps she did, but that was the moment she suddenly lost her hold. Khalid had been gone a long time. From the door she could see the hedge, the front garden and the wooden floor of the verandah. It had never looked so hollow. It began slowly, but in the end it swamped her, and in the deep middle of it she sobbed without control.

Catherine and Roger

It was too simple. She was sitting opposite the frangipani on the far rise of the open garden, and she was surprised at the simplicity. In a few days she would be in England. She sat back looking at the torn flesh of the frangipani. It had been struck during the storm the previous night, sliced into two.

The garden now seemed bigger, and the expanse of the sky was alive, she felt, and wonderful. Pure joy.

The President returned with fresh drinks.

'Thought it over?' he asked as he sat down.

'Yes. We should say that I'm away for the monsoon, you're right. People will ask though, after some time.'

'By then the interest will have dwindled into irrelevant formalities,' he said.

She sipped on the drink. It was bitterly cold. For a moment she considered how much like a government official he could sound. Irrelevant formalities, she thought. What the fuck does that mean? Then she thought: Here I am in the garden saying fuck to myself. What a naughty bitch I am. Oh well, here it is, nineteen sixty-seven. Keats would've said fuck, fuck, fuckity-fuck.

A smile felt as though it was spreading over her jaw, and she tried keeping a hold of it. It was very springy and very strong. It was really giving her a hard time, so she thought of something that would not make her smile. Soon, she quickly thought, she would be in Exeter, then in Bristol. Breakfast in dirty bed linen, late lunches washed down with champagne, from summery balconies to dimly lit dinners in dark corners, shows up in London, and the best thing of all, their lovemaking. It never let anything get in the way. There were wars to think about, the poor to think about, Fidel Castro and the CIA, the KGB, the bomb, the British recession; the world abounded with activity to set the conscience alight, but she knew that they would not let all the wars in China stop them. They would soil yet more linen and slake yet more thirst. Too lovely for a smile, she thought successfully.

'I've had the bank manager make your traveller's cheques,' he said.

'Thank you.'

She felt that things were progressing with such simplicity that she decided she ought to make small talk.

'Have you found a suitable replacement for Brian?' she asked idly.

He did not answer immediately.

'Abdul has suggested a graduate from the polytechnic,' he said.

'You'd employ a local as the foreman? You do surprise me from time to time.'

He did not see any point in engaging. He thought, She loathes the place, loathes the people, I love the place, love the people.

But his remark fell out anyway.

'You do not understand me. That's why I surprise you. From time to time.'

'Oh yes I do. Your cunning I do. You are more than

likely planning to train the blighter in order to sell the business to him so that you can retire to Hackney,' she said lazily.

'I don't intend to retire to Hackney.'

'Wherever.'

He was right. He decided to keep his remarks to himself. Keeping his remarks to himself, he reasoned, would conclude the matter. The first part of his plan. Persisting to be free.

'Is the money all right with you?' he asked.

'Yes,' she said, 'fine.'

'I mean the monthly instalments.'

'Very generous, yes, thank you,' she said.

'There is only the one condition,' he said quietly.

'Not five?'

'Just the one.'

'I shall be away for the monsoon, yes yes.'

'No. Say nothing about the oven.'

'The oven? ... oh yes, the oven ... do you intend returning it to its rightful owner?'

'That is none of your concern.'

'As if I care—I'm just asking, that's all. Fine, I shall not mention the damn thing.'

'Good.'

This, she thought as she sipped, is too simple. She regarded the frangipani high up on the rise of the garden. Poor thing, she thought.

'Do you think that tree will recover?' she asked with an ice cube rolling in her mouth.

'What?'

'The frangipani. I think you should have Ali dig it out.'

'He says it'll keep going, leave it to Ali,' the President said vacantly. He got up and went inside.

She remained outside and took in the expanse of the garden. A final look. It was not the tall trees and rich flowerbeds that she saw; it was a tumbling flow of bits of her recent life in Chittagong. She thought vaguely of how, maybe, her poets had saved her. Big changes, she knew, had visited her spirit. And though she wanted to erase the place from her mind, she was a smart enough memsahib to also know that these disruptions would become precious memories. She also knew she would miss Fatimah. They had met for a last lunch at the club. They drank, ate, shed tears and hooted with laughter. She had banged her fist on the table. Sang out happily that she now hoped everyone found out about her and the Theatre-sahib. She also gave Fatimah an open invitation to visit her and the Theatre-sahib in England. Fatimah said she would.

Where Ignorance comes from

Akram the Chief Bearer arrived at work, and he spat to step: 'Damn President!'

But that, according to Khan the sabjantawallah, is not what he meant. What Akram meant was something like this. Every time someone goes off to work they lose a grain of the self. They cough, they get up and they look into what the hands might do today. Vigilant against ignorance, they contemplate what the day will bring. Maybe not boredom. Hope not a loss of will in the hands. Hope not the creepy and slow dissolve. Fraught with fear, they spit, look at the thumb and forefinger. What is it I will do today? Anything useful? They yawn like a cat and then make a silent wish. Wish becomes desire, and desire tumbles over the sink into something they willingly lose. Like this the soul seeps. It is normal.

In Chittagong it is different. You are not fiddled away. You are gone quickly. The cloud comes down, mumbles 'not my fault'. It just descends. Or the disease does. One day you are off to work, one day you're not. Sabjantawallahs up and down the coast heard about Chittagong. They came there like flies to a dung. I could never understand it.

'Iqbal?'

'Yes?'

'Can you explain that?'

'Explaining mysterious things that sabjantawallahs do is folly.'

'Give me something at least, please.'

'No. Explain explain explain. It is for dunderheads. The hobby of explaining is the place where ignorance comes from.'

'Stop your bulldust. Why did sabjantawallahs flock to Chittagong?'

'Maybe they decided there is much more work available, more disasters to squeak about, more people taken away quickly, like you say.'

This little mystery bothered me, but it did not bother the President. To him, it was plain and simple: Chittagong is a paradise. Abdul agreed, but added: An ancient paradise. The cement at the poolside was rough. It gave your sole a grip. You could run if you wanted. Laugh too, sing, dance. It would let you think that Chittagong was all beautiful. Was the centre. If you fell in love in Chittagong, they did not say *ey*? They would say nothing. If you ran around the pool, you might run around the world. If you fell into it, well you were only drunk. Nobody fell into the pool. The beautiful rough cement had been laid too well.

Candles at the Poolside

Abdul the teacher. Here he was, this sahib, following up Fatimah Westcott after work. He decided finally to set up a plan to give his pung-goo what it wanted. Earlier in the evening Mahfouz the Spitting-bearer fixed up a table under a big Cinzano umbrella with a fine white tablecloth and the cutlery and crockery from the dining room, and a silver platter of candles. When it rained, disaster. Abdul came down to put his finger on the progress. The whole set-up had to be replaced. He quickly had Mahfouz string a tarpaulin over the umbrella. Two layers of shelter. The tarp was tied off at four far corners, and it was so large that they had space to dance around the table if they wanted. An hour later the rain lashed again. The trick worked.

'Good job, Mahfouz,' Abdul said.

'Thank you, sahib,' Mahfouz said as mightily as he could without Abdul getting smells of arrogance or bulldust. Mahfouz knew how to deal with the teacher.

'Take this money, use it wisely.'

'Thank you, sahib.'

Abdul climbed up to the club to shower and change. Fatimah was due any minute.

He was sitting in the lounge when she arrived. He felt pleased and clean.

'Are we going to the hotel?' she asked as she looked him over. It was up and down, the look.

'Greetings!' he said. 'The hotel? No, we are dining here at the club.'

'You seem to be dressed for the hotel.'

'I have arranged a special table,' he grinned.

'Oh?'

'Please,' he said as he stood, 'take a seat.'

He ordered drinks and they talked awhile. When the drinks were finished they walked out of the clubhouse. Down the hillside, the glow came into view. A drizzle had arrived. This did not matter. It made the candle-lit atmosphere under the umbrella more intimate.

'It looks like a tent,' she said with cheer as she strolled over the cement.

'We have drinks in a big tub of ice, and we have a torchlight to signal the bearer, and we have the place to ourselves,' he said. 'Please,' he added with a hand held out to a chair.

Mahfouz sort of knew the teacher's views on things, so he looked after the evening at the poolside with special care and attention. Besides, Abdul had promised a fantastic bucksheesh. Mahfouz climbed the steps all night. In one hand he balanced a tray, in the other he held a brolly. He exaggerated the bucksheesh to the other bearers so that he would not look stupid either at the club or at the teahouse with his independencewallahs. Darting up and down the hillside looking like a puppy was not Mahfouz's idea of a good time. But if he exaggerated the money, then it was roughly okay. Cranking it up five times made him big. And the Chief Bearer could not interfere. Mahfouz had simply 'told Chief-bastard: Get lost'.

Also, Mahfouz had heard the main rumour about Abdul. The teacher was one of those students who marched at the Language Riots in Dacca long ago, demanding equal status for Bengalis. In '52 Mahfouz was a one-year-old baby, but now, at fifteen, it burned his imagination. Police had shot dead some of the students, Mahfouz had heard. To him, it was the birth of the struggle against Karachi. He and his teahouse friends celebrated the tall, sleek martyr's monument they had seen in pictures on the twenty-first of every February. They held a Shahid Minar evening at the teahouse. With guys like Abdul showing the way with protest, things were good. Yes, Mahfouz had a special place in his burning mind for the teacher.

For Abdul, the complicated plan came up perfect. The night was warm, the rain seemed reasonable. He had Mahfouz turn off all the lights except one at the far end that was left to wash over the surface of the oily looking water. The wind was down, and the pool moved molten and emerald. The water tank rose like a cliff face fading away into the high darkness. The big almonds dripped with vines, and the frangipani stuck to the night. Hidden world on hidden world of water had crashed to the plains, and tonight the poolside took a fine drizzle which was just right.

Mahfouz gazed down from the rear verandah. Other bearers had come to watch, but had gone back inside to work. One stayed, sitting on a stool.

With his elbows on the railing, the bearer said, 'I hope you are shaking your head, Mahfouz. Because I am.'

At the pool Abdul lifted an icy bottle of wine from the

tub. He poured two glasses, and the thrill was complete. Now he could get started with the evening.

'This soft rain makes a pleasant change from the storms of the past week,' Fatimah said as she raised her glass.

'Yes,' he said.

'The floating frangipani in the pool, it was your idea?'

'As you can see from the display, it is very lovely,' Abdul said.

'How was your work today?' she asked. 'I always wanted to work in a college, for the sake of the quest. But somehow I got stuck in a trading house.'

'Quest? Do you mean for knowledge? That is a romantic mirage, I'm afraid,' he said and smiled broadly.

'Not quite. Giving knowledge; that I'd take for granted. What I mean is the co-operation, the mutual assistance, a quest as a whole institution—those kinds of things. It seems very honourable. Compared with my purpose: we scheme and plot and next thing the blighters are loading up another ship with all kinds of lovely inventions. Like these candles.'

'Do you enjoy the work?'

'No, I do not.'

'Then why do you do it?'

'I have to do it.'

'But you always look as if you like doing it.'

'I might as well feel as if I like it. If I did not feel as if I liked it, I would have a horrible time.'

'You invent cheer, that's what it is about you. I fumbled about searching for what it is about you and see? You define cheerfulness.'

'It is not cheer. It is simply the liking of things as they happen. You're the one who is cheerful.'

'Are you pulling my leg? I am a worn-out protester.

Anyway, people need candles.'

'For many years I travelled in a dream to work in languages. I speak and write French, Italian, English and Arabic. How I waste these tongues today. But it is a wistful night: you have done very well, Abdul, and I approve,' she said looking over the flowers afloat on the oily surface.

'Jinnah,' Abdul said, 'wanted Urdu—for the whole damn place. In '48, when he came to Dacca, he carried on like a typical Karachi cockroach. "Let me make it very clear to you," he proclaimed to the crowd, "that the state language of Pakistan is going to be Urdu and no other language." How do you think this vibrant speech went down with us Bengalis? One thing is for certain, these days the anger is bubbling up all over again. I can feel it in my bones. Soon there will be big trouble.'

Abdul felt it in his bones, fine, but soon the delta would erupt into an all-out civil war. For me it is easy. I can say this and say that, but for Abdul to feel it in his bones, well that is quite astute. Trouble always frothed away, just under the feet, ready to break the cement into pieces; anyone could have told you that. But to feel it up in the bones is another thing.

When Major Ziaur Rahman proclaimed an independent Bangladesh from the radio station in Chittagong four years after Abdul feeling it in his bones, there was already blood on the streets from the broken talks, broken promises and broken bottles. That was a day Major Rahman's boots would have shone so bright it would have stung or blinded the eye of any oppressor present, even absent probably. I knew the guy who polished the Major's boots, he was very finicky about it. Of course independence didn't come until later, and in the meantime Mujibur and the others formed a government in exile, in Calcutta of all the pleasurable places.

'Jinnah,' Abdul continued, 'then said, "Anyone who tries to mislead you is the enemy of Pakistan." Well, I became the enemy of Pakistan straightaway, that I think is the honourable moment a college teacher can claim years later, I suppose.'

'You like your politics a tremendous amount, Abdul, I must say.'

'It is not politics. It is the care for the people here, those who are totally rubbished by the Karachi fingerers and the foreign overlords. Present company excepted.'

'Yes, you mean the English, like Roger, I realise this.'

'Roger is a strange English fellow. He is okay, an oddbod. I have a sneaking suspicion he wants to take up permanent residency. Roger loves this country. Besides, his enterprising approach to life might cause the immigration people to hand him a fully proper citizenship—who can tell these days? Decision makers I notice are becoming much more lenient when it comes to international concerns. Roger is a topnotch candidate, and I will support his application if he requests it.'

Abdul was now gliding pleasantly in the damp air. He almost put his feet up on the spare chair.

'Guillaume agrees,' Fatimah said.

Abdul's air fell to the cement. All the air he had been flying with, thinking with, smiling at, swooped to the floor and settled on the texture of the rough cement. But he did go on.

'He will support Roger?'

'No, what I mean is Guillaume intends seeking citizenship—but from the Indians. He believes the nature of business has become too complex. Too sophisticated for the simplicity of nation states, he says. Actually Guillaume is so fond of saying it that it bores me to death.'

'More wine?'

'Thank you.'

'Shall we order this thing, the entree?'

'Why not.'

Abdul switched the torchlight on and off. In a short while Mahfouz stood at the table, and they ordered. Abdul suggested the chilli shrimp, which came from the catch at Cox's Bazaar, a platter, to share, and it was done with a tilt of Mahfouz's proud fire-eating head.

'He will be somebody one day,' Fatimah said as Mahfouz walked off under the brolly.

'Who? That boy?'

'Have you never spoken with him?'

'Well … quite often …'

'I have. He is an angry young man, quite intelligent too. He told me he belongs to an independence club.'

'Mahfouz?'

'Yes, I think that's his name. I don't know his name.'

'What independence club?'

'Some shabby group of irritated young men, no doubt. Well, cheers.'

'Cheers,' Abdul said. 'You really do surprise me.'

'I don't know if that is a compliment, Mister Rahim.'

'Oh no no. You seem to know totally everybody around here.'

'All the gossip, that is true. A spin-off from my work if you like.'

Fatimah smiled, and Abdul threw back his head and he laughed a little. He was feeling fine. All those times of looking at Fatimah and exploding into a dark seething mass of frustration now seemed to him like a rotten past. He felt really fine.

As the drizzle grew lighter they drank the wine and they made a feast of the curries, breads and tandoori duck Mahfouz brought down after the shrimp. He had also brought down a big assortment of pickles and salads. The smiles brought down were naturally not noticed. He took them up again and brought them down and they were just like the food and the wine, coming and going unnoticed in the idle drizzle.

The air cleared and the cement lay shining. Clear air is a good thing, but it does bad things to you if you pour wine into the night. Three empty bottles stood on it and Abdul opened a fourth. The trees were still. The audience from the second performance had gathered on the verandah for drinks and air. They could be heard buzzing in the upward distance. Fatimah looked up to the verandah, and her gaze swam.

'Seems like tonight's audience actually enjoyed the play,' Fatimah said.

'I myself thought it was pretty good,' Abdul muttered, placing his head to the side in support. 'Brian is making the point that locals no longer need to imitate the foreigners. It is a responsible theme, and these days it is deeply relevant. Thank you very much.'

'Poor old Brian,' Fatimah sighed as she looked up to the club. Then she looked down. 'What a mess we have made of this glorious table. Is it not truly wonderful?'

'Poor old bugger nothing. He is having a good time. He is a lucky bachelor.'

The cork came away with a sharp pop.

'He is sleeping with Catherine,' Fatimah said as she held out her glass.

'Rubbish,' Abdul snorted, pretending to not know. 'Who told you that?'

'She did. She's having a good time too. She's having an extremely good time, really doing all kinds of things. She is one heck of a dirty girl, I tell you. Brian ought to be having a good time.'

Abdul pushed at the clutter with his elbow and held his head up. He looked into the band of night over the wall, and he took a deep breath.

'Yes?' she said with a satisfied smile.

'Principles ... I have principles, why shouldn't I?' he said as he gazed.

'Is that why you stay in Chittagong? To teach? What? Values?'

'I suppose so,' he said without care.

'Why not Dacca? Maybe in Dacca the horizon is wide and respectful. Maybe loftier.'

'Don't start being funny.'

'Dacca University, why not?'

'I am a badly qualified tutor, that is why. And what about you? The beautiful Fatimah Westcott. Why does she stay here?' Abdul felt like taking a risk, and he continued, 'Why does she not stay with her fancy French husband?'

Fatimah laughed and drank from her glass.

'Well?' he said. He waited. 'You see. I knew it.'

'Oh? And what is it that you know?'

'I can easily admit to my humble origins, my forgettable stature. But not the grand Fatimah, no. I always suspected that you were a bit like that, yah, I knew it.'

Fatimah pushed her glass forward into the mess, and Abdul filled it. She said nothing for a moment.

'I am making the best of a shitty hand,' she stated.

This stopped him. He lifted his head and the alcohol rolled it up and down his shoulder like a ball instead of a head.

'You do not like it here?'

'Yes, it's fine. It's my work, only the work.'

He lifted his head higher. 'That is too bleak,' he said.

Then she held up a bottle to the candles, saw that it was empty and flung it into the pool.

'Nothing bleak about it. It's a crappy hand, plain and simple,' she said.

They drank the wine, and the sounds of the verandah filtered through the air.

'You are insulting me,' he said.

'Consider. Every morning, each and every day, I wake up, scooter off to work, lose a small piece of myself.'

'Fatimah …'

'There is no "joy"—as Catherine would say. She has plenty, good filthy girl that she is—believe that. But me, I go off to the damn office and send meaningless telexes and flatten the cushion on my swivelling chair. No joy.'

'Lose something—of you?'

Fatimah seemed surprised for a moment, and she looked at him directly.

'Yes,' she stated.

'I am sorry, so sorry …'

'I started off innocently enough. In a store by the harbour in Alexandria, then a big dull emporium in town, then a merchant gave me a good position in Cairo and then he transferred me to a dusty warehouse in Amman—where I met Guillaume, at the Hilton one night. We settled first in Delhi. Then me, I came here. To work, you know. For a friend of Guillaume's.'

'Please, Fatimah …' Abdul started. He wanted to somehow shift the talk away from the husband but the alcohol interfered with his tongue.

'Before I left Delhi we visited a special place. Nagercoil at Cape Comorin, 8.1 degrees north.'

'I've heard of it,' Abdul said with a slight relief that at least they were shifting away from Delhi. 'Where is that?'

'The bedhead of the Indian Ocean. A strange and touched place. We sat on the sand at the water late at night and further down the beach lay a couple making love. We did not make love. We just sat there and pretended not to watch. There was this eerie light far off. It was dark at the water and we didn't even touch. Just sat there, catching the shine of their thighs … hearing the hunger and starvation of their breathing.'

Abdul was becoming irritated. He liked the story, but to his alcohol ear the husband had been mentioned twenty times. Abdul wanted to change the direction of things back to his objective. He searched the mess on the table. He stood up to lift things and move them around and he finally found the torchlight. He began flashing it at the club. He stumbled sideways but caught himself and continued flashing the torchlight.

'No, there is no sparkle,' she said.

They sat in silence until Mahfouz appeared, and Abdul requested a tray of liqueurs.

'No hard stuff for me,' Fatimah mumbled. 'Bring more wine also, same as this,' she said to Mahfouz.

'Yes, memsahib.'

'Even he has something to do,' Fatimah said as she watched Mahfouz's form dwindle in the darkness.

'He is a bearer, he has plenty to do, but the hand he has been dealt is plenty worse than yours.'

'You do not understand. He is an irritated boy, an angry young man,' she said.

'That's right,' Abdul said, suddenly upright, 'I am a Bengali, and it is I who should understand this before you!'

'He will do something with it.'

'He cannot do anything constructive with a temper.'

'Oh yes he can.'

'What can he do? Abuse his master? Throw stones at the children?'

'For a man who teaches in a college, you make me nearly laugh.'

'I teach them to think, that is what I do. Plus, it works. I have a student who is the son of a paanwallah, and I taught the cook as well. Not only that, I have taught many kids over the years. To make themselves free.'

'It is plain that you do not understand a shitty hand.'

'I understand a shitty hand very good.'

'Well, we cannot complain too much. At least Khalid came up with a fine idea.'

'That's right, that's what I am saying.'

'It was quite beautiful, a real spark of talent.'

'He is a smart kid, there is always a notion running around in his head.'

'Remember the feast?' Fatimah said with a smile.

'What feast? There have been a hundred feasts this year.'

'The Monsoon Feast when Khalid pumped-out the five-star chicken and duck from his tandoor.'

'That is exactly what I mean! You see? The stupid bugger!'

'It is a great shame. I feel sorry for him.'

'Pity is pathetic.'

'Making that tandoor was very clever.'

'He copied it, he did not make it.'

'He made it.'

'Did he tell you that?'

'No.'

'Fatimah, you do not know Chittagong. Things are said in haste and heat, petty myths float about, people can be mean. I know that boy, and I have a lot of time for him—I recently gave him a letter of introduction to the Dacca Polytechnic …'

'Dacca?'

'… yes, he has gone to further his studies. He is a smart young man, full of promise, but, you know, these kids today are cracking fibbers. I don't blame them; it is the only way they believe they can somehow make it—and that is why I fight to instill in them the honour of an education, to hold onto dignity even if they are the clippings of dignity's nails and even if they are stained and yellow.'

'He really went to Dacca? When did he go?'

'Last week. Or the week before maybe.'

'For good?'

'How should I know? Yes, most probably, yes. And shabash to him, well done for looking to a better future.'

Mahfouz came down with the strong stuff and the wine and then he swung around and left. Abdul opened the bottle of wine and filled their glasses.

'Now there's a bad one,' Fatimah said.

'It's damn good—Italian.'

'A bad hand.'

'Ah Fatimah, Khalid is a lucky boy.'

'Kissed by the luck of the filthy camel driver,' she mumbled.

410

'Kissed by …?'

'I taught him to say it. Instead of swearing.'

'Wealthy foreigners like you still cannot grasp Chittagong,' Abdul sighed.

Fatimah gazed over the pool for a while. The bottle floated in the flowers.

'Let me convince you,' she said finally. Her eyes were empty.

'Roger,' Abdul interrupted, 'now there's a fellow who has a grasp on this place.'

'Do you know who told me that Khalid came up with that tandoor?' Fatimah asked. She spoke in a bored, declarative way. And her eyes were empty.

'Yes, half the servants up and down the coast probably.'

'Catherine.'

'Reid?'

'She ought to know.'

They fell silent. They were looking at one another. Fatimah did not look at Abdul so much. She felt comfortable. But Abdul was beginning to feel a discomfort.

From deep inside himself, from a big, spacious area of truthfulness, Abdul began to slowly realise what Fatimah was saying. And as the realisation grew Abdul felt a growing disgust. His stomach began to lurch.

'Also,' Fatimah continued, 'my ayah told me. What reason would Leila have to fib?'

Abdul settled down and breathed unsteadily. His eyes rolled.

'Are you all right?'

Abdul grunted and nodded.

'And where did the detail in the play come from? Thin

air? Brian's fat imagination?'

Abdul retched.

'Why don't you go directly to Roger and ask him. You're friends, the both of you. Ask.'

Abdul now knew what Fatimah was saying. His stomach heaved and he vomited over the rough cement. He heaved again and tried to stand up.

Fatimah got up and walked round to his side. She stroked his back.

'Are you okay?'

Abdul mumbled and stood shakily. He began to walk off to the change rooms. Fatimah went with him.

'I have asked him,' Fatimah said as she walked and held his shoulder, and Abdul heaved again.

'But you should obtain the answer for yourself,' she said, and Abdul vomited over the cement.

Abdul had done it. His very own soul-seeping cough and spit.

As Khan the sabjantawallah says: They cough, they get up and they look into what the hands might do today. Shaking with puzzlement at things like betrayal, they spit. Like this the soul seeps.

She took him to the showers, undressed him and put him under. When she felt he was all right, standing in the stream of cool water, leaning against the wall and breathing normally, she undressed herself down to a bathing suit and went outside. She walked up the rough cement to the deep end and stood poised for a neat dive into the pool.

The Imitator

Across the Sundarbans dipping heads stunned-eyed would drink from their day and contract cholera and typhoid; but at his small bungalow, Abdul suffered other fevers. For these, he had taken no inoculations. He sat on the porch to sort out how to confront the President. A bewilderment infected his head. He watched the rain fall in massive gusts, but saw moments that spanned the summer; moments that drifted around the samosas, the bright Tuesdays after work in the library. Vietnam. John Wayne. Ayub Khan. Functional Equality. The raising of his 'kids' the students from despair. His causes—his usefulness: gone, like the contents of a pot of boiling water long forgotten.

But bewilderment was nothing. The poison was disappointment. And from this came the bursts of anger. Fatimah, he thought numbly, was right. This is a fool's paradise.

I knew Fatimah back in those days. Better than Abdul knew her. People the likes of her made the Sundarbans bigger and bolder. More than that, if I give my praise full vent, people like her make the world. They give it shine, lustre, shape. They allow it to have unseen feelings. When they speak, it is not to make pronouncements; they speak to encourage curiosity. They make people like me understand—the ignorant fool that I was back then—that disliking the rotten bits of a day is not to hate the day, but in fact to like it quite a lot.

More or less, Abdul now knew this about Fatimah. He now liked Fatimah even more. He went inside to take an early sleep. There he was, lying on his back looking past the punkah, his feet sticking out from under the tangled sheet, deciding he now had *something*, in his sweating palm, with Fatimah.

'I am in a tangle with her,' he said aloud with his hands behind his head.

'I am in love with the lady,' he said to the little empty room.

Abdul's cook brought up a glass of water. On his approach, the cook heard the words drift from the door. He felt sorry for his sahib, but only a bit because he thought Fuck the sahibs anyway, and he looked forward to setting off home to his wife.

What a disease. What a mixture. Sticking-out feet full of bewilderment, then all that bitterness too, then the explosion of love. In a pot on a stove this is the sort of mixture that would bend a spoon in trying to get it to mingle to be good enough to eat. Poor bastard.

The next afternoon, Abdul hesitated. He lifted his hand to the door of the club library, but let it drop. I do not know, but I now say that the hand fell from a uselessness. Abdul's whole life was lived for change. Big vision done in small pieces, but what could he change now?

He walked back outside, along the trophies and the portraits, the Queen, Ayub Khan, and he took a seat on the verandah above the pool.

A bearer appeared, and Abdul ordered a tray of tea.

'Samosas, sahib?'

'No.'

He sat by the railing. Vacantly looked over the activity at the pool. No tarp, no table, and the green water was lively with a small crowd even though the rain swept the enclosure.

He gazed back into the lighted lounge. The Irishman and the Sikh sat at the bar. Then he gazed back down to the pool.

Jazz floated into the warm air of the big almonds, a light, cheerful tune that made it seem like the afternoon was full of wonder, not bitterness and bewilderment.

When the bearer strolled past, Abdul requested that the music be changed, and the bearer rolled his head with a level smile, saying he would see what he could do.

'No! *Just put it off!*'

'Yes sahib.' The bearer strolled away.

A Letter to President Reid

Abdul concluded the class early, and the paanwallah's son and girl from Yorkshire closed their books. Rain fell heavily, so they walked under cover to the offices. Abdul walked a distance behind, and they assumed he was following. But he only wanted the office.

He telephoned the Dacca Polytechnic, and he had a long and friendly chat with the bursar's assistant and then with an enrolments officer, and nobody could say that a Khalid from Chittagong, or a Khalid from anywhere, had enrolled or had approached the school at all. Abdul went home to write the letter.

Roger,

I do not know how to write this letter, so I am just going to blast away. What you have done is sickening. Stealing that tandoor from the cook is beyond reality. Don't worry how I found out, I have my sources.

I want to write a balanced note of remorse, but I am going to pen a missive of disgust instead. I came to see you at the club yesterday, but I thought about it and decided that this is the best way.

All these years of tricking me ... I can't believe it. I have broken my back putting hope into my people's lives.

I have suffered the bad breath of patronising idiots from all over the world. Yet here is you, making a secret mockery of my work.

This kind of hypocrisy is exactly the stuff of spoiled brats like you with their riches and their baby hands which have never seen a day's work.

The boy has now vanished into Dacca. I doubt anyone can find him.

Forget about counting me as your friend.
Abdul Rahim.

He then held up the page and read it half aloud. When he finished examining what he had said, he called out for his thin cook. Abdul gave the cook the letter to take to the President's factory.

Dazed

Abdul walked in circles until he wandered into the darkness and found himself outside the bungalow of Fatimah Westcott. He would not go in, he would not go away. He stood with his head low in his shoulders, looking into the house. He leaned on the gate, and its rusting backbone creaked into the night.

He was full of disgust and he was full of love. The letter to the President had brought back old frustrations, the student days of bitter campaigning, dark plans, hot nights of grim agreements. 'Nothing has changed,' he told himself.

But as Mookerjee said: 'Abdul-sahib is a typical living fellow, caking himself in a crust all his life to forget, forget, forget.'

Abdul pushed himself off the gate. It was a lift, a breath of love. 'It will get better,' he then told himself.

He walked up to the bungalow and stood at the verandah. Then he turned and walked away, into the night, down the road to the car.

A car here, he thought, in the old coastal dump, is funny. Look at it. Bashful in the darkness.

'Bloody fucking car,' he said suddenly. He kicked the door, making a dent. It was a big dent, and he regretted making it the second it was done.

Nobody knew if Abdul ever did jam his pung-goo into Fatimah Westcott's firm fat vagina. But Khan in his typical sabjantawallah fashion simply said 'maybe not'. Khan admitted starting the rumour about sahib types grunting like babies. He said the only proof he had that Abdul failed in his dream of grunting with Fatimah Westcott was Abdul's affair long ago with a lady from Dacca.

Khan explained: 'Abdul-sahib keeps his mouth closed. Only breathing sounds from his nose. The whole face becomes redder than paanspit. He bites his lips inwards and then badang-badang he goes fast and then when he is finished his mouth explodes, just *bah!* like that. A Fatimah Westcott type of lady will not like such a thing.'

On the President's Desk

'What do you want?' boomed the Karachi chowkeedar. His big chin was a useful foghorn.

'I have a letter for the sahib.'

'I have never seen you before, get lost.'

'From my sahib.'

'Show me.'

'Here,' the thin cook said, and he offered the envelope through the iron bars.

The chowkeedar pretended to inspect the envelope, 'reading' the name Roger Reid.

'Okay, I'll take it,' the big man confirmed.

'No, it is me who must give it to the sahib's office.'

The chowkeedar gave the cook a stare.

'You come back here in three minutes or I will come after you with this stick.'

He walked open the gate to an iron groan and the cook found his way to the office. He went into the air-conditioning and gave the envelope to a secretary at a desk.

He smiled at the Bengali secretary, but she did nothing to return the smile. She continued to work at the typewriter.

High-flying hag, he thought, and walked out. He

decided to ride home to his wife.

The President had been reading a newspaper on a new batch of deaths in Vietnam.

Who does this? the President thought. Generalisers, he decided. They create it. Fatimah Westcott is right. It's the generalisers.

The secretary came in, put the envelope next to the tea, and then went out.

The President opened the envelope. With his hand resting on the desk, he held up the letter. When he had finished reading it, he looked out the window. His hand did not move, the letter did not move, and he gazed out for a long time.

He could have taken action. Phoned the Old Man to see if Abdul had been passing on the news to his good friend. But he didn't. He could have phoned Abdul, but he simply sat at the desk and looked out the window. He could have done any number of things to attend to the problem, but he didn't.

For a moment he envied his wife her clear hand. She could do it with a flick of the finger. Get on a plane, ascend the heavy air, look out the window, and say quietly, 'Goodbye Chittagong, goodbye you horrid little place. Goodbye to all your petty problems. Goodbye to all your sodding mud. Goodbye to your stench. Goodbye goodbye.' Which is what she and the Theatre-sahib were about to do.

But for himself, no way. He loved Chittagong, and he was staying. That was what the final thing was with him. So kind and clear and simple. Besides, he had a plan. And he would persist.

The Sabjantawallah puts His Finger on It

You can sit right in the middle of things and know nothing. I used to sit right in the middle of the teahouse, and I knew next to nothing. This is when the sabjantawallah moans, as though his cleverness is being beleaguered by somebody very stupid, 'nobody knows totally nothing, be reasonable.'

You can pretend to know nothing. Trouble is, and tell Iqbal this, he will agree, you realise that one or two things pop up. But then to pretend to know everything is petty, like the quivering lip of the sabjantawallah. Howling 'doomed!' over walls and fences is not what you'd call knowing a lot. He didn't like me. He badgers Iqbal to find out if I have returned to tell the story. Iqbal grumbles because he detests to tell a lie, 'No, he has not,' but Khan pulls a fast grin, and walks off calling lightly, 'The monsoon is here, the borders of the living and the dead will be dissolved!'

The weeks rolled by with the rain bringing the stench. Outside, mud carried the disease off slopes in never-ending waves, and ballooned animals carried it down the river on floating islands. The wind ate the coastline and picked trees from its teeth. Inside, a festering dampness crept into the deepest pits of bones. Khan is one of those gloating sabjantawallahs who is not satisfied with his tag of Mister-Know-It-All. He also likes to see that you know he knows. Petty, we called it. Perfect, he calls it. He takes chai with no pleasure, and makes it with no humility. The milk just goes in like a bomb. He releases nothing from his calling: people and dogs, and ticks and lice, are dumped into his talent just like the milk in tea lacking pleasure.

'You can say what a tick is thinking?' the earth-carrier asked incredulously.

'Yah,' Khan said.

'What is this tick thinking?'

'On that step?'

'Yes.'

'This tick is thinking, "Of all the stupid cooks on the coast, my one and only favourite scalp is now back in Chittagong."'

'Who do you mean?'

'Who do you think the tick means?'

'Khalid?'

'Ask the tick.'

Khalid Returns

All his life the Chief Bearer had believed he would be rich. His reasoning was simple—'There are so many rich guys around, all you have to do is be around too.' The ringing manner he excitedly said *Too!* is what I can remember easily. Same as everyone flung hope in the teahouse: keep an eye on the opportunity. A beady eye.

The Chief Bearer had finished work for the day. He lifted his raincoat off the hook in his corner behind the club. He rode off to Iqbal, sat down, and recited a letter to the woman living by the Hoogly in Calcutta who had given him the flick. He enjoyed talking, and he attempted, as with all the letters he sent off to her, to make himself seem important and yet kind. When he had finished his natter into the air, he asked Iqbal for an opinion.

'What do you think?'

'It is fine.'

'Not too high and mighty?'

'No, it is fine.'

'Too begging, you think?'

'No.'

When the letter was done he got on his bike. To hear a learned man like Iqbal say 'fine' a few times gave Akram pleasure. He wanted to hear fine a bit more but he knew it would look stupid. The rain had stopped a while, and drizzle drifted across the air, but the monsoon drain flowed with noise and gusto. He was forced to meander the long way on higher roads as a lot of ground lay under a foot of water. This made the journey twice as far, so he cycled like life did not matter. If it now rained, he would fling open his brolly. A raincoat and a brolly. He felt quite rich. But he believed he would be richer. Akram was confident he could 'twist the President-bastard's arm' for more payment. This was the substance of his letter to the beautiful seamstress on the Hoogly, and he added that he would 'just wait for a ripe moment' to mention the matter. And 'have a meeting' with the sahib. Meetings were something he really liked, and he arranged meetings of the 'minions' at the club whenever he could find a reason. A meeting with the President-sahib he had never arranged. He thought with excitement, What stink, and shabash to me!

But the Chief Bearer had no idea that the President had other plans. 'No inkling,' as Iqbal would say.

He cycled along, contented and tired, until the teahouse formed in the drizzle. When he came closer he saw the damage. The wall was smashed. A lorry had sailed off the bend in a storm, and the rain had helped to loosen the bad cement. The bonnet tipped into a window of the building, bursting the window frame from the wall.

Today the teahouse is a ruin. Too many monsoons, too many baking summers. Maybe a very long time from now if it is left to dissolve into the stream the teahouse will be a cluster of mounds pushing from the grass. Passers-by in the distant future will suppose these are boulders resting at the foot of a hill where they belong.

Akram went inside and stood at a clean table. He ordered tea—for he only took a strong drink after a pot of sweet tea.

It was early, so there were only three customers.

When the tea was brought over, he asked the boy about the lorry.

'They say some idiot was walking in the middle of the road when it was dark.'

'When?'

'Last night.'

'And the driver?'

'They say he is okay, but the police took him to the doctor just in case.'

'What about the idiot?'

'Into the trees.'

'Lousy bastard.'

'Yah.'

'Why was he walking in the middle of the road?'

'Because he is an idiot.'

'What I mean is, was he taking drink?'

'I do not know.'

'Was he walking straight?'

'I do not know. You want some food with the chai?'

'No. Bring me the English lager. I want it ice-cold.'

'Okay,' the boy said and rolled his head.

'Is the cook making food from the tandoor?'

'Yah, the tandoor started lunchtime.'

'The new one?'

'Yah, the funny one.'

'Give me chicken.'

'Okay,' the boy said, and he strolled off hitting a table here and there with his cloth.

The Chief Bearer looked around.

'Anybody upstairs?' he called to the boy.

'Yah, one guy.'

'Who?'

'I do not know.'

Akram sat back disappointed. He decided to wait. Maybe the place would pick up. He drifted into idle thoughts about Calcutta. Someone had told him that Calcutta was beautiful when it was on the bay and spreading on the beach. Sometimes, in the morning, it had a pinkish colour, like Chittagong's setting sun. Calcutta must be a very funny damn place, Akram thought, why be pink when the sun is coming *up*? He felt pleased with the letter he had sent to the woman who had given him the flick, and Akram was the kind of bastard that was so heavily full of ignorance that he felt confident the letter would change her mind.

Upstairs Khalid sat on the balcony. It felt strange to be back in Chittagong. He could feel his breathing, slow and sleepy. He could feel his hollow gaze. It felt like he had been away for a hundred years. But he wasn't seeing too well. And he wasn't bursting with sunny excitement. He did not go to the house, and he did not see Zeythi, the Minisahib, Mookerjee, Leila, Lall or Iqbal.

One fellow he did see. Last night Khalid had sat under the balcony up against the building. The moment he felt his back on the damp wall, he slept, though not well. His head ached, the night heaved and rolled, and he turned under thunder cracks against the hillside. His arm hurt, and his knee was badly bruised. Out front, earlier in the evening, he had swung to the side to avoid the headlights that came from out of nowhere and had slipped against the sharp shoulder of the monsoon drain. The current swept him away. With a shaking hand, he had caught a hold of the other side, and placed his legs against the current to climb out. The current had carried him a long way, so he fled into the guava grove. In the darkness of the trees he rested, and the headstones falling to the river, which was flowing quick and dangerous, gave his arms less shake. The trees were not brollies but they were fine and they smelled good and gave shelter. In rain a tree does nothing but in the night a tree is a house. Up on the road there was a commotion, blazing lights, police calling orders, and the rain scrubbed away any firm sounds. As he gained his breath, he felt the shaking of his hand melt away over the gravestone and into the dark river. But his head ached like a bruised bone.

Then, the figure had stood directly at his feet. The figure was broken by the darkness, but the lights from the road made an outline of his legs. He leaned on a tall headstone with an elbow. He was not concerned with the rain, and he simply stood. Staring. He might have stayed all through the night, using his insolent backbone to lean on the headstone.

Khalid did nothing. His hands lay upturned in the mud. His head felt like it was in a vice. He stared back. The rain's persistence closed his eyes, and, when he awoke, the figure had gone. The lights on the road had also gone. It was dark, and it was still, but the stream could be heard rushing. He picked himself up. His head seemed lighter. He decided to keep off the road, to follow the swift-flowing stream was the best way. Huddling up to the wall of the teahouse underneath the balcony, he had tossed and turned between the thunder and lightning.

In the morning he woke but fell back to the rough sleep. Early afternoon he woke again and walked to the stream, and from a low rock he washed himself awake. He squeezed the last water from his eyes. He took the path up to the teahouse and then put his foot on the steps up to the balcony where he sat away the afternoon. They were the first proper steps his feet had felt for a long time.

A boy came out. He put his eyes down. This was to pretend to be low. He knew results could be bucksheesh, maybe big.

'You want some more tea?'

'No,' Khalid said. 'I want duck—from the tandoor.'

'We do not have duck. The chicken is good.'

'Get some duck.'

'We do not have duck.'

'Then goat.'

'We have goat, yah.'

'Good. And English lager—cold. Like ice.'

'It is cold.'

'I want it to be like English ice, English.'

The boy went off and hit the door with his cloth. In his mind he looked at the odd man.

He turned around. He was an odd Dacca type, for a Dacca type. Dacca travellers came here a lot, like people coming up from Cox's Bazaar. You get these types, the boy said to himself, always you get them.

'You are this guy,' the boy said turning around with his cloth. 'You are Khalid,' the boy said.

'No.'

'Yes.'

'Who,' asked Khalid, 'are you?'

'Me? I am nobody.'

'You are a bastard to say that. Everybody around here says he is nobody.'

'Are you Khalid?'

'No.'

The boy stood there for a moment.

'I want to tell them,' he said with a sudden burst.

Khalid was unconcerned.

'I want to tell them all.'

'Give me duck.'

'I will get for you ten ducks!'

'Tell nobody I am Khalid.'

'Why?'

'You know that tandoor downstairs?'

'You are!'

'Come here, quickly. You are new in this place?'

'Yah.'

'You know Mookerjee?'

'No.'

'You are useless.'

'I am not!'

'You do not know Ajit the gardener?'

'I know Ajit-sahib, yes!'

'Tell him I am here.'

'I will run like the wind!'

'Run like the damn monsoon.'

'Yes!'

Khalid called out to the boy, 'Run like the damn monsoon!'

'*Yah?*' the boy sang out, 'watch this!' And he smacked the door with his cloth. The crack echoed around the old cement balcony.

Cement lay all over the place. Who had so much of it nobody knows. But even your hand in Chittagong could be cement. The boy's cloth smacking the door did sound a bit like dry, crusty Chittagong at the height of summer, and Khalid looked at the hide of the wet Sleeping Camels. The dry crack and the wet hillside together did not seem right or true. But his finger on the cement seemed right, and his toe on the floor seemed right. Then what was true? Dacca was not, that any blasted Leila could tell you. Leila was okay. He realised it was not Chittagong here anymore. But then, back in those days, he was very slow to know certain things. After all, Chittagong changes with every new monsoon. Even if someone pretended to know nothing, this he knew very well. Well enough. Chittagong changes.

Places, others will assert, stay the same, and it is the people who change if not the butcher or the letterwriter. But once you know a couple of things like I, you come to accept it is the place that will change.

A different boy brought up a serving of goat, and Khalid looked at it. He sipped at the cold beer, but did not touch the goat. He cut away a slice and brought it to his mouth. He chewed for a long while and then swallowed, but he left the rest. His head ached and he felt unstable.

Squeeze your Hands

Ajit Mookerjee never let his hand get in the way of the garden. He let the plants gain on himself, and he let the water do the good work. His garden was neat, yet he laid few plans, only those which were necessary like the grassy dips which made the water run without harm down the slope.

'Nobody can see a hand growing faster than a leaf,' Ajit Mookerjee always said. But he said it with a sense of glee.

'I can,' the earth-carrier said with a tone of importance. The earth-carrier was a friend of Mahfouz the Spitting-bearer. He was another fire-eating guy heading into the explosions of independence. Sometimes he had more anger than Mahfouz.

'No, you cannot,' Mookerjeee said, 'a hand is the servant of a leaf.'

They worked in the Mayor's garden. Mookerjee tended to work without talk, but the boy talked a lot. The compound fell away off a small cliff, and the slope dropped steeply to the back wall where a large monsoon drain collected the run-off. Over the seasons the previous gardener had fixed the rise with fruit trees, and Mookerjee added shallow grassy trenches across the plateau. These grass-lined dips which came out from the house like the spokes of a wheel escorted the monsoon over the cliff and down the slope. It was a good view from the rise. Past the roses and orchids you could see a sweep, and on a clear day the teahouse jutted from the foot of the Sleeping Camel Hills.

'You say Khalid is back?' Mookerjee asked.

'Yah. Sabjantawallah says so.'

'Are you talking bulldust?'

'Khalid made that tandoor! Like a bastard! Like a great man!'

They went on a bit about Khalid. Bad good nice stupid.

Mookerjee did not worry. Dunderheads who did not know Khalid were all right to bumble around with ideas of bad, good, nice and stupid. Mookerjee sucked his teeth and decided to go along with it. Mookerjee had been Khalid's friend for a long time, and he had seen all kinds of things that were stupid and bad in the cook.

The boy from the teahouse ran into the garden. He was excited and breathless, but he did not stop and he ran from the high entrance with a big jump. He landed on a fresh mixture of turned mud.

'Ajit-sahib!' the boy called, his foot a bit stuck.

'Get off my work!' the earth-carrier shouted.

'Leave the boy to climb out.'

'Get off, or I will dive in and throw you off!' the earth-carrier persisted.

'If,' said the gardener, 'you say this one more time, I will take a tree to your ear like a brush and let you forget your wages.' The gardener turned to the boy. 'Are you okay?'

'Yah!' the boy shouted, bobbing up and down.

'Why are you dancing in my flower bed?'

'Ajit-sahib! Khalid is here!'

'Are you telling lies?'

'Sahib?'

'Come here.'

'Ajit-sahib, I am sorry about my feet.'

'Nothing wrong with your feet.'

'You,' said the earth-carrier to the boy, 'are a dirty beggar.'

Mookerjee had never held a man by the collar. In all the time they gave him the excuse to hold a collar, he had said no. But he took the earth-carrier by the collar of his shirt. He did not know what to do. The gardener found he said, 'Talk to him with some uplifting stuff.' He pushed the earth-carrier away.

Mookerjee washed off his hands. He also washed his face and the back of his neck. He left instructions with the earth-carrier. 'Move that bed over there, and move this bed to the back corner. When that is done, you can go.'

'These are big, they will need one extra day.'

'If you do not want to do it, you can go now.'

Observation of the weather was Mookerjee's wealth. A knowledge of what it does to the dust and earth; and what the earth does to flowers and trees was the gardener's love and wonder. Nothing stood between Ajit Mookerjee and his beloved earth. Except the earth-carrier. One of the guys had recommended the young man. But Mookerjee would let him finish the two beds and then he would let him go elsewhere. What a funny world, Mookerjee thought, of all the things that can come between my garden and myself, it is an earth-carrier.

Mookerjee showed the teahouse boy the tap. The boy washed the mud from his legs and then followed the gardener to the shed.

They rode off on his bicycle. Khalid is back? thought the gardener, is this a dream? Mookerjee cycled eagerly, but he did not look ahead with concentration. He took in the flats and the hills, scouting for anything strange, a missing hill maybe, a field folded in two. The road gleamed, and houses and shops glistened in the pale grey afternoon. The cloud was very close to the road, and the sheen of the wet trees made a strange colour in the haze from the touchable sky.

After a mile it became clear. This lull would soon be gone, maybe later in the afternoon. No, this was not a dream. The monsoon is still with us, he thought, why has Khalid returned so quickly?

'I will come back next year, just before the monsoon,' Khalid had said at the bus depot, 'if I come back.'

Dacca in the Eyes

Ajit Mookerjee threw his arms around the cook. Khalid embraced the gardener with a small laugh. The boy brought up cold drinks and plenty of rice with a large serving of chicken from the tandoor.

'I asked for duck,' Khalid said with a smile.

'We have no duck,' the boy said. 'But this chicken is good, it is not dry. It is very special because the tandoor keeps all the juices inside the meat.'

'Oh, I see,' Khalid said as he leaned across the table. 'Looks good.'

'Yah,' the boy said standing back, a hand clutching an elbow. He lingered a moment, but he was not asked to stay and so he went reluctantly inside and down the stairs.

Mookerjee settled into the table. He moved the glasses and the plates into a better position, placing the chicken at the centre. They ate and drank slowly, and often left the meal for minutes at a stretch. Khalid did not eat much; he seemed not to eat at all. Their talk was slow too. Chewing on things slowly. Especially Mookerjee. Rushing was not his game.

'Six weeks,' he said.

'Yah,' Khalid said.

'Not long. Dacca no good?'

'Dacca is a bastard of a place.'

But Mookerjee was not satisfied. Something was wrong.

After a while, Mookerjee leaned back and picked his teeth.

'Come,' he said standing up. 'Let us give Zeythi a surprise.'

Khalid hesitated. All he did was look off into the distance and say nothing.

'Come,' said the gardener with a flick of the head.

Razia Iltutmish

They strolled quietly down the side of the house. Khalid continued to the mangosteen, Mookerjee veered up the back steps and knocked on the door. He called into the gloom behind the gauze.

'They seem to be out,' Mookerjee said.

'Okay, let's go.'

'It's all right, I can wait awhile,' the gardener said.

Khalid's old quarters stood silent. Freshly painted for protection from the rain, the tiny structure looked like new quarters. The rear of the house had been painted too. The big frangipani had been trimmed. The break in the wall at the end of the compound had been repaired, and a gate had been installed. Things were looking new. The only sign of neglect was the flying fox. Also, Khalid was no longer accustomed to true and fine silence.

But the calm was broken. Shouts of the Minisahib and Zeythi came filtering through the house.

The door flung open with a great smack against the wall, and the Minisahib came flying down the steps with Zeythi in pursuit. They ran down the compound for the back gate. The Minisahib flung it aside and vanished into the jungle. His footsteps sounded with muddy squelches.

Zeythi turned and walked back to the steps. Halfway up the compound, she froze her small head; a sharp breath left her mouth.

She turned to settle into a steady standing position with her hands at her sides. The Minisahib called from somewhere, but she remained in the centre of the compound, standing, staring.

Mookerjee very slowly rose from the bench and strolled off up the side of the house.

Here was Zeythi who had been sending letters to a mother and a father who no longer existed. Zeythi who infiltrated the President's wife's dreams. And laid a curse on the hawker. Yet she could not decide if this Khalid sitting on the bench was real—or, maybe, she was too frightened of hoping.

She watched him a moment. Then she ran across the compound and threw her arms around his shoulders. She almost fell off the bench with him. She stood back and she felt Khalid's hands and his face.

The Minisahib's head appeared at the gate, and when he saw Khalid he shouted out and ran across the compound to the bench. He jumped on Khalid, and this time the cook fell off the bench.

Ibrahim the new cook came outside to check on the commotion. He stood on the back step, but then came across the compound with a concerned expression. But as he walked, nobody had to tell him.

Khalid suddenly felt as if he looked back a long time. It was a scene he knew: these three had come from the club. The new cook had been to the bazaar for the week's goods and then to the club to collect Zeythi and the Minisahib; on his bicycle Ibrahim had followed beside a rickshaw, maybe also set down the French girls if they were still in Chittagong.

Ibrahim asked Zeythi, 'Shall I bring out pakoras?'

'Yah.'

'Chai?'

'Yah.'

Ibrahim went inside.

Ajit Mookerjee came strolling back with a smile. He stood by the bench, saying hello to the Minisahib, who was seated next to Khalid.

'And Madam?' Mookerjee asked, 'still keeping Ibrahim under control?'

Zeythi did not take her eyes from Khalid. 'He calls me madam nowadays.'

'You are Razia, that's why,' Khalid said.

'How is work?' Mookerjee continued.

'Fine, thank you,' she said, without removing her eyes from Khalid.

'Did you see the Kutubdia woman when she came to town last week?' Mookerjee asked.

'Yes. She came here,' Zeythi said, looking at Khalid with a big smile.

'To the house? Really?'

'Yes,' Zeythi said lightly without taking her eyes from Khalid, 'she is my friend.'

'Ajit is talking to you,' Khalid said.

'She knows he's talking to her,' the Minisahib said, 'that's why she's talking back.'

'Ajit is a grown man,' Khalid said with a smile, 'you must talk to him when he addresses you.'

'Ajit is my friend,' Zeythi said.

'Has he looked after you?'

'No, he has been a bastard,' she said, smiling.

'What is this?' Khalid said.

'He has not visited for a long while,' Zeythi said.

'She is right, I have been busy moving earth at my place. What I am doing moving earth in the rains, I do not know.'

They all sat back like paan munchers, and the talk flowed. After a while Ibrahim brought out tea and pakoras. Ibrahim gave Khalid much respect as the talk filled the air. It was talk that was clipped and tight because there was too much excitement, talk that was eager and much too happy to make much sense. The tin mugs were filled and the pakoras were passed around. Khalid took a pakora but he did not eat it.

One of the sahibs came out. He stood on the back step a moment. But he then strolled across. There was nothing unusual in a clutch of servants far down the back, but he had not been able to find the ayah and so he went down to ask if anyone knew where she could be found.

As he approached, he decided that he saw the ayah's back. Then, as he approached further, 'Oh ... hi Khalid.'

'Hello sahib.'

'How was Dacca?'

'Very good,' Khalid lied.

The sahib was about to turn to the ayah, when he continued.

'By the way, was the rain as bad as they are saying in the newspaper?'

'Very bad, sahib.'

'Terrible business this monsoon, ugly. Now, Zeythi ...'

'Sahib?'

'Have you done the washing?'

'Yes, sahib.'

'Where are my underpants?'

'On the dining table, sahib.'

'Good.'

After the sahib went into the house, they resumed the eager talk—which suddenly changed in tone. Zeythi noticed it.

Khalid again looked up at the flying fox. It was broken. Nothing more than a dangling rope. The end, which lay in the mud, seemed frayed.

'What happened to the flying mongoose?' he asked lightly.

But Zeythi caught the other tone. It was the same bitter growl, she thought, which had infested his heart after he found out about his oven and then spent the last hot weeks baring teeth in the nights. Chasing Mohendra and the Chief Bearer, dumping a curse on the hawker … simply being eaten by a beast. And here it was once again.

'It all came apart,' the Minisahib said, 'and we couldn't fix it and nobody wanted to fix it for us because they said it was too dangerous, until Uncle George fixed it but it broke again.'

'We fixed it,' said Zeythi.

'No,' the Minisahib said, 'Uncle George fixed it.'

'We fixed it,' said Zeythi.

'No!' the Minisahib shouted.

'We fixed it.'

Khalid looked around the place once more as Zeythi and the Minisahib continued, and that was it. He could not stop himself feeling the horrible sadness rising inside. He let it gain a hold and he sat quietly on the bench.

The eager talk flowed after the Minisahib and Zeythi ran out of interest in the flying fox, but Khalid did not hear it. Ibrahim made a bed for him on the floor of his quarters. Zeythi, feeling bold, told Ibrahim to move the bedding to the floor of her quarters, but Ibrahim stood his ground and warned her what would happen if someone from the house found out. The bedding remained in Ibrahim's quarters. Mookerjee went home. The early evening began to brew, and the rain came in bands to smash and shatter more stuff, to swallow up Chittagong for the night. Khalid took with him to sleep the echoing sounds of the Minisahib and Zeythi fighting over who fixed the flying fox. He liked it. Took some small comfort from it reminding him of the happy time before the monsoon.

The Second Monsoon Feast

It is true that you look forward to the rains. A thousand celebrations come to life. But it is the outsider who regards the monsoon with single-minded reality: destruction.

'Remember,' Ajit Mookerjee would gently counter, 'the monsoon brings also bud and blossom.'

The gardener is right: the Sundarbans is the most fertile delta in the known world. Or Abdul: the Sundarbans could put food on the tables of Pakistan *and* India, and everybody can forget about 'Functional Equality'. But when the rain has settled in and the papers are counting the dead in their thousands, celebrating the monsoon seems very far in the past.

In the morning Khalid waited until the house was empty. Zeythi would be busy with the last burst of the morning's work. Ibrahim too would be finishing the activity of the morning, and the Minisahib would be crumpled in a tangle, half asleep and dreaming of a scary school humming in the middle of hundreds of houses stuck together at the sides. But the memsahib and the others would be gone into the day, and the Old Man was in Karachi on urgent business. So Khalid strolled from the door of the quarters up the other side of the house, into the tunnel of bougainvillea to emerge at the front garden. At the corner he stood silently and gazed upon himself cooking the chicken and the duck at the feast back before the monsoon.

So he was home, the young cook. Yet he stood on the matting of wet grass, feeling like an outcast.

'Remember to remember the good things,' Mookerjee had said as his friend boarded the bus, 'for it is only these that will bring success in Dacca.'

But what had Khalid done in Dacca? What was that splinter of darkness Zeythi had noticed? Had he simply walked in circles the deep, narrow lanes of old Dacca, hearing murmurs fall, along with the rain, from the latticed balconies?

Or did he take Mahfouz's advice? Did he follow the Spitting-bearer's directions to visit the decrepit palace of the nawab of Dacca with its columns stained by the seasons, and arches faithful to the secrets of the meeting over half a century in the past which clinched the founding of the Muslim League? Probably not. Khalid was in search of his own fortune, not the collective fortune of the entire delta like Mahfouz. In any case, Mahfouz wouldn't know how to find the palace if his high good breakfast counted on it: Mahfouz was simply repeating whispered, inaccurate navigation, young Chittagong stuff feeding on dusty Dacca legend.

Or did Khalid find himself lost in the massive outer fringe of giant old Dacca, stumbling upon a wetland rising up as factories? Stumbling upon the Adamjee Jute Mill? What would he do here? Wander into the back office and cheerfully suggest that he cooks lunch for the millers?

A young man working as a household cook in a small town who has a bit of get-up-and-go. Goes to Dacca no less. Yet it seems to strip his spirit, fling him back to the small town, where he suddenly tastes the rancid flavour of the outcast.

Standing at the front garden, he observed himself cooking the chicken in the new tandoor. An image of the President arriving with the Old Man. No scolding, only high praise. Balloons, filled with the praise, floated between the chairs. And the garden of candle-lit tables looked like a restaurant out in the warm, dry night. Khalid felt delirious, and the images continued rising. Like the balloons, the oven multiplied and floated far and wide, to Dacca, Karachi. The President and the Old Man strolled into the party with their filled plates, into the night of colourful saris, but Khalid's heavy fatigue engulfed his head and he collapsed on the morning grass.

Khalid

Khalid woke on a sweaty bed. He felt nauseous. The doctor had informed the Old Man that it was the second stage of typhoid, and that care was needed to avoid the dangerous part of the third phase—perforations in the intestine and eventual haemorrhage.

So much for the bud and blossom of the monsoon.

But compare: three years later they suffered a worse monsoon. A cyclone ripped through the place, killing 250,000 East Pakistanis. Tidal waves burst miles inland. Villages were swept out to sea. It was the worst in memory, and when President Yahya Khan called by after visiting China, he dragged his feet for so long that it was only after help came from England and America that Karachi got into gear. By then, President Yahya was being spat on with every word uttered by the survivors. Eventually he had to say something to account for the slow effort, and he said, 'My government does not consist of angels, it consists of human beings.'

I remember the week the household was scheduled to visit Doctor Matheison's rooms in the bungalow he shared with the Australian Consul. These were the inoculations the Old Man insisted everyone had to have, including Khalid and Zeythi, and so the annual event was taken for granted. For Zeythi, it had been her first, and she went along with the Minisahib and the Minisahib's mother. Khalid was supposed to have gone to Doctor Matheison's rooms the next day. But Khalid had not been thinking of anything beyond his stunning new tandoor.

Khalid now had no energy to properly turn his head, but the clinic was full of beds, patients wall-to-wall, up and down the corridors. Khalid felt hotter than he had ever felt, and he sweated heavily. His head was swimming and aching. Delirious and seeing things, he passed out.

When he woke, a blur of the Old Man stood by the bed. The memsahib was sitting. They spoke but Khalid caught only a muffled stream and he passed out.

Over the next two days he woke and passed out to visitors in the rickety chair, or standing in a kind of line down the bed—Ajit and Leila first, then Lall, then the household over another day or two, Aranthi the potterywallah, Fatimah Westcott and Abdul. And the Minisahib with his mother. But Khalid could not recall if Zeythi had visited.

The doctor came by to request the memsahib's attention for a moment.

When they had walked away, down a few beds, Khalid spoke urgently to the Minisahib.

'Where is Zeythi?'

'We can't find her.'

Khalid was silent. He breathed heavily and waited a long time.

'Go to Iqbal ... ask him to come.'

The memsahib returned with moist eyes. She stayed and she talked a while.

Mahfouz did not visit the clinic, but in Chittagong the monsoon fuelled frustration against the overlords in Karachi, and when it had turned to anger Mahfouz bitterly caught the clinic. Mahfouz caught it and shook it. Talked about the clinic, beat the ears of the bearers with his Mukti Bahini slogans.

'For proof,' he shouted, 'see what has happened to Khalid!' But he did not visit the clinic. When a junior bearer pointed this out, Mahfouz said he fought bigger and higher things.

'We must fight the bastards in Karachi!'

Later that afternoon Iqbal arrived at the bedside with his pencil and paper. Khalid lay asleep, so the letterwriter sat on the thin chair. Iqbal studied the cook's face. He was surprised at the sharpness of the bones that showed from the pale, pallid skin. A long time seemed to hang in which Iqbal recalled the times he and the cook took too much drink at the teahouse where they joked that they were slipping off the balcony. All that colour the cook had, deep, sturdy colour, was now a damp flesh sunken into the cheeks.

Khalid woke. He felt brighter.

'Iqbal!'

'Yah,' the letterwriter said quietly. He edged forward, and the chair squeaked.

They talked about nothing at first. For Khalid it was pleasant. But soon he asked after Zeythi.

'Nobody knows where she is,' Iqbal said, 'but I see her when she comes to do the letter to her mother and father, so do not worry.'

'She is still sending those letters?'

'Oh yes.'

'But how?'

'I just put: To Mother and Father of Zeythi, Barkal.'

'And then?'

'She takes it to the post office and puts it in the postbox.'

Khalid felt tired, and he drifted off to sleep, but woke later.

'Iqbal!'

'Yah,' the letterwriter smiled, and he leaned forward.

They talked about nothing, and Khalid seemed to like it. Then he asked a favour.

'Can you do a letter for me?'

'Yah. But why not do it yourself when you get out?'

'It is to Zeythi.'

When Iqbal commenced, he had to wait between deep breaths for the lines to appear. It took the rest of the visit to take it down, and when he emerged from the clinic, the place was already dark and rain swept the road in violent sheets. But it was not a long letter. It came straight to the point.

To Zeythi,

I like you very much. I believe that you like me. When the tandoor was to be okay, I wanted to ask you to marry me.

Khalid watched Iqbal's hand as it led the pencil. Hand of a good man, he thought, not one of these ignorant hands.

I thought of you in Dacca every day. The photo I was always bringing out of my pocket. Somehow, I lost the photo, but we can take another. Even now, in this hospital, I can see your beautiful face. Maybe I am very stupid, and maybe I do not understand this world like some others. I will never get the tandoor back because now it is all over town, and it will never become ours again. It is too late.

But it is not too late for us. You have chosen. I have chosen. When I get better I would like to marry you. No need to be straightaway, you can grow up first if you like. The sahib and the memsahib can marry us later on, when it is right. I can still cook like the best, and this will bring opportunities for us.

I have told Iqbal he might find you in the room upstairs where you met the Kutubdia woman, so if you get this letter please come.

Your Friend,
Khalid.

They sat quietly for a while. A man down the hall screamed. Nurses rushed in. There was a violent confusion, and then the patter of normal activity.

Iqbal re-read the letter.

'You should sign it,' he suggested quietly.

Iqbal arranged the small board on the sheets on Khalid's chest, and Khalid wrote his name under the letter. Khalid fell asleep and Iqbal took the letter away.

During the night, the clinic transformed into an echoing den of shadows. Howls and screams rode the air. Abrupt thuds rode along the damp cement floor. And the figure rode the corridors until he was standing at Khalid's side. The figure said nothing, Khalid said nothing.

The next morning Zeythi entered the grounds of the building. This is what she did not want to see. She hesitated. A chowkeedar strolled up to the lost-looking girl. After a plea in which she explained the situation, he brushed her away. She produced her green headband, showing it briefly, and he stood back to allow her to pass. She took a while, but arrived at the verandah and then went inside. Staff crisscrossed the big floor into doorways and corridors, and she did not know which way to proceed. A nurse came up.

'What do you want little girl?'

'I wish to see a friend.'

'As do many, but I cannot allow you inside,' the nurse said. 'This place is strictly out of bounds. Go now, go home.'

'That is okay, I have had the jabs from the English doctor in town.'

'And who are you?'

'I am the ayah from a house on Zakir Hussein Road.'

'You are here to see Khalid?'

'Yes.'

'Come with me.'

The duty nurse took Zeythi into the clinic and up a series of corridors and then through a tunnel of dormitories. Here she was, to see what she did not want to see. Not again. She fell behind, but the nurse slowed down and walked with her to show her the way, until she came to Khalid.

He was asleep, so Zeythi stood quietly. The duty nurse then gave instructions to a nurse nearby to let the two alone. Zeythi stood for a very long time. She instinctively reached out to touch his exposed shoulder, but her slow hand sought the letter inside her shirt instead. When she felt the paper, she relaxed and sat on the chair. It had been many days since she had seen him lifted from the grass and taken away. The look of his face was now a shock. She began to see not the Khalid that lay before her eyes, but the Khalid the night before he was found on the front garden. Ibrahim had kindly shown him the tandoor in the kitchen and told him how much he liked using it. 'What a fine and fantastic thing,' the new cook had said. She recalled that the compliment had given Khalid a smile. Not a smile as big as the day he came back from the history class singing 'Ra ... zia!', not as big as that, for that was the afternoon the tandoor had at last come to life—and smiles were thrown out the window for laughter.

She also saw the Khalid who sat in his quarters after dinner so long ago. Upright on his jute bed, wise, helpful. Making a plan to save the swimming pool. She also saw the Khalid who had welcomed her into the house. She saw the Khalid who danced with her for no reason. But she did not see this Khalid on the crumpled bed: she barely noticed when the nurse came and set about lifting the sheet over his sunken face.

The nurse had come along and put an arm around her small shoulder. She reminded Zeythi that it had been a long time. He was asleep, and maybe she should return later. But then the nurse, who was not seeing other Khalids, had noticed that this Khalid no longer breathed, and she gently trailed the sheet over the shoulders to his head.

A Fragrance of Guava

So there I was. Hovering a moment over a hole in the wet ground which slipped around with mud. As I was lowered into the grave, someone bit on a guava, I think it was Mahfouz, and someone standing beside him caught the tang of the scent.

'Smells good,' he whispered.

'Sweet,' Mahfouz whispered.

'Give me some,' the other said.

'Get your own,' Mahfouz said.

They carried on pushing elbows until Ajit Mookerjee strolled behind to carry out two sharp slaps to the back of the head. Fatimah Westcott nodded approvingly at Mookerjee.

Lall Thankee was there, Leila, Iqbal, and one or two club bearers. Teahouse people came. Even shining-shirt Mohendra, that damn chicken-bastard turned up. He tried to stop complaining of a snotty nose full of 'a terrible flu'. Winter flu, he liked to call it. The word 'winter' to him was all high and mighty.

The Old Man was there with the memsahib. The household uncles and aunties were there. Also the President, and Abdul. And the Minisahib was present, pale and steady by his mother's thigh. He was steady because he was told I was asleep.

So, you know, not a big funeral. But an average one, particularly for a petty cook. Cooks do not get big funerals in Chittagong. In fact, nobody does. Not gardeners, bearers, ayahs. In Chittagong you take what you are given, and then you realise you are in love. But you are too late. Cooks are very lonely creatures. Ajit says so too are gardeners. Lall says butchers are as well. Leila says ayahs also.

Later in the afternoon the gravedigger and his son returned to work. The strong young son wheeled the cheap cement headstone down the grassy avenue and spent the next hour setting it to the grave. And there it was, the name. My name. Before the moss had covered it up.

At the Old Man's request, Ibrahim made snacks on the front verandah and a bearer from the club made a bar. Those who attended the funeral went back to the house.

'Quite a sight,' Iqbal said, 'Khalid's pals and the household friends mingling. Well, almost mingling. Mingling quite a bit. Khalid used to say that about mulligatawny—"make it mingle a bit more. If you don't make it mingle it will be boring and nobody will want it."'

The President arrived later, but he did arrive. He stood with Fatimah Westcott for a while, and she accepted his silent presence. Fatimah had enough strength and warmth together to let him stand with her as long as he wanted. He didn't say anything, just stood next to her in silence. Fatimah always spent a minute talking with me in the kitchen when she visited the house, and she now talked with Ajit Mookerjee. They talked a bit about me.

Fatimah mentioned the beauty of the tandoor, but Mookerjee said the real beauty, the deeper sorrow, was another thing. He told her about Zeythi and I. He said he had come to know the feelings she had and the feelings I had.

But when night came, Mookerjee and the rest left the house, thanking the Old Man and the memsahib at the door. They made their way to the teahouse to continue.

Zeythi walked in the dark across the field of mud and water. Inside the graveyard she did not know what to do and so she wandered. When she found my grave by simply walking she lay on the freshly turned earth beside the headstone. The Minisahib had followed, and he sat away in the darkness. It was very dark and though his eyes were wide open he could see only velvet blackness. All he could make out was the sound of her talking. It sounded like she was whispering.

President Reid in Pursuit
of the Ayah

Countless seasons have come and gone since the funeral. Back steps have baked under the heat of other destinies, and the delta still belongs to the monsoon.

The destruction of independence has come and gone. Chittagong belongs to a new creation, Bangladesh. Mahfouz got his 'yandee-pandence', but he is now tired and, he claims, less better off. I would have made less better off into a song. Less-Better-Off. What stink. Mahfouz sees Iqbal regularly, bemoaning being tricked. Iqbal quietly suggests that things are better.

But Mahfouz shakes his head, and with a slow, crumbling voice, he says, 'I am still a bearer, and up there the bastards are still kings. Not Karachi kings, but now Dhaka kings ... Khalid used to talk about a slave who ate Delhi. Crunched it, like the head of a snake—what utter bulldust.'

Chittagong is still a filthy paradise. Giggling in the dark goes on with fun and vigour. How can anyone be Less-Better-Off if they keep giggling in the dark?

These days, laughter from the teahouse belongs to echoes and memories of Mookerjee, Lall Thankee, Leila and Iqbal. Mohendra likes to say he is older and wiser. He is older and still jumps into a boasting binge when he gets the opportunity. Just that now he has learned to show off in a more pleasant way. In a more sneaky way. So that nobody can say he is boasting. If anyone said he was boasting Mohendra would let loose a bit of indignation.

The Chittagong club still holds a show in the hall where the night belongs to the member who wishes to be an actor.

I always suspected the club President was a bastard. But I was convinced from the moment we were hiding under his feet. When his wife moaned out the omens, when she told the guests at the table that he had stolen the tandoor.

But I was wrong. It was Akram the Chief Bearer and Mohendra the featherduster who were the bastards. Not that President Roger Reid was a glass of rosewater.

Zeythi took up her meagre belongings, including the fish skull, polished the brass eyes, and took off with the few rupees she had put aside. She folded the skull and the money into the green headband and walked out after midnight when the house lay in darkness. She stole only one item—and it had always belonged to me. A worn old brolly. She departed as she had arrived, with little disturbance, invisibly.

The household concern, and two days of police interviews, made a mess of the week. The Minisahib was stunned. His real world had collapsed. All he had left was the pretend world of the adults. Within a week, a new ayah was employed. The household was now the domain of one Ibrahim and one lifeless young woman of immense efficiency. The Minisahib knew he was soon to be sent to a different school. His high summer full of excitement was finished. All he now did with the days was imagine a faraway place. His mind made four repeating images from which he could not escape even if he rode out back to the pond. They were: cold grey walls, boiled potatoes which had gone cold, thick woollens blowing in a cold wind and iceblocks hanging from cold trees.

But it was the President who made a strange move. He began a search. It was not a big search where everyone is asked to chip in. He did it more like a thief. But he also did it in a planned and careful way.

First, he called Chief Stinker into the library.

'Sahib?'

'Take a seat.'

'Sahib, we are very busy outside for the lunch.'

'Take a seat,' the President ordered.

This new boldness gave Chief Peanut a bit of a surprise. He sat on the red leather chair.

'I did not see you at the funeral,' the President said.

'I was very busy, sahib.'

'Then you do not know, perhaps, that the ayah has gone missing.'

'No, sahib.'

'Why would she just disappear like that?'

'She is from the hills, sahib. A Chakma I think. With them, you can never tell.'

'Do you remember my new factory manager? He is a Chakma,' the President said firmly, 'and he is a good man.'

'Yes, sahib.'

'Here is what I want you to do. Ask around, find

Zeythi, and bring her to me. Start tonight.'

'Sahib? Ask who?'

'I'm confident you will strike a good idea.'

Akram fell silent, but he had not heard the President speak to him like this in a long time.

'You can go now.'

'Sahib.'

That afternoon Akram felt horrible. He knew he would have to seek out those who hated him. Mookerjee, Thankee, Leila, Aranthi, and guys at the teahouse. Horrible.

He started with his cousin at the chicken stall, and he hoped like the blazes. Featherduster did not even know that she was missing, so Akram commenced his rounds. He took a glass of whisky, and in one powerful moment he decided this hateful job could be done in a jiffy, but five nights on he was still asking around. Nobody knew where she had gone, but he suspected that nobody would tell him. After a week of irritation and then frustration and then failure, he decided to try Iqbal.

He came to the corner and sat with exhaustion on the stool under the brolly.

'Hard day at the club?' Iqbal smiled.

'The club is nothing. I need your help.'

'Still no reply from Calcutta?'

'Something else.'

'Oh?'

'This ayah who was working in the Anglo-Banglo house with Khalid. Do you know where she is?'

'If I may say so Akram, she is a bit small for you,' Iqbal said helpfully.

'Don't be stupid, I do not want the Chakma bitch. It is

the sahib.'

'The President-sahib? But why?'

'You are asking me? You know these English fools—half the head is filled by their balls.'

Iqbal knew where she was, but he shook his chin, smiled and made good apologies.

Akram stood up and called down a rickshaw. It started to rain and then it crushed things in a roar. The rickshaw's plastic sides flapped and leaked.

At the club he climbed the steps to the rear entrance. He was wet through and he was annoyed. He became calm by changing into a dry uniform.

'Mahfouz,' a bearer hissed, 'he is coming!'

Mahfouz waited by the doorway. Behind him the kitchen was in full flight.

As Akram came in, Mahfouz blocked the doorway.

'What are you doing? Get back upstairs.'

But Mahfouz did not move. He smiled.

'You want to know where she is?'

'Get up to the bar,' Akram said flatly as he looked down at Mahfouz.

'I will eat the damn bar!'

'Soon you will be eating nothing if you do not get upstairs.'

'You want to know where she is?'

'What are you talking about?' Akram scoffed.

'Twenty rupees.'

Akram regarded the boy for a moment.

'Okay. Where is she?'

'She is staying with the Kutubdia woman.'

Akram laughed. He pushed Mahfouz aside and walked into the kitchen.

But Mahfouz followed him. Upstairs, he swung aside

the door and the cold air gripped his skin.

Akram strolled out to the lounge. Mahfouz followed.

At a table two guests ordered lunch from a bearer. Akram stood back. He favoured these two because they were good with their tips. He had made a small fortune from their hands over the seasons. Mahfouz came to a stop where he could stand facing Akram. Here, I give Mahfouz his credit. He was keeping faith with the boom. Back then, the boom swept like a fire through those with initiative. If some were pesky, so what? A boom can make you pesky. Akram tried to get rid of him. He glared with his usual threat in the eye. Then he flung his nose in the air in sharp hits. Mahfouz did not budge. He had twenty rupees coming, there would be no going. Akram made the move. With a smile and a small bow, he walked off. Mahfouz followed him across the lounge into the service entrance.

In the dark passage Akram stooped right down into Mahfouz's face.

He said, 'If you are telling bullshit, you can forget about working here. You understand?'

'Yah yah, give me the money.'

'You will get it when I find her. Go back to work.'

Akram waited until the office crowd filtered in around six o'clock. The President arrived with the Irishman. They went to the bar. Akram waited until a crowd gathered and then he signalled the President.

But in the library, where Akram thought things would be fine and shabash, bad news lay in waiting.

'Excellent,' said the President, 'I want you to take this note to a letterwriter for translation. After that, take it to the ayah.'

'Sahib? How?'

'Take the bus, here is the fare and expenses.'

'No, sahib,' Akram said plainly. 'I will not go to the Kutubdia woman, no,' he insisted quietly.

'You will do as I tell you.'

'No,' he said calmly.

The definite tone caught the President.

'Why not?'

Akram remained silent.

'Think of it as a paid holiday, stay a day or two at a coastal teahouse.'

'No.'

'A hundred.'

Akram paused. He paused a long while.

'Five hundred,' Akram said.

'Two.'

'Three.'

'Fine, you leave tomorrow.'

Next day he rode the bus down the coast going over things in his turning mind. The last time he had to contact the Kutubdia woman was bad enough. Why in the heck was the damn ayah staying there? This would be no good.

He decided to pass the note onwards, not to see her directly. Yes, he thought, that will be okay.

The task turned out to be not too difficult, and he returned to Chittagong the next morning.

As the days passed, it did not look promising. The President waited. An image of Zeythi's face, a large image, very close, drifted in his mind. Her big, beautiful eyes floated in his own eye.

Many days later, the Kutubdia woman approached the

factory gate with Zeythi at her side. The big Karachi chowkeedar stood up off his stool and came out from under the corrugated tin shed. He bounced his nose at her and motioned with his hand, but she remained standing at the gate.

'Go away!' he called.

'We have a meeting, let us in.'

'Fuck off.'

'Your mouth is a toilet, young man, just like this town. Let us in or I will wash your rotting teeth with petrol.'

'Take your little girl and go home, there is no begging allowed here.'

'When I see your sahib in my meeting, I will tell him to sack you.'

'Yah, good—now get lost before I bring this stick down on your head.'

'Show him the letters,' Zeythi said quietly.

'No, let us give him something to think about.'

'No, just show him the letters.'

'You are right,' the woman said, and she smiled and placed her hand on Zeythi's shoulder. She produced the notes. One was written on letterhead, and when he saw the company symbol, he opened the gate.

'If you do not come back in ten minutes, I will come for you with this stick.'

At the main office they waited. After some moments the secretary invited them inside, but Zeythi remained seated.

'Come,' the Kutubdia woman said.

'I do not want to go. I will wait outside.' She turned and walked out.

The secretary took the woman to the President's office. The secretary didn't mind. She looked the woman up and down, but she didn't mind.

For all the things the Kutubdia woman had seen and done none of it prepared her eyes for the moment she walked through the door. The room was huge, she thought. It was filled with the cold air they talk about. It was filled with shelves up the walls, files, three desks, chairs, a sofa, and the softness under the sandals gave her a floating sensation. But in a moment she recovered.

'We have come,' she said.

The President was also stunned, and he said nothing for a moment. The woman towered above the secretary. He saw freshness, a neutral eye, poise. When he finally stood from his desk the secretary had left the room. The search had taken a fortnight, but here they were at last. He felt very pleased.

'And the ayah?' he asked pleasantly.

'She is waiting outside.'

'Won't she come in?'

'She does not wish to come in.'

'Is she … all right?'

'She will wait.'

'No—what I mean is: how is she?'

'She is fine.'

The President then indicated a chair at the coffee table, and the woman sat down. He sat opposite.

'Would you like tea or a cool drink?'

'No, thank you.'

'All right then, we'll get straight down to it. You have my letter? Do you understand it?'

'Yes. You wrote that you wish for us to come to Chittagong so that you can give Zeythi money. That is English.'

'No. Not once, today. But monthly.'

'Every month you wish to give her money?'

'That's correct.'

'Every new month?'

'Yes.'

The woman sat silently for a very long while. She looked at the carpet.

'Why?'

'That is my business.'

The woman fell silent again.

'How much will you give her?'

'That depends. Do you know of Khalid the cook?'

'Yes.'

'The tandoor?'

'Yes.'

'What I want to do is this,' the President said. 'Money will be transferred to the bank in Cox's Bazaar. The amount will be one-fifth of the total amount of the tandoors which we sell from my factory. We produce many of these ovens, and they are sold around the country, so the amount will not be small.'

The woman sat silently, but she rolled her head.

'Are you Zeythi's mother?' he asked out of curiosity now that he had done what he had set out to do.

'No.'

'Are you a relative?'

'No.'

'But she stays with you?'

The woman rolled her head.

It was done.

After the woman left the office, the President sat back and gazed from the window. An image of Zeythi came up. It was after the funeral when they had gathered on the verandah. The President wanders down the house passing silent rooms and cool, damp corridors. He strolls as if aimlessly, but he is headed towards the working end of the bungalow to the grey cement of the servants' quarters. At the end of the house a curious whining sound floats from a window of mosquito gauze. Seated on a high ledge is Zeythi. She seems to be whispering. The President steps closer. He is puzzled. He stands still and watches. It is strange, he thinks, to see the ayah up this close. That face, he thinks, what a sublime impression. But the features seem to want to separate, to fall away from a centre. She has larger eyes than he thought. Staring, only staring, in the direction of the hills. A long and full mouth on a chin of definite firmness; and so, he thinks, maybe a strength. An open face, he thinks. The sound of her whine filters through the gauze. She is rocking.

He makes no movement, but glances down to see that his foot does not tap a stray object.

Outside, the rain has stopped and the afternoon has become a lull of dense quiet. Only a distant parakeet makes a shrill sound, and it echoes on the damp air. The other sound is the wake, but the murmuring and laughter of grief is too far at the front to disturb the deep lull.

He has stopped for so long, and the quiet is pressing his ears with such a force, that he notices something else. It's the shine suddenly on all things, the shine of the wet afternoon light. A kind of silvery yellow like a factory light—but it is faint and it is everywhere. It looks beautiful, he thinks. What a paradise, he thinks. But he is cast suddenly back to Zeythi. He can see clearly her lips moving. Some kind of incantation, he thinks. Her knees are held tightly to the chest, and she rocks back and forth inches from his face until the whispers burst into the barking of hard sobbing. The President throws a sudden look up the corridor and grips the window to steady himself. His heart is pounding. Zeythi's mouth gapes widely: the disturbing burst has ceased. In the silence that follows he can see only the big stretch of her mouth and eyes. She is unable to breathe, and then the hard burst explodes again.

For many days this small picture behind the gauze prowls the President's mind until one morning he decides to send for Zeythi, but is told that she has vanished. This does not deter his resolve, and he depresses the button to call for the Chief Bearer.

Kutubdia Island

What a beautiful breeze it is bringing me a clear night when I am standing in a raining day. What is this magic breeze? When I was a cook I did not know that the rest of the town talked about what comes next. I thought it was just me that did. Now I know that the country is in endless concern about what comes next. The first salty scent of a breeze arriving at the beach gives the coast pause.

What can you do? You have dreams and you have a vision of yourself as a comfortable sahib type. Do you see past this glorious stuff clear into the palm of your hand? I didn't.

As Khalid the cook I once told a small story to Iqbal and Khan the sabjantawallah about Zeythi and the Minisahib fiddling in the jungly patch behind the house. It was not too long, maybe two cups of chai. When the story was done Iqbal sat contented and quiet.

But Khan said, 'Yah, holes and lies. These are what is the ruin of a whole village. Stupid cooks like you who leave things out and exaggerate. Nothing but useless gossip you have just told us. You have no idea what is really going on.'

I told Khan I did not like being lumped in with 'stupid cooks'.

'Sit in the dark,' Khan said with a wave of his hand.

Now I can see what he meant. I've learned a little bit about seeing what is there. Without wishing for more. Maybe it is difficult to see the future. It might be difficult to see the past. But it is hard to see what is in the palm of your hand. That is what I would also like to say.

Zeythi lives on the island learning the ways of the Kutubdia woman, and the manners of the monsoon. She no longer sends letters to her mother and father. This is not out of neglect, you'll understand, but out of gaining a feeling for life. Out of knowing what lies in the palm of her hand. Soon after my funeral she thought about sending letters to me. These thoughts she placed aside.

Lively Leila once said, 'Khalid, I do not like cooks.'

Stupid thing to say. What, all cooks? All over town? But never mind, that was Leila who was trying to match what her daddy-sahib decided.

She wanted to say, according to Khan, 'You are a stinking pig.'

Mookerjee once said, 'Khalid, I will give you from my garden a pound of garlic, ginger, anything, but I cannot give you my idea of what will happen next. This country is about to burst, but you will still be my friend.'

Zeythi once said to me, 'Khalid, please be silent, please please be quiet. Hold my hand.'

I now see moments come and go like small waves, but there is that other moment which will cross the bay like a breeze. The moment when you do things before you understand. Not after.

I now see plenty. But what good is that? It is useful as stale rice. Sour. And after two days, watch how the grains make that see-through slime. I am not sour, and the only thing I will say in regret is that I should never have gone

470

away to Dacca because instead I could have maybe stayed with Zeythi. That's all. If that is sour, I say Chittagong is sweet.

I now see the great song of the dead riding on that mysterious breeze that brings me the feel of a clear night when I am stood in a raining day. So now I am supposed to understand. And what good is that? I see a giant circle of glowing dead, calling for the progress. What good is that to Zeythi? She keeps my old transistor radio. Can it play the great song of the dead on this magic breeze?

Khan says the borders of the living and the dead wash away when the monsoon brings plenty.

'Khalid, do not go to Dacca,' he once said and rolled his head in a huge dip of expression which was maybe sympathy.

Seeing plenty doesn't matter. You can have a good eye, a good instinct too, but it doesn't matter. Having a good eye and a good instinct is shit compared to knowing what is in the palm of your hand.

The Theatre-sahib once visited the house to show the Old Man the play he had written. He was excited and so he jabbered on with anyone who was sitting around. I brought out the drinks.

He said to me, 'Cook! You are a good bloke!' He was very drunk, but happy, and he liked our place.

'Thank you, sahib,' I replied.

'No, I mean it, I like this place, I like you and your people!'

'Thank you, sahib,' I said again, for what else could I say to a jolly and drunken sahib full of giant things to say?

'You are not getting my meaning,' he said, 'I am an artist, and I have a good eye and a gifted instinct! I see a lot!'

Very late into the evening the Old Man fixed up the night and threw him out. He called the driver and sent the artist home.

'Boring bugger,' the Old Man groaned as he waved goodbye.

But I was left thinking in my quarters about his drunken passion for seeing. I thought, Well, me too. It was like my wonder at Abdul's Iltutmish and Shamsudin. These possibilities were mine too.

Zeythi is now learning that seeing means nothing too big. She is learning many things and many ways. She is now so fine. People stream to the Kutubdia woman's house to request many different what-comes-next problems that need attending. They come with irritations to be solved. With disputes to resolve. And with hopes of fertilising fancy hopes and schemes. The house is a busy place of clutter, yet it is quiet and clean, and the time of most work comes with the darkening weeks of monsoon. Zeythi has become known as the woman's assistant. But this situation does not have to be forever—maybe one day she will become the Razia Iltutmish of Kutubdia.

Once a month Zeythi takes the small ferry to Cox's Bazaar. She spends the morning in town, visits the bank, strolling safely through the lanes looking for good vegetables, maybe a new comb and shirt, and returns to the island.

Patience

It was long ago when I first tried to speak to Iqbal. His third ear was not too perky back then. But one thing in life leads quietly to the next. Without sound.

'Iqbal?'

'Yes?'

'Do you agree?'

'I agree. I was a letterwriter. Not some twisted kind of sabjantawallah.'

'Then what are you today?'

'Letterwriter.'

'Is that all?'

'Yes!'

'You are annoyed?'

'No, I am fine.'

'Iqbal, you seem to be angry.'

'Yes, I am!'

'Why?'

'Never mind.'

'Iqbal, tell me.'

'Okay, I will tell you. I am tired of these endless letters to Zeythi! I gave her your last letter when she came to Chittagong a few days ago. Just like all your letters—full of regret and longing. Do you know what she told me? She said, "Iqbal, please do not make up any more of these letters, they do not make me feel better."'

'One day she will accept it, keep trying.'

'She is only a sorcerer, she will never accept it. Khalid, I tell you, leave it alone. I am tired. You—you definitely must be tired. Plus the monsoon is coming again.'

'Please do not give up … Iqbal?'

But we decided to stop my letters to Zeythi. Iqbal was right, she was no longer a small child sending letters off to a mother and father who had passed away. She was now a young woman, and only a sorcerer after all. Another monsoon fell to the place, another summer.

'What do you think? A story maybe?'

'Khalid, that is a good idea. Your letters through me are no good. But a story? They will see the exact stuff that happened. Everyone will know in the heart. How can they deny it?'

'Only the cynical bastard can.'

'Yah, and those who were here cannot!'

'Iqbal, let us do the story.'

'Yes, where do you wish to begin?'

'I would like to start when Zeythi and I were holding hands on the roof of my quarters after the feast.'

'Why?'

'Because we were both depressed by the tandoor being stolen, and we thought we liked each other too and these things together were damn fine.'

'No. I think make it before.'

'Okay. The swimming pool. When the Minisahib and Zeythi were sad.'

'Earlier even.'

'You think so?'

'Yah.'
'Earlier … yah, okay, when she arrived at the house.'

Cracks in the Wall

The teahouse broke down step by step. Lall and Mookerjee kept an eye on it. Mookerjee lived nearby, and Lall had to ride past.

By the end of the Minisahib's summer holidays from school in England it was given the first order. The rain had done more work shifting the slope, and the balcony began to split off the building. The council inspector needed one look to put a sign out front, and that was it: the big bungalow continued to crumble and crack.

For a while, Mahfouz and his gang held meetings downstairs in the dark emptiness. Sitting on the floor by the flickering truth of candles, the brave and bony young guardians ate fire and stones. Outside—across the delta—independence was the thing, but it would take them by surprise, because a breath away the country was to be torn from the ground by its roots: how close they were to eating real fire. One dark evening Lall strolled inside.

'What a sight,' he told Mookerjee. 'A secret huddle of young guys burning with desire to fight the overlords from Karachi.'

Mahfouz was the first to find his way into the Mukti Bahini.

And plenty used the teahouse to sleep the night. They slept in corners and under the stairs and on the floor, but took no notice of the fire-eating guys around the candles.

The following season, a piece of the roof collapsed. Nobody was hit.

After that, in a new summer, a fire turned it into a place of black sticks. It was like a bat still clinging to the electricity wires when it somehow got shocked. And that is how it is today, a stone ruin on the way to the guava grove embraced by a jungle of vines thick as thighs.

After the teahouse you will arrive at the guava grove, and the headstone. These days visitors bring along baskets to fill.

The Visit

Iqbal was the first. But he was not alone. The Minisahib was now older, and Zeythi was now older. They came all together to the headstone. Three quiet friends. Tall girl, tall Minisahib and smiling letterwriter.

'Place the flowers,' said the Minisahib. School put a new thing in him. Stuck-together houses.

'I will put them when I want,' replied Zeythi quietly.

'He looks nice,' said Iqbal looking down at me, 'he looks nice.'

'You cannot see him,' said Zeythi.

Iqbal looked up. He smiled.

'I am sorry,' Zeythi said.

'Put down the flowers,' said the Minisahib. 'Please.'

'Shut up,' Zeythi said quietly.

'Let me have them,' Iqbal said.

'No,' Zeythi said.

'Then put them down,' Iqbal said.

'No,' Zeythi said.

'Then give them to me,' the Minisahib said, 'I'll put them down.'

'No.'

'What do you want to do?' Iqbal said.

'I want nothing.'

'Zeythi, I am Iqbal.'

'Yah, you must go.'

'And the Minisahib?'

'He must go.'

'Will you put the flowers down?'

'Yes.'

'You have become someone else.'

'Yes.'

The Minisahib and Iqbal walked up the rise to the road. They talked as they climbed up the grass.

'What is England like?'

'Fine.'

'Really?'

'No, it's horrible.'

'Never mind, one day you can stay here.'

'Here has become horrible.'

'Yah? Why?'

'I don't know.'

They walked past the teahouse. They walked in silence.